THE
FAMILY
BUSINESS

THE
FAMILY
BUSINESS

BYRON BALES

ASIA BOOKS

Published and Distributed by
Asia Books Co. Ltd.,
5 Sukhumvit Road Soi 61,
PO Box 40,
Bangkok 10110,
Thailand.
Tel: (66) 0-2 715-9000 ext. 3202–4
Fax: (66)0-2 714-2799
E-mail: information@asiabooks.com
Web site: asiabooks.com < http:asiabooks.com >

© Byron Bales, 2003.

This book is a work of fiction. All names, characters, and other
elements of the story are either the product of the author's imagination
or else are used only fictitiously. Any resemblance to real characters,
living or dead, or to real incidents is entirely coincidental.

Typeset by COMSET Limited Partnership.
Printed in Thailand.

ISBN 974-8303-75-6

For my long-time partner in crime,
Nancy Dzupin-York

Acknowledgements

The author would like to thank the editorial staff at Asia Books, particularly Chris Roarty and Richard Baker, without whose invaluable assistance this book would not have been possible. If any writer believes they can do without the expertise of people such as these— well, they probably haven't been published yet.

1 Manila

"I think that sucker's dead," the ponytailed backpacker shouted across to his buddy. He thumbed towards the lone figure at the far end of the communal table, face down in spilt beer. "He ain't moved since we sat down."

Buffalo Joe's was packed, the volume deafening. Glassy-eyed hookers followed his thumb, looked over indifferently. Alcoholic blackouts featured nightly at Buffalo Joe's. But the guy at the end of the table wasn't breathing.

"Yeah, you're right, man." His buddy drew on his reefer, zombie-like, exhaled a thick plume of smoke, and added hoarsely, "Look at that crap comin' outta his nose. Dude's history."

"Where did she go?" one of the bargirls asked, looking around for the girl with the oversized purse who'd been sitting with the dead man. Then her eyes fell on his gold wristwatch, and she forgot about the other girl.

The manager came over to investigate. He looked at the body from several angles, afraid to touch it, then called a waitress over. She felt for a pulse and announced that there wasn't one. She asked if anyone knew CPR, but no one volunteered—not with all that slop on the guy's face. She called for someone to phone the police, and at this, johns and whores, drunks and hopheads scattered to other tables with extraordinary haste for people in their condition.

No sooner had the call been made when a police officer kicked open the screen doors. He was a large, chesty, dark brute in a tight-fitting blue uniform. He ordered the staff into the kitchen, pointed to the manager, and ran his finger across his throat. A chorus of bitching rippled across the saloon as the music died and blinding overhead lights came on.

"All right, everybody. Hit the bricks. Outside," Officer Reno Marcellus shouted. He scanned the saloon, spotted the dead man's co-ordinates in a sea of emptying tables, then walked over and stood behind the girl who had been eyeing the watch. She tried to dart past him, but he grabbed a clump of her hair and spun her around, tore the dead man's wristwatch from her hand.

"That'll look better on me, *puta.*" He held it up to the light and admired a genuine diamond-studded Cartier. He kicked the girl into the crowd pushing towards the door. When the last person was out, Marcellus began emptying the corpse's pockets. In the back of the joint, the manager cut off the air-conditioning. Marcellus yelled at him to turn it back on.

It was a typical Manila night—hot and sticky. Soon, the dregs milling about outside began thinning away, some to find another beer joint, others back to their cheap hostels with a hooker in tow.

Just in front of an ambulance, an old battered Ford screeched to a halt at the curb. A news photographer jumped out, ran up the steps into Buffalo Joe's. As the EMS team approached the saloon, a flash-bulb exploded inside, followed by a torrent of curses from Marcellus. The newsman flew back out onto the street, taking off the screen doors and bowling over the paramedics coming up the steps.

Officer Marcellus rode with the body to the hospital. On the way, he ordered the driver to pull into an alley, and to step outside for a cigarette. The driver started to say that he didn't smoke, then got the message and did as he was told. Marcellus turned off the light in the back of the ambulance. He took the corpse by the shoulders, hung the head over the gurney. He withdrew his nightstick, but thought better of it, rummaged around the ambulance, found a crowbar in the vehicle's emergency kit. Gripping the metal bar, he took aim, smashed it down with all his might. The dead man's skull split open, caving in an inch between the eyebrows and the hairline.

Marcellus lit a cigarette, examined his work. It was a bit of overkill, but so what. Satisfied, he honked the horn and the driver came running back. Marcellus stepped out of the ambulance, looked at his newly acquired Cartier. It was 2:30 a.m.

———

Just before sunrise, Marcellus sat at the wheel of his patrol car in the alley behind Buffalo Joe's. He zipped up his fly as Lolita moved away and began crying.

Marcellus withdrew a pint of rum from the glove compartment, took a swig. He watched drunks stumbling past his car, heading up the alley, dispossessing the rats in a pre-dawn search for old pros well past their prime—Blowjob Boulevard.

Lolita wiped her eyes with the back of her hand. "Brian was a nice man, Reno. He never hurt nobody."

"What do you care? You got Jordan now."

"You said the pills would just make him sleep."

"Get your pussy back on the street, girlie."

When she didn't move, Marcellus leaned over, opened the door on her side, and kicked her out. The contents of her purse spilled across the alley.

"I'll call you when I hear from Jordan," he said, slamming the door. He put the car in gear, cruised slowly up the alley with his lights off, looking for drunks to roll, hookers to extort. He was having a banner night, although the stiff from Buffalo Joe's had been the real windfall on this shift.

Lolita squatted in the alley sniffling, and scraped her things into her purse: clean panties, tampons, cigarettes, a few pesos, and a vial of downers. "You bastard," she screamed, knowing he was too far away to hear.

2

The door of the go-go joint flew open, shooting daylight through the darkened club. The few customers inside shielded their eyes, shouted at the intruder to close the fucking door.

"Hey! I got limitations here," Max Pollock returned with equal indignation. He grunted and tugged, trying to force his electric wheelchair over the door jamb. A diminutive, scantily-clad bargirl hurried over to assist him. She managed to get him through the door, for which he rewarded her with a pat on the ass. Max surveyed the girls shaking with minimal enthusiasm up on the catwalk. They returned his look, a few wondering if a paraplegic was able to get it up.

He spotted Roth at the end of the bar reading a newspaper. On the stage above him danced a well-endowed girl who gave Roth her full attention, jiggled especially for him. She looked to see who was entering the club—and certainly got Max's attention. But she ignored him; crippled pensioners were poor spenders, and from the looks of this one, clean clothes weren't a priority.

Max wheeled over to Roth, ordered a drink. He wiped sweat from his forehead with his hand, flung it on the floor. "Fuckin' furnace out there," he said to announce his arrival. He craned his neck to read the newspaper headline: "CANO'S *LAST ROUND-UP AT BUFFALO JOE'S.*" A photo of a dead man, taken from behind, covered the front page. A wide-eyed police officer, bent over the body, was caught in the frame.

Roth acknowledged Max with a grunt, then turned his attention to the girl on the catwalk. She'd make a credible alibi. "Hey! Titty City," he called, beckoning her down. She squealed, slapped high fives to the other girls in the meat review.

"Whaddya doin' over here in Manila, Roth?" Max asked, his eyes glued to Titty City.

Roth shrugged.

"Whoremonger," Max accused light-heartedly.

"Nothing wrong with whores. They're honest about what they are."

Max tapped the newspaper headline. "I heard about this guy. People at the hotel were talking about him this morning. Guy boozed himself to death."

"Bet he won't do that again," Roth mumbled.

"You working over here?"

"Yeah," Roth said tiredly, watching Titty City's anatomy jiggle as she negotiated the narrow steps at the end of the catwalk. Her six-inch heels didn't make it any easier. She threw a shirt over her shoulders, a loud red nylon job with the club's logo embroidered on the back, her number on the front. She scurried up to Roth. Her height on the catwalk had been deceptive. Even in her come-fuck-me spikes, she didn't reach his shoulders.

Roth wrapped his arm around Titty City's waist. She snuggled up under his arm and gave him a well-rehearsed innocent smile, her eyes starry with adoration.

An enterprising scheme was working in Max's mind. "Listen to this, Roth—"

Roth said to the girl, "Get your civvies on. I'm bar-fining you."

"Hey, Roth, you listening?" Max pulled his sleeve to get his attention.

"Hanging on every word, Max."

Titty City skipped back to the dressing nook by the DJ's booth. Her cheeks bouncing around the G-string distracted Max momentarily, but he won the struggle, regrouped his thoughts. "When I get back to Bangkok, I'm gonna write my insurance company, tell them I was wheeling across Sukhumvit Road, see. Mindin' my own business, crossing with the light, when this bus comes barreling down on me at fifty, sixty miles an hour, and damn near runs me over. Hell, man, everybody knows Thai drivers are crazy." Max threw his shoulder into the action as he narrated. "But I jumped clear, threw myself outta my chariot, see, crawled to the curb and barely made it as the bus flattened my chair. Flattened it to shit." He made a spurting sound, spraying the newspaper on the bar. "This baby's insured for three grand. Whaddya think?"

"Won't work, Max." Roth shook his head, drained his glass.

Max was indignant. His scam certainly sounded feasible to him. "Why not? You gonna snitch me out?"

"Only if your insurance company is my client."

"What! You wouldn't lie for me?"

"To friends and my priest, I lie. To clients, never."

"Bullshit!" Max spat. "I know how you claims guys cheat your clients."

Titty City returned in hot pants and a low-cut tank top that threatened fallout. She smiled at Max now, seeing how he was acquainted with her new customer. Maybe they were good friends. A girl could never be sure in this business; it paid to be nice to people connected to anyone she connected with. She really didn't like him though; crippled customers had a strange hunger that made most of the girls uneasy.

Roth threw some pesos on the bar, shot Max a dark look, and headed for the door. Titty City trailed after him, waving goodbye to the cripple.

Max called out, "See you back in Bangkok, huh?" But Roth was already out the door. He turned to the bartender, threw out his arms in innocence. "What did I say? Huh?"

The bartender ignored him. But Max was used to that.

3

Roth's rental car sat in front of the Immaculate Heart Hospital. It was a run-down medical facility so named to invoke some spiritual healing power stronger than what was practiced therein. Across the street, Roth occupied a child's four-seater swing in a mini-park, licking an ice-cream cone and reading a paperback.

The Avis driver sneaked glimpses at Titty City in the rear-view mirror. She knew he was checking her out, but ignored him.

"Isn't he taking me to his hotel?" she asked, her pride injured from Roth's indifference.

The driver shrugged. "Meester Roth has to see the owner of the hospital."

Roth swung the four-seater absently. A toddler came along with his grandmother, an ancient crone whose toothless face was crisscrossed by a thousand lines. The boy watched Roth, instinctively offended by this interloper. The swing was his domain. He inched forward.

Roth glanced at the boy, ignored him.

Finally the boy scowled and stomped his foot.

"Beat it, kid. I was here first," Roth snapped. To drive the point home, he leaned forward and tantalizingly licked the ice-cream.

Uncertainty swept across the boy's face. Did he want his God-given rights to the swing, or the ice-cream?

Grandma rattled off a rebuke in Tagalog just as Dr. Ignacio pulled up across the street in his car. Roth watched Ignacio extract his 300 pounds from behind the steering wheel. He locked the door, polished the chrome side-view mirror with his sleeve.

Roth looked back at the grandmother, flipped the boy a casual salute. "Smart kid; always bring your muscle with you." He abandoned the swing and shuffled across the street, intercepting Ignacio as he waddled towards the hospital entrance.

"*Yo*, Doctor!" Roth called out. He extended his arm and pumped Ignacio's hand.

"Do I know you, sir?"

"You will," Roth said. "Here, hold this, Doc." He handed him the cone of melting ice-cream and dug around in his pocket for a business card. He found one, stuffed it in Ignacio's tunic pocket.

Dr. Ignacio offered him back the cone, the cream beginning to run down over his fingers.

"Nah, that's okay, Doc. You can have the rest of it." Roth pointed over to the mini-park. "See that kid over there?"

Ice-cream was dripping on Ignacio's shoes. He held it away from him, looked around for a trash can, then at the boy in the park. "Yes, what about him?"

"Just don't give him any ice-cream," Roth said. "I don't like him. He's a bully." Roth linked arms with Ignacio and walked with him towards the entrance. "Gus didn't write you about me? Gustavo Clemente? My *amigo*. I work with Gus in Tacoma."

"Ahh, Gustavo! Yes, my nephew. He is well, I hope?" There was no place to throw the ice-cream. Finally, Ignacio tossed it in the gutter.

"Your nephew? Right," Roth said. "Gus is in the pink, Doc. Asked me to look you up."

"It is my pleasure, sir."

Roth led Ignacio into the foyer, where he stopped and turned around to show him Titty City sitting in the back seat of his car. She returned their gaze, wondering if Roth had a sick-dick problem.

"Doc, I need a very large favor," Roth whispered. "You see, I gotta report back to the plant next week, or I'll get fired." He pointed to Titty City. "But Titty, uh, Theresa has agreed to marry me, sweet darling that she is. So, I need more time for a honeymoon. You understand." He winked at Ignacio. "Gus thought you could fix me up with a medical certificate; give me an excuse, buy me some extra time." He guided the doctor inside, past an attractive receptionist, and slipped a 1,000-peso note into Ignacio's breast pocket.

Fifteen minutes later, in the doctor's office, Roth reviewed the fictitious certificate that Ignacio had created for him. "This is perfect, Doc. Let's see, 15-day hospitalization, starting today. Typhoid fever. Terrific."

Dr. Ignacio smiled proudly. He stood, extended his hand.

But Roth just stood there, a wicked smile coming to his mouth. "But you see, Doc, the truth is, I'm such a good fuckin' liar, I oughta be a lawyer."

Ignacio's smile faded. "I don't understand, my friend."

"Don't you? First, I ain't Gus's *amigo* and we ain't friends." Roth stuffed the bogus medical certificate into his coat and pulled out another with an insurance claim form on Gustavo Clemente. "Second, Gus is nothing more than a fraudster. And you gave him this phony medical certificate. Just like mine. It's a fake, Doc. Bogus. Fraud-u-lent. You've been caught out. Right along with ol' Gus, trying to dick his insurance company."

"But—but, I was only doing Gus a favor. He also needed time off."

Roth laughed. "Of course you were, Doc. Hell, I know you didn't do it to split the 18,000 dollars he's claiming." Roth read the certificate, chuckling. "For a two-week hospitalization, round-the-clock nursing, medications—oh, Christ, this is rich—consulting physicians, therapy, x-rays, lab work-ups, ambulance, private room at 500 bucks a day, plus, plus, plus." He threw his arms open and turned, taking in the room. "Eighteen thousand dollars is a lot of ice-cream, Doc—for this fuckin' toilet?"

Ignacio plopped down in his chair, rested his head in his hands. "Doc, your picture should be in the post office."

Ignacio jerked his head up. "I'm not a crook."

"Doc, Doc, Doc!" Roth shook his head. "That line is reserved for presidents. Okay, you're no thief. You're no sleazy, lying, two-bit scam artist. You'd never do it for the money." Roth reached over, plucked the 1,000-peso note from Ignacio's tunic. "So, I'll tell you what we're gonna do, Doc. Write me up a statement. Something that reads that good ol' Gus was never hospitalized here. That it was all a big mistake. A clerical error." He snapped his fingers. "Better yet, blame it on that luscious little secretary sitting out front. Save your face, keep the Philippine Hospital Association off your ass, and get me out of your life."

———

Roth walked out of the hospital, tucking Ignacio's signed statement in his jacket.

The doctor hurried after him. "Couldn't we come to some sort of an arrangement, Mr. Roth?"

Roth opened the rear door of his car, turned to Ignacio. "For a piece of 18 grand? Don't insult me." He got in and rolled down his window, pulled a miniature tape recorder from his jacket. "And Doc, don't even think about recanting your statement. My little witness heard it all." He rewound the tape and they listened to Ignacio's excuse: *"But—but, I was only doing Gus a favor. He also needed time off."*

Dr. Ignacio bit his knuckle, spoke through his fist. "I'll tell you the truth, Mr. Roth. Gustavo was counting on the insurance money. What shall I tell him?"

Roth chuckled, his eyes hard. "Why, tell him that you betrayed him, of course!" He reached over and tweaked Titty City's nipples as the car pulled from the curb. She giggled, happy at last to have her customer's attention.

4

Lori MacMillan crossed Roxas Boulevard and walked towards the US Embassy. The late afternoon heat was oppressive, and her lightweight cotton suit had already lost its crispness, her blonde bouncy hair now flat. She envied the Filipinas whose thick, black hair defied humidity, who always looked fresh and never perspired. On her flight over from the States, she'd read that Southeast Asians had a lower body temperature; immunity against blistering heat with matching humidity.

She passed the long line of Filipinos waiting outside the embassy, drawing attention as she usually did. Lori was 23 years old, five feet eight, slim, busty, and curvaceous. She carried herself with a model's poise; the beauty mark high on her right cheek seemed to suggest this, in fact.

The crowd near the heavy steel gates funneled open as she passed through and asked directions to the American Citizens Services section. The Filipino guards didn't bother to check her passport, for she was obviously an American. Women with her looks filled fashion magazines.

But there was something different about this *cana*. Americans are quick to smile, Filipinos say, because life in America is good. But Lori MacMillan wasn't smiling. She looked miserable and her black outfit told her story: a recent widow on the verge of tears. Typical of Filipinos, they sympathized with long faces as whispers followed her progress. Filipinos are great mourners—a trait well-practiced—for the country is awash in tragedy, the most dangerous on the Pacific Rim. Violent death is common here.

The gates closed after her, barring the flow of humanity desperate to set foot on American soil. Inside the gate, Lori waded through another, smaller crowd snailing up the stairs into the consulate. Again, the hopefuls yielded immediately.

Inside, visa applicants formed long lines at a dozen service windows while hundreds more sat waiting to be called. The US visa office in Manila is the busiest in the world.

Huge air-conditioners labored full-blast against the heat of this humanity. After a few moments, Lori felt cold as the air chilled the perspiration crawling down her back. She asked a Marine for the American Citizens Services section. He pointed to an area where only a few people waited at windows reserved for Americans. She thanked him, walked on, and the Marine discreetly conducted a visual reconnaissance of her ass.

In the American section, Lori looked around. A little girl squirmed restlessly in the seat next to her mother—a Filipina-American service wife—pestering her when they'd be going home to Oregon.

Lori took a number and sat as far away as possible from the little girl. She withdrew a handkerchief from her purse, wiped perspiration from under her eyes, dabbed at her hairline. She looked around for a ladies room to freshen up, knowing she looked haggard. Don't bother, she thought; it was just as well.

Players from a semi-pro basketball tour poured into the section and lined up against the wall, their youthful energy working overtime. They jostled each other and horse-played until, one by one, they noticed Lori. Hormones kicked in and demeanors improved immeasurably. When her number was called out by an attractive brunette at Window Three, Lori stood and walked over. Predatory eyes followed her every movement.

At the window, Lori presented a telegram, pushing it under the glass to the brunette who smiled at her. Until she read the message. Then Lori watched the smile fade.

"Hello, Mrs. MacMillan," the brunette managed. Through the thick security glass, her voice over the intercom sounded like a long-distance telephone connection.

"We weren't sure when to expect you. I'm Millie O'Hearn. Mr. Towers—he sent you the telegram—just stepped out from his office. He'll be right with you."

Lori nodded and made a mental note of Millie's name.

"You have our sincere condolences, Mrs. MacMillan."

Lori forced a faint smile to her lips.

Millie scanned out front, took in the jocks propping up the wall, their eyes glued to Lori MacMillan, and as only a woman can about another, reached a conclusion.

"Here he is now. Just one moment, Mrs. MacMillan."

Lori looked back behind the counter to see William Towers coming over. He was tall and pleasant looking with the nondescript features that typified State Department personnel.

Millie intercepted Towers. "Hard-on country out there," she whispered.

"What?"

"I said, handle Counter Three out there. It's Mrs. MacMillan."

Towers glanced at Lori. His expression went somber. He nodded to Millie, walked over to the window. Off to the side, Lori saw another consular officer—a man of about forty—lean sideways to get a glimpse of her. The late Peter MacMillan was obviously a topic of conversation.

"Good afternoon, Mrs. MacMillan. I'm William Towers."

Lori sensed that he wanted to shake hands, impossible of course through the window. He gave his condolences, then excused himself, said that he'd get Peter's file.

Peter MacMillan reportedly died five days ago, his body discovered in a packed honky-tonk on Mabini Street at 2:00 a.m. No one knew how long he'd been dead. They all assumed he'd passed out.

Towers returned with the file. He laid it on the counter on his side of the glass, slipped the tacky newspaper headline beneath the stack of papers. Lori's eyes fell on the typed label that ran across the file tab: *"MACMILLAN, PETER—REPORT OF THE DEATH OF AN AMERICAN CITIZEN ABROAD."*

She blinked wide, mist in her eyes.

Towers avoided eye contact, although he knew he must—at least intermittently—look at her. Every consul hated this part of the job. He imagined what terrifying thoughts had haunted the widow MacMillan this past week, starting with his telegram. Confusion, disbelief, denial of the horrible truth, and finally, accepting the unacceptable. Then the hasty travel plans followed by an interminably long flight among unknowing, uncaring strangers. A sad journey, he thought. People in Lori MacMillan's predicament should be entitled to wear an insignia, like battle ribbons, a sign bearing their grief to the world: *I lost someone dear and I'm alone and going to get him, what's left of him. I want the world to understand that I'm miserable and frightened by the unfairness of what's happened to me.* The sign should flash whatever her emotions dictated at the moment: *Leave me alone to grieve*, or *approach me with genuine sorrow for my loss. Understand my loneliness and my pain as though it were yours. Grant me a special dispensation from all worry, fear, heartbreak, and loneliness, just for these first few horrible days.*

Towers cleared his throat. She made him feel awkward. It wasn't just her fabulous looks. He sensed an inner strength, a quiet resolve that enhanced her very obvious charms. He'd met others on similar missions, visiting the embassy as though they were on an errand, like picking up the laundry; or worse for some, like picking up the garbage. The family garbage: black sheep and deadbeats, deserters and absconders who disappeared in these islands to live squandered lives; men whose eventual demise brought relief from further family embarrassment, answered long-held doubts, brought closure. But that wasn't the case here. No, he could see that hers was a real loss. A painful one.

Lori spoke first, and Towers realized that she probably thought he didn't know where to begin, even though he'd been through this routine a hundred times.

"My husband's associate—" She fumbled to find a facsimile in her purse and read the name. "A Mr. Morales, left word at my hotel that he couldn't meet me. I'm checked in at the Manila Hotel. He had to leave for Zambo—uh." Lori dabbed her eyes with the handkerchief, then stuffed it back into her purse and focused on the paper. She couldn't pronounce the city.

"Zamboanga?" Towers offered.

"Oh, yes." She looked up, tried to smile. "I guess that's it. I always thought it was some mythical place, like Mandalay or Pago Pago." She grimaced at her own ignorance.

"Actually, those places also exist," he said, then smiled, assuming most Americans didn't know where these places were.

"Oh! Well, that's where Mr. Morales is, I guess. He won't be back in Manila until next week. What day is it? Friday? I seem to have lost a day somewhere. Isn't that silly."

"No, Mrs. MacMillan. Not silly at all. You lose a day when you fly to Asia. We're a day ahead of the States."

"Yes, of course. Stupid of me. When the flight landed, they announced it was Friday morning, but I really didn't think about it." She shrugged. "Mr. Morales has been very helpful. I only wish he could be here, although I've never met him. In fact, I'd never heard of him until I received your telegram."

"Did anyone accompany you from California?"

"No," she said, looking down, blinking away tears. "Mom couldn't get away and there was no one."

"I see," Towers said. That was unfortunate. This business was bad enough without a widow being alone. "This Mr. Morales had been notified by the police who, in turn, contacted us. He has your husband's business papers and a few things from his hotel room. We have his personal effects and passport. We found your name and notified you immediately."

"You have his things?" She held back no longer, tears began welling in her eyes. She dug into her purse again for the handkerchief.

The little girl from Oregon stood by her mother at the next window, holding her skirt. She asked why the lady was crying.

"Mrs. MacMillan, please come inside the office," Towers offered quickly, pointing to a door off to the side.

She collected her purse and papers, heard the little girl ask her mother again why the lady was crying, and passed into the office. A sign on the door read: *"Staff Only."*

Inside, Towers pointed to another door beyond. "Let's use the staff lounge."

Employees glanced at Lori, trying not to be obvious. Yes, Lori thought, word on Peter MacMillan had certainly gotten around. She followed Towers to the unmarked door leading deeper into the consulate. The lounge was spacious if sterile, a typical government space with tile floors. Nestled at one end of the room were four leather couches squared off around a huge coffee table. A Filipina clerk was brewing a fresh pot of coffee.

"Please sit down," he offered. He edged around the coffee table to one of the couches. She sat at the end of one abutting his, their knees almost touching. She tugged at the hem of her skirt, but it didn't cover her knees.

"Would you like something to drink?"

"Tea, if it's no trouble."

"Of course, no trouble at all." Towers pulled his attention away from her knees, turned to the clerk. "Maria, could you, please? A tea?"

As he turned back, Lori asked, "Do you have Darjeeling tea?"

"Uh, I'll check." He turned again and inquired, then shifted back.

"And honey?"

"Yes? Uh, excuse me?"

"Honey rather than sugar."

"Oh, uh, let's see." He twisted again, relating this request, then turned back, feeling rather like a puppet.

"I'm sorry to be such a bother," Lori concluded.

"No bother at all," he said, nonplussed with her preferences at such a time. He started to say that this was his job, but checked himself. That would sound too impersonal. "That's what we're here for," he managed diplomatically. But the business at hand was unpleasant. He'd just have to slip in the necessary details matter-of-factly. But her closeness was disturbing and he had trouble organizing his thoughts as he felt her warmth, absorbed her heady, musky perfume. Dizzying. He held the file in his hands, inches from the distraction of her legs.

Maria brought their drinks on a small tray. There was only Liptons and, sorry, no honey. Towers shrugged his apology, but Lori pushed the cup and saucer away.

Towers opened the file. The preliminary police report—completed by an Officer Reno Marcellus—read that Peter MacMillan died an ignominious death in a sleazy dump where prostitutes trolled amongst Manila's wasted expats. Buffalo Joe's was legendary, the inspiration for lewd jokes in the American community. Towers wondered how a guy with a wife like Lori MacMillan could end up in such a rat-hole. It just didn't make sense. But this was Asia and a lot of things didn't make sense here.

MacMillan had eventually been identified through a hotel room key found in his trousers. At the hotel, Officer Marcellus reportedly found MacMillan's passport which had been hidden somewhere in the room. Naturally, by the time the police tossed the place, there were only a few pesos found amongst his belongings. Just his clothes, toiletries, and some business papers. No wristwatch, rings, camera, laptop; nothing negotiable aside from a return ticket to the States and a few traveler's checks in small denominations. Mr. Morales had offered to keep the business papers for Mrs. MacMillan, adding that he had removed anything that would injure her feelings, specifically a photograph of a young Filipina, and condoms from his toilet kit. In retrospect—now sitting only inches apart from the widow MacMillan—Towers was grateful for Morales' astuteness, because in the Philippines, philandering is the national pastime.

He handed Lori her husband's passport. She opened it and looked at the smiling face of Peter MacMillan. His handsome features and clear blue eyes stared back at her.

"I hadn't seen him for a while." She sighed. Her eyes watered and before Towers could distract her—could deflect what he feared most—the dam broke and tears gushed forth. He bit his lip, eyes downcast, helpless to comfort her. He felt compelled to shift next to her, to hold her, soothe her, but he didn't dare. Her face contorted in anguish, her hands moved as if to reach for him—for someone, anyone—but instead she clutched her knees so hard her knuckles turned white. He covered her hands with his, impotently muttered, "Now, now." But there was nothing to say. She cried hard, shaking her head back and forth, and gasped for breath. She withdrew her hands from beneath his and clutched her handkerchief to her face, wiped her eyes and nose.

"I'm sorry," she breathed quietly.

"No need to be, Mrs. MacMillan. It's quite all right." He suddenly realized his hands were on her knees just as Millie pushed open the door to the lounge. He jerked his hands away, but Millie had seen it. He wished she'd seen the deluge. Millie just stood at the door, studying them.

They'd been an item six months back. It hadn't lasted long; just long enough for an occasional pang of jealousy on Millie's part, punctuated by frequent bouts of sniping. As for him, losing what could have been hurt more than he let on. After a cooling-off period, they settled back into the friendship that preceded their affair. They were compatible as friends, but as lovers the worst in both of them came out: absurd competitiveness, jealousy, inane pettiness. They squabbled over everything, and the affair ended one morning in a shouting match over who used the hairdryer first.

But the diplomatic community was close-knit, and, after all, they still liked each other, had similar interests, which was their mutual appeal in the first place. They just shouldn't have been lovers. They kept each other company, which encouraged gossip that they still had a thing. But they didn't and never would again. Eventually their post-affair returned to what it had been before the sex. They went off together on weekends, usually with friends, but they no longer shared a room. This weekend—a three-day holiday, since Monday was Labor Day—they planned to visit a resort at Puerto Azul with John Warbell, the section head.

Towers stood, walked over to Millie. She studied his face, her eyebrow arched—worked to perfection—her way of asking pointed questions that always made him cringe a little.

He leaned close to her, whispered, "She's a mess. I'm trying to console her."

"Starting with her thighs?" Millie whispered back, wide-eyed, mock confusion on her face.

"I'll explain later."

"No need to. It's not my business. But maybe it's good therapy. I should've tried that last week. Remember when old Mr. Walters came in all broken up over his wife's death. I should have held his dick, don't you think?"

Towers pulled his attention from Lori MacMillan. "What do you want?" he snapped.

"Just to remind you: Puerto Azul? We've got to leave by four if we're going to beat the traffic."

"Oh. Right." Towers grimaced. "Okay, this won't take long. Are we going in John's car?" he asked absently, again looking over at Lori.

"Yes, Bill. In John's car. Where our bags are. Where our bags have been since this morning. They were still there when we talked at lunch." She mimicked telephone static and white noise. "Earth calling Bill, lost somewhere up Planet Your Anus. Are you all right, or has Mrs. MacMillan caused you to run a fever?"

"Hmm? Oh, very funny, wise ass. I told you, she's a mess."

Millie peeked around Towers. "She looks pretty good to me. You didn't see how she stopped traffic out in the section." She turned to leave and called back over her shoulder, "Puerto Azul won't wait."

Towers returned to the couch and sat down. Lori MacMillan had stopped crying and held the handkerchief to her nose. He gently took the passport from her. "Well, then, I'll just have this—" He started to say "canceled," but thought that might open the floodgates again. "Taken care of."

He went to the door and called Maria over. "Have this canceled and bring it right back," he whispered.

Passports of Americans who died abroad were canceled and returned to the next-of-kin. Otherwise, they had a way of disappearing, since they carried a high street value, selling for as much as 10,000 dollars, depending upon the statistics of the bearer and the length of validity of the passport. For those who could afford one, it was, literally, a ticket to freedom and opportunity.

Towers returned to the couch and opened his file. He pulled out State Department Form 180—a Report of the Death of an American Citizen Abroad. "This form will assist you with matters back home. For changing records, creditors, insurance, that sort of thing. Also, you might like to know, when a credit card holder dies, many of the institutions have a built-in life insurance feature which automatically kicks in, canceling the outstanding balances on the card."

"Oh? I didn't know that!"

He smiled, feeling like a bearer of gifts, relieved that they could talk now. He'd just have to watch how he said things. Her crying jag had subsided, and he didn't want the flood to start again. Lori MacMillan had obviously been deeply in love with her husband. He admired her loyalty and wondered if Millie could ever be that devoted. Maybe she could be, to the right guy.

He continued: "The report isn't finished since we haven't received the, uhm, medical certificate yet." Medical certificate sounded better than death certificate.

Lori nodded and read the document. "Do I need to sign?"

"No. In fact I sign it once we have the medical certificate. I can give you as many copies as you like. Most families require a dozen or so."

"What's the purpose of the report? I don't see why I need it. Won't I need a death certificate?"

"There'll be a local death certificate also," he answered, thinking that since she felt comfortable using the D-word, there was no reason he shouldn't. "In fact, I need it first to complete this report. You see, in many countries, death certificates are naturally in the local language. Fortunately, here in the Philippines they're in English, but in other places they're often in a strange format, sometimes extremely brief, even vague to the point of being unclear, so the State Department long ago devised Form 180 to make things easier for surviving family members."

Lori looked confused. "You mean the local death certificate isn't any good?"

"Yes. Yes, of course it is. But Form 180 is like a death certificate that people recognize at home. Back there, you'll find that people—financial institutions, that is—will prefer seeing this. Some foreign death certificates are even spurious."

"Spurious?"

"Questionable."

"I see. I guess. Then I'll be needing one of these?"

"It's best you have one, yes."

"What else will I need?"

"That's about it. Just this, really." He tapped the Form 180. "And the local death certificate."

"Nothing else?"

"Not really. I'm sure the NBI will provide you with a copy of the post-mortem report if you like, but I don't see why you'd need that."

"Post-mortem?"

"Autopsy," Towers said, as softly as he could. "It's necessary in matters such as this." By "matters" he meant a violent death. Autopsies were conducted so that coroners could rule out foul play, although in this case it appeared as though Peter MacMillan had just fallen down in a drunken stupor and cracked his skull.

Lori's eyes watered, but she kept her composure. "NBI?"

"Yes. The National Bureau of Investigation. Sort of like our FBI, but unfortunately nowhere as efficient. Cases such as this are turned over to the NBI whose pathologists handle post-mortems."

"The death certificate, where is that?" she asked, paging through the file.

"Ordinarily, in America, it would be available by now. But this is the Philippines, *mañana* is always another day. We should have it by Monday. Oh! I forgot, Monday is Labor Day, and we're closed. Tuesday then. It'll be here Tuesday."

"Where is my husband?"

The NBI had no medical facilities, and conducted autopsies at funeral parlors. MacMillan's autopsy had been performed at the Las Flores Funeraria in Ermita where his body remained. He handed her a slip of paper with the address. "As for some of your husband's things, I tried calling this Mr. Morales yesterday," he said. "His number just rings and rings. But you said he was away?"

"That's what his fax said."

Normally, the embassy inventoried a dead American's personal effects if no family members were available. Towers had sent Ernestine Scales, an intern with the consular section, to the post-mortem once they were notified by the police where the body was. Ernestine then went to MacMillan's hotel with the police where she collected his personal effects. Towers pushed a large manila envelope towards Lori. "This is all there is, I'm afraid. Mr. Morales has his clothes and business papers, which we assumed appropriate, since they were in business together, and we made certain there was nothing negotiable amongst those things."

Lori looked at the envelope, felt the wallet through the paper. She put it aside, studying the incomplete Form 180.

Maria entered and stood by the door. Towers excused himself again and went over to her. The cancelation stamp was nowhere to be found, and she'd looked everywhere. Towers couldn't recall where he last saw it. He told Maria to keep searching and asked her to make a photocopy of the preliminary police report.

He sat down again and explained the delay as Lori read the Form 180. She pointed at a blank space under *"Disposition of the Remains."*

"You can provide me with that information afterwards." He trailed off. After the funeral, he meant, or however she decided to dispose of the body. This was the part where delicacy was nearly impossible. "Mrs. MacMillan, after the NBI's post-mortem, most families prefer, uh, cremation."

He studied her face as she digested the words. Her expression asked *why*. How could he tell her autopsies were horribly ugly, and that here, the NBI pathologists did such sloppy work, that when they released the body to funeral homes, embalmers had to practically reinvent the human body to meet a family's expectations. Especially if the body was to be repatriated to the States. Consignees in the States always complained about the condition of corpses they received, and usually recommended a closed casket service to the family.

"Of course," he added quickly, "if it isn't against your faith."

She kept her eyes on his and he resisted an impulse to squirm, wondering why she made him particularly edgy. He'd given this talk countless times. But her eyes were like magnets.

"It's simpler," he went on, "and of course far less expensive than shipping to California. This is your choice, of course, but I must warn you not to expect too much when you view your husband."

Thankfully, there were no more tears on the way. She'd probably cried herself out, he thought, emotionally numb by now—a stage that grieving relatives eventually reached—unable to process further trauma to the psyche. Her eyes sank to the carpet and she nodded her understanding.

Maria returned with copies of the preliminary police report, but still couldn't find the stamp used to perforate the word 'canceled' through the passport cover. Towers snuck a look at his watch: 3:50 p.m. He was running late and still had a stack of papers that required his signature before he left for the weekend. He excused himself, went out into the general office, quickly reviewed what still needed attention.

Too much. He found Millie at Window Two, finishing with the last American for the day, a businessman who required extra pages added to his passport. He trailed her to her desk as the office staff stampeded for the doors.

"Look, there's no way I can make it. I don't know what happened to the time. It's like I lost the afternoon."

"Did you look for it up Mrs. MacMillan's skirt?"

"Cut it out, will you?"

"So what else do you have to do? When can you split? John's anxious to hit the road."

"I gotta put my signature on a pile of papers and I've got to finish with her."

"She's *still* here?" Millie asked incredulously, a little too loudly.

"*Shhhhh!*" Have you seen the cancelation stamp?"

"No, I haven't."

John Warbell came up to them. He'd changed from work clothes into Bermuda shorts, a tropical print shirt, and tennis shoes. "Hey, you guys, ready to rock 'n' roll?"

"Running behind, John. Very behind."

John glanced at Millie and asked, "Translate 'very.'"

"It's not me," Millie objected. "Ask Mister Fondles here."

"Will you cut it out?" Towers said through clenched teeth. "I need an hour, maybe more."

"Damn!" John exclaimed. "That'll put us in the middle of traffic. It'll be bumper-to-bumper all the way down to Puerto Azul." Late traffic on the National Road meant sweltering behind rolled up windows. Traffic crawled at that hour, with diesel-belching trucks sputtering long trails of nauseous, black plumes.

"I know. I know," Towers said testily. "Look, you guys go on without me. Take my stuff and I'll drive my car down. Have the resort hold my room. I'll be there for a late dinner, but you guys can have a swim before dark." He turned to Millie. "Just go with John."

John looked at Millie. "Okay by me. Whaddya say?"

"Sure," she said, slamming her desk drawer closed with her knee. "Why not?"

They watched her storm off, exchanged shrugs, and John headed for the exit. Towers was sick of Millie's attitude. If the weekend was going to be like this, who needed it. He headed back to the staff lounge. Midway, he spotted the cancelation stamp sitting on a windowsill and started for it. But he stopped short and looked around. Maria was hurrying to leave but hadn't given up the search.

"Maria, you go on home. I'll find it later."

"Oh, thank you, Mr. Towers. Have a good weekend."

"You, too," he said, staring at the stamp. He left it where it was and went back into the staff lounge to find Lori MacMillan paging through the file. She was certainly entitled to whatever he had, but he didn't appreciate her taking the liberty of going through government papers. Moreover, he wanted to protect her from reading the unsavory details of the incident or seeing that newspaper article. The reporter—a muck-raker named Otero—liberally salted the story with repeated references to whores, drugs, and the dregs that patronized Buffalo Joe's. Peter MacMillan's body had been looted, or so the NBI presumed. There was a slight bluish lividity impression of a watch or band on his left wrist, and the item didn't appear on their inventory of his personal effects. That, plus his body had been callously treated. Some drunks had flipped cigarette butts at the corpse, angry that the dead man had given the police cause to empty the joint.

But maybe it was better that she read it for herself, rather than have him tap-dancing around her emotions. She seemed to be handling the situation much better now. Her handkerchief was in her hand, held next to her cheek, but she was soberly digesting the file. Logic was replacing emotion, he guessed.

He handed her the preliminary police report—a three-page summary—and an envelope. "We still can't find the cancelation stamp," he lied. "It's around someplace. Tell you what, I'm running late as it is, and there's still more I need to do. Perhaps you'd like to visit Las Flores in the meanwhile to finalize things. I'll drop the passport at your hotel when I leave. Would that be all right?" The Manila Hotel was a two-minute walk from the embassy, just across Luneta Park.

"Yes. That would be fine. Las Flores . . . is it far?"

"Maybe five minutes in traffic. You can catch a taxi just outside, on Roxas Boulevard. I'd suggest you have the driver wait, then have him return you to the hotel or wherever you're going next."

Lori stood, digesting his instructions. "I have nowhere else to go," she said quietly, looking lost. "I don't know anyone here."

Nowhere else to go, he thought. Her husband's death was bad enough, but being on the other side of the world on such a mission had to be the loneliest thing imaginable.

"I understand Manila is dangerous," she said.

"Not as dangerous as road rage in Los Angeles." He smiled. "And not unless you're looking for trouble. Then you'll surely find it."

Lori's face went white.

Shit! Towers thought. He had to go and say that. Obviously, Peter MacMillan wasn't at choir practice in Buffalo Joe's. He thought again of the stash of condoms Mr. Morales had found in the hotel room.

"Uhm, just take normal precautions," he mumbled.

He showed her to the door, confirmed that he'd drop the passport by her hotel no later than six o'clock. He watched her walk out through the visa section, his eyes sliding down her form. Fabulous looking woman. Fabulous everything. He cleared his throat and closed the door.

He wouldn't reach Puerto Azul before nine o'clock once he'd met Lori, then went home, showered, changed, and drove down. Suddenly, going down there this weekend didn't seem so urgent. *Yeah, Millie. You just go on with John.* Towers was due for another posting in the New Year. Wherever it would be, it couldn't come soon enough. Transfer. A clean break. Maybe settle down. Maybe find the right woman.

He went into his office, waded into the paperwork on his desk.

Shortly after, Joselita, the section telephone operator, peeked in on her way out. "Call for you, sir."

"Who is it?"

"A Mr. O'Toole. He's called from Boston several times this week about his missing brother."

Towers looked at his watch. It would be 6:00 a.m. in Boston. "All right, put him through. Then close the switchboard." He punched a key on the telephone. "William Towers here."

"And Kevin O'Toole here," a brusque Bostonian accent came back at him. "I've been calling you people all week to see what you're doing about finding my brother."

Towers remembered seeing a note. He rummaged through the mess on his desk, and not finding it, asked a few general questions, not really paying attention. He summarized by telling O'Toole that since his brother hadn't registered with the embassy when he arrived in Manila, all they could do was file a report with the police.

"Look," O'Toole objected, "I know there's something wrong. Brian calls me every day while he's there. You people can do a lot more than that."

"No, sir. That's really all we can do. Except maybe refer you to a local investigator who might be able to assist you."

O'Toole told him to check around, insisting that the embassy must have started a file on the matter after all his calls. Towers lied that the files were locked away for the night, and started to provide him with the number for the Tourist Police.

"I've already talked to them," O'Toole cut in. "And I've got a private investigator flying over from Boston. You people just be damn sure you're doing everything you can." He slammed down the receiver.

Towers, stunned, responded in kind. "You're very welcome." He steamed for a bit, waxing defensive. *It's not my fault if your brother didn't register.* The embassy tried to help in cases like this, supplied a menu of emergency telephone numbers and a list of local attorneys.

He brushed off another call from a young Filipina married to a World War II veteran who recently expired at the Makati Medical Center. He'd been comatose for the last day—his death imminent— and his 20-year-old bride had been calling all week inquiring about veteran's benefits, social security, widow's benefits and—of course— whether she was still eligible for a visa to the States. She'd married the old boy on his death bed, and Towers wondered if the ancient campaigner was under medication when he said "I do" to the little gold-digger.

"Is that switchboard closed?" he yelled.

There was no answer, Joselita had gone. Good. She was a sucker for callers in distress, had a hard time saying no to anyone. Well, he didn't. No sir. Office hours are posted and they should be adhered to. Everyone seems to have an emergency these days. Well, he also had a life, and emergencies—real or imagined—would just have to wait.

His thoughts returned to Lori MacMillan. He'd see her again shortly. If she wasn't back at the hotel, he'd wait for her. Couldn't leave a US passport with just anyone, could he? Even if it was canceled. No, he'd wait at the hotel until she returned. But since she'd be returning to the embassy on Tuesday, there really wasn't any reason to take it to her tonight.

But he knew why he'd offered to.

5

At 5:45 p.m., the giant air-conditioner went off with a violent shudder. Towers finished the last of the reports, sorted them in the mail room. There were five death reports, a busy week. Most were for older veterans who'd retired to the islands after military service, many settling in Angeles City, outside the old Clark Air Base. Life in the Philippines was easy and inexpensive. Paradise. These deaths were expected, whereas MacMillan's had been the only death out of the ordinary.

But then, he'd probably thought it was paradise, too.

Towers thought about the widow MacMillan, as he had a dozen times since she'd left. There was something special about her, not something any fool could obviously see, but something more than her beauty. An inexplicable depth he couldn't define, couldn't put his finger on, a knowledge and maturity beyond her years. He rechecked her date of birth on the photocopy he'd made of her passport. She was not yet 24 years old. Incredible. But then Lori Mac-Millan *was* incredible.

Within minutes, the building warmed noticeably and the general office would soon be a sauna. He remembered the cancelation stamp. He took Peter MacMillan's passport from the file, went into the general office as staff cleaners began coming in. He pressed half-inch-high perforations which read, "*CANCELED*" across the face of the passport, then entered the cancelation into the logbook.

———

The Manila Hotel was a famous establishment, a hundred-year-old tradition. Towers asked for Mrs. MacMillan's room at the desk. The clerk found a note in her box instructing callers that she was at the swimming pool.

The pool area was nearly deserted. He walked out to the patio and spotted her at the far side. Her lounge chair was wedged between those of two older, chunky American business execs who were trying to engage her in conversation.

She ignored them, got up, and stood at the edge of the pool, drawing quiet stares. Towers was mesmerized by her figure, the way she filled out a modest one-piece tan swimsuit. She dived in, surfaced. One of the businessmen hoisted his bulk off his lounger, sucked his gut in, and toed the edge of the pool. He tried to execute a smooth dive, but belly-flopped next to her, splashing water in her face. She sprang out, shot him a look that could kill, and then spotted Towers.

"Hi," she called, and waved to him. The exec turned around in the water to see a man skirting the pool towards Lori. Disappointment etched across his face as she went up and took Towers' arm, conveying a definite message that a significant someone had arrived.

"Let's sit over there." Lori pointed out a table at the other end of the pool. She threw a towel over her shoulders, picked up her cigarettes and lighter, and walked ahead of him, tossing a departing scowl at the jerk in the water. Towers tried but failed to avert his eyes from her shape.

She led Towers to the table where they sat down. He felt good just being with her.

"Beautiful, isn't it?" She pointed with a cigarette past Towers. He turned to watch the spectacular evening light show as the sky changed colors, while the sun—an orange ball—slowly dipped behind the mountains on Bataan. The reflection gave Lori a warm glow on her face, which, he wanted to believe, was from his company.

"Thanks for coming," she said. "I got out here ten minutes ago and found that area deserted." Her eyes shifted cat-like to the lounge chairs. "For all of two minutes, that is."

Towers looked over at the paunchy executives commiserating, probably fortifying themselves that it didn't matter. It didn't really, there was certainly no shortage of available women in Manila. But Lori was a blonde, a rare item in Asia, like a trophy compared to the local talent. Hell, like a trophy compared to any woman.

"They'll survive," he said, turning back. "Manila's a friendly town." *Damn! Watch what you say, Bill. Searching for companionship probably cost Peter MacMillan his last night on earth.*

Lori's smile evaporated, replaced with a look commensurate with the business at hand. "Yes, I suppose," she said flatly. "Care for a drink?" Without waiting for an answer, she summoned the waiter, a smart-looking young man with a drinks tray tucked under his arm.

"Sure," Towers agreed. He forgot the time, forgot his plans to drive home, shower, change clothes, and head down to Puerto Azul.

"I've just had a marvelous concoction," she said with a curious mood swing, rolling her eyes. "A Sunset *something* or other, and, yes, I think I'll just have another."

"Sunset Surprise," the waiter corrected. He was tall, trim, ever smiling, and smooth. Towers read the name tag on his jacket.

"Of course, Antonio. That's it," Lori affirmed. "Sunset Surprise. Two, please." She gave Antonio a smile and looked back at Towers. "And it's really a surprise."

Towers thought that she was a little under the influence, maybe trying too hard to lighten up.

She pulled the towel from her shoulders, and began drying her hair. Towers stirred in his chair as her breasts jiggled like two plates of jelly. He looked up to see if anyone was around, certain that even an eighty-year-old monk would do a double-take. No question about it, Mrs. M. was stacked. A heart-stopping, drop dead handful. When she finished, her hair hung across her face like a mask. She smiled from behind the cascade of smooth blonde fleece, blew it out of her eyes. Towers laughed. She was definitely under the influence. He wondered what a second Sunset Surprise might accomplish given the effects from the first.

Lori flung the towel back across her shoulders, combed her hair back with her fingers, then asked, "Now, why in the world did I bother doing that? The water's marvelous and I'm going right back in." She stood and dived into the pool, back-stroked towards the other end, her breasts dipping left then right as she glided through the water. At the far end, she turned, upended to dive deep, her long legs and perfect buns descending.

"Damn, damn, damn, son," Towers muttered. He shook his head and followed Lori's watery shadow returning to their end. She popped up near their table as Antonio came out with their drinks. She sprang out, turned sideways, and perched herself on the pool's edge.

"Here, please," she directed Antonio, patting her thigh. He sat the tray on the ground. She signed the charge and Antonio left. "Come on over," she motioned to Towers.

He walked over, squatted down.

"I'll bet if you remove your shoes and socks, dangle your feet in the water, not a soul will care," Lori whispered.

He laughed, eased himself down next to her, took his drink. Lori tapped glasses, said "*Mabuhay.*" The moment seemed preposterous, but then his entire afternoon had been strange, starting with the moment he first laid eyes on her. She seemed a normal person now, frolicking in the pool, her spirits high. So what if she was trying too hard? Everyone heals differently.

"Have dinner with me," she said suddenly, looking into her drink. "Here." She pointed her drink straw towards the hotel restaurant. "I really wish you would. I want to have dinner, then I want to drink myself to sleep, or until I'm stupid, whichever comes first. Yes. I've thought about it. That's the thing to do." She looked up at him, pleading in her eyes.

You twisted my arm, lady. "Sure," he said. "I'd be happy to." It seemed like the most difficult thing she'd ever asked for, assuming she had to ask for anything.

"Good," she said, smiling. "I'm told the food here is excellent."

He wouldn't reach the resort until midnight at this rate. But so what? Why not have a few drinks? Instead of driving down to Puerto Azul, he'd just hop in a taxi, leave his car in the embassy compound. It would run him thirty, maybe forty bucks to Puerto Azul— subject to haggling—but what the hell! His bag was waiting in his room at the resort and he'd return Monday evening with Millie and John as planned.

"Did you know that General Douglas MacArthur once lived here?" Lori said. "In the penthouse?"

Towers nodded. It was common knowledge in Manila.

She gave a mischievous smile. "When I asked if I could stay in his room, they informed me it was a huge suite. One thousand dollars nightly. Imagine that! But I had to have a peek at it, don't you know. So I shrugged as though price was of no consequence. It's absolutely gooooorgeous. But then I told them—in an uppity fashion, you understand—that it just wouldn't do at all."

Towers cracked up.

"I'm ravenous," she announced. "How about you?" She didn't wait for his answer. "It was too hot all day to eat. Or maybe it's the Sunrise Surprise. Oops! Sunset, I mean. What do you think?" The second drink was making her loquacious.

Towers said that he could eat something. Lori asked him to wait while she went up and changed. She stood unsteadily and struggled into the robe provided by the hotel.

"Don't you *dare* run off," she said, then wavered towards the doors leading into the hotel. She negotiated a table, but bumped into a chair near the entrance.

Not likely I'd run off from you, lady. Not likely at all. He finished his drink and picked up her cigarettes and lighter, wandered into the cocktail lounge where he ordered a vodka tonic. He sat at the bar, playing with her lighter, practiced flipping the top open and striking a light. It was heavy. Gold. He turned it over. A small engraving read, *"To Rachel With Love, Bobby."* Towers shrugged; apparently it was someone else's.

An hour passed and Lori didn't come down from her room. Towers was working on his third drink, pleased somehow to be slightly tipsy. He meandered around the lobby, appraised the paintings that lined the walls, and settled into a large leather armchair. Another twenty minutes passed and he started to wonder if she'd fallen asleep. He was about to ring her room when she emerged from the elevator. She wore a flowing tan crepe dress which clung to her figure and, as usual, she turned heads. Towers admired her openly as she approached, smelling of honey and lilac, her cheeks rosy, radiating health. He wished he could have at least showered. He struggled with his thoughts; the poor woman was a widow all of five days and trying hard to forget it. And he was trying to forget that she was on a widow's mission. A shitty way to meet a beautiful woman.

The Mabuhay Room was darkened, quiet, less than half full. Tables with starched white linens glowed under small, brass candle fittings. A romantic place for all intentions. Towers took in the room, certain that many of the couples weren't married. At least not to each other.

They were seated at a table near to where a trio was setting up. Towers pulled the envelope containing Peter MacMillan's canceled passport from his jacket, pushed it across the table to Lori. She didn't open it, but put it in her small purse.

"Tomorrow," she said at length.

"Absolutely," he blurted without thinking, but recovered with a quick, "What about tomorrow?"

"Peter's funeral. I've decided. Tomorrow morning. The funeral director, Mr. Florentino, has been very helpful. He agreed with what you said. About cremation, I mean. We'd never spoken about it, Peter and I. That's not the kind of thing people our age think about. I don't see what difference it makes. Do you?"

He assumed she was comparing cremation to burial. "No. I don't think it matters."

She nodded, as though his approval had been necessary, and stared into the candle for long seconds. Fire.

Blinking, she looked up at him. "It's awfully inexpensive, isn't it? The funeral and everything."

"Yes," he said, almost adding that at least one benefit about dying in the Philippines was the nominal cost. "Yes, it is. Life is inexpensive here. It's a hard economy." He patted her hand, pulled his away, but sensed that she wished he hadn't. Her eyes shifted back to the candle.

Cremation solved many problems. No delays or paperwork necessary to transfer MacMillan's remains back to the States. No health certificates, no hermetically-sealed coffins, air freight waybills, or permission to remove a corpse from the country. One just carried the ashes back home. That was at this end. In California, there'd be no need for a consignee; again no paperwork, funeral home, burial. Most families just conducted a memorial service, the urn taking center stage.

He made a mental note to prepare a memorandum for Lori to carry Peter's ashes aboard the plane back to LA. It might save indelicate questions at airport security. Just an ash urn, a small aluminum vessel that the *funeraria* would neatly box and label *"The Ashes of Mr. Peter MacMillan."* Most people never bothered with documentation, instead they just placed the box in the overhead bin. Passengers would be surprised, he mused, if they knew how many spirits rode the Pacific in the luggage bins above their heads. One thing's for sure, it'll be the cheapest flight Peter MacMillan will ever have.

"They do it right," Lori said with sad eyes. *"Poof!* It's done. No trouble." Her eyes watered. "'No muss, no fuss,' is what Mom said when Dad passed on. No bother. Nothing. All very convenient." She dabbed her eyes.

Towers reached over and patted her hands again, this time not pulling his back. His heart picked up pace; damn if he didn't get a charge out of simply touching her. But she slowly pulled her hands from beneath his and glanced up at him, a question in her eyes. She opened her small purse.

"I've lost my cigarettes."

Towers dug into his pocket. "No, you haven't." He offered one of her own cigarettes, then lit it for her, somehow disappointed that she smoked. The one imperfection about the otherwise perfect Lori MacMillan.

"Didn't Peter have family?"

Lori shook her head. "He was an only child. Orphaned at 12. An aunt raised him, but she passed on when he was away in the army. We met down in Mexico, both on vacation, both from LA. We were married a month later." She smiled, her eyes sliding away, as if lost in memories.

Towers thought she was at this instant with Peter, back on some Mexican beach. He sipped his water, waited for her to return from her reverie.

Shortly, she did. "That's enough of that."

She ordered another Sunset Surprise and Towers said to make it two, although he really didn't care for them. Lori asked him questions about himself. She listened, hands folded under her chin, eyes intent on his life story. She was a good listener. The only thing preventing him from thinking he was on a date with this gorgeous creature was the wedding band on her finger. Beautiful fingers, perfectly manicured. He wondered how long she would wear the ring. When did a woman take it off? One year? Never? Until she remarried? He'd ask Millie. No, check that; bad idea.

They had dinner with more Sunset Surprises, and after they'd eaten he wanted to ask her to dance to the soft music by the trio. But that would be improper. By ten o'clock, it seemed they'd hardly been talking long at all. Lori was tipsy, laughing at whatever he said, which encouraged him all the more to weave humorous stories about life in the Foreign Service.

He paid the check and they carried their drinks outside. They made their way past the deserted pool to a pier behind the hotel overlooking Manila Bay. There was no moon, but the festive lights around the pool lit the area to similar effect. Lori said that the moon was beautiful, all seven of them. She cracked up and fell against Towers. It was high time she retired and he suggested this reluctantly. She agreed, her laughter trailing off, and then said that she had to rise at ten for an eight o'clock service.

They laughed for a while at her state of inebriation. All too soon, he thought, the night had to end. They headed inside.

At the elevator, he asked if she'd be all right. She said she would, then fell back against the elevator door. He steadied her again and got into the elevator with her. At her door, she managed to unlock it and turned to bid him goodnight.

"I'll see you Tuesday," she slurred. She patted his coat lapel, left her hand there and stroked the material. "You are a very nice man."

She wavered, and backed into her room. As she closed the door slowly, her eyes regarded him with a strange, probing stare.

It was after midnight when he walked out of the hotel. He thought about the look on Lori's face as she closed her door. Was she also unhappy that the evening ended all too soon?

He caught a taxi at Roxas Boulevard but headed for home—not Puerto Azul—inexplicably feeling empty, replaying Lori's every word, her every expression. And her parting look.

In his apartment, he telephoned the resort. Not wanting to wake Millie, or maybe not wanting to explain, he left a message for her that he'd be down in the afternoon.

6

Lori stopped short at the sight of Towers, arms crossed, leaning against the fender of his car. He was dressed in a dark blue suit, smiling at her. She shielded her eyes from the sun. "What are you doing here?"

"Funerals are lonely enough as it is. I thought I'd take you."

"You *are* a dear," she replied, her voice choking a little. "Just a sec."

She returned inside to the transportation desk, canceled the hotel's car.

On the drive to the Las Flores Funeraria, she said she'd received a fax from Mr. Morales earlier. He couldn't return to Manila on Monday, maybe not even Tuesday. "He wants to discuss some things with me." She shook her head. "I hadn't planned on remaining that long. I have to get back to the shop."

"What does he want to discuss?"

"Haven't the foggiest," she answered. "I really didn't know anything about Peter's business. Just import, export. Did Mr. Morales
mention anything to you when he came into the consulate?"

"No, but I didn't inquire. As a gauge, if he says the business is
pressing, that probably means money, which probably means *your*
money. Filipinos are never eager to discuss money *they* owe."

"You mean I could owe him money?"

"Don't know. But if he says you do, I'd suggest you carefully
examine whatever it's for. There'd have to be records, air-freight
bills, things like that. We maintain a list of local law firms if you
need one. Can probably find an accountant for you, too."

She looked at him, said softly, "I don't know what I'd do without
you."

At the Las Flores Funeraria, he parked his car in the compound.
Inside the main building, a small sign next to the chapel read, "*Mac-
Millan.*" In the chapel, a closed casket lay on a draped gurney in
front of a rostrum. The director's son, a young, heavy-set man, led
them to the office where they met Mr. Florentino. He was a heavier-
set, middle-aged original of his son. Lori signed some papers, then
asked for the ladies room. Young Florentino led her out of the office.

Towers asked Florentino if Mrs. MacMillan had seen the body.
She hadn't wanted to, he said. Not after he delicately explained that
the NBI pathologist's work hadn't been the best, particularly the
cranial closing. He'd been left with an extremely difficult cosmetic
job, particularly the cranium which had been difficult to seal closed,
plus the ugly bashed-in forehead. Florentino caught himself, shrugged, and belatedly asked if Towers was a relative. Towers shook his
head and handed Florentino his card.

"Ah, it is fortunate," Florentino said, "that Mrs. MacMillan has
the good services of your embassy."

When Lori returned, Florentino explained that he could crate
the urn for shipping, unless she wanted to carry it with her. She
asked him to pack it. They went into the chapel where a non-de-
nominational minister waited to begin. The coffin was a simple
rectangular pine box painted white with ornate, gold-colored wood-
work on its top and sides. It was inexpensive and crude by most
Western standards.

A wreath from Morales lay at the foot of the casket, and another elaborate one hung on an easel.

"Mom sent those," Lori whispered. "That was sweet of her. They never really got on well. She and Peter. She felt that Peter wasn't, well, wasn't the most attentive husband."

Towers nodded, curious to know more. But it wasn't his place to ask.

In attendance were Florentino and Junior, their secretary, plus an organist, and an older couple who worked for the *funeraria*. The service was brief, dignified, during which Towers sensed Lori's distance, having steeled herself for this moment. Her eyes watered briefly when the minister spoke what little he knew of MacMillan, having the barest statistics from Florentino, perhaps from Morales. Towers held Lori's arm and she leaned into him as the final prayer was read.

The organ whined out a solemn number in conclusion. Lori stared blankly, as though lost somewhere in time. Finally, her eyes misty, she uttered, "It's like he never existed."

Towers looked at her. It was a strange thing for her to say.

A worker wheeled the gurney back through a curtain to the crematorium at the rear of the building. Lori turned to leave. "I don't want to stay for this. Please drive me back to the hotel."

"Of course," he said.

They refused the offer of tea in Florentino's office. Lori thanked him, added that she'd telephone in a few days about the ashes, and instructed him to send any necessary papers to the hotel. Florentino said that he'd take care of everything.

Back at the hotel, she invited Towers into the coffee shop for tea. A secretary from the transportation desk approached as unobtrusively as possible, handed Lori an envelope. Her circumstances were apparently known to the hotel staff, who seemed to mouse around her with near reverence.

"It looks like I'll just have to wait until Wednesday," she said to Towers. "If that's how long it takes Mr. Morales to get here. A lot of waiting."

She dismissed the secretary curtly. "It seems like a lifetime, these past 24 hours. Do you realize I've been in Manila less than a day.

It was difficult sleeping last night, even after those lovely Surprises. Time is different somehow, and I still feel foggy."

"Jet lag," Towers offered.

"I suppose that's it," she said. "Whatever it is, I can't face getting back on a plane for a few days, so I'll wait for your report." She shot him a glance, immediately adding, "I mean, I'll wait for Mr. Morales. I asked the travel desk for suggestions for the weekend. I don't want to wait in Manila. They suggested a place nearby. Puerto Azul or something."

"Puerto Azul? That's where I'm heading!"

"Oh!" Lori looked at him suspiciously. She opened the envelope and read the reservation slip. "They've put me into—" She peeked up at him. "Oh, some bungalow. A car will take me down there at noon." She looked at her watch. "I've just time to change. Is it far?"

"Not too far. Two hours with no traffic. It's Saturday, so you can make it in less time. Most weekenders left yesterday. That's why the restaurant was quiet last night. I was going to leave last night."

"You stayed because of me?"

"I had some paperwork at the office," he lied. "So I went in for a few hours this morning. Uhm, we're staying at the South Seas Resort. Some friends and I. There are lots of bungalows along the beach, but I've never stayed at any of them. South Seas is about the nicest place in Puerto Azul. There's a casino and everything. Place will probably be mobbed." He realized that he was rambling on, leading up to suggesting that she drive down with him.

But she stood abruptly, signed the check, and extended her hand. "Well. Tuesday, then?"

He stood up. "I'll complete my report as soon as I have the death certificate Tuesday morning."

"There doesn't seem to be a rush since Mr. Morales won't be back for days." She grimaced. "My shop. I don't think Irma—she's my assistant—can handle it alone. She's terrific, but I'd better send her a fax before I leave, telling her where I'll be for the weekend." She started to leave. "Mr. Towers. I want to thank you for everything. You can't imagine what it's meant to me. You've been wonderful."

"Bill. Call me Bill."

"Thank you, Bill," she said, turning towards the elevators.

Watching her leave was like turning out a light in his world. She glanced back, waved goodbye, and at being caught with a long face, he forced a smile.

Contact with the lovely Mrs. MacMillan had been severed all too soon, all too suddenly.

7

On the road to Puerto Azul, Towers replayed their parting for the tenth time, cursed himself for not offering to drive her down. After all, they were going to the same area. But her expression when he announced his plans had put him off. As if he'd invented his trip to Puerto Azul. What did she think? That he'd fabricated all that? That he was going down just because she was?

A note from Millie was waiting for him in his room. She'd gone scuba diving with John and would return by dinnertime. Good. He wasn't in the mood for them. All he could think about was Lori. He called around to the other resorts and the few bungalows that were listed. Unable to locate her reservation, he went out to the beach where bungalows north and south skirted the coastline. He walked north, suddenly realizing that this whole weekend seemed flat. Hell, his whole life seemed pointless. Like a monotonous chore before returning to the salt mines Tuesday. That's what it was; just marking time. That's what these past two years had been, except for those few months with Millie. The futility of it all, waiting for his life to take on meaning.

He gave up the search along the north shore, returned to the resort as night was falling. He ran into Millie and John near the restaurant, but made excuses for dinner, saying that he wasn't feeling well. He showered in his room, but instead of retiring, he slipped out through the casino and headed back for the beach.

This time he proceeded south. Lights dotted the beach from jungle outcrops where beer bars and bungalows lined the shore. As he walked into the blackness at the resort's perimeter, he felt the sensation of being watched. But Puerto Azul was a safe area so he shrugged off the feeling.

He abandoned the search at midnight and returned to the resort.

———

In the morning, Towers was jolted out of a deep sleep by someone banging on the door. He flew off the bed, scrambled across the room, and opened it wide, ready to fly out.

Millie, in a tennis outfit, was bouncing a tennis ball against the door. It hit him in the face. She laughed at the picture he made: hair disheveled, sheet lines across his forehead, dumbfounded look on his face. He immediately closed the door to a narrow slit, so she couldn't see the bed. Until he realized it was empty. He'd dreamt of Lori; the dream seemed so real, so passionate. He rubbed his face, let Millie in.

She looked around, then drew back the curtains and opened the balcony door. She picked up the telephone, studying him as room service came on the line. She ordered coffee for him, pointing to his crotch. His fly was open. He turned away from her and buttoned his pajama bottoms.

She shook her head. "My, my. Such modesty." She hung up, and going out the door, called back over her shoulder that they had a reservation for a tennis court in thirty minutes.

He shuffled into the bathroom to piss, but stopped midstream— no easy feat with a full bladder—at what Millie had said. No, it wasn't what she'd said, but how she'd said it. What? She'd looked over her shoulder, called back that she'd reserved a court. He shrugged. So what? A déjà vu thing, he guessed.

They played tennis, but to Millie's disappointment—*court reservations aren't easy to get, bub*—he forfeited after one set, which relinquished the court. He apologized, said that he just didn't feel up to working-out.

They sat and had drinks by the pool. Towers was quiet, listless, and Millie casually inquired how things had gone with Mrs. MacMillan on Friday afternoon. He looked out over the water, shrugged off her question, unwilling to reveal that he'd attended MacMillan's funeral. Millie wouldn't leave it at that. So what kept him in Manila, she asked. He lied, said that a screen full of e-mail awaited him at home, that he'd worked through the evening, sleeping late yesterday morning.

After a while, their talk trailed off. They read and napped until John returned from diving and found them poolside. Towers again begged off having dinner with them, lied that he wanted to look up a retired air force buddy who'd settled near Batangas, an hour's drive south of Puerto Azul. Millie became short and went off to her room to change for dinner. She'd been looking forward to the dance in the ballroom that evening.

John looked at Towers. "How generous you are, pal, tossing away something that lovely. That's what you're doing, you know?"

Towers grunted, stood, and gathered his things. "Be my guest."

He went up to his room, showered, and dressed in shorts, a print shirt, and sandals. He left at dusk to comb the beach again. At the water's edge, he watched the dying sun reflecting off the bay. Soon it was dark.

He thought how this business was becoming ridiculous. He hardly knew Lori, yet could think of nothing else.

He walked south again. As with the night before, the feeling of being watched gripped him in the darker areas. Aside from petty thievery, he'd never heard of any crimes around the resort. This wasn't Manila where phantoms of the night had claimed Peter MacMillan. He walked on, looking over his shoulder whenever a soft breeze kissed the edge of the jungle, rustling fronds.

"Who's there?"

Small breakers lapped against the shore, and music from beer stalls drifted up the beach. But there was no one there.

He passed a bungalow colony set back off the beach. High bamboo walls surrounded the compound, and no signs advertised the place. He wondered how people ever found it. He passed a string of beer bars and some darkened bungalows, passed a cluster of backpackers lazing around a bonfire, swigging down San Miguels and roasting fish. They spoke German, and he caught a whiff of marijuana.

He stopped at a beer bar further up the beach. He was the only customer, but strangely he still didn't feel alone. He looked around again, but saw no one else. Another night remained in this lonely paradise penitentiary. Another night of longing, of rethinking his life, whipping himself for being 10,000 miles from home and realizing he didn't want to be here at all. He finished his beer, then doubled back towards the resort.

As he approached No Name Bungalows, he saw Lori up ahead. His heart turned over almost painfully at the sight of her. She stood at the water's edge, looking out across the dark void, towards a hard streak of pink that cracked the blackness to the east. She wore bikini bottoms under a sleeveless T-shirt. Her hair was slicked back from a recent swim and her breasts stretched the undershirt. Prominent nipples poked against the material as proudly as her stance. The vision of her was breathtaking.

She was barefoot, her arms were folded, and she held an empty glass up next to her cheek, scrunching her breasts together. She turned to him as he approached, her face smiling a hello. He marveled at how the beauty mark on her cheek turned up. Weak-kneed, he came up next to her.

"Thought that was you," he said the obvious.

"Funny, I was just thinking about you."

"Oh?" Towers felt his heart tug.

"Wondering if you'd made it down," she added.

"How's the food here?"

"Marvelous. They have a Belgian chef. Try for yourself."

"I think I will. Join me?"

"I've already eaten, and my dance card is jammed." She turned her empty glass upside down. "Buy a lady a drink?"

Inside the gate, Towers took in the pool surrounded by tucked-away bungalows, creatively landscaped for maximum privacy. A small restaurant was at the end of a walkway. Two security guards were on duty, disguised in knee pants and loud Polynesian shirts. One was a teenager, but the other was an older, thick-set man whose easy smile didn't hide a tougher side. A few couples sat around the bar near the pool, waiting for tables inside.

Lori wrote Towers' name on a slip of paper, gave it to a waiter. This was the *in* place in Puerto Azul and he'd never even heard about it. He felt like a holiday nub from Podunk, the kind of tourist who never ventured beyond his balcony, while a newcomer had found *the* place.

They perched on stools at the bar, ordered drinks from the bartender who addressed Lori as Mees Mock-me-laan in his cheerful sing-song accent.

They were called soon after, bumping—Towers thought—two other parties. The small restaurant was first-class, expensively decorated, with a superior menu.

Lori drank while he ate, and soon a pack of yachties came ashore, congregating around the bar outside, waiting for tables along with other arrivals from off-premises. As his entrée was served, Towers braced at the sight of Millie and John entering. They were shown to a table and Millie looked around, taking in the restaurant. She froze when she spotted them in the corner. Towers cringed. From the corner of his eye, he saw her alerting John.

Millie and John sat down and ordered, looking over occasionally, obviously talking about him. Soon he excused himself and walked over to their table.

"Look who I ran into," he said, almost apologetically.

"Your old air force buddy?" Millie confirmed to herself, then shot him that look of hers. "She looks *so* young to be retired."

"I ran into her on the beach."

"Walking down to Batangas, were you?" Millie batted her eyelashes innocently.

"No," he said coolly. "I decided not to go down after all."

"No kidding? How *is* Mrs. MacMillan this evening?" Her eyes slid over to Lori's table. "She seems fine."

"Strange that she should end up here," John said. "Did you invite her?"

"Of course not!" Towers objected, a little too strongly. "She decided to get away for the weekend and the travel desk at the Manila suggested this place."

Millie and John exchanged glances. Exasperated, Towers said that he should get back to his table.

"Casino later?" John asked.

Towers shook his head, said he didn't care to gamble tonight.

Millie gave him a concerned look as he withdrew. "Take care, Bill."

He ignored her.

Back at their table, Lori seemed not to have noticed Millie and John. In fact, it seemed that she'd kept her face towards the window so that they wouldn't see her. Was she embarrassed to be seen with him? Towers lingered over his dinner, making certain that Millie and John finished and left first. He saw them walking around the pool, inspecting the place, before going out through the gate.

Lori languished over several more cocktails between appetizers she picked at, and didn't seem to mind his slow pace. She was becoming more tipsy, more talkative with each drink—potent fruity concoctions.

Towers paid the bill and they went back out to the poolside bar. No one was there now except Alberto, the bartender, who flashed a gold-capped front tooth and stationed himself, awaiting their order. Lori ordered a drink and walked off towards the cabins without a word, staggering slightly. She returned wrapped in a towel, and dropped her key on the bar. She lifted her glass, tapped it against his, and sipped as she let the towel drop to her feet. Her outfit—what there was of it—nearly jolted Towers off his stool. It wasn't the modest one-piece she'd worn at the Manila pool. This job was a skimpy Day-Glo lime-colored bikini held together by a few strings, an outfit absolutely guaranteed to make that eighty-year-old monk do back flips. The bikini top was cut an inch or so wide over her nipples, and the bottom was a triangle not much larger than a Band Aid. A string ran around her hips, disappeared between her buttocks.

Towers held his breath as she turned and dived into the pool. He exhaled, then peeked at Alberto who muttered something in Tagalog, turned his back and pretended to inventory the shelves behind the bar.

Lori surfaced at the shallow end, beckoned Towers in. But he dare not stand up, his shorts resembling the oft-referenced home of Omar the Tent Maker. He shrugged helplessly, pinched at his shirt to show he had no trunks.

"Take my key," she called. "Use my bungalow, drop your shirt and loafers. You can swim in your shorts."

He refused, she insisted. He declined, she relented, whereupon he acquiesced in cavalier fashion, saying that no lady should be thrice refused. Besides, the stalling tactic eased his erection. He felt his retort witty until Alberto muttered that only a fool would have refused once.

"And grab another towel," she called as he crossed the lawn to the bungalows. He thought that he might also be a bit under the influence. Or maybe he was just happy being with her. Whatever it was, he felt great.

In her bungalow, Lori's clothes were strewn about. The appointments were excellent, far better than his sterile room at the resort. King-size bed with rich linens, a well-stocked wet bar, cable TV, a library of porno videos, and a Pullman kitchen. Beyond a sliding glass door, a private, walled-off sunbathing patio nestled next to a large Jacuzzi, exclusively for this unit. Towers whistled. In such a place, one had no need to ever venture beyond the door. This was also a place for lovers. He ran his finger across the file of porno tapes. Maybe seven or eight lovers.

Feeling impropriety, he emptied his pockets and left his keys, money, shirt, and loafers in the bungalow. He pulled an oversized Godiva from a heated towel rack and returned outside.

Lori was still in the pool, standing at the darkened shallow end—drink in hand—speaking in hushed tones to the big security guard who squatted close to her at the edge of the pool. Their conversation seemed conspiratorial, and a moment later, she laughed. The guard saw Towers, abruptly terminated their conversation, and stood up. Lori turned and ran her thumb down the inside of her bikini top, adjusting the patches that covered her nipples. The guard wandered off as she waded across to where Towers stood.

He smiled at her, curious about her conversation with the guard; too familiar with him being an employee. She was adjusting the bikini top again. Maybe it was precarious keeping the sheer cloth perched across those beautiful summits. A scant millimeter shift to either side and *las coronas* would peek out and say hello.

"C'mon in," she coaxed, patting the water. She slurred her words.

He sat at the edge, scooted in. The water was warm. Lori summoned Alberto over with his drink, then handed hers to Towers, taking the fresh one. She backed against the side and sipped the drink quietly, studying Towers, a pert smile on her face.

"I love the water," she said wistfully. "I could live in it. There's a pool where we live, in LA," she added. Then hesitatingly, "Where *I* live. But it closes at nine, and I'm rarely home from the shop by that time."

"What kind of shop do you have?"

"Antiques, collectibles, that sort of thing," she answered, suddenly testy. She seemed to want to tell him something, was thinking how to say it. He sipped his drink, waited.

"Peter traveled a lot," she said at length. "At least lately. I thought he was just trying to keep away from me."

How could a man possibly want to stay away from you?

"I didn't think all the travel was necessary, since he had agents wherever he did business. People like Mr. Morales. But, he insisted it was. We argued about it and he suggested I go with him, knowing that wasn't possible with the shop. Anyway, he finally admitted that the trips weren't all that necessary, but he liked globe-trotting and said he wouldn't stop. Then I found out why."

Lori sipped her drink. "I don't think I would have been welcome on his trips, after all." She bit her bottom lip.

It was nearly midnight and the lights around the pool area went off suddenly. Two couples emerged from the shadows for a late dip, having waited for this moment. One was a middle-aged tourist and a young Filipina who looked suspiciously under-age despite her considerable physical charms. In the pool, they closed like magnets in intimate conversation as the other couple joined them—a younger man with a Filipina of Buffalo Joe's caliber. An exhibition of giggles, fondling, and cross-embracing followed, the couples unaware or uncaring that others were poolside. Lori watched them quietly, Towers waited for her to continue.

"I'd gone through his things one morning after he returned from a long trip to Manila. He was asleep, dead to the world. He hadn't touched me when he came in during the night. After a month! That wasn't like Peter.

"So, I went through his things. Women do that, you know, when they suspect something. His boarding pass showed that he'd left Manila three days before. He hadn't just arrived, he'd been in LA for several days. There were condoms in his toilet kit." She stopped, seemed to be thinking where to go with this.

I could have told you that, Towers thought, still unable to fathom how a man would prefer other women to Lori, especially those tarts that patrolled Buffalo Joe's.

"I looked in his address book," she continued. "I'd never looked through it before. Never had a reason to. There were names and addresses of women. All over, even in LA. Right under my nose, and I had no idea. Snapshots of pretty little Asian sluts. I'd been a naïve fool. Peter was a *very* handsome man." She swallowed hard, and said bitterly, "I should have guessed it."

She snapped her fingers and Alberto looked up. She pointed to her glass, held up two fingers, although Towers had hardly touched his drink. Alberto grinned, his gold tooth aligning perfectly with the brass buttons on his tunic.

Towers chug-a-lugged his drink to keep up with her. What the hell! It was Sunday night and he could sleep in tomorrow morning. Let Millie and John play tennis; he was here to relax—and finally, with Lori, he was doing just that. He couldn't remember feeling so good.

He peered over at the couples in the corner of the pool. They spoke in hushed tones, laughing intermittently, then an occasional burst of pretend outrage when one of the girls was fondled.

"I told Peter I wanted a divorce," she went on, watching their antics dispassionately. "But he wouldn't hear of it. He asked for time, saying he had some important things he was working on. I suggested at least a separation, but he didn't want that either, although as things were going, we might as well have been separated. I insisted he sleep on the couch when he came around. I only saw him twice in the past six months, when he dropped in—a detour to somewhere else. But he paid his share of the bills and I devoted myself to the shop, doubting that he'd straighten out. He was drinking. Heavily."

Their drinks came and Lori turned light again, as suddenly as she'd gone sullen.

"Whatever these are, they're heavenly. I'll sleep well again tonight. Come on," she commanded. She climbed out of the pool, stood unsteadily above him. "Bring your drink." She held out her hand. Towers took it, and climbed out, wondering where they were going. To the Jacuzzi in her room?

"The towels," she whispered drunkenly, although no one was close enough to hear her. Towers gathered their towels and she led him around the pool to the compound exit.

"The pool's too crowded." She giggled. "Well, too busy at any rate."

"We can swim at the resort," he gestured in the opposite direction. "They leave the pool open until one o'clock." He nearly tripped on a sand mound.

"So what?" she protested, pulling him along. "They leave the ocean open all night! And we have no school tomorrow."

Towers turned the 'we' over in his mind.

She pulled him across the sand until they were well away from the lights from the bungalows. The bay was silent, the water still, aside from a faint lapping on the sand. Lori tried to sit down, but fell sideways, giggling. Towers sat down clumsily, spilling his drink on his arm.

"Oops!" he said.

"What oops? Sit on a crab?" She laughed.

"Spilled some on my arm."

She reached for him, falling across his lap. "Where? I'll just drink that," she slurred, pulling his arm to her mouth, slurping at the wetness. Towers began to swell.

"Not bad," she appraised smacking her lips, her breath hot against his skin. "But next time, hold the hair, please." That struck them as terribly clever, and they laughed for long moments, caught their breath, then she repeated, "Hold the hair," and they laughed again, launching into contagious giggling. She stood up reeling, gained her balance, stripped off her tiny bikini, and dropped it on his head.

He pulled a string away from his face, held up the tiniest strip of material, and looked up. *Oh, my Lord!*

She waded into the water. "It's wonderful," she called out.

"It certainly is," he said to himself, focusing on her ass. He tried to stand up, but fell sideways. He tried again, succeeded, and followed her.

Splash. She had dived, disappeared. Towers dived shallow, and scraped his body on sand and seashells. He was drunker than he thought. He stood up, spat water—the salt burning his eyes—thinking this wasn't such a good idea.

Lori was a short distance away, facing him. She upended, her buttocks glistening as she descended. Rock hard now, Towers was aware of the water's coolness at his crotch for the first time. She surfaced, treading water. He waded out a bit further, wishing he liked water as much as he professed. But in truth, he didn't feel at all comfortable in the ocean, especially in the dark.

"Do you think there are sharks?" he whispered, trying for mature indifference to her nudity, trying to tread water effortlessly.

She moved closer, her face near his, her eyes intense, preying. Then she screamed, "Shark!" She grabbed his manhood, laughed out loud. "And what a big fish he's caught!" She drew closer and threw her other arm over his shoulder, nearly pulling him under. Her hand worked feverishly on him as he struggled to keep his head up. He took in water, choked, and fought to keep from panicking, relieved when his toes touched bottom. With considerable effort, he edged them closer to the beach until his feet were squarely on the bottom.

And she still held his member, tugging at him, squeezing so hard it positively hurt. And his heart thumped madly.

"You'd swim easier if you weren't overdressed," she said, the liquor on her breath strong. Her hand searched through his fly, groping him knowingly. His heart hammered in his chest and his brain pounded with excitement. She tugged at his shorts, jerking them down around his knees to where he obligingly stepped out of them. He threw her legs around his waist as his shorts floated to the surface and away from them. She put her arms around his neck, hoisted herself out of the water, and body-scissored him, moaning. She grabbed his penis, her nails like razors, guiding him into her.

"Oh, my god," she cried. "It's been *so* long." Her arms were strong around his neck, her fingernails tearing the flesh on his back. She screamed and jerked, her legs squeezing his waist so tight he winced, almost unable to breathe. Then, all of a sudden, she was still, hanging limp around his neck, panting. She then pushed him away and waded back to the beach. He looked down at himself, grimaced in frustration.

Lori sat on the sand, drew her knees up to her chin, and covered her nakedness with a towel. She seemed to be crying. Towers waded ashore, painfully erect, hoping her scream wouldn't summon the guards from the bungalows. He sat down next to her, looked around for his towel, and draped it across her shoulders.

She *was* crying! He put his arm around her but she made no effort to lean into him.

Eventually she spoke without looking up. "God, I'm despicable."

"No, you're not," he said, wishing she'd been despicable just a little bit longer.

"That's the first time I've ever been unfaithful to Peter."

Towers felt like crying out his frustration, but nearly laughed at her words. Their briefest coupling could hardly be called infidelity; shaking hands took longer.

"I had no right to take advantage of you," she said.

"You haven't," he replied. "And you haven't been unfaithful to Peter."

She looked at him, her face blank, her tears stopping, as if realizing her new status for the first time. "No, it isn't infidelity now. Is it?"

He shook his head, wanting desperately to take her again. His erection was scheduled for eternity if he didn't.

He was indecisive and she offered no encouragement. "Just the same," she said. "I had no right to presume with you. I'm sorry."

"I'm not sorry, and you have nothing to be sorry for."

She glanced at him. "Maybe. Maybe not."

"Where do we go from here?"

"Back to Manila," she answered.

"That's not what I mean."

"I know it's not, Bill. But I need to understand where I've been this past year before I know where I'm going." She stood without another word and walked back into the compound.

Towers replayed what had just happened, wondering if she would return. When it was apparent she wouldn't, his disposition withered while his erection persisted. Should he follow her into the compound? He stood up, and that's when he realized he was still naked. He looked around for his towel, then slapped his forehead; he'd thrown it over her shoulders and she'd taken both in with her. He couldn't very well steal naked into the compound, creep up to her bungalow, and knock on her door with his boner. His shorts! He searched in the blackness, checking along the beach where, hopefully, they'd washed ashore. Not finding them, he went back into the water, and waded up and down the shore, searching but mostly feeling around in the pitch dark.

Voices were coming up the beach. The group of German backpackers were returning to their bungalows, their banter booming across the sand. Several carried flashlights, their beams jerking this way and that, bouncing between their paths along the beach and occasionally out across the water. Towers cursed his predicament. Nakedness took on a new meaning. Being discovered alone and naked on the beach with a boner would look peculiar. The damn thing just wouldn't go down. He thought to call out, ask them to help look for his shorts with their flashlights. Bad idea. They'd probably just have a big laugh at his expense, maybe keep their spotlights on him all night. He backed deeper into the water, hunkered down, ridiculously feeling like a commando on an enemy beachhead. When the group passed, he resumed his search.

Near dawn, he skulked back to the resort wrapped in a banana leaf. A suspicious security guard followed him to his room, then listened at length as Towers tried to convince him that he was, indeed, a guest.

He took a long, hot shower, cursing his luck. But he couldn't blame Lori. She was drunk. Drunk and ashamed. No. It wasn't her fault. It was him; he'd been a size-ten asshole, guilty of taking advantage of a widow. Christ! A widow for all of one week and he'd gotten into her pants. He should be shot. Yet as he relaxed in bed, a broad smile came to his lips.

8

Towers waited for a respectable hour before making his way back to Lori's bungalow. Ten o'clock seemed right. Over breakfast, he'd regale her with his naked adventures after she'd abandoned him last night.

But she'd already checked-out, leaving his things and hotel key in a paper sack with his name on it. Inside, was a note:

I'm so ashamed, I don't know how to face you.
But I guess I'll have to Tuesday.
Lori.

He was devastated. She could have at least telephoned him at the resort to tell him she was leaving. But she was probably too embarrassed. Outside the gate, the heavy-set guard looked away, pretended not to notice him. Did he know? Had his conduct been so dastardly? He shuffled back towards the resort, his disappointment monumental.

However, it was a capital conquest, after all. He didn't admit to himself that she'd been blind drunk from firing down cocktails as fast as Alberto could mix them. He'd make it up to her, though. He should have resisted her. She might have respected him for that. Good grief! What was he saying? Weren't women supposed to think like that?

He avoided Millie and John, and left the resort without saying goodbye. He telephoned the Manila Hotel as soon as he dropped his bag in his apartment. Lori had checked back in but wasn't in her room. Or maybe she just wasn't answering the phone, too embarrassed and ashamed to talk to him. He left a message, but she didn't return his call by 10:00 p.m. Maybe she thought it was too late to telephone after that, but he waited up until midnight just the same, then set the phone ringer volume on high. He fell asleep, dreamt of her and woke several times during the night, resisted the urge to call her.

On Tuesday morning, he received the death certificate from the Civil Registrar's office at City Hall. He completed Form 180 by hand, based on the autopsy findings which showed that MacMillan's stomach had contained massive traces of barbiturates. Combined with alcohol, it proved fatal. Plus, there was a fracture of the skull. Towers shook his head as he read the certificate. He had a clerk type out and photocopy a dozen Form 180s, then he pressed the government seal on each copy.

At two o'clock, his heart lurched when Lori entered and sat down in the American Citizens Services section. She wore a simple cotton dress and a straw sun hat. The section was busy, but he called her out of turn to a window.

"Hi," she mouthed, coming up to the window, then she lowered her eyes. She peeked at him from under her hat, shifted her gaze, saw Millie watching them. Towers had no excuse to take Lori back to the staff room this time. He almost wished she'd start to cry so he'd have a reason to get her alone.

"How are you?" he whispered.

She nodded. "Is everything ready?"

"Uh, yes. Wait one moment," he said in his best official voice. He took MacMillan's file from his desk, feeling Millie's eyes on his back, and returned to the window.

"Here," he said, shoving a wide envelope beneath the window. "I've signed and sealed a dozen copies of the 180 for you. Extras usually come in handy. And here's the death certificate."

Lori read them carefully and Towers watched her eyes pause on the entry next to Contributory Cause Of Death: *"Substance abuse,"* according to a Dr. Locanto of the NBI laboratory. He shrugged even though she wasn't looking at him. Hopefully, she wouldn't have to show it to many people.

"Can I see you later?" he asked, almost mouthing the question because the mike required a certain volume to be audible.

"Mr. Morales made it back to town after all," she said, equally conspiratorial. "I have to see him later. He'll call. Maybe for dinner."

"Dinner's fine."

"I mean, I may have to see *him* for dinner."

"Oh! Uh, well, when are you leaving?" Towers' eyes slid sideways, his voice low. Millie was busy at another window, John was in his office.

"I'm not sure. That depends on what business Mr. Morales has."

"I'll call you later," he said. "Say, around eight tonight?"

"That'll be fine." She folded the envelope, stuffed it in her purse, started to turn away, and then looked back at him. A frown. "Was what happened Sunday night part of the American Citizens Services?" Her sober expression was accusing, and Towers cringed inwardly until he detected a smile coming to her lips, the beauty mark rising.

"Shucks, ma'am. We try to help," he quipped cheerfully, feeling nothing at all like that. He needed desperately to see her again, to hold her. He gave her a broad smile. Maybe tonight they'd swim at the Manila Hotel and afterwards, well!

"And you certainly did, Bill. You'll never know how much you've helped me." She turned and walked away with a provocative gait he felt certain was for his benefit.

He was due for some home leave. He'd planned on saving it, adding it to other time accumulated once he returned to the States. But now that had changed. He'd tell her tonight. He'd go home to

Denver, but stop off in LA to visit her, maybe take her home with him. Better yet, maybe they wouldn't even make it past LA. Maybe by then she'd be clear of Peter's memory. Maybe then she could think about the future. He turned to find Millie standing directly behind him, her eyes questioning. Had she overheard their exchange? He felt foolish, but what the hell, he didn't care. He brushed past her and went into his office.

———

He made a point of working late, to stay near the Manila Hotel. He telephoned her at exactly eight.

"I'm sorry, sir," the operator said. "But Mrs. MacMillan checked out this afternoon. Just after three o'clock."

Again, she'd vanished! That was odd; three o'clock? Right after she visited the embassy. Odd also since she had to meet Morales this evening for dinner. Perhaps Morales had invited her to stay at his home. Well, Filipinos were very gracious, hospitable to a fault. That's probably it. He realized Lori didn't have his home number. He opened Peter MacMillan's file and noted the number given by Morales. He called the number, but the phone just rang. He called back several times. Same thing. He kept calling up until midnight, letting the phone ring on and on, each call more desperate than the last. Finally he left the office and drove back to his apartment. Maybe she'd call him in the morning.

Throughout Wednesday, he hovered near the switchboard, eavesdropping as incoming calls were answered. But hers wasn't one of them.

9

Roth skipped around passengers disembarking the flight from Cebu, dodged a family congregating near the ramp, and hustled through the Domestic Arrivals terminal.

He'd taken Titty City down to the islands where he'd worked another case, and had now abandoned her in her seat with a wad of 1,000-peso notes. He told her he had to catch a connecting flight, and yes, of course, he'd look her up when he returned to Manila.

He raced to International Departures and checked in for the flight to Bangkok on Thai Airways. The staff at Gate Seven, alerted by the check-in counter, waited anxiously as an agent hustled him through Immigration.

Next to Gate Seven, Lori MacMillan was hurrying to Six, to board Philippines Flight 631 en route to Los Angeles, where she'd connect with a New York flight.

Had she been thirty seconds earlier or Roth thirty seconds later, they might have met. Had Roth seen her, they surely would have met. If so, she surely would have blown him off. His eyes were rheumy and he was sweating and disheveled, smelling of booze, day-old clothes, and Titty City's cheap, syrupy-sweet perfume.

He slumped into his Business-Class seat, ignoring several icy stares condemning him for the late departure, and smiled at the hostess, his bartender for the three-hour flight to Bangkok.

10 New York City

Mrs. Julia Warner entered the Fifth Avenue apartment building at four o'clock, Tuesday afternoon. Gus, the doorman, smiled and tossed a casual salute. She tipped her sunglasses down on her nose, winked at him. She was always friendly that way, a knowing smile on her lips. Gus wondered again if that mole on her right cheek was real. He'd read somewhere that moles were fashionable, that women just pasted them on here and there. Fake or not, it was far more attractive than those bimbos who stapled their faces these days.

"How was Chicago, Mrs. Warner?"

"Windy. Is my husband in?"

"All day. Hasn't gone out yet."

She'd called the apartment from Kennedy Airport, but Robert hadn't answered. The numbnuts was probably glued to the TV, hadn't heard the phone ring. She was exhausted; thirty long hours since she left that toilet called Manila.

Hank, the elevator man, took her up to the fourth floor. She didn't bother finding her key, knowing Gus would buzz the apartment ahead of her. At her door, she detected a shadow behind the peephole. Then Robert opened the door.

"Surprise, Jordan, darling," she greeted him, making certain Hank overheard his name. "I finished up sooner than I thought."

"Rachel! Uh, Julia, darling!" Robert answered.

Hank smiled, pleased with his small contribution to this joyous reunion. Robert swooped her up in his arms, planted a kiss on her mouth. He kicked the door closed with his foot, kissed her again, harder this time.

"I've missed you, Rachel."

"Don't overdo it." She pushed away from him, throwing down her bag. "And goddammit, keep my name straight."

Robert grimaced. He'd screwed up again.

Rachel went to the bar and made herself a martini. Barbie, her toy poodle, scurried in from the bedroom yapping frantically, and flew into her arms.

Robert went over and sat on the couch, turned his attention to the TV for a stock quotation he'd been waiting for. A ticker tape paced across the bottom of the screen and he scribbled figures on a notepad before him.

"How was my baby?" Rachel nuzzled Barbie. "Did you miss mommy?" To Robert: "Was she all right?"

"No matter how well I disguise it, I just can't get her to eat the poison," he said distractedly.

"That's not funny," Rachel snapped, then made a pouting face to Barbie. "He isn't funny, is he, precious?"

"How'd it go?" he asked, turning back to her.

"It went," she said tiredly.

"May I extend my condolences on the loss of your late husband, the unremembered, unlamented Peter MacMillan."

"Good riddance."

"Tell me about it."

"Later. I'm tired. And filthy. Thirty hours from Manila. Routed through LA, laid-over for five hours."

"Don't complain. I've hauled my ass to Manila and back twice in the past six weeks."

"Haul this," she said, kicking her bag across the floor. She put Barbie down, but the dog protested with a shrill bark, the fluffy ball at the tip of her tail wagging like a metronome to an eight count beat.

Robert got up, hefted the bag, and followed her into the bedroom, Rachel leaving a trail of clothes: shoes, coat, blouse, and skirt. She disappeared into the bathroom, slammed the door. Barbie, on her heels, scratched on the outside.

She called through the door, "Fetch my drink, won't you?"

Robert looked down at Barbie. "Fetch? Isn't that your job, you ugly little furball." Briefly, he heard the bath running. He toed Barbie away from the door, but the poodle protested. "Yeah, yeah, Mommy Slut's home, you little bitch." Barbie looked up at him, growled, and then pawed again at the door. Robert dumped Rachel's clothes into the laundry basket, returned to the bar for her martini, and carried it into the bedroom. He knocked on the bathroom door, and Rachel's hand poked out through the steam. Barbie seized the opportunity, squeezed inside. Rachel slammed the door shut and Robert heard the lock turn.

He went back into the living room, plopped down again on the couch in front of the TV. A moment later, he was lost in financial reports. Their stocks were doing poorly. He clamped the earphones on his head, listened to a CD as he watched the screen.

Rachel emerged from her bath an hour later wearing a robe, her hair bundled in a towel. She went into the living room and behind the bar to make herself another martini.

"How are we doing?" she asked. She looked up when he didn't answer her. Headphones again. No wonder he hadn't answered her call from the airport. The phone sat directly in front of him on the coffee table.

"You're really a sad sack of shit, you know that, Robert?" She leaned on the bar. "A real class-A idiot." She snickered at her solitary game, picked up the cellphone on the bar, and dialed their apartment number. Robert tilted his head, thought he heard the phone ringing. He removed his headset, picked up the receiver.

"Uh, hello?"

"You're a fucking idiot, you know that?"

"What? Who's this?"

Rachel threw an olive that bounced off the back of his head.

"Huh!" Robert jumped, turned around surprised. "Oh!"

"You can hang up now, Einstein." She replaced the receiver. "How are we doing?"

"Hi-tech's are down. Way down. Bonds are up." He looked back at her. "Why don't you take a nap. We'll go out later for dinner."

"I will. But first, another. I can't go, go, go for thirty hours and then just fall asleep." She came around the bar and perched on a stool, sipping her martini and studying the stock reports. Occasionally, Robert picked up pad and pencil, scribbled down a stock quotation.

"There's a really good window opening up for some stuff I've been following," he said. "You'll have to cut loose with about three, four hundred grand." He put his headphones on again.

Rachel watched the screen for a few moments, then finished her drink with a gulp. She went into the bedroom and closed the door.

———

Robert woke her at eight o'clock. The bedroom was dark. He scooted Barbie off the bed, lay down and pressed up against her, cocooned beneath a quilt. She stirred, gave him a shot with her elbow. He grunted.

"Don't, Bobby."

Robert moved back. "Why, Rachel? Why?"

"You know why."

Fuming, he got up, walked to the door. "We could've gotten two bedrooms," he snapped.

"I did it to save money. It's only for another few months and you said you didn't mind the couch."

"I was hoping it'd be the way it used to be."

"We can't ever go back, Bobby." She sat up. "I'm famished. What time is it?"

"Just after eight." He resigned himself, sighed. "How's steak sound?"

"Moooooo?" she answered, earning a chuckle from him. He could never stay angry with her for long.

———

On Third Avenue they found a steakhouse and took a table in the back. She told him about Manila, Puerto Azul, the cremation, and Towers, laughing at the buffoon.

"Fuck him?"

Rachel let out a deep sigh. Whatever she did lately dominated Robert's thinking. "I wanted to come away with the 180. I did what I had to. How's it going with what's her name?"

"Lolita? She's gonna make trouble. Says if she's gotta die off and disappear, she wants more money for her family before she comes to the States."

"She really believes you'll marry her?" Rachel shook her head at Lolita's naïveté.

"Of course she does. I can be pretty persuasive, you know. Pretty good in the cot, too."

She ignored his self-promotion. "She's getting greedy, huh?"

"What do you expect? She's just a streetwalker that cop fixed me up with. Dumber than a sack of hammers. Uses drugs, some local shit called *shabu*. Something like crack." He opened his hands in protest. "I didn't know it until I saw her again the other week. Reno will keep her in line. But she ping-pongs: nice, then bitchy, flirts around in front of me, like I give a rat's ass what she does. Then she puts on a jealousy act when I look at a skirt. She asked who you were when she called last month."

"Tell her I'm your sister."

"She didn't believe me. Says if I cheat on her and don't cut her in for more money, she'll talk. Get that; cheat on *her*. If she had as many dicks sticking out of her as she's had stuck in her, she'd look like a porcupine."

"She understands that if she runs to the authorities, she'll get nothing?"

"Says she doesn't care. I'm telling you, she's not reliable. That *shabu* shit makes those girls crazy."

Robert and Rachel Tierney, also known as Jordan and Julia Warner, also known as Peter and Lori MacMillan, studied each other for a moment.

"Do what you have to," she said finally, looking away.

"Don't we always?" he replied, concentrating on his steak. "Anyhow, I'm outta here first thing in the morning. St. Louis. Don't forget to file the claims on MacMillan."

"I'll wait until next week." She crossed her silverware on the plate, lit a cigarette.

"Why?" he asked.

"Peter MacMillan is a pile of ashes one day and I file the next? No. Makes a widow look too anxious. A widow needs time, grieving and all that shit. Then, she thinks about security, goes through the safe deposit box, and surprise, surprise, she discovers the insurance policies. Think about it."

Robert shrugged. "I suppose so. Still, some of these stock opportunities don't stay around long. I told you I needed three, maybe four hundred thousand."

"I'll look at it first."

Temper again: "Don't you think I can choose stock?"

She didn't answer. Robert was too impulsive. Too fast with investment decisions. And he snubbed her insurance research: what companies wrote what lines of business, how they paid, who they hired to investigate their claims. They'd been over this. Too many times. Robert didn't listen. He lost in the market chasing glamour stocks, anything new, promising, regardless of how she stressed blue chips—solid risks with solid track records. Last year, their portfolio had eked out four percent, taking his losses into consideration. Had he followed her advice, they'd have earned 12 percent.

He waited for a reply, arms akimbo, challenging, like a martinet.

She ignored him. *Buster, you're reducing your importance around here to only one thing: passing for an insured—something anyone with half a brain could do.* She changed the subject. "I need another place before I file the claims."

"Use this place. Tell them you're staying with a friend."

"No, Robert. Too easy to connect the MacMillans with the Warners. All I need is some adjuster coming to interview Mrs. Warner who says, 'Hey, weren't you Mrs. MacMillan last month?' I like to think I'm not easily forgotten."

Robert shrugged. "Use LA."

"Maybe. But we've used that place too much."

"What are you thinking? Another apartment?"

"Not necessary. Don't want to spend the money or bother with new bonafides. Which reminds me, you didn't have the security camera installed. I told you that I want to see who's at the door without having to peek through the spy hole."

"Been too busy."

"One call. That's all it would take."

"Okay. Okay."

"You don't think people know when someone's peeking at them from behind the door. Hiding behind doors in an apartment like ours looks suspicious."

"I'll call someone in tomorrow."

"You're leaving in the morning. Never mind. I'll handle it."

"You're too careful."

She stubbed out her cigarette. Again, he'd let her down. A simple telephone call was all it took. An hour or two for a technician to install a pin-point camera lens and a monitor. Too busy, like hell. All he did was sit on his ass and watch the market and hit the singles bars, trying to get laid.

"And you're not careful *enough*," she said quietly. For the hundredth time.

———

Back in the apartment, Rachel brushed her teeth, did maintenance work on her complexion, retired. Later, she felt the bed shake as Robert got in, and later still he started touching her, his hand warm on her thigh, sliding up beneath her panties. She reached around, withdrew his hand, threw it off her.

"You want *me* to sleep on the couch?" she asked.

The bed shook again as he got up. He took a pillow, left the room, stopping at the door. "You screw everybody but me."

Rachel rolled over, her back to the door. The expense of a two-bedroom apartment wasn't necessary and he'd agreed to use the couch when they took this place on a six-month sublet. But he was starting again, becoming more insistent. He probably wasn't getting laid; with his attitude, she didn't wonder. He counted on his good looks, but as soon as he opened his mouth, he turned women off. They wouldn't be here much longer. January at the outside. Until then, the couch wouldn't kill him. As for their next place? She had some hard thinking to do on that item. She was getting sick and tired of his tantrums.

The next morning, she woke just after seven o'clock to the smell of cooking. She threw on a robe, went into the breakfast room adjoining the kitchen, poured a cup of coffee.

Robert was dressed for traveling. Slacks, crew-neck sweater, and sports jacket. She liked the way he dressed. Or rather, she liked the way she taught him how to dress. "What time's your flight?" she asked.

"Noon. I'll stay in St. Louis tonight, head north in the morning, maybe up to Iowa. I've written out my itinerary for you. On the desk. A few weeks should do it. But I'll need more than three grand for the trip."

"Three is enough."

Robert scowled at her, but didn't want to argue. She was squeezing him too much, never enough loose cash for a guy to have a little fun.

"I think I'll go down to Mom's next week," Rachel declared.

"File the claims on Mr. MacMillan, Mrs. MacMillan."

"I told you last night. It'll wait until I get back."

"You tell me!" he said snidely. "Who died and left you chief? I don't see any fucking Indians running around here."

Rachel sighed, didn't answer. Robert was looking for an argument again. This was happening too much, and sex, or lack thereof, was behind it. That, plus he always needed more pocket money. Well, she wasn't going to screw him or throw away money just to keep the peace.

He served her a plate and sulked quietly. After a while he said, "Say hi to Doc for me."

"It's been two years since you've seen them, Robert. They always ask about you."

"Tell them I'm just fine, Rachel. Maybe I'll go down at Christmas."

"My name is Julia," she sang impatiently, rolling her eyes.

Robert blew up, threw the skillet into the sink. "How come I gotta remember that you're Lori, or Julia, or whatever flavor of the month you are, but you can always call me Robert? Huh? Huh?"

Rachel stood and threw her cup at him, barely missing his head. The cup shattered on the wall behind him. "Because I don't screw up like you do," she screamed. She headed for the bedroom, slammed the door, and didn't come out until she heard the apartment door bang shut. Barbie looked up from her pillowed lair beneath the bed, her eyes sympathetic.

"Asshole," Rachel spat.

Barbie yapped agreement and jumped on the bed for a cuddle. She liked it when Robert was away.

11 Hannibal, Missouri

Robert drove past the city limits heading northwest towards Palmyra, Missouri. Rachel's initial data had developed three search possibilities for establishing faked personas: two in Northeast Missouri and one in Southwest Iowa; courthouses that had burned down over the past 25 years. Around the time Robert was born.

Unfortunately, in two of the courthouses he checked, birth and death records had been saved, but in the third, birth records had been partially destroyed. He drove through Lewis County, on up into Clark County, arriving at the county seat at dusk. He stopped at a roadside motel, registered under the name of Jordan Warner, and went out in search of the best restaurant in town. It wasn't hard to find since there was only one place, a countrified steakhouse attached by swinging doors to a honky-tonk bar. The waitress, a buxom girl of 17, came over with the menu. Robert selected a tenderloin steak, with California Burgundy to keep it company.

By the time his steak came, the restaurant was crowded. This was *the* place in town; his first bite of tenderloin confirmed that. Not bad for a Wednesday night in Hayseed, Missouri. He surveyed the place, doubting he'd find any action, or at least anything he'd care to wake up next to in the morning. The local women looked corn-fed: full breasted, round bottoms, easy manners. Pretty much like the local cows. They didn't interest him. He liked sophisticated-looking women; tall, willowy blondes. Women like Rachel. Maybe the first woman in a man's life forever determined his preference. He and Rachel had been in their teens when they discovered each other in that way. Damn! He'd called her Rachel again, even if it was to himself. When he admitted it, he *was* afraid that one day he'd use the wrong name at the wrong time. She was Julia, Julia, Julia. Until three months ago, she'd been Lori, and before that, Clara, and before that, hell, he couldn't remember.

He finished his meal and transferred to the bar, perusing the room for single females, flirted with the waitress who seemed impressed by his cover story: a reporter up from St. Louis. She called it the big city. That was good for a chuckle.

He saw no worthwhile opportunities. Besides, these girls would-n't be easy. He knew the type: even if they secretly galloped the seven dwarfs in the back of their pick-up, they'd first elicit a pledge of marriage, demand a respectable period of pleading before they even gave up a little stink-finger.

He paid his bill, drove back to the motel in time to catch the start of the "Tonight Show." Life in these Midwest troughs was a drag. He'd rather be back in Manila. His thoughts turned to Lolita. He'd love to have the little tramp here in the sack, then kick her ass across Missouri for the way she'd treated him last month. But she'd get hers. Soon.

———

He visited the local newspaper office the next morning, and by noon had a list of males born 25 to 35 years ago, taken from announcements. The certificates read, *"Live Births."* He chuckled at that; these yokels were brain dead from day one.

He also had four obituaries from this same period, two of which matched the birth announcements. The other two were probably born elsewhere. Of the two local obituaries, one died of pneumonia at three years, and the other was killed in a highway accident at nine years of age. Of the two born elsewhere, one had died in a fire, and the second had been run over by a farm tractor. Stupid shit, Robert thought. The kid had probably been in sexual bliss porking some pig when his daddy sliced him up with his International Harvester.

His next stop was the library. There he learned that two of the four families were listed in the town directory and the local telephone book. The infant who died of pneumonia and the boy who died in the fire still had family locally.

He headed for the cemetery, found the headstone for the boy killed in the highway accident, but there was no registry or headstone for the boy who'd been blended with the corn stalks. Maybe he'd been buried on the farm, Robert mused, or, depending on the job the tractor had done, all over the farm. Robert checked two other cemeteries. No burial registry or headstone. Very likely, the kid had no family locally. Robert smiled. It was beginning to look like his next persona would be a plow-pushing bugger named Wallace Bishop.

Don't be hard on the local yokels, he thought. He and Rachel just might be setting up in Chicago next. Maybe in February, after the claims on Peter MacMillan were paid and they killed off Lolita Perez, then, of course, Jordan Warner.

He returned to town. In the courthouse, he researched Wallace Bishop's family. The Bishops—Elmer and his two sons—had farmed a few hundred acres. The older boy, Willard, went off to the army at 17, a year before Elmer shredded pig-fucker in the wheat field.

Elmer Bishop hailed from Iowa, moving here a few years before Wallace was born. Wallace's body might have been returned to Iowa for burial. He would have been thirty had he lived, four years older than Robert. Close enough.

He next checked birth and death records. Death records for two years preceding Wallace's death, and up to four years following his death, had been destroyed in the fire. Many records, perhaps as many as sixty percent, had been reconstructed and refiled, using affidavits and testimonials. In the birth records, he found Wallace's certificate on fiche. That was good and bad. Good because he wouldn't have to scrounge up testimonials, and bad because the document provided leads which Robert needed to research in order to circumvent close scrutiny in a background investigation.

He learned through yearbooks that Wallace hadn't attended school locally. No one recalled him. The birth certificate showed that his parents, Elmer and Lydia Bishop, nee Walker, were born in Muscatine, Iowa, and Rock Island, Illinois, respectively. That was some fifty miles north, both towns on the Mississippi River. Robert studied the clerks working in the records section. None were old enough to have worked here when Wallace was killed. In the past, Robert had come across some old, decrepit civil registrars who'd chiseled their first statistics in stone. Those throwbacks had memories like elephants. But now, record keeping was automated, impersonal; Americans didn't know each other anymore. That was good.

When he checked out of the motel, he paid in cash and drove up to Muscatine. Wallace's older brother, Willard, was also dead, having been killed in the army during the Gulf War, an accident when a helicopter fell on him during a training exercise in Saudi Arabia. Robert wondered how anyone managed to have a helicopter fall on him. He put the Bishops down as truly stupid fucks, fatally attracted to anything having blades.

Elmer Bishop was 73 and said to be taking up space in a nursing home in Davenport. At the Muscatine cemetery, Robert found the grave for Wallace Bishop. Eureka! No one at the Clark County courthouse recalled Wallace, whose death certificate had been destroyed in a fire elsewhere. But his birth certificate was on file here.

Robert drove to Davenport, found the nursing home, but learned that old man Bishop croaked two months previously. Tough luck, but "Mrs. Witt is here with us," the nurse yodeled as he was walking away.

Robert turned, shrugged. "Mrs. Witt?"

"Mrs. Norma Witt is Mr. Bishop's sister. She's with us also," the nurse-curator smiled, proud of her Bishop Family fossil collection.

To Mrs. Norma Witt, Robert spun a combat tale he said he was researching, a story in which Willard may have played a part in a secret operation during Operation Desert Storm. If so, Robert claimed, there might be a posthumous Silver Star in it for Willard. Maybe even a Medal of Honor. He needed to research the family's records. But Mrs. Witt only had a collection of family photographs. He studied these as Mrs. Witt spoke proudly of Elmer, Wallace, and Willard, and directed him to her sister living in Cedar Rapids who maintained more family records and memorabilia.

———

The next day, Robert left the home of Auntie Maxine Sayers with a box full of photographs and documents under his arm. The kindly old woman gave him Wallace and Willard's birth certificates, baptism records, and school records, only too happy to help the nice young reporter from the *St. Louis Post-Dispatch*, especially if nephew Willard might be a real American hero. Would the nice young reporter promise to return the documents after his research?

"Certainly, ma'am."

Robert walked down the steps of the Sayers home. *Don't hold your breath 'til I get back, you old cunt.* He rethought that. *Better yet, hold your breath.*

He was elated. The Backward Bishop Bunch had served up two bonafides just for the asking. He wouldn't even have to write the Clark County courthouse for a photostat of Wallace's birth certificate. Better still, he could build another persona around Willard, despite him being from the same family—it was a common name. Plus, Rachel would select different insurance companies to insure with. He sat in his car outside the Sayers home, studied the photograph of Willard in his army uniform. Then he found Wallace's picture, taken the winter before he was killed in the wheat field.

Robert laughed at the gangly youth. "You really looked like a bacon-maker, boy."

He swung up into Minnesota where preliminary research showed a total of four county courthouses that had burned at least partially over the past thirty years. Fires were much more likely in cold climates, most occurring during the bitterly cold winters that swept the plains. He spent four more days skulking around small towns, researching backgrounds, eating in country restaurants, watching Jay Leno, and jerking off to thoughts of Rachel. The Bitch.

———

By the time he returned to New York City, he had a few more solid candidates, but the success with the Bishops—a fluke—had been the real score. He had everything he needed to develop their identities and create a backdrop for their continued existence. But he would have to avoid the social security on the older boy, Willard, who would have been issued a number in the army if not before. His death would have canceled that number. Robert would either apply for a number for Wallace, then confuse the number when it came time to use Willard's persona to build bonafides, or just invent a number. Then, he'd insure himself under both names with different companies.

For the remaining possibilities—the identities garnered in Minnesota—he contacted a skip tracing company, providing them with whatever information he had, except, of course, that the person was dead. He instructed them to locate families, but never to contact them. The more difficult the locate was, the more likely the candidate for creating a bogus persona. The skip tracers believed he was an independent consultant engaged in heir searches.

Robert and Rachel Tierney maintained multiple mail drops, but post office boxes made civil registrars and insurance companies suspicious, so Robert recruited a woman he'd met in a singles bar. Marcia Post, homely to a fault, predictably and immediately became infatuated with him. He asked her if she'd mind him using her address for a mail drop, since he was on the road most of the time. She wasn't the brightest motor-scooter in Manhattan, so to her, Robert came across as brilliant and witty.

He and Rachel collected friends, many friends, whose addresses became the object behind lightening-fast, chummy acquaintances.

12 New York City

Rachel's tan was deeper after two weeks in Florida. On her instructions, Robert invited Marcia Post to dinner that evening at The El, a trendy coffee shop just across 68th Street from Marcia's apartment building. His sister, Julia, was in town, he said.

Marcia hurried to the restaurant, arrived late as usual although she always tried to be punctual. Especially for Jordan. She caught her breath, saw him through the window, sitting in a booth with Julia. She watched his easy laugh, adored his handsome looks, and always garnered envious looks from women whenever she hung on his arm, something she did at every opportunity. She briefly wondered why Jordan didn't use Julia's address for his mail. Well, siblings could be strange sometimes. Besides, she liked having Jordan depend on her. She thought it made them close.

She studied Julia, who was as beautiful as Jordan was handsome, and thought she could see the strong family lines in their faces. Both were tall, fair, and lean. Marcia had to diet constantly, but was eternally twenty pounds overweight. She often fantasized what a child fathered by Jordan might look like, but when she was honest with herself, she wondered what Jordan saw in her.

She entered the restaurant and stood by the entrance, waiting for Jordan to notice her. He spotted her and waved her over. He greeted her with a wide smile and a kiss on the cheek, and Julia smiled, too, when Jordan introduced them. Several guys at another booth stole furtive glances at Julia, as did the women at Jordan. Now that Marcia had joined these beautiful people, she entered the spotlight, feeling attractive. She wondered what having Julia for a sister-in-law would be like.

She withdrew a bundle of mail from her purse addressed to Jordan, in care of her apartment. She knew that people at work called her a doormat behind her back, but nevertheless took advantage of her many kindnesses. But Jordan wasn't like that. He genuinely appreciated her help. He'd said so several times.

Marcia perched on the stool next to their booth, gave Julia a shy smile and watched as he sorted through the mail. "His work is fascinating, isn't it?" she said to Julia. "Searching for heirs."

Rachel smiled, shrugged.

"Maybe someday he'll be asked to find me," Marcia bubbled. "Maybe I've got a filthy-rich old auntie out there who's left me a million dollars."

"I hope so." Rachel smiled. *Not in this lifetime, sweetie.* For a split second, she considered using Marcia in other ways. Maybe as a stand-in for insurance. No. Bad idea. Marcia was too straight. Plus, she was dumber than Robert, and he was enough of a risk.

"I like scholarly men," Marcia announced. "He's writing a book, you know, something to do with veterans from the, uh, Gulf War."

Rachel raised an eyebrow, nodded.

"But I didn't know there'd been a war in the Gulf of Mexico. Maybe I was too young when it happened." Marcia thought to research it, to give her something to talk about with Jordan. But she'd forget it the instant she dropped onto the couch in front of the television. She checked her watch and announced the latest episode of "Sex and the City" was on TV tonight. She commented that she didn't understand why Sarah Jessica Parker's boyfriends always left her, because she had such a beautiful smile.

Robert cleared his throat, winked at Rachel. Yes, Marcia was for real. She was perfect.

Rachel and Marcia made small talk—it could only be small with Marcia—while Robert opened his mail. Most were from county clerks, asking for affidavits of birth or payment in advance for birth certificates.

He turned away from their conversation and continued thumbing through the stack of envelopes. It was about time he received a certain correspondence. He froze momentarily when he saw the envelope. *Yeah, there you are, you little darling.* He shot a quick glance at Rachel who was busy working on Marcia for something or other. He stuffed the envelope in his pocket. It was a claim form for a hospitalization policy he'd purchased in Brisbane last month, when he'd taken a quick side trip down under from Manila. He snapped the rubber band around the envelopes and rejoined the conversation.

"And can you imagine," Rachel was saying, "they have absolutely nothing available in my building while they're painting my apartment."

"Crash at my place," Marcia offered.

"And I absolutely refuse to pay hotel prices."

"Really, it's no trouble," Marcia almost pleaded.

Robert smiled admirably; Rachel was working on the temporary apartment she needed for the interviews with the insurance adjusters on MacMillan's death. He *had* to admire her. God, she was good! She'd just met Marcia and already had the run of her apartment.

After dinner, Rachel paid the tab. Marcia glanced at Robert who seemed aloof. But it probably bothered him that his sister was paying. Outside, Rachel gave Marcia one of those cheek-to-cheek girlie kisses that miss by a mile, then hailed a taxi. Robert offered to walk Marcia home. At her building just across from the coffee shop, he declined her invitation to stay the night, complaining about project deadlines. He kissed her tenderly on the mouth, holding his embrace just long enough to convince her she was special. They'd have more moments the next time he was in town, he said. As Marcia walked up the stairs of the brownstone building where she rented a small, one-bedroom apartment, Robert made a face behind her back. She turned at the door, waved goodnight, and he smiled. Once she was inside, he hailed another taxi, arriving home just after Rachel.

"Rachel! Julia, I mean," he called out, entering the apartment. He threw his coat on the couch, dropped the mail by her computer, and found Rachel in the bathroom, her face plastered with some sticky, gooey, green shit as she ran a bath. "How is a woman like a tile floor?"

Rachel gave him a dirty look in the mirror. "Do tell," she said indifferently.

"Lay 'em right enough the first time and you can walk all over them forever." He laughed at how he'd duped Marcia. "I made a copy of her mailbox key. Don't want her looking too close at everything. A bar of soap did the job." He checked her mailbox most days before she returned home from work. Until today, Marcia thought he'd been away, planning a move to New York sometime soon. To be close to her, he'd said.

Rachel caught his reflection in the mirror. "I wouldn't take people for granted if I were you." She tested the water, adjusted the temperature. "I've got a lot of entries to make tonight. I changed my mind and filed on MacMillan while I was down in Florida. All three companies. I've talked with two of them. They left messages on the machine in LA and I got back to them, made appointments for the week after next. I'd rather put them off until I hear something definite from the third company and finish them all at the same time.

"You'll see them in LA?"

"I guess so. Even though I've got Marcia's place lined up. I thought it over: no sense drawing anyone's attention to New York with Warner coming up."

"Who's investigating?"

"Both companies farmed the claims out to local investigators. A guy named Dubbs on one case. A one-man shop. I checked him out. He's a young LA guy who mostly does domestic work. A divorce dick. American Travelers apparently farmed it out to a guy named Loggert in Chicago, and he in turn passed it on to this Dubbs guy. He's not too bright. Wasn't even sure where the Philippines were.

"It's unlikely there'll be much of an investigation, since the policies are incontestable. They have my claimant's statement, the police report, and the local death certificate along with the embassy's 180. That'll satisfy them. I asked Dubbs—nicely of course—that since the policy wasn't contestable, if I should have my lawyer with me, and he said no. That makes him a dummy in my book."

Dubbs had violated the industry's Statement of Principles, as it related to attorneys and adjusters. Ethics dictated that an investigator refrain from discouraging a claimant from getting legal advice, and once retained, the beneficiary could only be contacted through their attorney. Dubbs would have known that if he did insurance work.

"That's the 200,000, right? American Travelers?" Robert asked.

Rachel caught his reflection in the mirror, rolled her eyes. Robert had trouble with details, all the juggling they did with ongoing claims. Too many insurance companies, too many policies. Too many balls in the air at one time.

She worked the goop around her nose, answered tiredly, "Right." For the second policy with Chase-Hampshire, a young woman with a national inspection company had contacted her from San Francisco. That policy was for 300,000 dollars.

Rachel walked into the bedroom. Robert followed. She switched on her laptop sitting on a small secretary in the corner of the room, and went back into the bathroom. Robert trailed her, Barbie followed him.

"Do I always have to tell you? Feed Barbie."

He went into the kitchen, looking for dog food. "Nothing from the third company?"

"Just an initial call from them. That's the big one. Amalgamated Life of Illinois—500,000 dollars with double indemnity."

"Call 'em back!"

"Not yet. I don't wanna seem pushy. Some secretary called me at the LA number, said she's handling everything. Going over her head would look suspicious. If I don't hear from her soon, I'll call back."

Robert came back into the bathroom. "Weeping, of course."

"I won't overdo it. I'll sound unhappy, and confused by the delay."

Rachel started to slip off her bathrobe. She pushed him out of the bathroom and slammed the door. Robert went back into the living room, built himself a drink, and carried it back to the bedroom. He called to Rachel through the door, asked if she wanted a drink. Maybe she'd let him carry it in to her.

"I've got too much work tonight," she called back.

He heard Barbie munching down her food in the kitchen, and leaned against the door jamb. "Such a chilly night. Perfect for a bubble bath with a friend."

"If you've got one, send him in," she replied. "Now get away from the door."

He sipped his drink, tried the door. Locked.

"Go see Marcia," Rachel called.

"I told her I'm flying out tonight."

"Tell her you've changed your plans." She eased herself into the bubble bath. "Tell her you can't stand being away from her for another two weeks without seeing her one last time. Women love that sort of thing."

"She's too fat."

"So what? William Towers was too stupid."

"Why mention him?" Robert spat.

"To point out that we all have unpleasant duties."

"He wasn't a fat pig!"

Rachel sponged water over herself and cursed Robert under her breath. What she'd done with Towers was no more pleasant than what he'd complained about with Marcia. Besides, Marcia was kind of sweet, even if she was dumber than a broom handle.

Barbie scurried up behind Robert and scratched at the bathroom door. Rachel reached over and opened the door just far enough for her to squeeze through, then locked it again, eased back into the tub.

"You hear me?" Robert rapped on the door. "He wasn't a fat pig."

"You don't know what Towers was," she said, sick of this. Time he understood that they couldn't go back to how it was before. Talking about other men usually put him into that 'size' mode until he'd extract believable confessions, that some guy's penis was smaller than his, or he'd assail her with accusations, that she refused him because she wanted other men. He just wouldn't face the simple truth.

"Towers was an inept, bumbling idiot who hadn't been laid in years without—I'm sure—buying it off the street. He couldn't hold his liquor and he was a buffoon. Like taking candy from a baby." She added, nonchalantly, "So what if he had ten inches?" *There, asshole.*

"*What*! He had a ten-inch dick?"

"No, Robert. Ten inches is called a cock. *You* have a dick."

He hit the door with his fist and swore. Rachel cracked up and made eyes at Barbie who perked up, her tail wagging furiously, as though she understood the joke.

Cursing, Robert retreated to the living room and settled on the couch. He put on the stereo headsets and contented himself with finally breaking from Rachel. Not in the way she rejected him, but in another way. The hospitalization policy was his secret, the first he'd ever kept from her. She didn't allot him enough pocket money. Never had. He'd caught Marcia's expression when Rachel as usual paid the tab, and as usual, he looked away. It was humiliating when she did that in front of others.

He'd paid for the hospitalization policy with his own money when he was setting up the MacMillan scam. He got an Australian visa in Manila and jumped down to Brisbane, bought the policy through a travel agency. It was a one-time travel policy that went into effect immediately. It covered theft, accidents, and emergency treatment confinements while on the road. He returned to Manila, finished up the details on MacMillan with Reno Marcellus, then stopped off in Budapest. He faked a fall-down accident, and spent a week allegedly convalescing in hot baths, then filed the claim out in Missouri, using Marcia's address. Rachel would never know, and it was safe, since life and medical claims from different companies didn't share claim databases. Besides, the travel policy was issued in Australia. The claim totaled 10,000 dollars, when and if it paid. Not much, but still, it would be more pocket money than he'd ever had before. And he planned on working more of these as the opportunity presented itself. Rachel wasn't the only one who knew this game.

They'd banked 3 million by June, with another 1.5 coming on MacMillan, and 2 million more in the pipeline on the Warner and Lolita claims. Still, Rachel cheaped him, doling out a miserly 300 a week. Runaround cash. No more, she said. The money was for their future, she said.

Yeah, yeah, yeah.

13

Another week passed without further word from Amalgamated Life of Illinois, a giant mutual life insurance company licensed to write business in all states. Rachel decided to proceed with the interviews for American Travelers and Chase-Hampshire, and arranged to meet their representatives at the LA apartment the following Tuesday and Wednesday.

She flew out on Sunday, stopping off in Chicago to attend a fraud conference sponsored by an insurance association. Through the Internet, she'd contacted the association and got on its mailing list just for the asking, representing herself as an employee from a third-party administrator. The association didn't bother to check her out, questioned not one detail on her membership application.

At the conference registration area—her fee gladly accepted as a delegate—she circulated amongst an army of claims examiners, investigators, and law enforcement types. As a brunette, and from behind large-framed, tinted glasses, she mingled with a thousand claims professionals from across the Midwest.

During the seminars she wandered around, inspecting the vendors' exhibits, which were set up in a separate room. She scooped up promotional material of investigative agencies whose brochures outlined their services, geographic areas handled, and—more importantly—company personnel. She reckoned she would have a solid week of indexing when she returned to New York. Without doubt, her database already held more information about investigators than those of most insurers.

She sat in on one seminar which dealt with foreign claims. Many investigators boasted this service, but few actually traveled themselves. Instead, they farmed out assignments, especially now with the Internet. The panel focused on spotting fake death claims, but the audience concentrated on cost containment. One woman from a Texas insurer bent her spleen over high overseas investigative costs. Atta girl, Rachel thought. Cheap your investigators, honey.

One alarming development: one investigator addressed the assembly on State Department Form 180—the death report—citing examples of bogus death claims despite the existence of a 180. Fortunately, his talk made little impact on the audience. That their government could be duped was unthinkable.

She circulated at cocktail hour, listening to examiners and asking questions, all the while thinking that if any amongst them were worth their salt, they'd be suspicious from her queries. Instead, they rambled on about their experiences. War stories, as they liked to call them. Mostly they related the escapades of their field investigators.

Older claims execs were eager to appear claims savvy, and not one admitted to *ever* being scammed. Denial permeated their way of thinking. This knowledge alone was well worth the price of admission.

Some spoke about SIUs, special investigative units mandated by law. Rachel saw that the laws had no teeth. Better yet, some companies outsourced this function, even contracting accounting firms. She'd researched SIUs through the Internet, fearing the worst. But, for the most part, these units concerned themselves with filing reports with state insurance commissions. It was just so much bean-counting, with attention paid to filing compliance reports rather than actually fighting fraud.

The conference had been more educational for her than the defenders of the coffers. There'd been no need for anxiety about entering their arena; they were the Christians—she was the lion.

———

In LA, she crashed on the couch in the apartment she had illegally sublet last year. The renters, a young couple who bore an amazing resemblance to Lori and Peter MacMillan, hadn't been easy to find. Maureen and Larry bussed tables between acting jobs, and made themselves scarce when Rachel was being interviewed. They assumed she had business meetings.

It was expensive maintaining multiple apartments, creating and back-dropping personas. Rachel roped in young couples who met her and Robert's general descriptions. They unwittingly passed for whoever the Tierney's posed as during any given period. Rachel charged low rentals in exchange for keeping the sublet quiet. She leased the furniture, and when a scam ended, she skipped out on the bills, always maxing-out the credit cards issued to their fake personas. Why not? Credit card companies just wrote off the losses. Damn, but America was a great country!

Rachel sat through two separate beneficiary interviews over the next two days. She feigned bitterness with Debbie Brubaker, a thirty-year-old housewife and mother who'd flown down from the Bay Area to interview Mrs. Lori MacMillan on behalf of Chase-Hampshire.

Debbie sipped Darjeeling tea that Rachel had brewed especially for her, and listened intently to confidences of Peter's infidelity—the same sob story that Towers had bought into. Such revelations created plausibility, put life and drama into the claim, gave amateur investigators something negative to report, something juicy, however immaterial. But it deflected Debbie's questions and wound down the clock as Rachel related her heartbreak, then abruptly terminated the interview, declaring that she had to rush off to a job interview. After all, with Peter gone, she had to find a job, didn't she? Yes, of course, Debbie was free to see her again if she needed more details. But a second interview would require that she remain overnight in LA, and with a precious nine-month-old daughter at home. Well! Any further details could be discussed over the telephone. It escaped Debbie that Rachel knew far more about her than she'd ever know about Lori MacMillan.

Dubbs, representing American Travelers, had been predictably distracted by the widow's legs. Rachel covered the same ground about Peter's infidelity, adding tearful details. Dubbs became very chatty, even volunteering information about himself, not the least being that he was planning to separate from his wife. Hint, hint.

With the policies out of the contestability period, the companies wouldn't bother—according to the insurance contracts—to inquire into Peter MacMillan's medical history. Therefore, his background wouldn't be scrutinized. Neither investigator thought to question if an actual death had even occurred, or, if it did, that the dead man was really Peter MacMillan. Beyond that, neither came close to suspecting that Peter MacMillan never existed. After all, the good Mrs. MacMillan reported that she'd actually seen her dead husband. And wasn't there a Report of the Death of an American Citizen Abroad?

Rachel signed releases for both companies, authorization for them to check whatever records might be necessary. When the interviews were over, both investigators were impressed with Mrs. Lori MacMillan. Her courage to carry on after such a tragedy was uplifting.

She wasn't surprised at how the interviews went; her research had been very good. Before the policies for American Travelers and Chase-Hampshire were purchased, she'd telephoned their claims departments, introduced herself as a claims examiner new to the area, and wanted recommendations for claims investigators.

She knew what companies she'd be facing long before the claims were even presented.

But the big score, Amalgamated, had been silent after the initial contact, advising her that they were investigating her claim. Would Amalgamated contest accidental death for double indemnity, even though the dead man's skull had been fractured? If not, what was the delay?

———

Within two weeks, American Travelers paid up. Their check was deposited in a joint account for Lori and Peter MacMillan in LA. When the other companies paid, the account would be closed out and Rachel would erase their personas and then vanish.

This was another juggling act at which Rachel excelled. While the IRS had greater resources, they moved too slow. Before deposits could be traced, particularly on Social Security numbers that didn't exist, she emptied out their accounts with wire transfers. Rachel and Robert Tierney were long gone before discrepancies were even noticed.

Also, IRS task forces were reserved for high profile players— drug lords and money laundering folk—and by comparison, the Tierney's were small players, particularly since they couldn't be singled-out on more than any one scam.

"Never piss off the Feds," Mom always said. "And never give them a challenge. Slide into anonymity, evaporate, and they'll leave you alone. They chase commendation letters, accolades to validate their budgets—and small potatoes don't taste good."

14

Chase-Hampshire hadn't paid yet, and Amalgamated Life of Illinois hadn't even recontacted her. Rachel telephoned Amalgamated in Chicago, spoke with a claims examiner, a Miss Walsh, who sounded young and inexperienced. But Miss Walsh wasn't very talkative. Noncommittal actually, saying only that the claim was being looked into. Rachel didn't push the fact that the policy wasn't contestable and, therefore, there wasn't any reason for the payment to be delayed. She backed off, offered whatever assistance she could, puzzled by the fact that Miss Walsh didn't mention that someone would interview her. Finally, she asked if she shouldn't obtain the services of a lawyer, to which Miss Walsh replied that she couldn't advise her on legal matters. Rachel looked at the receiver; maybe Miss Walsh wasn't so inexperienced after all.

After she hung up, Rachel entered the details of the conversation into her computer, and on the other end, Miss Walsh made notes in her claim file. She didn't know what was going on, only that her boss, Jim Kincannon, was personally supervising this file. He'd sent it to Nina Davis of Premier Services on Long Island, New York because he couldn't trace the Macmillan's back further than two years. Nina promised to have the senior partner, Mike Roth, handle the case.

And in New York, Nina Davis had been trying to reach Mike Roth, who was traipsing around Asia.

15 Kaohsiung, Taiwan

Roth waited outside the medical records department of the Min Sheng Municipal Hospital. This was the last stop on a case he'd been working for three days between here and Hong Kong. The claim was on a 37-year-old Taiwanese who died of lung cancer before the second anniversary of his policy. Contestable death claims were suspicious, and most investigations developed pre-existing medical history that the insured denied at the time of underwriting.

But the insured's cancer had metastasized like a forest fire, taking him in under six months. The policy, for 50,000 US, had been taken out in Hong Kong, just before the insured married. It was fortunate he'd had the foresight; his wife gave birth to their child a month after his death.

Roth paid for copies of the medical record which, along with the charts he'd gathered in Hong Kong, showed no serious medical history. Just as he thought, the case was clean and the policy would pay off.

Roth checked the airline timetable, made a dash for the airport. With any luck, he'd be in Bangkok that night, sopping up drinks on Soi Cowboy.

———

He awoke the next morning in his bedroom in Bangkok next to a girl he didn't know. It was noon, and he was still drunk, having only slept a few hours. It was a humid day, but at least the sun was out. Night would bring another rain storm, similar to the one the night before, when the skies had opened up as he pulled in from Taipei.

Between the trips he used to make from New York and all the itineraries around Asia, he had decided to set up in Bangkok, and henceforth handle Asian cases exclusively. He had reps in most regions now and he could afford to lay back a little. He'd covered half the globe, and at the last count, had worked cases in over a hundred countries and territories. Now he wanted a steady diet of the Orient, the ease and freedom of Buddhist cultures, the weather—and all the little lovelies.

Nina, his next senior partner, handled the New York office. Her fax on his desk read that more claims were coming for the Philippines, in particular a curious one involving the death of an American citizen. There were too many documents to fax, Nina wrote, so she was sending it along with the other cases by DHL.

He sat up in bed, looked at the girl. She was maybe twenty, not much older. Her hair was cut pageboy style, and she wore no make-up. She was balled-up under the sheet against the air-conditioner. He threw the covers off to see what he'd dragged home. She was petite, not very shapely, and looked a bit butch. Roth craned his neck, looked between her legs to reassure himself. He shook his head, wondering what her appeal had been last night.

He rousted her out and sent her on her way with a handful of baht. In the bathroom, he nearly slipped on a used condom lying on the tile floor. He picked it up daintily, as though it was a dead rat, and flushed it down the commode. He checked his trousers. His money was still there, most of it anyhow. Dirty clothes from his trip were heaped in the laundry basket.

Mac, his macaw, squawked from his cage out on the terrace. Aside from his clothes and business equipment, Mac was the only thing Roth owned in Bangkok. He wrapped a towel around his waist, went out to Mac. The water cup was bone dry, so Roth opened the cage to retrieve it. Mac squawked and scurried across the perch for a finger snack before his owner could close the door. Roth filled the cup and again risked the jaws of death.

His apartment was on the ground floor, less than twenty feet from the swimming pool. Two girls, somebody's playthings from last night, were frolicking in the water. Playful bargirls in the pool during the day was common, one of the perks that induced Roth in taking this apartment. He recognized one of them, a dancer from a club on Soi Cowboy. She looked over at him and waved.

He shook the fog from his brain, rubbed his eyes, yawned, and farted. He threw the girls a casual salute, headed for the shower.

———

Over the next few days, between carousing by night and suffering through daily hangovers, he finished two weeks of reports on his laptop. He e-mailed the reports to the New York office and express-mailed hard copies as well, since some documents were originals.

On his third morning back in Bangkok, the express package from Nina arrived. He sat at the desk in his office and opened it. There were two death claims in Manila. One involved a young Filipino who'd been shot by his girlfriend's *other* boyfriend, while the second concerned an American named Peter MacMillan. This one aroused his interest. Nina had attached a Post-It note to the front page, which read, *"Don't you just love it? Marcellus, again."*

When he read the police report, he saw where Nina had circled the name of the cop who attended the scene: Special Police Officer Reno Marcellus of the Manila Traffic Division. A familiar name from a couple of scams he'd previously investigated in Manila. Usually, the deaths hadn't even occurred, and often there hadn't even been an accident. Marcellus was a known plant—a guy who slipped bogus documents into the pockets of dead men. It was a simple trick, one that Roth had seen countless times; cops were recruited by persons holding large life insurance policies issued in the States. Usually they were Filipino-Americans, Chinese-Americans or Whatever-Americans. They furnished cops like Marcellus with their personal ID papers and when he came across a stiff meeting their description, he'd plant their documents on the body. Things took a natural course from there; the stiff was identified as the insured. When the falsely identified corpse never turned up, families filed a missing person's report, but their case was never solved because the deceased was in someone else's coffin. Eventually, the family figured the man just ran off, and in places like the Philippines, with over 7,000 islands, the archipelago was the perfect place to disappear. *Tago ng tago*, baby; hiding and hiding.

Roth saw the photocopy of the tabloid headline: "CANO'S *LAST ROUND-UP AT BUFFALO JOE'S.*"

"Oh, yeah, yeah, yeah. This one," he mumbled.

Someone in Manila had said they saw the body. Nope. That wasn't it; someone said they heard about this dead guy. Whatever. Oh! Right; Max the Mangled had said that. Roth wondered if Max had made it back to Bangkok. If so, he was probably out on Sukhumvit Road studying traffic patterns.

He reviewed the proofs. Everything was there: the Filipino death certificate, Reno Marcellus's police report, the funeral parlor's bill, autopsy report, newspaper clipping, and, of course, the ever helpful State Department Form 180.

Jim Kincannon at Amalgamated was one of the few people who shared Premier's view that 180s did little more than parrot local death certificates—themselves often bogus—created by corrupt municipal clerks.

But the fact that the embassy completed a report likely meant that there was an actual dead body involved in this claim. Not necessarily, but probably. When a Filipino-American died in the country, their families often didn't bother informing the embassy. But few visiting Americans had families in the islands, and thus came to the attention of the police when they died. Police protocol was to inform the embassy. But embassies handed out these 180s a little too freely. Sometimes a death never even occurred.

So, if there was a stiff, this was a variation from the scams Marcellus usually figured in. Roth checked the name of the wife and beneficiary shown on the 180—a Mrs. Lori MacMillan. He knew many consular officers across Asia by name, but he didn't recognize the name of William Towers. He opened his laptop, slipped in the Sidekick disk where several thousand names were stored, along with comments of when, where, and in what connection he'd met them. He scrolled down his list of American embassies, and under Manila, came up with the name of John Warbell. He'd met Warbell before, the date and case name was shown. However, he couldn't recall his face.

Of course, it was possible that this case was legit. After all, Marcellus was a traffic cop and he handled real accidents as well as fake ones. And accidents did happen.

MacMillan's death occurred just a month after the two-year contestability period had passed. Therefore, Amalgamated wasn't interested if the insured had made a material misrepresentation on his medical history. Even if he had, Amalgamated would still have to pay out. Jim Kincannon wanted the actual death verified and the accident checked out. Faking deaths for insurance benefits was an international business. Everyone was doing it: the Lebanese, Jordanians, Syrians, the Haitians, the Nigerians, and the Filipinos being amongst the better practitioners. The cases were usually easy to break. Once you'd done a few hundred of them, the patterns were simple to spot. Either there was no actual body, or if there was, it belonged to someone else. In most of these scams, accomplices were involved: cops, doctors, undertakers, and primary witnesses such as family members. It was easy to uncover the confederates once the investigation started.

Kincannon knew his business and trusted no one. He'd handled international cases himself. Pushing sixty, he rode a desk now and sported a limp, compliments of a claimant who ran him down with her car twenty years ago. Kincannon hadn't always been an armchair detective—unlike most clients these days.

There was also a third case in Nina's package, a death claim in Burma. Roth decided to handle that one first and called his travel agent for tickets.

They'd also handle his visa application.

Roth closed his laptop, built himself a drink, and carried it out to the pool. Unfortunately there were no girls splashing about, so he dived in, started on laps.

16 Los Angeles

Towers' flight landed at LAX from Denver shortly after midday. He was happy to escape his parents. Good to see them and Sis, but enough was enough, especially with Lori MacMillan waiting in the wings—hopefully. He had tried to reach her from Manila several times, but she hadn't answered his letters or returned his calls.

Within weeks of submitting MacMillan's 180, the Social Security Administration returned their copy with a form advising that the deceased's social security number was incorrect. They wanted a correction. He rechecked his paperwork, saw that he'd correctly reported the number from the card found in MacMillan's wallet. Lori had also confirmed the number. He remembered being quite impressed by that. What wife these days knew her husband's social security number by heart?

On his personal e-mail, he'd asked a State Department buddy in Washington for an informal social security check. Actually, he wanted more than the usual information. The friend balked, eventually relented, and wrote back that while the social security numbers for Peter and Lori MacMillan originated in California, the one for Lori checked back to an 86-year-old widow in Burbank, while Peter's number matched the one for a 45-year-old aerospace engineer in San Diego.

Then, the Veteran's Administration—to whom a report had also been copied, since Lori said Peter had been in the army—advised Towers there was no record. Towers assumed he'd just gotten the numbers wrong.

When he rechecked the files, he saw that two insurance companies had written, asking for verification of Form 180. He blew them off with standard form letters, directing them to obtain copies from the State Department in Washington, D.C., and circled the ten-dollar fee request shown on the form. He was annoyed that insurance companies would bother him with such details. He had more important things to do than send out copies.

He telephoned Lori's apartment from LAX. As before, her phone was answered by a machine. He'd heard this many times from Manila and Denver. It was Lori's voice all right, but she didn't identify herself, just said that she'd return shortly, to please leave a message. Well, he'd left messages. Six of them, in fact. If she didn't want to see him again, the least she could do was say so. He deserved a straight answer.

He took a taxi to Lori's address, an investment of forty bucks. The La Crescenta Apartments, three blocks off Ventura Boulevard, surprised him a little. It was stark. Concrete lawns. It was decent enough, simple actually, well maintained, but with an air of desolation, impermanence. And there was no swimming pool! It was also well off the beaten path, and while all Los Angelinos used cars, La Crescenta still seemed too remote. He wondered where her antiques shop was.

The building manager, an elderly Mexican-American named Colon, directed Towers to apartment A-4. He added that Lori wasn't in, but that her husband might be.

I doubt that, my man, thought Towers as he headed for A-4. It was just after 3:00 p.m. and Lori wasn't home. The mailbox was full with envelopes. Towers took a furtive look around, then pulled the letters from the box. There were a dozen or so, mostly from insurance companies, various state government offices, and some addressed to other people carrying this apartment number. He assumed those from the insurance companies were in connection with Peter's death. So, they were pestering her, too. A folded copy of *Variety* lay in front of the door. He stuffed the mail back into the box and returned to Colon's apartment, asked when he'd last seen Mrs. MacMillan. Yesterday, Colon reckoned. He said that both Mr. and Mrs. MacMillan worked, should be in later. He last saw Mr. MacMillan two, three days ago.

Husband?

Towers doubted whether Colon saw the tenants frequently, and certainly couldn't have seen Peter MacMillan for over a month! He decided against leaving a card on the door, saying that he'd return. He walked for a mile before he found a restaurant where he sucked down coffee until seven, then hiked back to La Crescenta, wishing that he'd rented a car.

A-4's mailbox was empty. Towers edged up against the window covered by a curtain. He could make out a man and a woman in the kitchen. Had Lori already hooked up with another guy? His gut wrenched. Well, what did he expect? A looker like her certainly wouldn't suffer lonely nights if she didn't want to. Maybe that's why she never answered his calls or his letter.

Still, he deserved an answer. An explanation. With a knot in his stomach and feeling like he'd caught a cheating wife, he knocked on the door. After a few moments, a tall, attractive blonde in her mid-twenties opened it.

"Hi," Towers began, relieved that it wasn't Lori. He glanced over the blonde's shoulder to see the young man working the controls on the oven. They were preparing dinner. "I'm looking for Lori MacMillan."

The woman hesitated, then: "Uh, she's out at the moment. Can I help you?"

"When will she return?" Towers could see that these people were comfortably settled into the apartment, which was only a one-bedroom unit. Now that Peter was dead, maybe she was sharing it, but he wondered what sort of sleeping arrangements these people had. His face asked a thousand questions.

"What's this about?" the woman asked.

"I'm Bill Towers," he said.

"Yes?"

"Uh, I met Lori last month."

The woman nodded, waiting for him to continue.

"When she visited Manila." The young man came up behind the blonde. He was also in his mid-twenties. "When her husband died."

The woman looked over her shoulder at the man. "Oh, yes." she said. "Wasn't that terrible. Lori told me. Remember, Larry? I told you about it."

"Yeah," he said indifferently. "Terrible."

"Why don't you come in, Mr—?"

"Towers. Uh, call me Bill."

"I'm Maureen. We're just about to have dinner, so if this won't take too long."

Maureen and Larry never met Peter, and only once met Lori who informally sublet the apartment to them for 400 dollars a month, far less than the actual rental. Lori told them that she and Peter might return in a year or so, and didn't want the hassle of looking for a new apartment. Since subletting violated the lease, Maureen and Larry let the management assume they were the MacMillans. Lori insisted they keep a low profile so that she wouldn't lose the apartment.

They didn't know how to reach Lori aside from a post office box in New York City. Lori received a lot of mail here, which Maureen bundled off to New York weekly as part of their agreement in exchange for paying such a low rent. Lori told them that she wanted to keep her California insurance license active, another reason why she needed to keep the address.

Towers screwed up his face. Insurance license?

"She was here for a few days the other week," Maureen volunteered. "She needed to meet some people here in the apartment."

"Wait a sec," Larry said, remembering that she'd called the day before. "She left something on the machine. I wrote it down." He looked on the bookcase, found a slip of paper. "She's staying with a girlfriend in Manhattan. Here it is, Marcia Post. East 68th Street. But no phone number."

"She never leaves a phone number," Maureen added. "Guess she bounces around too much."

Towers asked where Lori's shop was. Larry and Maureen looked at each other, asked what shop. They knew nothing about an antiques shop, only Lori telling them she and Peter were insurance consultants. They didn't know anything about that either—and didn't want to—grateful that Lori hadn't tried to sell them insurance. Towers asked where Lori's mother lived, and got a big "nope" on that one, too.

"Oh, yes. You called before." Maureen pointed a finger at Towers.

"Several times," he said, almost indignant.

"Lori calls occasionally. I gave her your messages."

In a last ditch effort, Towers quizzed Larry and Maureen about Irma who managed the antiques shop. They shrugged at each other, said they'd never heard of her either. Maureen gave him the post office box number in New York City and the address of Lori's girl-friend on 68th Street.

Towers returned to LAX more confused than ever. At least it explained why Lori's voice was on the answering machine. So, she'd received his messages, and also his letters since Maureen forwarded her mail. Maybe she wanted to start a new life, make a fresh beginning. Maybe she wanted nothing about Peter MacMillan in her new life. Maybe that included him as well. Back at the airport—another forty dollars blown on a taxi—he checked with the New York City operator.

"Yes, sir. There is an M. Post on East 68th Street, in Manhattan. Would you like that number?"

Towers dialed the number. It would be 10:30 p.m. in New York, but what the hell. If he could stop off in LA, spend eighty bucks on taxis, the least Lori could do was answer the phone at this hour. He still had two weeks vacation time and if Lori wanted to see him, well, he'd hop the red eye to the Big Apple.

"Hello?" A woman's voice, but not Lori's.

"Oh, uh, hello. May I speak with Lori, please?"

"There's no Lori here. I'm afraid you have the wrong number."

Towers nervously rechecked the number the operator had given him, and read it off.

"That's correct, but there's no Lori here."

"Does this number go to M. Post, East 68th Street, Manhattan?"

Silence. Then, "Who is this?"

Towers rattled off his name, where he was from, why he was calling, said that Lori MacMillan had given this address to friends in LA.

"Yes, I'm Marcia Post, but I'm sorry, I don't know any Lori Mac-Millan."

"Have you a roommate perhaps?"

"No. Well, lately a friend stays here sometimes," Marcia said.

"Is she there now?" Towers assumed a 'friend' was a woman.

"No. I don't know when I'll see her again."

"What's her name?" Towers immediately realized the question was untoward. "The reason I ask is that maybe she knows Lori MacMillan." He again explained the connection, wishing he'd introduced himself officially, inquired about the screwed-up social security numbers. But that wouldn't fly at this time of at night. "Lori definitely gave your name and address to these people in LA."

"Well," Marcia said, "I don't know how that happened and I don't know a Lori MacMillan. My girlfriend's name isn't Lori Mac-Millan."

Towers assured her officiously. Government people were, after all, not prank callers. "Do you have a number for her?"

"Come to think of it, I don't. She never gave me her number."

"When will you see her again?"

"I have no idea."

Defeated, Towers thanked Marcia Post and hung up. Maybe he'd gotten the wrong M. Post. He checked the New York City operator again. No other M. Posts. There were two other Posts in Manhattan and he called them both. It was eleven o'clock when he finished the second call. A guy told him to fuck off.

He decided he'd write her one last time, at the New York City post office box, and at Marcia Post's. If she didn't reply, well, he'd have his answer. He refused to face the fact that any man in charge of his hormones would already have it. With a heavy heart, he boarded his plane. He just couldn't understand how he'd gotten *both* social security numbers wrong.

17 Manila

Lolita Perez stared out of the window in the Aristocrat restaurant on Roxas Boulevard, her head propped in her hands. She sat quietly, studying people passing by, waiting for Reno Marcellus, but lost in her thoughts about Jordan Warner. She'd been waiting for an hour, and when she thought about it, got angry at this latest slight by Reno. He'd become more abusive, especially since she'd taken up with Jordan. Reno acted jealous sometimes, yet Jordan had been his idea all along. He'd introduced them.

Maybe Reno just wanted her out of his hair. Lolita found that the jealous act paid off. Men were suckers for guilt. But Reno never acted guilty. Nothing close to it. In fact, he dispatched her to johns, and made her sell pills he got from Morales—that Customs guy. Lolita had no illusions other than Marcellus stomping her to a pulp if she even thought about snitching to his wife. Or his crazy brother-in-law, who was the only person Reno feared.

Jordan was okay. For a *cano,* at any rate. Even if he did think he was God's gift to women. He was very handsome, very smart, and he wanted to marry her as soon as he secured their future. She'd have a home in America, and her family would have the most lavish home on Masbate Island. Jordan was going to make lots of money from insurance by faking some papers for her, an old game in the Philippines. She'd go *tago ng tago*, then come back to life and go off to America with Jordan.

Lolita didn't know how Jordan was going to do it, but it was going to happen soon. That's what Reno said on the phone this morning. She watched Reno pull into the parking lot. She loved the way he looked in his tight uniform, his gun, nightstick, and hand-cuffs dangling all over. She also liked his knee high motorcycle boots, although he never rode a motorcycle. It was fun to flirt with him when he was in uniform. It gave her face, and also let the world know that she wasn't being arrested for prostitution again.

That's how they first met. He caught her nodding in some guy's lap behind the Traders Hotel one night. He ran the john off before she was paid, and threatened to arrest her, unless they could re-solve the matter out of court, so to speak. So, she gave *him* a blow-job in the back seat of his car. He called his penis his nightstick, and Lolita thought that was terribly funny until she learned that he administered said nightstick similarly to half the street girls in Ermita.

Still, once she'd met Reno, other cops stopped hassling her. Also, Reno did important things for her. Introducing her to rich *canos* like Jordan for one thing.

Reno spotted her from the entrance. He beckoned her outside, returned to his car while she paid her bill. He drove her to a short-time motel near Ninoy Aquino Airport. He didn't have the money Jordan promised to send to her, so she wondered what all the sec-recy was about until she realized that he just wanted his way with her again. But this might be the last time she ever saw Reno since he was going to arrange for her passport under a new name. She consented to his demands, complaining that since she was now Jordan's fiancée, he shouldn't be doing this to her. Reno only laughed. He used her as never before, as she never allowed even good paying customers to use her—that rear-end business none of the girls liked. Well, she certainly didn't, anyhow.

Afterwards, she sat on the bed, naked except for a towel wrapped around her, sulking childlike. Her rectum hurt terribly, and she wondered if he hadn't torn her down there.

Reno was showering with the bathroom door open, giving her instructions. "Pay attention," he called out. "I want you to wait on the corner of Roxas and Vito Cruz. Tonight. Midnight exactly."

That was the corner near the Trader's Hotel where they'd first met, her favorite trolling place.

"Midnight exactly," he repeated. "Have your passport, ID card, three passport-sized photographs, and anything else that can identify you."

"Why can't I just give you that stuff here and you get the new ID?" she whined.

"Because the guy who makes this stuff deals only with the person he's working for. And that's you, honey buns. And he doesn't meet people openly. Tonight, you're gonna give him all your ID. Over the next few days, he'll make up new papers for you."

"Okay. But I told Jordan I wanted 100,000 pesos more for my mother. He said you'd have that for me."

"Tonight. Jordan's wiring the money this afternoon. I'll have it and the ID guy in my car."

Lolita shrugged. "Okay."

"I'll be parked in front of the convention center, across the street. It'll be dark in front of the building. Don't approach the car until I flash my lights."

"Why all this sneaky business? Do I look like James Bond or somebody."

"Because people know *me*. That's why." She watched Reno step out of the shower and examine his nightstick. She turned away and he laughed, amused by her pretended indignation. He checked his watch—more time to spare—and for the first time she noticed Brian's gold Cartier on his arm. He walked over to the bed, stood in front of her, and dropped his towel.

"Have a cigar," he said, chuckling.

———

She dozed off after Reno left. Later, a room boy banged on the door. The time on the room had expired. The boy carried fresh linen, and beers to replenish the small refrigerator. Seeing her with only a towel wrapped around her, he quickly offered to let her remain for a few more hours in exchange for favors, namely a blowjob. She refused huffily. What did he think she was, anyhow? She threatened to tell her boyfriend, the police officer, if he wasn't more polite.

It was dark when she left the motel. She went home to her single room. She locked the door behind her, then moved the bed. In a hiding place under a floorboard, she took out her passport—the one that Jordan had paid for. She hadn't gone any place with it yet, but she felt important just having one. None of the other girls who worked the streets had one.

This was Jordan's proof that he loved her. Proof that he was taking her to the States. Why else would he insist she have a passport? And he guaranteed that he'd wangle a fiancée visa for her from the American Embassy. He had connections, he said. She once tried to get a visa to America, but had been refused. The embassy kept a record of visa denials. Maybe Jordan knew that, and wanted her name changed. She rummaged through her hiding place and took everything she needed, replaced the floorboard, and pulled the bedpost over it.

She washed behind a screened-off area on the back porch, dousing herself from a rain barrel while she scrubbed her hair and soaped down. She felt her rectum. Still tender but not as bad as before. Reno was a bastard for doing that on their last time together. She was glad she'd never have to see him again after tonight. Maybe he was jealous that she'd be living in the States soon, living a life even better than his. Yes, that was it. Reno was envious. The thought pleased her until she started to worry if he'd be mean enough to tell Jordan what he'd done to her. She'd refused Jordan a blowjob. Nice girls didn't do that, she'd told him. He didn't have to know that she could vacuum-seal a missile silo. A smart customer would just put her face where he wanted it. But if a guy like Jordan was dumb enough to ask, well of course, the answer was always no.

But Reno probably wouldn't tell. Jordan had money and paid Reno to do things for him. She should have refused Reno. What could he have done? Beat her up? Not likely, with Jordan calling the shots.

Lolita was just smart enough to know that she wasn't particularly bright, but lately she'd felt absolutely stupid. Ever since Reno made her drug Brian at Buffalo Joe's. The pills would only knock him out, Reno had said. So he could roll the American, he'd said. But the pills had killed him. Reno said they hadn't, that Brian just had a weak heart and drank too much. But Lolita knew better. Too many downers with liquor had killed Brian dead as hell. Reno said to drop the whole bottle into his drink, but she thought that was too much. So, she only put 15 in his beers. And why Reno wanted to rob Brian was curious, too. Brian didn't have much money left. He'd already blown his wad on her, and was useless otherwise. He was a nice man, treated her and her son well, and had sent money this past year. Not much, because he had an ex-wife and a kid back home in Boston. But he didn't deserve what happened to him. Brian drank like a fish for three days straight after Reno told him about Jordan. Reno was mean enough to do that. She'd already latched onto Jordan, so she told Brian to go home as nicely as she could, that she was finished with him.

She dressed in her prettiest outfit, a one-piece fire-truck-red cotton shift that Brian had bought for her. She went out, took a taxi downtown. On the way, the driver propositioned her, offering to waive the fare in exchange for a little bit of lip service. She refused huffily. Why did men always think she was a whore? She got out on the corner of Padre Faura and del Pilar and, just to show the driver how wrong he was, she gave a twenty-peso tip. Unusually generous. What whore would do that? The driver thanked her, apologized for his mistake, and watched her strut—nose in the air—into a restaurant well-known in Manila as a hooker's hang-out.

The place was nearly deserted. She met up with a group of colleagues eating at a table. As usual, the girls brightened when she entered, for Lolita always spun funny stories. They talked about johns, the places that were hot, places off-limits to their profession, current prices for their services. A little while later, they adjourned around the corner to a dance club on del Pilar and converged on a large table, strategically situated just inside the main entrance where johns had to pass. There were some thirty girls already in the joint, but the place—seating hundreds—still seemed empty. Although they'd just eaten, several of the girls ordered kebabs and soft drinks. A house rule, if they plied their trade here, they had to order something. Most of the girls just nursed a mango juice all evening. If they didn't score a customer by 1:00 a.m., they took to the streets, each having their special patch.

There were few johns in the place yet, and the band was just warming up. Lolita was anxious to talk about going to America soon, but Reno and Jordan had warned her against that. She was to tell no one, and she knew herself if she began talking she'd tell everyone everything. Ten times over. So she wouldn't talk about the passport, which just ached to hold it back, especially when that Theresa bitch from Bohol Island began boasting about a Japanese customer who wanted to take her to Tokyo. Everyone knew that Japanese men only took Filipinas back home to sell them. Lolita wrinkled her nose at Theresa. Did she think they were all stupid?

Lolita still had the stash of downers to sell. They were something like Demerol, Reno said, but with a different name. The other girls wouldn't buy them. Too expensive. She carried her drink into the ladies comfort room. She took a pill, washed it down with a gulp of beer. When she returned to the table, Theresa was holding court, jabbering away obliquely to impress two johns who'd taken the next table. Lolita sat down quietly, looked over indifferently at the johns. One of them, an older man in his fifties, winked, motioned her over. She ignored him.

Working girls missed nothing, and Theresa just had to say something: "Oh ho," she blurted in Tagalog. "Miss Hoi Palloi is too good for customers now?"

The girls turned to Lolita. She tried to ignore Theresa, but her pride took over. "I don't have to work any longer."

"Sure. Girlie. Maybe you found Yamashita's gold, huh?" Theresa teased. General Yamashita was rumored to have buried a huge cache of gold in Manila during World War II. It was never found, and rumor had it that crooked politicians had recovered it.

Lolita bit back her anger, but couldn't ignore the baiting, couldn't hold it back. "After tonight, you won't see me again."

A girl who'd seen Lolita with Jordan chimed in, "She has a rich boyfriend now."

"He's taking me to America," Lolita confirmed.

Theresa laughed. She'd become popular over the last few weeks, ever since she'd bragged about scoring 500 dollars for one night with that Japanese guy who—she claimed—also sent her money from Tokyo. Lots of money.

"Sure he is," Theresa hissed. "Your boyfriend's going to get you over there and make you sell your pussy." Theresa held her drink up, flaunting a gold bracelet her Japanese customer had brought her. Lolita went back into the toilet. She sat in a stall and fumed. All she had to do tonight was meet Reno. Why not pop another downer?

At a quarter to midnight, she announced her departure, now very subdued from the beers on top of the pills. But still she laughed at almost anything the girls said. The place was packed with hookers and johns, but she paid no interest to a table of Japanese businessmen nearby, engaging the girls in conversation. She said she was going home, an air of independence in her voice. She no longer needed to troll for johns, she was going to marry her *cano* and have everything she wanted. Reno was waiting for her right now with 100,000 pesos from Jordan. He might think that's all she wanted, but next month, she'd hit him up for another hundred or refuse to go to America. A Filipino would knock her into the middle of next week if she tried that. But *canos* were suckers, easy to control. Brian had been an absolute fool for her, and Jordan wasn't much smarter in that regard. He'd fallen head over heels for her the minute Reno introduced them.

She caught a taxi in front of the club, feeling different about herself now. An air of indifference, of freedom, of complete independence. She'd never walk another street, never suffer the indignity of hanging about on a corner as cars cruised slowly past, drivers inspecting her body, some stopping and just staring without calling her over. Inspecting flesh for sale. She'd known a thousand johns, yet it still hurt when one sat in his car at the curb for long minutes, then cruised on without at least talking to her, pricing her, negotiating, requesting her specialty. What did the bastards want? That she should strip her clothes off right there, maybe pass out photos of her in action.

The taxi dropped her off in front of the Trader's Hotel on Roxas Boulevard. The second downer was kicking in and she felt sluggish, overly relaxed. She paid the driver, walked unsteadily across the service road that ran parallel with the boulevard, and reached the corner of Roxas and Vito Cruz. An occasional car flew by on Roxas, but Vito Cruz had no traffic and there were no pedestrians around. In another hour, the place would be infested with johns cruising past. She looked at her watch, had difficulty focusing. Yes, she giggled, Senor Downer was kicking in. Midnight exactly. Across the street, set back off Roxas, was the Manila Convention Center, its darkened facade silhouetted against a blacker sky. Lolita couldn't see Reno's car, but that didn't mean it wasn't there.

The area was dark. She stood beneath a street light and waited, occasionally squinting into the shadows around the convention center, wondering if she would see his headlights if he did flash them. She moved to where it was easier to see. She felt light—giddy actually—and thought that after she met the documents man, maybe she'd go back downtown after all and take a guy for the night. Not for the money. Great sex of her own choosing suddenly seemed like a good idea. Maybe she'd show the 100,000 pesos to the girls, especially to Miss Theresa Bitch. Maybe she'd even pay for a guy *she* wanted. Wouldn't that be a kick!

But first she had to finish this business with Reno. She watched a taxi approaching slowly from the direction of the airport. It slowed, then stopped near the corner. The driver was probably waiting for someone to come out of the Traders Hotel, Lolita thought. But if he was looking for a fare, he ought to pull into the service road and cruise past the hotel. The taxi idled quietly, and soon its headlights went out. The glow of a cigarette punctuated the darkened interior. Was the driver watching her? Did he think she was a fare? She certainly hoped he didn't think she was working the street.

She saw Reno's headlights flash in the darkness beneath the convention center. She stepped off the curb and crossed the inbound lanes. The taxi slowly pulled away from the curb, but she paid it no attention. She reached the grassy median, crossed that, and step-ped off the curb onto the outbound lanes. She swore as she turned her ankle, her foot slipping off her high heeled shoe. As she bent over to adjust the straps on the shoe, the taxi picked up speed and headed in her direction. She thought the driver was going to U-turn, until he gunned the engine and shot straight for her. She stood paralyzed, sluggishly trying to comprehend what was happening. Then she suddenly realized Reno's treachery; he'd marked her for a hit. She dropped her purse and tried to dart for the sidewalk, but the taxi—a low-slung Nissan—hit her in the middle of the street, sending her flying and crashing to the pavement. Metal ribs beneath the bumper caught her body and dragged her fifty feet along the roadway. She thought she could hear herself screaming, but in reality she uttered nothing at all until the back tire ran over her and spat her out from beneath the carriage, spinning her against the curb like a rag doll. She felt wet, numb, heard the taxi's brakes screeching. The driver looked back, saw that she was moving. He reversed the taxi, burning rubber as it sped backwards. This time, the rear tires ran over her, the carriage bouncing over her body, tearing flesh and snapping bone. The tires spun her sideways, until they ejected her into the middle of the road.

Car headlights appeared in the opposite direction. The taxi driver U-turned without looking back. If he tried to hit his victim again, it would be obvious that it was a murder. *If* the oncoming driver was courageous enough to stay around for the police.

The oncoming driver slowed, saw something in the roadway. The taxi was nearly out of sight, its headlights and tail-lights turned off. The driver thought he'd seen something he didn't want to witness. He drove by slowly, looked anxiously at the body at the end of a blood splattered trail along the roadway. He sped ahead, down the boulevard. Cars were coming from both directions now, and one of the drivers stopped and got out of his car. Other vehicles began stopping and the doorman at the Traders Hotel was looking over, although he'd seen and heard nothing. Several men came walking over from the hotel.

Soon, a dozen cars had pulled over. One of the drivers directed traffic around the body that lay in the middle of the outbound roadway.

Marcellus—in uniform—coasted down the convention center ramp, turning on his headlights as he reached the street. He pulled up and positioned his car between Lolita and the median, got out.

People stood back. He asked what happened. Several drivers and pedestrians began talking at once and Marcellus, who'd watched it all, knew that none was an actual witness. A dozen other people stood on the steps of the Traders Hotel, a few more walked over to the scene of the accident.

Reno ordered everyone to stand back on the curb and shouted for someone to call for an ambulance. He knelt down next to Lolita, cursed softly. She was still alive, though just barely. The back of her head was split open. Blood covered her head, face, and shoulders, a crimson pool forming under her back. Lolita recognized him, tried to move, to get up, her mind screaming for her to get away from this man. But she was paralyzed, floating in and out of consciousness, crazy thoughts racing through her mind, like just how incredibly hot the underside of an automobile was, wondering if her skirt was up and if her panties were clean. She murmured something, blood bubbling from her mouth. Marcellus' back was to the growing crowd. He leaned over as if to listen to her closely, his body shielding what he was actually doing: kneeling on her throat.

Lolita thought of little Pauley, her son. How would he react when he learned she was never coming home again?

"Die, you *puta* bitch. Die," Marcellus hissed. His eyes slid sideways to make certain that he wasn't being detected, called out again for someone to get an ambulance. Someone shouted back that one was on the way.

Lolita choked on her blood, thought that she was forming words but that Reno wasn't paying attention to her. What could she have expected? She'd let Reno beat, cheat her, even punk her. Of course, he thought she was his to do with as he pleased. Even to kill her, if that's what he wanted. Maybe that's what she'd been put on this earth for. For someone like Marcellus to use, then to kill. She began a silent prayer. *Our Father who art in heaven. . . .*

A doorman called over, "Here it comes now." Emergency lights flashed at the end of a line of cars funneling into one lane, slowing, passing behind Marcellus.

"Good," he yelled back, cursing Lolita as her blood soaked his trousers up to his knee.

Lolita never finished her prayer.

18

The claim in Burma was clean. Roth had traveled up to Mandalay where he tracked down the family of an insured who reportedly died in a road accident. It was legit; the man was killed as reported, and his family had transported his body to Rangoon for cremation.

He rerouted back through Bangkok without stopping over. The following morning in Manila, he started on the death claims for MacMillan and the young man murdered by his girlfriend's lover. It had been three weeks since Mrs. MacMillan filed the claim against Amalgamated Life, so he e-mailed a status report to Nina that he was starting the job. He doubted the case was dirty, and wouldn't take but a day to finish it.

He paid a visit to the Manila Local Civil Registrar at City Hall, where, at Window Six on the ground floor, he spoke with a clerk named Boy Carrera. Boy was as well-known in scam circles as Reno Marcellus—as corrupt as they came. While most death filings at the registrar's were legitimate, with Boy Carrera there was always a possibility of fraud. Boy was in his mid-twenties, pleasant, impervious to insults, and quick to flash a smile as he overtly solicited bribes. A dream come true for cops like Marcellus.

Roth asked him to match up his photocopies of both death certificates against the register—a manually kept ledger.

Boy looked at the photocopy of MacMillan's death certificate and immediately said that it hadn't been entered into the ledger yet. Roth's ears went up. That was impossible, since the registry number could only have been placed there by this very office, and the registration number clearly appeared at the top of Roth's copy. The number seemed logical according to the expected number of deaths for Metro Manila by late August, which is why Roth hadn't been overly suspicious, even with Reno Marcellus' accident report. Until now.

Boy reached into the bottom drawer of his desk, pulled out a bundle of death certificates. He rummaged through them, found a copy of the death certificate for Peter MacMillan. It matched the certificate and registrar's number on Roth's copy, which had been furnished to Amalgamated Life by Lori MacMillan. A Doctor Locanto—a pathologist with the NBI—had filled in most of the details.

But if Boy kept a copy handy in his desk instead of entering it into the manual log and keeping it on file, he'd done so for a reason. The handy certificates in his stack were spurious for one reason or another. This was Boy's private enterprise stash, a pile of documents in which he had a financial interest. Most people wouldn't have recognized such an obvious ploy, and to those who did—people like Roth—Boy couldn't have cared less.

Boy held it up, asked Roth if he wanted a certified copy. Roth smiled a please. The routine was for Boy to give Roth a fee slip to pay at the cashier's window, but Boy offered to go to the cashier himself and pay for a certification. Of course, he'd pocket the fee.

Roth gave him a 1,000-peso note, knowing that it would take him ages to get it changed.

Boy smiled. "I keep the change, yes?"

"In exchange for a few hours with your younger sister, sure." Roth smiled back.

Boy shrugged, said he had no sister, disappeared to press the registrar's seal on the document and get change. Roth turned the death ledger around and ran his finger down the list of people who'd died on August 25th. The name in the log for Peter MacMillan's registry number read, "*Reyes, Arturo*," with an address in Tondo, a suburb. Peter MacMillan's name appeared nowhere on the pages for September. Roth pulled out his miniature camera and took several snapshots of the page.

The claim on Peter MacMillan was bogus. No doubt about it. Roth was a little surprised, since most faked death claims in the Philippines involved *balikbayans*—Filipinos who'd lived in the States, bought policies there, then returned to the islands to fake their death. When Americans did it, they were usually either Filipino-Americans with no interest in returning to the States, or Americans who insured themselves under phony names, then did a disappearing act.

Boy Carrera returned with the change and the certified copy of the death certificate on Peter MacMillan. It was the same certification that Roth already had. But no record existed in the ledger, and the registration number had been assigned to another deceased.

Roth also had Boy certify the copy of the death certificate on his other claim, checked the manual ledger to make sure that the death was properly entered, then spent the afternoon working on the case of the rival boyfriends. The scenario was logical here in the Philippines, but anywhere else it would sound stupid. The policy was an old one, 25,000 dollars death benefit with double indemnity, and would pay 50,000 dollars if the boy had been murdered, since homicide met the policy's language under accidental death.

Roth substantiated the actual death, and there was no question about the boy's true identity. He spoke with friends and family, interviewed the tearful fiancée, and visited the church where the funeral service had taken place—even the funeral home and the cemetery—before wrapping up the case. It all fit, and Roth had no doubt that the death was legit. The boys had argued, the jealous suitor had been sniffing around his fiancée while he was off studying in the States. It was also clear that the fiancée hadn't tried to discourage the interloper's attentions. But she'd cried at the boy's funeral, then she cried at his killer's trial, and now tearfully visited him daily in jail, all the while dating yet another young man. Soap operas weren't invented in the Philippines, but they should've been.

That night, Roth faxed New York about the dead student, and advised that although he'd started on the MacMillan case, he'd need more time on that one. Clean cases usually required only a day to handle, like the boy in the coffin wearing a bullet in his brain. But fraudulent cases took days to disprove, sometimes weeks, even months. The MacMillan case could be one of those, since litigation would be likely if Amalgamated didn't pay up.

He instructed Nina to work up the background on both Peter and Lori MacMillan, and to tell Jim Kincannon that if they heard from Mrs MacMillan again, to say only that a Mr. Mike Roth would be in touch with her in due course.

He ate dinner in his room, then visited Buffalo Joe's, a few blocks from his hotel. He drank and flirted with the hookers until around 2:00 a.m., the time of Peter MacMillan's reported death. The place was packed. He bought drinks—guaranteed to attract attention—and chatted-up the girls, inquiring about where he could get his hands on some barbiturates. A pretty little hooker from Romblon Island professed knowing someone who could get downers, but it turned out that she really knew little about drugs, and offered to get him some marijuana. Roth declined, saying he wanted the *real* thing. Confused, she asked if he wanted a Cola-Cola.

———

In the morning, Roth obtained a certified copy of the police report on MacMillan from Traffic Headquarters. The report read that the undersigned, SPO Marcellus, was the first officer on the scene. Marcellus later met an American consular officer—a Miss Ernestine Scales—at the autopsy and went with her to MacMillan's hotel. Roth knew the place. It was a dump of a hostel just off del Pilar Street. Marcellus reported that amongst MacMillan's personal effects, there was a business card for a Mr. Morales—no first name given—describing him as an associate. Morales' telephone number was shown in the report.

117

The report went on to say that he contacted this Mr. Morales who—shocked by the news—rushed to the hotel. MacMillan's body was picked up earlier from the hospital by the Las Flores Funeraria. Marcellus notified the NBI. Later that day, he reported the death to the US Embassy, making contact with a William Towers there.

But conspicuously absent throughout Marcellus' report was a timeframe. It only read, "*later in the day*," with respect to his contact with the embassy.

Roth next visited the *Manila Night Beat*, a nightly news rag, but published by a respected Manila daily. He'd been here many times. He checked in with the City Room and located the reporter on the MacMillan story, Nestor Otero, down in the cafeteria.

Otero likely visited other accident scenes involving Marcellus, so when Roth sat down opposite him, he couched his inquiries matter-of-factly, in case Otero was buddy-buddy with Marcellus. Otero, in his late twenties, was pleasant, well educated, and co-operative. He tuned into police-band calls nightly, beginning at 8:00 p.m., and had heard the MacMillan call. He was ten minutes from Buffalo Joe's at the time, so he covered the story. Otero finished his meal and took Roth back up to the City Room where he dug out a copy of the edition his article appeared in. There were three headlines, all in red letters, each covering a ghoulish scene. Under the "CANO'S *LAST ROUND-UP*" headline, a kicker read, "*American found dead at Buffalo Joe's, OD suspected.*"

"Any other pix?" Roth asked.

"No. I only got this one, from about ten feet away."

"Why?"

"That preeck Marcellus. He threw me out."

"Again, why?"

"Who knows? Sometimes Marcellus is okay. Lets me take all the shots I want. Up close, you know? Whatever I want. Even with some john stuck in the hooker he got blown away with, you know. Then, other times, Marcellus gives the press a hard time, won't let us get near an accident or crime scene. I tip him, you know, for letting me get some good photos. A few hundred pesos, sometimes more." Otero shrugged. "I can't figure him out, you know."

"Got the negative on this?" Roth tapped the photo in the headlines.

"Sure. I keep all negatives, you know."

"Let me have it."

Otero wrinkled his forehead. If a *cano* wanted something, then there must be value in it. "I don't know, you know."

"It's worth nothing to you. You know," Roth replied, annoyed that Otero's habit was becoming infectious.

"Still. You know."

"Okay, tell you what. Blow it up for me, you know. I'll give you 500 pesos for an eight by ten."

"But I keep the negative?"

"You keep the negative."

Sucker, Otero thought, nodding. He would have sold the negative *and* the blow-up for 200.

Chump, Roth winked. He'd have paid 1,000. He exchanged telephone numbers with Otero, said he'd speak with him later.

———

The Las Flores Funeraria was a large building inside its own courtyard on Adriatico Street. Mr. Florentino had been contacted by a Mr. Morales at 3:00 a.m., Monday morning, August 25th, as soon as the body was refused by the hospital. This was an hour after the reported time of death. Morales said that his American business associate, a Mr. Peter MacMillan, had just been found dead. "How he knew that fast, I'm not sure," Florentino explained. "Mr. Mac-Millan had no family in Manila."

"Why did *you* get the call for the body?" Roth asked.

Florentino shrugged. "We're well-known in Manila. Six branches. Mr. Morales gave a deposit, said that the widow would pay the balance."

"What did Marcellus say?"

"Marcellus who?"

"Reno Marcellus?"

"I don't believe I know him. Is he a friend of Mr. MacMillan?"

Roth shook his head. He believed Florentino; one funeral director was the same as another if the perpetrators had an actual stiff. No reason to involve an undertaker if they didn't need him as part of the scam.

"You knew it would be an NBI case?"

"I assumed as much. We picked the body up at the Manila Hospital. They didn't admit him because he was DOA. Plus, the man had died in a saloon."

"The NBI boys post him here?"

"Yes, downstairs in our morgue, later that evening. Want to see?"

"No. Did you take any photos?" Roth hoped.

"What for?"

"Did the NBI?"

"Yes. They always do. After the autopsy they left the body here."

"And you prepared it for burial?"

"Cremation. Mr. Morales said that it would be a closed casket affair. How he would know that, I don't know, unless the wife, Mrs. MacMillan, told him so. Anyhow, it is usually a good idea. Those NBI pathologists are most untidy. They don't leave me much to work with."

"Wait," Roth said. "Let's back up. You said the body was autopsied in the evening?"

"Yes. Around 8:00 p.m."

"But he died at around 2:00 a.m. that morning. Eighteen hours earlier." Roth bit his lower lip, thinking. "Remember what Mac-Millan looked like?"

"Yes. Somewhat. Average height."

"*Cano* average or Filipino average?"

Florentino smiled appreciably. "You are correct, sir. Filipino average. *Cano* short. My height."

Roth estimated that Florentino was about five feet seven.

"That will all be in the autopsy report," Florentino went on. "Wavy hair. Very, uh, dark red, uh—"

"Auburn?"

"Yes, that's it. Auburn."

"Build?"

"Stocky. You will see it all in the NBI report, also."

"But you prepared the body. I wanna know what you remember about him."

"He had, how do you call it? Permanent, uh, pimples. Not pimples. Dots, uh—"

"Freckles?"

"Yes! Those. He had freckles across his face, his shoulders, and back. Many." Florentino tried to run his fingers across his own shoulder but his suit was too tight.

"Age?"

"Maybe thirty. A little less. Not more."

"What else?"

"Nothing. Regular features. Oh, karate."

"Karate?"

"Yes. Karate, I'm sure. His knuckles were large. Both hands. Like they'd been broken many times and mended bigger, thicker. Karate, I am certain."

"Color eyes?"

Florentino shrugged. "I didn't pay attention. I don't like them looking at me when I work on them, so I tape the eyes shut."

"Tell me about his clothes?"

"Casual. American jeans. Levis, I think. A baseball T-shirt."

"Which read what?"

Florentino shrugged apologetically. "I don't know. I don't follow baseball. I like basketball, though. And I like baseball caps, so they ought to have basketball caps, too. Ever wonder why they don't?"

"Night and day I wonder about it. Mrs. MacMillan took his ashes, huh?"

Florentino's eyes widened. "No! That's the thing. She came for his funeral with a man from your embassy. I have his card somewhere. Mrs. MacMillan asked me to crate the urn."

"And?"

"I never heard from her again. I sent her a letter, I think in Los Angeles, but I've heard nothing back from her. The good Mr. Mac-Millan still rests with us here."

He led Roth into a tiny room where several urns were stored on shelves. The urns, most containing the ashes of Chinese-Filipinos, had photographs on the face of the pottery, but not MacMillan's. His ashes were in a recepticle placed in a cardboard box, which was in turn packed in a small wooden crate.

"I crated it for her to take aboard the plane when she returned to America. But she said that the experience would be too much and asked me to ship it."

"Did she pay for shipping?"

"No."

"Did she pay all of the funeral expenses?"

"No. She promised to return a few days after the service and settle the bill, and tell me where to ship the ashes."

"I'll get back to you about the ashes," Roth said. "Tell me about Mrs. MacMillan."

A slow, awkward smile gathered on Florentino's lips.

"You'd like to jump her, is that what you're saying?"

"Pardon?"

"One more thing. Has anyone else been around asking questions about MacMillan?"

"An adjuster. I have his card upstairs. A local man."

———

Roth next visited the National Bureau of Investigation offices on Taft Boulevard. Dr. Locanto, the pathologist who performed the autopsy, was out. His secretary said that he'd be in the following morning, and made an appointment for Roth to see him.

It was nearly three o'clock. Roth dropped by the American Express office on United Nations Avenue and purchased some travelers checks on his corporate card. He crossed the street, grabbed a cheeseburger at the McDonald's opposite the Holiday Inn, stood outside and ate it, mulling over the case.

An old, dark woman sat on a mashed-down cardboard box on the sidewalk, leaning back against the building. She held an ill-kept infant in her lap. Both were dirty and nattily dressed. A coffee cup sat on the sidewalk in front of her with a few pesos in it. She looked up at Roth devouring his cheeseburger, then her eyes slid away. Above her head, inside the restaurant, chubby youngsters from prosperous families sat eating. None looked at the old woman, although she was just inches away, separated by the plate-glass window. Roth dug into his pocket and pulled out a 1,000-peso note. He walked over, bent down, and stuffed the money into the coffee cup. The old woman's eyes met his, then she looked away. Several Filipinos waiting at the curb for a *jeepney* watched him and looked dispassionately at the old woman, then looked away. Beggars were a common sight in downtown Manila, with hundreds sleeping on the streets. *Bahala na,* Roth thought. 'Come what may,' the Filipino's philosophy that kept the country in the toilet fifty years after independence. Once the richest country in Asia after World War II, the nation was sinking under patronage and crooked politicians.

Roth stood at the curb, ruminating over the MacMillan matter. Whoever the perpetrators were, they'd done a good job except for the screw-up with the death certificate at the registrar's office. The wife, Lori MacMillan, had to be involved. She was the beneficiary for one million on this policy, presuming double indemnity kicked in. For anyone else to profit from this, the money would first have to go through her. Never mind that she cheated Florentino, but abandoning the dead man's ashes had been dumb.

It was more likely that the MacMillan's cooked up this little trick together. Maybe Mr. and Mrs. MacMillan had another name altogether and were planning to disappear after the policies paid. Couples who did that were usually petty fraudsters, losers who bounced between scams until they hit the jackpot. Namely, a caper like this.

Maybe MacMillan wanted to do a Lazarus; return to life after death, to live out his days in the islands. A million bucks here was like having twenty million in the States. On the other hand, maybe they were pros, moving from one scam to another. A lot of maybes.

But there was a body. The body of a Westerner, if not an American.

Someone bribed Boy, who purposely failed to enter the case in the ledger that would later be sent to the NSO—the National Statistics Office—making the death official. Instead, Boy was waiting to hear from the person who orchestrated the scam, then destroy his copy of the death certificate. No death would be on record with the registrar's office or with the NSO. That someone was probably Marcellus. Filipinos used this scam to claim a death without actually dying, because, in the Philippines, one wasn't considered dead until the certificate was finally registered with the NSO. This was a form of check and balance, since no one trusted civil registrars. They shelled out bogus certificates for pennies, particularly after a Filipino was turned down for a visa to the United States and needed another name, another birth certificate.

Roth, and just about every one of his guys, had bought death certificates on themselves to show clients how easy it was. He had a few framed in the New York office. And although he'd been hospitalized only once in his life—for a broken fibula when he was in the Marines—he also had a collection of bogus hospitalization certificates for himself, compliments of fraudsters like Dr. Ignacio.

But here was the rub: the US Embassy knew that civil registrars were corrupt, and visa officers wanted birth certificates certified by the NSO before they issued a visa. Yet they accepted death certificates from those same civil registrars. Selective thinking. Visa officers covered their asses against issuing a bad visa, but when it came to death certificates, the insurance companies could piss off and die if they paid a fraudulent claim based on a bogus 180.

Roth finished his cheeseburger, rolled up the paper, dunked it in a trash can ten feet away, wiped his hands with his handkerchief. This was getting to be an interesting case, one that would dispel his general boredom, maybe offer up some unexpected perks as well. He'd been working these cases since around the time Christ was a corporal, and few challenges remained. Just getting to these places was what annoyed him most. Traveling to far-flung destinations had lost its allure long ago.

There was no point speculating further on this. The NBI autopsy photographs could clear things up. He walked back to his hotel, had dinner, and settled in for the night with Senor San Miguel and a paperback.

19

Next morning, to avoid long queues, Roth arrived at the NSO thirty minutes before the windows opened. The sun was already hot, although it was just eight o'clock. He mopped his face with a handkerchief, counted only eight people in front of him.

The NSO was better known by *Manileros* as the National Census Office and it was only necessary to fill out a form and come back for the answer. The lines continued all day, thousands engaged in another popular national pastime—waiting.

At a window, he applied for a certified copy of the death certificate on Peter MacMillan, paid forty pesos for a rush search. The results would be available by 4:00 p.m. He also applied for a certified copy of the death certificate on Arturo Reyes, the man whose death was reported on the same day, and whose registry number was shared with the death certificate on MacMillan.

He returned to the NBI offices for the meeting with Dr. Locanto. Locanto pulled the autopsy report, read through it with Roth.

However, there were no photographs of MacMillan's corpse. A note in the file read that that particular roll had been inadvertently overexposed when the camera popped open. Accidentally, of course. In addition, the film had been stripped apart somehow when it was removed from the camera. In either event, it had been destroyed and thrown out. On that particular roll of 36 exposures, there had been photographs of three other autopsies. The death mask—that being a facial shot—was always included.

Locanto appeared genuinely upset and wanted to speak with the technician responsible for processing the photographs. But the 'technician,' as it turned out, was merely a young morgue attendant named Bing-Bing who'd been processing film for only the past few months, after the regular photographer quit the job without giving notice. Locanto railed at Bing-Bing in Tagalog. Roth leaned against a filing cabinet off to the side, watching Bing-Bing's reaction. Bing-Bing snuck a glance at Roth as Locanto's tirade ran down. He was excused after Locanto waved off his excuses.

"Inexperience and negligence," Locanto said, shaking his head at the sad state of affairs within the NBI. More likely, Roth thought, Bing-Bing had been bribed to destroy the film.

Locanto couldn't recall any aspects of the autopsy. He performed three or four daily, and had to refer to his notes. Had it been otherwise, had Locanto been able to recall the particulars off the top of his head, Roth would have suspected him as being involved. Locanto struggled with his memory, but in the end recalled less than Florentino had.

"One thing," Roth said. "The cause of death? Did he drink himself to death or did he fall?"

"There was hardly a trace of blood around the skull wound. That would suggest he was dead before he fell."

"Let's see if I have this right: he was dead, then he got up and then fell down?"

"No. Of course not. Perhaps his body was dropped. But the trauma to the cranium is massive. As though he was struck by a blunt instrument with great force."

"After he was dead?"

Locanto shrugged. "Yes. But I admit there seems no point to that. Unless his assailant didn't know that he was already dead. Otherwise, why on earth assault a dead man?"

"For double indemnity. Are you calling the death accidental, or natural?"

"Oh, I see. For insurance, of course. I would have to say heart failure, induced by massive doses of barbiturates. But the trauma to the skull, while certainly enough to kill him, wasn't the cause of death."

Still, in court, it might come down to a pissing contest. Roth requested a photocopy of the autopsy report and thanked Dr. Locanto. There was no point pushing Bing-Bing around. He'd never admit accepting a bribe, because, for starters, he'd lose his job. But worse than that, cops like Marcellus had a reputation for rewarding treachery with extreme prejudice. Bing-Bing would end up on a slab himself. He wondered what Marcellus had paid Bing-Bing. Probably only a few thousand pesos.

Roth's next port of call was the flophouse where Peter MacMillan had stayed. To see what the registration drill would be, Roth asked to register for a room. The manager—an ever-smiling young man in his early twenties named Sonny Santos—gave him a registration card to complete. No ledger was used, at least by the guest. Roth said never mind, and told Sonny that he wanted to see the registration cards for the last week of August through the first week of September. Sonny asked him why.

Roth gave him 200 pesos, said, "That's why," and Sonny gladly pulled the cards. Finding no card for MacMillan in the stack, it was Roth's turn to ask why. Sonny went into another drawer where a card for Peter MacMillan was conveniently on hand, just as his death certificate had been handy in Boy Carrera's desk.

Roth quizzed Sonny if anyone else had been around asking questions about MacMillan. There hadn't, which told him that other insurers were not interested in the claim past a perfunctory check, believing it was legit. Still, there could be more insurance companies involved that he didn't know about, who hadn't investigated yet.

Sonny said that MacMillan's clothes and some papers had been taken by his friend—a Mr. Morales—after the authorities had gone through the room and collected MacMillan's passport and personal effects.

"Who took those things?"

"A woman from the American Embassy."

"When?"

"Later that day."

Roth leaned into Sonny's face. "Again, when?"

"Uh, it was dark."

"Morning dark or evening dark?"

"It was in the evening."

Evening. That would have been about 16, maybe 18 hours after MacMillan's death. "Let's see your register."

"Register?"

"Yeah, your daily register."

"Uh, we don't keep a ledger if that's what you're asking for. We only have the registration cards, which we keep chronologically."

"And this is MacMillan's registration card?"

Sonny nodded.

"You kept it handy, eh, Sonny?"

"In case someone wanted to see it. I thought that people would be needing it."

"What people?"

"Uh, like, uh."

"Insurance companies?"

"Yes. Exactly," Sonny replied.

"Who told you to do that?"

Sonny almost answered. He wasn't the smartest guy in Manila. He shook his head. "Nobody. I just thought people might want to see it."

The registration card was completed by hand with neat lettering. The handwriting was a Filipino's, in the familiar architectural style drilled into schoolchildren, a common script that stayed with them throughout their lives; a script as telltale as a typewriter model. The signature of Peter MacMillan was signed by the same hand, using the same pen—an ink pen rather than a ballpoint. Roth compared the signature on the registration card with the signature on the photocopy of MacMillan's passport, which had been submitted by the beneficiary with the claimant's papers. It was similar, but not the same. A graphologist could attest to that.

The residence address shown on the registration card was the same LA location as on Mrs. MacMillan's claimant statement.

"Okay, thanks Sonny," Roth said, tucking the card into his pocket.

"Hey! You can't keep the card."

"You're gonna take it away from me?"

"But you can't."

"Can," Roth said firmly. Another 100 pesos settled the question. Sonny scooped up the note with a shrug.

"By the way," Roth asked. "Where is Traffic Police Headquarters?"

Sonny started to answer but Roth cut him off. "Write it down for me, will you. My memory's shot to shit. Too many San Miguels."

Sonny laughed, and obliged by writing the directions on a slip of paper. He wrote with his right hand. The writing on the registration was also by a right-handed person, but it wasn't the same handwriting. Someone else had completed the registration card. As Roth turned to leave, Sonny asked what he should do if anyone else inquired, since Roth was taking the card.

"Tell them to see me. And, Sonny, I'll pay you 1,000 pesos to know who comes around." Roth threw his business card on the counter, his hotel card stapled to it. "Call me at the hotel or, if I've left, try me in Bangkok." He pointed to the Bangkok number on the card. "Call me collect."

"Okay."

"I gotta go over and see Reno. Anything you want me to tell him?"

"Say 'hi' for me—Uh, Reno? Reno who?"

Roth laughed. He went out to find a payphone and called Nestor Otero, who said he'd blown up the negative. They agreed to meet half an hour later at the Savory restaurant, opposite Luneta Park.

———

The enlargement did nothing in the way of identifying the dead man, so Roth asked Otero to provide him with blow-ups showing the back of the dead man's head, left arm, and wrist. Maybe that would tell him something. The film was black and white, which didn't help.

He gave Otero another 500 pesos, told him to have the enlargements ready that evening. They arranged to meet at the Blue Hawaii dance club on del Pilar Street.

From the Savory, Roth returned to his hotel, showered and changed into cotton slacks and shirt, and took a taxi back to the NSO where his responses were waiting. The death certificate on Arturo Reyes was on file, but the request made for the death certificate on MacMillan came back with *"NO RECORD"* stamped on it.

Roth smiled as he read the form. Not only would the death certificate on Peter MacMillan be controversial since it shared the same registry number as the certificate on Arturo Reyes, but it hadn't even been filed with the NSO. Technically, no death certificate existed despite there being an autopsy report and a record with Las Flores Funeraria for Peter MacMillan.

It was rush hour and he waited 15 minutes for another taxi. He ran to a cab discharging passengers, but a woman beat him there, jumping into the back seat. The average fare in Manila was less than eighty pesos, about two bucks. He offered the woman 200 to relinquish the taxi. She gladly did. The driver, seeing a 'rich' *cano*, asked for a larger fare. Since he was running late and had several stops to make, Roth told the driver to leave the meter running and he'd double the fare.

He directed the driver to the address on the Reyes death certificate where he met Arturo Reyes' widow. She lived with her three children in a two-room apartment over a *sari-sari*, a neighborhood store. Arturo Reyes had died on August 25th, at around 7:00 a.m. He was 56 years old and dropped dead near his home while walking to the bus stop to go to work.

Typically, neighbors gathered around Mrs. Reyes as Roth interviewed her. She didn't know Officer Marcellus, hadn't met any Peter MacMillan, and couldn't understand what Roth's inquiry was all about.

It was simple: Arturo Reyes, a brewer at the San Miguel Bottling Company, had actually died on the same day Peter MacMillan supposedly died, so instead of assigning MacMillan's dead body an actual registry number, Boy Carrera had used the death of the next individual to be reported—in this case, Reyes. Boy assigned that same number to MacMillan's death certificate, then purposely neglected to enter the MacMillan death into the ledger, or send a copy of the death certificate to the NSO. So, once the insurance companies paid up, the real Peter MacMillan could return to life. That's what Filipinos did when they wanted to fake a death without dying 'forever.' Had the MacMillan's wanted this? Not likely. This was a Filipino trick. An American, with extensive personal histories on paper, would more likely want an end to his persona, especially if it was bogus to begin with. The MacMillan's probably just wanted to collect and to hell with returning to life. But Boy Carrera had gotten his instructions wrong.

With two death certificates bearing the same number and no record of the MacMillan certificate at the NSO, the death certificate would arguably be disallowed into evidence if the case ever went to court in the States. No death certificate—no death. No death—no claim.

Roth took a statement from Mrs. Reyes, and had neighbors witness their signatures. Now it was too late for the MacMillan's from a legal standpoint. Despite the fact that there was a body involved in this claim, the death certificate on Peter MacMillan was compromised by conflicting information. Unless Lori MacMillan could come up with an actual eye-witness to MacMillan's death as Mrs. Reyes and neighbors had for her husband, she'd have a problem proving her claim in court. Roth doubted if this Morales would ever be found. That left only the cop, Marcellus.

This was getting interesting. Happy with his first real challenge in a long time, Roth did a little jig on the sidewalk to the amusement of the neighborhood kids, then walked towards his waiting taxi.

Still, there'd been a death. Since Marcellus and a bogus death certificate were in the picture, Roth ruled out an overdose suicide. A despondent nutcase wouldn't need confederates like Marcellus and his cronies to drink himself to death.

That presented one of two possibilities: either Marcellus body-shopped until he happened upon a dead *cano* to fill the part, or he'd guaranteed a body, then switched identities. Dead Filipinos were common, but dead *canos* couldn't be found in every gutter. Roth smelled murder.

He grinned at the taxi driver taking him back to his hotel. "Finally, I get something nasty."

The driver looked back at him. "You want a girl, sir?"

Roth laughed. "No. I mean a different kind of nasty."

And nasty raised the stakes, didn't it?

At the hotel, he called Otero, who said he hadn't gotten around to doing the enlargements yet. Otero explained that a huge fire had engulfed a tire factory out in the suburb of Paranaque that morning, and photographers were lining up to use the room. Still, Roth arranged to meet him at Buffalo Joe's later.

After dinner, he walked to Joe's to meet Otero. He wanted to make certain Otero's excuse was legit, that he wasn't stalling for more pesos or—more importantly—wasn't betraying him to Marcellus. Otero wasn't stupid. The case involved Marcellus in some way, and he understood the value of information. But Roth sized him up as playing it straight.

The girl known to peddle downers hadn't been seen for a couple of weeks. Several of the girls in the bar assumed she was with a customer. When girls went missing, it usually meant that some john had taken them off for a holiday. By two o'clock, few girls were entering Buffalo Joe's, so Roth called it a night. He fixed the next meeting with Otero for ten o'clock the following night.

———

Roth mulled the situation over while having breakfast in his room. It was time to see Reno Marcellus, maybe also take a few snaps of him. He dropped a 35-mm camera in his kit, picked through some rolls of film, threw them in.

He waved down a taxi in front of his hotel. Thinking that it would be another long day, he arranged for the cab by the hour. He directed the driver to traffic headquarters over by South Pier. On the way, he studied MacMillan's accident report again. But his photocopy was fourth or fifth generation, and while the handwriting looked similar to that on MacMillan's hotel registration card, he couldn't be sure.

He ordered the driver to stop off at a drugstore, where he bought gauze and adhesive tape. In the back of the taxi, he bandaged up his right hand to where he could hardly move his fingers.

At headquarters, he missed Marcellus by only a few minutes. He had the dispatcher call around, and he finally caught up with him at the Southern Manila Traffic Command station near the Harrison Shopping Plaza.

Walking into the command station, he spotted Marcellus talking with some other cops. He was just coming off duty. Roth hadn't seen him for a year or two, and the big Filipino seemed to be even darker, even bigger. Maybe he was just fatter. Marcellus saw the desk sergeant pointing him out to Roth, who motioned him over. Marcellus broke off his conversation with the officers, not thrilled at being summoned by a civilian. But he smelled money, and *canos* were his best-paying customers. He recognized Roth, but couldn't remember in what connection. Roth led the big cop into a custodian's room off the corridor. Marcellus followed cautiously, his eyes moving down Roth's frame for a bulge that might be a pistol.

"Officer Reno Marcellus," Roth began, offering his hand. "Long time no see. How you been, man?"

Marcellus shook hands, wondering what he wanted. *Canos* bought bogus accident and hospitalization reports to present to their insurance companies back home. The claims were small, but paid for their vacation in the islands. For bogus accident reports, Reno Marcellus was the man to know in Manila.

"Okay, man, I'm okay. How you doin'?"

"Never better, Reno. Never better. Hey, look at this, will you, man?" Roth handed him the accident report. Marcellus recognized MacMillan's name instantly, but pretended to read, playing for time during which this *cano* might reveal his objective. Was he one of Jordan's confederates, an investigator, or maybe someone from the American Embassy? Investigator, Marcellus concluded, and finally placed him.

"I know you, don't I?"

"Of course," Roth said, looking offended. "Smash up over in Quiapo 'bout a year ago. Death in Paco Park two, three years ago."

"Yeah. That's it. What's this about?" Marcellus handed the report back to Roth.

"I got a hundred for the real story, Reno. Dollars, not pesos. Just between you and me."

Marcellus took the report back and studied it, his mind working. He'd met Jordan—or whoever the fuck he was—through Montilla, aka Morales, his chum in the Customs Service. Montilla peddled contraband and brokered fraudulent insurance claims, anything from lost and damaged freight to bogus deaths, while Marcellus matched bodies up at accident scenes and lined-up the players—people like Boy Carrera, Sonny, and the NBI photographer. Whoever was needed.

Montilla's price to Jordan had been 2,000 dollars, which he split with Marcellus who arranged a *cano* stiff, changed ID, cleaned out the guy's room, and did the leg work. Easy money for Montilla, especially since the cop handled everything.

Marcellus' expenses had been 100 bucks, and Roth represented a chance to recoup that.

But this *cano's* death was a little out of the ordinary, a special case requiring special handling. For nearly a month he'd had to search for a stiff, and growing tired of Montilla's griping, took matters into his own hands, using that *puta*, Lolita, who had a convenient customer all lined up—a real loser.

He handed the report back to Roth again. "This is the real story, man. What are you talking about?"

"Okay, Reno, tell you what: I'll tell *you* what happened and you just nod or shake your head. Okay? The 100 will still be yours."

Marcellus said nothing, just eyed Roth cautiously. Before Roth said anything, two officers opened the door, seeking privacy themselves. The tiny space served as the station's conference room where cops acted as franchise scam brokers. The officers apologized to Marcellus even though one was senior, but Marcellus said never mind, motioned Roth back out into the corridor. Roth was squeezing him, and the closet put a fine point on that.

"Gimme five minutes to sign off duty, then we'll go for some beers, okay, man?"

"Fine," Roth said. Murder wasn't a simple fender-bender and Marcellus didn't like being caged; wanted time to think this over. But maybe he'd be willing to give something up; Benjamin Franklin was a popular guy in the Philippines.

Roth already knew the story. He'd seen a few cases tumble like this over the years. He wanted confirmation, even if it was silent. What wasn't said in an interview spoke volumes. Marcellus was a source, and impertinent questions elicited pertinent answers. So why not simply ask him?

They left the building and walked across the street to a small beer bar opposite the police station. They sat at a table and ordered San Miguels. Roth's eyes fell on the gold Cartier on Marcellus' left wrist. If it was real, it would've taken years to pay for it on a cop's salary.

Marcellus folded his hands, right forefinger over the left; he was right handed. He stared at Roth.

"So, like I said, just nod or shake your head. Easy as that," Roth instructed. He held the folded bill in his hand, just a tip peeking out. "If you don't know, just shrug."

To expect Marcellus to sell out for 100 bucks wasn't as preposterous as it would seem. For starters, he was practically immune. Manila cops were like politicians—their peers being very sympathetic—particularly when there was bribe money to spread around. Besides, the average Filipino never thought past tomorrow. That was the trouble with this beautiful, fucked-up country.

"The dead man wasn't Peter MacMillan," Roth stated matter-of-factly.

The cop remained expressionless. Roth tapped the bill on the table, Marcellus' eyes following the action. He glanced around, shook his head, though just barely.

"What was his name?"

Marcellus' face showed amusement, a reminder that this quiz was multiple choice, not an essay. He swallowed a mouthful of San Miguel.

"The dead man was definitely a *cano*?"

Marcellus blinked lazily.

"This Morales guy, he would know who the stiff was?"

Marcellus shook his head, barely noticeable.

"You knew who the stiff was?"

Marcellus did the slow blink again, suggesting that the answer was obvious.

"Where can I find Morales?"

Marcellus shook his head. Roth understood, no co-operation on that one. Morales was obviously a close confederate.

"Peter MacMillan's wife. Did she know about this?"

Marcellus shrugged. But that still didn't rule out the wife.

"You ever meet her?"

Marcellus shook his head.

"What did the photographer at the NBI cost you?"

Marcellus smirked, reached over, and pulled the bill from Roth's hand. "You got all that's worth, brother."

"Yeah, right," Roth said. "Enough business. Although I'll tell you, Reno, when I get it figured out, put names on faces, that sort of thing, I'm gonna hold MacMillan up for a lot more than he paid you. I think a third would be fair, don't you?"

Marcellus shrugged, wondering for the first time how much insurance money was *really* involved. He glanced back across the street at the station house as he had several times since they'd sat down.

"Four hundred million pesos, Reno. A cool 10 million Yankee bucks," Roth lied.

Marcellus kept a straight face, but Roth knew that the figure had hit him like a ton of bricks.

The cop's mind raced. *Montilla, you prick! You said it was for 10,000 measly dollars. A thousand for me, same for you, 8,000 for Jordan. Then another 1,000 for doing Lolita. Did you lie to me, or did Jordan lie to you, or is this* cano *pulling my dick?*

Roth could see Marcellus thinking, smell him thinking. The Amalgamated policy was for only a million dollars—if double indemnity kicked in—but he wanted to fuck with Marcellus, maybe turn him against Morales, or the MacMillan's, or whoever they were. Maybe he'd open up. Squabbling over the spoils often puked-out a disgruntled partner, and Manila cops usually got the smaller piece.

Marcellus twisted around again, looked across the street at the police station.

"But, hey, the hell with it," Roth said cheerfully. "Tell me Reno, where can I get some quality pussy? I don't mean bargirls. I'm tired of them. Something sweet, like young virgins. Maybe some college girls?"

"Sure, man. No problem." He rattled off a telephone number.

"Hold it," Roth said, taking out a small notebook and a pen with his left hand. "Write it out for me, will you?"

Marcellus noted the thick bandage on Roth's hand. "How'd you mess up your hand, man?"

Roth leaned forward, whispered conspiratorially, "Got it caught between a girl's legs."

Marcellus chuckled, taking the notebook. But he used his own pen, a Montblanc, which he pulled from his shirt pocket. He unscrewed the top officiously—obviously proud of its prestige—and wrote the name and telephone number of a woman. He shoved the notebook back at Roth, and called the waitress for more beers. He recapped the Montblanc with similar ceremony, as though he'd been a signatory to the Magna Carta. He looked towards the station again. A thin police major stood on the steps at the entrance, arms akimbo, staring at Marcellus like a hawk eyeing a field mouse.

Marcellus swore under his breath. "Shit. That crazy Rodrigo." He began talking fast as the major walked down the steps. "You call there, anytime after five, and she'll send you whatever you want," he said, winking at the waitress's bottom when she brought their beers. She returned his look with a smile. "Anything you want," Marcellus went on. "Juicy young college girls, man. Even 13-, 14-year-olds. But I don't know about virgins, man. I ain't never seen one." He tapped the notebook with a meaty finger. "Just tell this woman you got the number from me. Reno, the Manila Connection."

"Thanks, Reno," Roth said, holding his smile. The Manila Gorilla would be more like it. Marcellus surely had a financial interest in the call-girl service.

Marcellus shot a look across the street. "Damn, man. Here comes my brother-in-law." The dapperly dressed major was crossing the street, coming their way.

"Don't talk about pussy, man," Marcellus ordered. "This guy's the only man in his family. Eight sisters, and I'm married to the youngest one."

Roth looked over. "So?"

"So? Rodrigo was raised in a seminary, man. By the Jesuits. Crazy fuck. He'll cut my dick off if he knows I jump other pussy. Fucking fanatic doesn't understand men like a change sometimes. You know, eat different rice." He straightened up, whispered, "Got the Lord Jesus on his shoulder and a .45 that speaks his sermons. Check out his hands. Crazy fuck had himself crucified last Easter. You know the Philippines, you know the type."

Roth nodded. The islands were rife with religious zealots. Each Easter, dozens crucified themselves under the scorching sun, their equally zealous relatives praying at the foot of the cross. Few died, but spikes through your hands. . . !

Rodrigo came up to them, hovered over Marcellus. "Benita's not feeling well," he said. "I've been trying to reach you all day."

"On my way now, Rodrigo. Just had a little business here."

Rodrigo wasn't interested in Marcellus' business or in Roth. He just wanted Marcellus to go home and take care of his ailing baby sister. Roth read the masked resentment on Marcellus' face. No one talked to him this way or told him what to do. No one except Rodrigo, that is.

Rodrigo took in Roth at length, his dark eyes burning the image of him in his mind. He wasn't the kind of man who forgot faces— or insults. Marcellus hastened to add that he was meeting with Roth about an accident he'd handled.

A group of officers passed their table. One stopped and reported to Rodrigo briefly, his deference obvious, his manner rigid, wary, reserved. Rodrigo was a feared man. His blank, ball-bearing eyes locked on his subordinate as he made his report. Roth estimated that he was probably the only cop in Manila who wasn't on the take. He studied Rodrigo, who studied Marcellus, who studied his boots. The Gorilla was right on that point: Rodrigo wasn't too tightly wrapped.

Roth stood to take his leave. He tossed some pesos on the table, threw a mock salute to Rodrigo and Marcellus, and walked down the street to where his taxi waited. He compared Marcellus' handwriting in his notebook against the hotel registration card where MacMillan had stayed. Bingo! Likely even the same pen, which, knowing Marcellus, was probably lifted off some corpse. Roth tucked the papers in his jacket, waited, watched.

Ten minutes passed during which Rodrigo did the talking and Marcellus the listening. He gestured defensively as Rodrigo read him the riot act with regard to his beloved sister, Benita. Rodrigo ended his lecture, tapping with emphasis on Marcellus' forehead. Then he walked back across the street to his car parked in front of the station house. Roth watched Marcellus' face, read the seething rage—anger built up over the years married to a woman he no longer wanted. The day would come when one of these men killed the other. Roth's money was on Rodrigo doing the whacking. Marcellus stood, back-kicked his stool, and sent it crashing against another table ten feet away. The waitress and other customers avoided his eyes. Marcellus looked at his Cartier, then walked to his car, a puke-yellow Datsun, parked in a lot behind the beer bar. He turned onto the street and Roth had his driver follow.

At Roxas Boulevard, Marcellus looked around to make sure that Rodrigo wasn't behind him. He pulled into traffic, which was beginning to get heavy now. Roth followed him for about a mile down to the Admiral's Hotel. He parked by the side of the building and took a suit on a hanger and a gym bag from his trunk, walked into the restaurant. He sat by a window facing the parking lot, ordered a beer, and chatted with a waitress. A short while later, he carried the suit into the men's room and returned wearing it, his uniform on the hanger. After another beer, he left the restaurant, his arm wrapped around the waitress he'd been chatting up. She'd also changed into street clothes. She was a dark, long-haired beauty in her thirties. Roth snapped off several shots of the entwined couple, Marcellus relishing a handful of butt. The taxi driver checked Roth in his rear-view mirror, anxious because he was surveilling a police officer. Marcellus and the woman got into his car. He pulled back into traffic and drove towards the airport. Traffic was bumper to bumper now.

"Just stay with them," Roth ordered. "You lose him, Chico, I'm not paying." He always called Filipinos Chico if he didn't know their name. The driver checked his watch. He'd been working for Roth for over three hours. That would mean losing 400 pesos. He could argue the point if he blew the surveillance, but Roth didn't look the type accustomed to losing arguments.

In his car, Marcellus necked passionately with the waitress whenever he stopped at some lights. Roth snapped off a series of photos, the driver moaning with each shot. Following a cop was a very scary business.

It was nearly dark when Marcellus cut off from Roxas into an alley. About 100 meters up, he pulled into a short-time motel that provided garages beneath the rooms. In the Philippines, to hide one's car while philandering was essential. Roth photographed Marcellus registering in the reception area—and with the waitress's features framed under a neon light—photographed them as he pulled his car into the garage, and again when the cop tried to eat the woman's face as the door closed. Roth checked his camera; 33 exposures had been shot. He rewound the film, removed it, and reloaded another roll, this one a black and white slow speed for night photography. Roth told the driver to settle in, and after a while, snoring reverberated from the front seat.

Shortly before midnight, the garage door opened and Marcellus pulled his car out. The waitress was in the front seat, working on her make-up. Roth snapped some shots, doubting whether he got much with the limited amount of light. He nudged the driver awake and they followed, staying a car behind and on the right—on the blind side of Marcellus' car—until there was an opportunity for the driver to swing to the left. He clicked off a further half dozen excellent shots under street lights; images that would be clear.

His lust spent, Marcellus was cooler now, indifferent to the waitress who hung around his shoulders, kissing his neck and cheek. She was apparently the type who liked pock-marks. Thirty minutes later, he dropped her off on East Avenue in Quezon City, where a bus was just pulling away. She ran after the bus, but couldn't catch it. Marcellus, ever the cavalier, pulled away with a wave of the hand. The woman waved back, sat down on a bench to wait for the next bus.

Roth tailed Marcellus another few miles to his home. A cop who supposedly earned 300 dollars a month could never afford such a home. Properties like this were in the 4-million-peso range, about 75,000 dollars. Yeah, Marcellus did all right; Roth raised his estimate of what he'd gotten for his part in this scam. He noted the address on his tape recorder, then told Chico to cruise past the bus stop. He saw the girl about to board another bus with a few other passengers. He told Chico to follow, suspecting there was a very good reason why Marcellus hadn't dropped her at her home.

She got off a mile away and walked into a quiet residential neighborhood. Not on par with Marcellus', but decent, middle class by Filipino standards. The street was narrow and dark. Roth told Chico to wait while he took the woman on foot, following close around a winding lane where a slow-moving taxi would have attracted attention. She entered a small, modest home at the end of the block just after midnight. Lights came on in the living room, and soon he heard a man shouting. The woman screamed her rebuttal, and while he could only pick out a few words of Tagalog, it was enough to know that hubby was very upset at the hour. Roth crossed the street and slid up near to the entrance. He noted the address, sauntered back to the taxi.

Downtown, he left the taxi beneath the Blue Hawaiian dance club. He paid the fare and tipped the driver 500 pesos. He'd done a good tail job.

"By the way, Chico, I wouldn't think about scooting back up to Quezon City and telling that cop you followed him around all night." Taxi drivers in Manila were notorious for selling information, details on adultery being an especially valuable commodity. "He'll surely blow your brains out. Got it?"

Chico said nothing, just glad to get the *cano* out of his taxi. Shit like this, he didn't need. Anybody crazy enough to tail a cop around Manila at midnight was bad news.

Otero was waiting for him in the club. He had eight-by-ten matte blow-ups of Peter MacMillan's back, and close-ups of just his head, arm, and wrist. All that Roth could make out aside from MacMillan needing a haircut, was that his hair was wavy, almost curly. Color couldn't be ascertained; MacMillan could have been a brunette, or even a redhead. There was a pale band around his wrist where a watch or bracelet had once been. Also, something appeared to be written on his upper arm, partially hidden under the sleeve of his T-shirt.

He told Otero to concentrate on the arm and wrist with yet closer blow-ups, paid him 500 pesos. They had drinks and sat around bullshitting about accident scenes, nasty deaths, nastier women. Roth flirted with a bosomy 18-year-old from Mindoro who gave the improbable name of Lisa Lane. He nicknamed her Mammary Lane, and they went around to Buffalo Joe's. Otero located the table where he'd taken the photograph of Marcellus leaning over the dead man. It was a table with a charcoal grill in the background, same as in the photo.

Whores were territorial, occupying a usual venue where they could be found by their johns and colleagues alike, so with any luck, some of the same girls might be around who remembered the morning of August 25th. Buffalo Joe's was a big place. He and Otero drank on, flirting with the usual fixtures, which worried Lisa who feared she might lose her customer. Roth again asked around about buying some downers. None of the girls could help him, not tonight, but there was one girl named Lolita who had some. But she hadn't been around lately. The girls surmised she'd gone to America with a boyfriend. Boyfriend, of course, as in customer.

He told the girls to scout around for anyone who handled down-ers, and offered a reward to any of them who could make a good connection for him. He had a few more beers, tipped Lisa a few hundred pesos, but decided to forego a stroll up Mammary Lane.

20

"Peter MacMillan didn't exist until three and a half years ago, chief," Nina said over the telephone. "I've got Amalgamated's underwriting report. A nickel and dime fluff job, only requiring a two-year background. But I went past that, and there's nothing. This guy didn't exist before then."

Roth had worked with Nina for the past 15 years and he'd made her the first of four partners. She specialized in background investigations. She'd taken family trees back to the American Revolution, and if she couldn't find a history, that meant MacMillan didn't exist. Of this, Roth had no doubt.

"Apparently, Kincannon also tried running a few checks on MacMillan. Came up with zip," Nina added.

An underwriting report was a background investigation that underwriters ordered on new life-insurance applicants. In MacMillan's case—because of his age—only a brief background check had been requested. These reports were inexpensive, and the inspector had been satisfied by the manager of La Crescenta Apartments—in a telephone interview—who said that the MacMillans paid their rent on time, and there were no complaints from the neighbors. The accounts manager at a Wilshire Boulevard bank reported that the MacMillan's maintained a checking account, average balances in the low four figures. No loans. No overdrafts. The account had only been opened a few months before the policies were applied for. Neither the La Crescenta manager nor the accounts manager could actually provide a description of the MacMillans, however. In fact, Nina pointed out, bankers these days rarely knew their customers by face. Currently, the balance was now in the low six figures, which could be anywhere between 100,000 and 333,000 dollars. Only a fool would leave that sort of balance in a checking account, so Nina figured that the money was recently deposited, and speculated that a life insurance benefit on Peter MacMillan had just been paid.

For the underwriting report, Peter MacMillan had also been interviewed by telephone, and gave his occupation as a self-employed importer-exporter. A business reference had been given: a Dr. Rossiter in Tampa, Florida. What the underwriting inspector hadn't known was that he couldn't possibly have checked MacMillan back further than a few months, because Peter MacMillan didn't exist before then.

MacMillan had undergone a physical examination by a paramedic for the Amalgamated policy. The paramedic had taken his blood pressure, listened to his heart, and taken a sample of blood and urine. His report read that Peter MacMillan was 5' 11", weighed 160 pounds, and was a healthy 26-year-old. Roth's mind raced back to the autopsy report that stated that MacMillan was 5' 8" and weighed 150 pounds.

Nina had also learned of two other policies: Kincannon stumbled upon the policy with American Travelers Insurance Company, while Chase-Hampshire had picked up on Amalgamated's investigation. Chase-Hampshire wasn't happy with the investigation carried out by Debbie Brubaker, and subsequently learned of Premier through Kincannon. They wanted to co-operate on the investigative costs, and contacted Nina.

Neither policy carried double indemnity, but it was obviously a build-up.

"Now, catch this," Nina went on. "The reason I called. A week after MacMillan died, he was sitting up to his ass in mud at the Gellert."

"In Budapest? No shit?"

"I shit thee not. A hospitalization claim came in this morning from a travelers assistance company down in Australia."

"How'd they find us?"

"Our website. They saw we handle Europe, and just faxed in the case."

The Gellert was a hotel-health spa in the Hungarian capital, an institution known worldwide for its therapeutic mineral baths and treatments, its specialty being mud baths. Many of Premier's investigators had examined hospitalization claims there, enjoying the sanitarium's services while they were at it. Each autumn, hospitalization claims for Hungary came flooding in; claims alleging treatments that had taken place over the summer. Most treatments were unnecessary, a convenient excuse for amateur fraudsters to finance a European vacation.

"A dumb mistake if it's the same guy," Roth said.

"Same date of birth, so I matched MacMillan's signature on the Amalgamated Life application against the claimant's statement for the treatment at the Gellert."

"And?"

"It's our boy. No doubt about it."

"What about American Travelers?"

"I've put a call in to them, to see if they also want to come in."

Roth thought for a second. "Who we got near Budapest?"

"Let me check." Nina put down the phone and went into the general office where a world map showed her daily where their reps were. The average rep handled ten, maybe 15 cases per month, covering a particular geographic area. Most returned to the States after a month on the road, finalized their reports, took a few weeks off, and then headed out again with a stack of fresh claims.

She came back on the line. "Laura left Budapest three days ago. She's in London now, but maybe she can get back over there." Nina mumbled to herself. "Wait, no she can't; she's got a biggie in Spain that's getting old, then she jumps down to Dakar—has to fly out to Cape Verde. She's been on the road for nine weeks. She needs a break, so I'm pulling her back. She can fly direct to the States from Cape Verde, a direct flight into Logan."

"Thanks for the tour. Like I asked, is anyone near Budapest?"

"All right, I'm checking." She dropped the phone again, and shortly came back on the line. "Ben's in Israel, then he's got three hospitalization cases in Greece, then, yeah, he can do it. It'll take him two weeks to get to Budapest because one of the cases is out on Crete and the another is up on Corfu." She mumbled to herself again. "But he can't fly from Corfu to Budapest. Has to reroute back through Athens and layover one day."

"Two weeks is fine. Get him up to speed on the MacMillan claim and be sure he checks for signatures, anything that ties the two Peter MacMillans together. Wait. . . ." Roth thought. An unusual opportunity might be presenting itself. "On second thoughts, don't bother Ben with details on MacMillan. Just send him a specimen of MacMillan's signature."

Nina went quiet on the line. "Why not bring him into the loop."

"Just don't," Roth said firmly.

"Okay."

"And another thing. Don't tell either company about this hospitalization claim."

"But that clinches the case for all three companies. Why not?"

"'Cause I said not to, that's why."

Nina was quiet again. This was irregular. Clients had a right to know these things. "All right," she said.

Roth heard the hesitancy in her voice. "Anything else?"

"Yeah. You're getting some cases. A dead guy fished from a canal in Bangkok; a dead guy in Kunming, China, and I'm getting in a tourist couple ambushed near Angkor Wat. Bandits shot up a convoy. It looks pretty straightforward, but the floater in Bangkok smells. I mean the case smells."

"I'm sure the stiff does, too. Okay, I'll be back in Bangkok soon. On MacMillan at the Gellert, I'd like to see the claim papers. Fax me that shit."

"Yuck! It'll probably jam the machine, but if that's what you want?"

"You're not well, lady."

"It's because I haven't been laid for so long, I'm growing cobwebs down there. Mexico, here I come."

"Why's that?"

"We got a pile of hospitalization claims down on the Texas border and we're stacking up Tijuana cancer claims. Thought I'd take a run out there myself, get away from this madhouse for a week. The crew can handle things at the office. Get this. In Tijuana, quack cancer clinics are administering coffee enemas to rectal cancer patients."

"No shit?"

"A lotta shit, apparently, *mi amigo*."

Roth chuckled. "One more thing. Get someone out to LA on MacMillan. Have them nose around on the beneficiary. She's out in the valley. Near Ventura Boulevard, I think."

"Check," Nina said.

"Anything else?"

"Isn't that enough?"

21

The next morning, Roth booked a return flight to Bangkok for the following day. He wrapped up a few details on the MacMillan claim, doubting Morales would ever be identified unless the consulate had this information, which wasn't likely. Morales was a go-between, used to convey information on MacMillan's death to the consulate, and introduce the beneficiary into the picture.

Roth called the US Embassy. Towers was away, on temporary assignment down in Cebu. He'd have to delay meeting him until his next trip.

He returned to Buffalo Joe's that evening, learned that the girl who peddled the downers had been killed in a street accident the week before. Roth's inquiries had prompted an enterprising girl named Maritza to look up the girl known as Lolita. That's when she learned of her death. A small blurb had also been in the papers at the time, according to Maritza, but few pros at Buffalo Joe's ever read the newspapers, and even if they had, none of them had known Lolita's surname. Last names weren't a requirement on del Pilar Street. It was thought that she'd been loaded with downers, and walked out into traffic. Lolita had been a long-shot, anyhow. There were a lot of places someone could get downers. Still, Buffalo Joe's was his only lead.

Roth tipped Maritza 500 pesos for her trouble, asked around for other sources. While he got leads for just about everything one could get only with a prescription, there were no further leads for downers.

––––––

Back in Bangkok, Roth started the case of the floater in the *klong*. He also had his travel agent take his passport to the Chinese Embassy for a visa. He sat in his office overlooking the swimming pool, completing reports and working up the case on the floater. It smelled bogus from the start, and while the police had actually pulled a body from the canal, there was a question as to its true identity.

The following week, he flew up to Kunming. The case on Yu I-Lung, the brother of a Chinese-American, was easy. Yu was very much alive, operating his brother's restaurant downtown. The notary, a government official in China, who certified the death, vanished when Roth visited his office, always a telltale sign when bogus documents surfaced. Or at least the ones they were a party to. The notary was involved in creating certain documents for the beneficiary—the insured's brother living in San Francisco. But the notary's disappearing act didn't matter; Roth located the restaurant, identified Yu from his passport photo, stood him up against the wall outside his restaurant holding a recent newspaper, and took his picture. Yu actually apologized for putting Roth through so much trouble. He complained that he hadn't been feeling well lately and thought he might die soon. He said that he wanted to be certain the insurance company would pay the claim.

––––––

Returning to Bangkok, Roth made preparations to fly over to Phnom Penh to handle the murdered tourists case. Just before 6:00 p.m., as he was building his first drink, a package from Nina was delivered. It contained paychecks, some personal mail, and new claims. Also in the package were the documents from Chase-Hampshire, and the claim forms from Peter MacMillan covering his stay at the Gellert in Budapest.

Roth pulled the MacMillan file. Just as Nina had said, MacMillan's handwriting on the life insurance application with Amalgamated matched his signature on the claim forms covering the treatment at the Gellert. It was a capital fuck-up, but unless Premier had been assigned both cases, there was no way in the world this would have been picked up. Still, the actual documents from the Gellert would confirm if he'd actually been there.

He was about to put on a steak when the phone rang. It was Nina in New York.

"Any word from our good Mrs. MacMillan?" he asked.

"Yeah. She turned up here in New York. Visiting a friend for a while. Says she'll be here for a few weeks. You want me to interview her?"

"No. Tell her that I wanna see her. Give her my name but don't mention anything about my having been in Manila."

"Check. When do you want to see her?"

"Stall her. I need a week before I can get there."

"Gotcha. Kincannon wants you to move on this."

"I'll get there when I get there."

"Okay. Just telling you. Did you get my last package?"

"Yeah, it just walked in the door. Oh, that guy in Kunming, Yu I-Lung. He's dirty. Give the customer a status and I'll get a report out in a few days."

"Was he dead?"

"Didn't look dead, and he said he wasn't. But his brother will probably kill him when he gets to Kunming." By this time, Yu would have contacted his brother in San Francisco, the designated beneficiary, alerting him that he'd been found.

"Just the same, ask the client if he wants us to follow up on the brother for a confession. I'll e-mail the photo of Yu picking his nose in front of his restaurant. You know what to do."

"Right," Nina said. Insurers didn't bother pursuing attempted fraud, so in these cases, Nina notified US Immigration of a reported death, and Immigration sometimes picked them up when they re-entered the States. Confused, Immigration would contact Nina, asking why she'd reported the man dead when he was standing right there in their office. Like it or not, clients were brought into the picture and made to come forward with their files. Let Yu I-Lung try talk himself out of this fix. He'd likely be deported even if the insurance company—the intended victim—couldn't care less once they'd gotten off the claim.

"Another thing," Nina said. "That third company on MacMillan. American Travelers. I spoke with Sid Sydow. Remember him?"

"Yeah." Roth recalled. "What'd he say?"

"They've already paid the claim, coughed up 200,000 dollars to Lori MacMillan, easy as you please. That explains the six-figure balance in the MacMillan bank account. I contacted Sydow, asked if he wanted us to handle this claim past the perfunctory inquiries their investigator had made. I told him in no uncertain terms that the claim reeked of fraud. Sydow's a snob, if you recall. He used that investigator in Chicago, a back-slapper named Loggert. Then Loggert farmed out the LA handling to a guy out there. Probably farmed it out in Manila, too."

"He did," Roth confirmed. "Associated in Manila handled it."

"Those fuck-ups? Anyhow, you met Sydow, remember?"

"Yeah, it's coming back to me now."

"At the Eastern Claims Conference three years ago."

"Right. Right. Arrogant dummy."

"That's him. We had drinks with him and Loggert. They're army buddies, and Loggert's retired Army Intelligence. So are most of Sydow's contacts. Old intel cronies. Sydow didn't like your manners."

Roth had called him an idiot, so Sydow never referred business to Premier, even when they tipped him off on mutual cases he shared with other clients. He also refused to reinvestigate bad claims he'd paid. Paying bad claims didn't look good for him. And he paid a lot of bad claims; so many that one had to wonder if Sydow wasn't on the take. Probably not, but what else could account for Sydow's supreme ineptitude?

"Let me know as soon as you have anything on MacMillan from Budapest."

"Ben was delayed on Corfu. He should be in Athens tomorrow, then up to Budapest Friday."

————

The next day, Roth wrapped up the case of the floater in the canal. The alleged deceased's uncle had filed the claim against a Canadian insurance company. Fortunately, forensics had lifted fingerprints off the corpse so a comparison could be made with those from the insured. These came courtesy of the Royal Thai Army, with whom the insured had once served. The insured's prints didn't match the dead man's. Case closed. The authorities would probably never learn who the floater had been; just one of dozens of unsolved cases at the Bangkok Medical Examiner's office.

Roth wrote up the report and instructed Nina to notify Canadian Immigration that the insured was dead. He had no idea where the guy was—maybe he was already back in Canada—but he'd get picked up when he passed through Canadian Immigration the next time. As with Yu, he could explain his apparition to the friggin' Mounties. Canadian authorities weren't much better than the Americans; they also refused to make inquiries on fraudsters playing games overseas. "Privacy laws, eh," a Canuck copper had once told him in Vancouver. Everyone had rights these days. No small wonder insurance fraud was fashionable. No penalty if you get caught. First, Roth mused, there'd been no-fault automobile accidents, then no-fault divorce, and now there was no-fault fraud. It made a guy think.

Didn't it?

22

The victims in the ambush up at Angkor Wat were dead, all right. The Cambodian police had done a good job of documenting the deaths, and the case was a simple open and shut matter. These American tourists had been in the wrong place at the wrong time.

From Phnom Penh, Roth transited back through Bangkok and flew on to Manila. He handled a pair of hospitalization claims in Makati, then decided to take a wild flyer on something that had been troubling him.

That Lolita girl.

He had Otero check the newspaper's archives for the past few weeks, and later, armed with her last name and the accident date, Roth poured through accident reports at traffic headquarters until he found hers. What were the odds against two lost souls from Buffalo Joe's meeting with a fatal accident within weeks of each other? Pretty slim.

One victim sold barbiturates, the other died from an overdose. What were the odds against them knowing each other? Slimmer yet.

Also, if one in a thousand people die violently, here he had two on the same case. What were the odds? When his eyes came to rest on the name of the investigating officer, a computer couldn't have calculated these odds:

SPO Reno Marcellus.

Lolita's autopsy photos matched her passport photo, and her landlady confirmed her identity for Roth. But Marcellus never bothered visiting her room. Not like the Manila Gorilla, who'd walk on his knuckles across town for ten pesos. Unless he knew he'd find nothing there. She'd been carrying every piece of ID she owned. Why was she carrying her passport to cruise the streets?

The cause of death was massive internal bleeding and subsequent heart failure. Her system had been laced with phenobarbital and alcohol, making 'misadventure' a logical assumption, according to the accident report. A gruesome death, and on this occasion the tabloid photographers were allowed to snap close-ups of her face. Good, sordid journalism.

The NBI's autopsy photos hadn't disappeared this time, and they were horribly clear. Lolita's mangled face was a ghastly death mask, but she was identifiable. There were no visa stamps in her passport, no arrival or departure stamps to anywhere. Little Miss Perez had never gone anywhere and never would.

The police report called the case an accidental hit and run. Well, Reno Marcellus was calling it that, despite multiple tire burns on her body. It wasn't Dr. Locanto's case, but Roth had gone to him anyhow. He was calling it a murder: there were two sets of tire tracks across the victim's body, yet only one car struck her. It was, of course, a crime to leave the scene of an accident, but nevertheless, the police report—based upon Marcellus' account—saw nothing sinister, despite the evidence suggesting otherwise.

"The police, they do not care," Locanto had said. "The girl was a prostitute and nobody cares about them. They will not work hard to find her killer."

Marcellus' investigation report speculated that Miss Perez had been out cruising for johns, perhaps peddling her services car-to-car in the middle of the street, delusional from booze and pills, and was accidentally struck by one or more automobiles.

———

The Philippine Airlines flight to Masbate Island took 45 minutes. Landing at Masbate City Airport, the pilot braked hard. The landing strip couldn't handle large planes, and even the 737 took every foot of runway.

Masbate was in the middle of the archipelago. Most places in the Visayas were paradise: clean, safe, inexpensive, the girls wondrously beautiful. But not Masbate. Here, remnants of the New People's Army were solidly entrenched. Called the NPA—or Nice People Around—the quasi-communist group controlled parts of Masbate just as they did in Eastern Samar.

As the plane came to rest, the ground crew rolled out the stairway. Roth took a last look at the preliminary police report on Lolita Perez. Her occupation was listed as *"hostess."* Maybe Marcellus did her a kindness; he could have listed her as a prostitute. That he'd handled the scene immediately after the incident wasn't lost on Roth. Just like MacMillan. Still, Marcellus' supervisor hadn't bothered to take a closer look at her case. Nobody cared.

Except her three brothers in Masbate City. Roth sat on the bamboo porch of the Perez home just outside of town, studying Lolita's brothers who studied him right back. They had NPA written all over them and didn't much care for Roth's looks. To the NPA, America was behind every problem the Filipinos had. But then, most Filipinos blamed America for something. So, nosy *canos* weren't particularly welcome to sit down over San Miguel beers, and for that reason, Roth told the biggest, oldest, and meanest looking of the bunch to fetch him one. Big Brother's eyes said that he'd just as soon crack open Roth's head as crack open a beer for him. But he rattled off something in Tagalog to a small boy answering to the name of Pauley, who jumped down from the porch and scooted beneath the house where the beer was kept.

Roth wandered inside the hut and looked around. The boys said nothing at this intrusion, and Roth reflected momentarily if he shouldn't piss around the hut to stake off his territory. The home sat about ten feet off the ground, up on stilts. It had four small rooms under a sleeping loft reached by a bamboo ladder. He asked where their parents were. Big Brother called into him that their mother was off somewhere in town, wouldn't return until evening. Religious posters and calendars were nailed on the walls here and there, and an old glass-framed photograph showed a young man and woman, Mom and Dad, taken back in the fifties. An even older photo depicted a young man in a soldier's uniform. Apparently, grandpa had served with the Americans back in the forties. In the muddy yard below the hut, a pig stood chained to one of the foundation beams next to the chicken coops. A rooster crowed from beneath the structure and forayed into the yard. He flapped violently, ascended up onto the pig's back.

Roth went back outside and settled on a railing that ran around the porch, took his beer from Pauley.

Lolita had been knocked up at 16, a common thing in the islands. No one spoke about the boy who'd done the deed, only that he wasn't around any longer, leaving Roth with little desire to inquire further on that point.

She was buried outside of town, and her death was still vivid in their minds. Big Brother ordered Pauley inside. The boy went in, but popped up shortly at a window overlooking the porch, staring at Roth. Pauley was a cute kid, friendly and outgoing. He wore a Boston Red Sox baseball cap and a T-shirt, and watched shyly whenever he thought Roth might not be looking. It soon became a game, Roth shooting him a 'gotcha' look every few seconds, which started him giggling. Eventually Pauley abandoned the game and openly stared, wondering what was being discussed about his mother. He didn't understand any of it, but his little eyes watered whenever he heard Lolita's name.

Once Roth got the brothers talking, or at least grunting, he ran through a list of questions. But they knew little about Lolita's work in Manila. From the money she'd sent to their mother, her occupation should have been obvious. He asked if Lolita was involved in any way with drugs. They didn't know, but in the Philippines, using and selling marijuana was no big deal.

Several months before, she returned to Masbate City on one of her occasional trips to see Pauley. She spoke of going to America soon, of marrying a *cano* who would take care of the family once she was in the States. She hadn't explained much, only that her *cano* fiancé would be coming into plenty of money soon. In the meantime, she'd return to Masbate and wait until everything was ready for her to travel to America. She'd been expected back just around the time they were notified of her death. Instead of meeting the ever-laughing, fun-loving, homesick Lolita at the pier, they'd met her coffin.

She hadn't shared the secret of her impending prosperity, trusting her fiancé to take care of them once they married. Roth pondered the fiancé's part in the hit-and-run. *Insurance?* Lolita hadn't mentioned anything about insurance to her brothers.

A classic scenario sprang to mind: an American applied for a Fiancée Visa at the US Embassy, thus giving him insurable interest. He stacked up policies on the girl, then had her greased for the benefits. A few US sailors had played that game and were spending the remainder of their lives in prison.

After he'd heard all he wanted, he asked to see Lolita's belongings. In the hut, there was a bed in a cubicle where she slept when she visited. Beneath it, a green army foot locker was pushed back against the wall. There'd been a lock on it which had been broken off. He opened it. Inside was the accumulated treasure of an uneducated girl who hoarded cheap mementos earned from her customers, collected and saved from vacations she'd taken with johns to places like Boracay, the Palawans, or Puerto Azul. There were imitation flowers, T-shirts and sweatshirts, a set of Heineken beer glasses, promotional coffee mugs, a cigar box of costume jewelry, island crafts, plush animal dolls. If there'd been money, the brothers had taken it. In another cigar box were photographs. Most were of Lolita alone, others depicted her man of the moment: Australian customers, Germans, Americans. On the back were dates and places, sometimes the john's name. In a third cigar box, there were letters from boyfriends overseas, and a few letters she'd sent to Pauley.

Lolita looked happy in the snaps, her eyes bright, smile wide. She'd been a pretty girl: large eyes, small nose, full pouting lips, and long silky hair. There were too many photos and letters to go through just now. Roth snapped the rubber bands around the cigar boxes with the letters and photographs and carried them under his arm back out on the porch.

"I'll send these back," he said. He shook hands with each of them and asked Big Brother to convey his condolences to their mother when she returned home. He went down the steps and walked across the yard, scattering chickens. His driver kick-started his motorcycle and Roth straddled behind him. He knew Pauley was watching him but he didn't look back.

———

Only one flight returned to Manila daily, the flight he'd arrived on. It was gone, so Roth arranged to fly back the next morning, then contented himself that evening by sitting at the hotel bar, flirting with two young pretties as he swigged down beers and idly foraged through the cigar boxes. There were silly love-bunny letters from johns, some promising to send Lolita money for her mother's imaginary operations. Others told her about their vacation schedules, when they'd see her again. Promises and lies. More than a few had PO boxes for a return address. Married men. None of the letters, several dozen in all, offered anything interesting.

The girls in the bar said that they were closing. In Masbate City, that meant locking the front door as well. Roth told them to pile a few beers in an ice bucket, close his tab, and lock up. He'd go up to his room when he finished. They complied and turned off all the lights except for a dim lamp over his table. As they were closing the windows back in the restaurant section and preparing to leave, he called over to the prettiest one to come up to his room later. She screamed with laughter and the other girl admonished him: "No, no, no. You must marry her for that."

"Sure," he called back. "But how about having the honeymoon tonight?"

They laughed and went out through the back door to a small house behind the hotel. All of a sudden, the night was dead quiet with only an occasional sound from a distant motorcycle, a dog barking, another answering.

Roth spent an hour looking through the second cigar box, the one with the photos. At the bottom of the box was an address book.

He thumbed through it. A snapshot fell out on the table. He lifted it and started to insert it back into the book.

Whoa! He stared at a snapshot of Peter MacMillan. It was a passport photo, the same picture that appeared on the photocopy of MacMillan's passport. He turned the photograph over. A single name was written in Lolita's handwriting: *"Jordan."* Written on the page where the photograph had slipped from were two names. One was Reno Marcellus, with a telephone number for the Southern Traffic Command. The other was Jordan Warner, with a PO box in New York City. There was also a New York telephone number, with area code 212. Manhattan.

――――――

Roth flew back to Manila the following morning. Upon landing at the domestic terminal, he reserved a room at his usual hotel, telephoned Otero, and asked that he meet him there.

His next stop was at the Immigration office in Intramuros, to look up a source he'd used a few years ago. He was gone now, so Roth made another friend for 500 pesos and requested a listing of the arrivals and departures of one Jordan Warner.

Warner had visited the Philippines three times, once in April and twice in August, the last time just a week before MacMillan's death. On the first and second arrival, he'd flown over from the States, but on the third he'd come up from Brisbane on Qantas. His last departure from Manila was on Lufthansa, to Frankfurt.

Roth returned to his hotel. Otero was there waiting for him. He had more blow-ups of MacMillan, these focusing on the wrist and arm. Part of a tattoo showed from under the dead man's T-shirt. Roth was certain it was the bottom part of the initials *"USN."* United States Navy. Now he at least knew that the deceased was an American.

He called New York for an update on MacMillan. One of their guys had done some poking around over at Lori MacMillan's LA apartment. Roth listened, took notes. It was interesting stuff.

23

Towers nodded to Millie, walked to Window Four studying the scant details on Roth's business card. "Yes, sir. You wanted to see me?"

Roth took in the brunette who'd handed off his card to Towers. She seemed interested—more than interested. Her antennas were up. Then he studied Towers. "Yeah. I wanted to have a look at you."

"Excuse me?"

"I wanna see your Missing Persons notifications. For August and September."

"Who are you looking for?"

"Won't know until I find him. Maybe I won't find him."

"Well," Towers said, hiding his glee. He just loved it when a brazen civilian marched in off the street and demanded service. "That file is confidential. Government business. You'll need authorization from the next of kin."

"Really?" Roth questioned. "What's the big secret? Missing an atomic scientist."

"You can't just go looking through government records." *This guy's a smart-ass who needs a good dressing-down.*

Roth sized him up. "Anal type, huh? Got all the rules and regulations stenciled on your hemorrhoids."

"Look, fella," Towers said. "If you have a name, I'll check. If not. . . ." He thumbed towards the door.

Roth smiled. "Try MacMillan. But I doubt you got a 'Missing' on him."

Towers stared at Roth. It spoke volumes.

"That got your head off the desk, didn't it?" Roth's smile was more pleasant. "Pull MacMillan's death file while you're at it. You know, the one that goes with this." He slipped a photocopy of Mac-Millan's Form 180 under the glass. "And before you ask, yeah, his wife's provided an authorization." He slid across a photocopy of the document Lori MacMillan had signed as part of the claim application to Amalgamated Life.

Towers had been dying to tell this guy where to get off. But this changed things. Maybe he had information on Lori. He'd get in his shot afterwards, tongue-lash this wise guy good and proper, maybe call one of the Marines to escort him off the grounds. He couldn't remember the last time he'd done that to some wise-ass. He motioned Roth to the staff entrance.

They sat in the staff lounge, Roth looking through the Missing Persons file. Towers sat opposite, tried to read upside-down the papers Roth laid on the coffee table. Roth paid him no attention. There were only two missing persons reports for August and September.

Towers never got a response to the letter he'd sent to Lori's PO box in New York, or to the copy he mailed to Marcia Post's address. Maybe Lori never received them. He'd send some more, just as many as it took to get his answer. He'd been composing a follow-up letter in his head that morning. A few weeks ago, a local insurance guy had asked about MacMillan. But the guy only had the same LA address for Lori, so Towers blew him off. Maybe there were times when he should give civilians more attention. Like now.

"That's it? Just these two?" Roth asked.

"Uh, yes. That's all for that period," Towers said, trying for a practiced voice of officialdom. One of the notifications had been retracted later, when a tardy daughter finally called home. When Americans went missing, families made inquiries on the off-chance they'd registered with the embassy when they entered a country. Except for the police, they had nowhere else to turn. In poor host countries, Americans took the precaution of registering, giving an approximate itinerary and a date of expected departure from the country. But few Americans bothered to register in Manila, and none had during that period.

The second notification was interesting. He compared it against dates in the MacMillan file. It was on one Brian O'Toole, whose brother, Kevin, had called several times from Boston during the last week of August. His last call had been on the very day Lori Mac-Millan visited the embassy. Shortly afterwards, a private investigator from Boston paid the embassy a visit on behalf of the O'Toole family. He spoke with Millie and telephoned several times thereafter, then they heard nothing more from him.

K. O'Toole. Sounded familiar, Roth thought. Oh yeah, KO for short: 'Knock Out.' It came to him. Middleweight contender, maybe 12 years back.

Roth jotted down Kevin O'Toole's details, and pulled the only photograph of Brian O'Toole from the file. It had been left by the private investigator. It was a glossy eight-by-ten of the family gathered around a Christmas tree, dated the previous year. Brian was circled with a magic marker. Roth rolled it up and stuffed it in his jacket, closed the file, then opened the file on Peter MacMillan. He read the particulars of Lori MacMillan's visit to the embassy.

"Wait a minute, you can't keep that photograph," Towers said.

"Why not? You gonna find him?"

"No, but. . . . Well . . . perhaps we will."

"Yeah, Towers, I can just see you humpin' your pasty ass out there in the heat, beatin' the bushes." He took in his white shirt and tie.

Towers objected, not at all liking Roth's manners. "Now, hold on, fella—"

"You went to MacMillan's funeral," Roth interjected. It was a statement, not a question.

"Huh? Well," Towers started. "I—I—"

"Did," Roth helped him.

"I did. Yes." *Well, it certainly isn't against the rules if I did.* The question had thrown him. He forgot all about the O'Toole family photograph.

"Did you see a body?"

"His body?"

Roth made a gimme gesture. "Try to keep up with me here. I'll go slower: Did . . . you . . . see . . . a . . . body? It's an easy question."

Towers' mind raced. Only the thought of getting Lori's address kept him from cutting into this guy. He was closer to it than he'd been since Los Angeles, but he didn't want it getting around that he'd gone to the funeral. He'd lied to Millie about that. Now the Social Security Administration was worrying him again for corrections on the numbers he'd reported to them. The Veterans Administration also couldn't find anything on Peter MacMillan, and he had tried as well, burning the midnight oil on his computer at home and calling in favors from State Department buddies to check other indices that he wasn't subscribed to. There was something seriously wrong with this whole affair.

"Uh, it was closed casket." Then, to dodge further questions, he added using his best bureaucratic voice, "As a matter of fact, I have a few open items I'd like clarified myself. Do you have Mrs. MacMillan's current address?"

Roth ignored his question. "You didn't see the body when it was being autopsied?"

"No. I didn't attend the autopsy. Someone else went."

"Yeah. A Miss Ernestine Scales. Did she see the body?"

"I imagine so." *Wait a sec, here. I didn't say her name!* "Uh, she met with the police officer and picked up Mr. MacMillan's passport. I remember now, she said the NBI pathologists were there, at the funeral home, conducting an autopsy. I don't know what she saw. We could ask her."

Roth already had. Ernestine had told him that when she arrived, the autopsy was nearly over. MacMillan's skull had been reflected—opened like a coconut—his brain plopped on a scale like meat in a butcher's shop. She'd remained well back from the autopsy table, and candidly admitted her squeamishness when she saw the dead man's facial flesh pulled down over the lower skull like a rubber Halloween mask. She'd become queasy, had to sit down.

She met Officer Marcellus there, who told her that he hadn't found a passport, only knew that the dead man was an American from the registration card at his hotel and from his associate, a Mr. Morales. From Las Flores, Scales had driven with Marcellus to the hotel. The passport wasn't in the hotel safe, so, at Marcellus' suggestion, they tossed the room. He found the passport hidden up in the ceiling tiles.

"Clever," Roth had said to her.

"I would never have thought to look up there," she'd said. "I guess the police know these things. Where people hide things, I mean."

"I'm sure that's what it is," he'd replied. It had taken Marcellus only minutes to find the passport. Surprise, surprise. Miss Scales surveyed MacMillan's belongings, but didn't think of going back to the pathologist with the passport to make an ID. When she did think about it, she shrugged it off; autopsy photos taken before the scalp was reflected would be available if anyone needed to see them. Aside from the passport, there were a few travelers checks in twenty-dollar denominations, some pesos, a few credit cards, and a return ticket to LA. Nothing else except for a few clothes, one piece of luggage, business papers, bills of lading, customs forms, and whatnot. No jewelry, no wristwatch, no cameras, laptop. Morales just happened to turn up at the hotel while she was there. She assumed that Officer Marcellus had contacted him, asking him to come at her convenience. Mr. Morales volunteered to hold MacMillan's clothing and business papers for the wife, saying that she was coming from the States. Yes, he'd contacted her already. Miss Scales had gone through the papers and, determining that there were no negotiable items, gave them to Morales who provided her with his local telephone number as well as Mrs. MacMillan's address in LA so that someone from the consulate could communicate with the widow. Towers had sent the telegram, since it was his case.

Roth thought of having Ernestine here now as he interviewed Towers, but decided against it. Towers wouldn't make any admissions before a witness, especially an intern.

"What exactly is this all about?" Towers asked. It came out more huffily than he intended.

Roth arched an eyebrow. "Tell you how this goes. I got the investigator's license, so I ask the questions. Now, if I lose my passport, and want another one, you get to ask the questions. Okay?"

Just keep pushin', buddy. Towers' facial muscles started twitching. *You're gonna go flyin' outta here on your ear.*

"You didn't see the body at Las Flores, either before or after the autopsy?"

"No," Towers said, shrugging. He took the file and reviewed his own notes. "I took the report on the MacMillan death from an Officer Marcellus at around 2:00 p.m. on the day he died. I was advised that the death occurred in the morning, but the officer didn't have the exact time." He went quiet, his mistake was glaringly obvious. He'd neglected to press that question. Marcellus had only said that he wasn't certain of the time. Later, when he learned that the death had occurred in the early morning, he never thought to question the delay, assuming there had been difficulties identifying the body. The man, after all, croaked in the infamous Buffalo Joe's, and wasn't exactly a dignitary. Had he been an important figure in Manila, Towers would surely have handled the entire matter himself.

He next heard from the NBI pathologists that afternoon, advising that they would perform an autopsy that evening, given the circumstances of the man's death—dying in a public place and not under the care of a physician—providing that the embassy had no objection. This was protocol. In essence, they were asking if an American consular officer wanted to be in attendance. Towers assumed an autopsy would still take place whether or not there were any objections, as this was a municipal requirement in violent deaths. He acknowledged the call and passed the task to Ernestine Scales. It would be good experience for her. Besides, he didn't like working past 4:00 p.m. and was expected at the ambassador's residence at 7:00 for a fourth at bridge.

On that day, Ernestine Scales had a stack of files on her desk— most of them passed down to her by him. She was late getting to Las Flores and didn't have MacMillan's passport in hand, essential to make a positive identification of the body. He knew the passport hadn't been found yet. Therefore, there should have been someone who could identify the dead man. He'd screwed up on that point as well, but wasn't sure what Roth was after.

"I saw no reason to question the identity of Mr. MacMillan—"

"You've only got a death certificate issued by the Local Civil Registrar. No certification by the NSO?"

"That's correct."

"You're a visa officer now, isn't that right?"

"Yes, deputy of the section, in fact."

"When a Filipino wants a visa, you want positive ID. Like a birth certificate. Right?"

Towers nodded.

"But you'll accept a birth certificate only if it's certified by the NSO. Correct?"

Towers nodded again, wondering when Roth would reveal something about Lori's whereabouts. Whatever this was about, he couldn't see how it concerned her.

Roth continued: "You won't accept a birth certificate from a registrar, because we know they're crooks. Right?"

"Right," Towers agreed.

"So," Roth pressed, "why accept a *death* certificate from a civil registrar?" He leaned back and stretched his arms across the back of the sofa. In his jacket were the two death certificates with the same registration number: the one on MacMillan, and the other on Arturo Reyes.

"I'm not sure I understand," Towers said. "I'm certain there was a body."

"No doubt," Roth said. But the question was, whose body? After all, it had been Marcellus who'd come up with a corpse. Anywhere else, when you saw a crook, you yelled 'cop,' but in Manila, when you saw a cop, you yelled 'crook.'

Towers shook his head, at a loss to grasp where Roth was going with this. Lori came to mind. What was new; she came to mind every hour of every day. He shook his head slowly, confused. But there was something here that Roth brought out. It annoyed him. That *something* in the back of his mind nagged at him once more. The time with Lori rushed back to him, but he couldn't put his finger on what it was. How Millie had called back over her shoulder in the staff lounge, telling him how Puerto Azul wouldn't wait.

Then, Lori's reservations at the bungalow for the weekend. Had she heard Millie? He ground his teeth, frustrated with something just beyond his reach. Lori's suspicious look when he announced he was going down to Puerto Azul also. Later, he felt certain she dropped hints where she'd be staying. And that creepy feeling on the beach those nights he went searching for her. Damn! There were times he wanted to scream out his rage. What is it? Where is Lori?

Roth shook his head, went for the throat: "Okay, you fucked Mrs. MacMillan. Right?"

Towers groaned.

That was clear enough. "What's your part in this scam?"

Towers jerked his head up. "Scam? What scam? No. Nothing. I swear."

"You may have to," Roth fired back. "You saw her again after she left Manila?"

"No. I—I didn't. And I don't know what you're talking about. What scam?"

"But you *tried* to see her."

"I, uh, yes."

"At her place in LA?"

"Yes," Towers said, incredulous, wondering how he knew.

Roth studied Towers. He was only a pawn. He didn't have the balls to pull off a scam like this, plus he'd left his card with the couple in LA and with Florentino at Las Flores Funeraria. If he was a confederate, he wouldn't leave tracks all over the place. It was simple: Lori MacMillan waited in Manila to be certain that she had the 180 in hand, rather than chance a snag coming up if she left without it. She got the report from this dummy and skipped out. Apparently to New York.

Roth stood up, putting away his papers. Millie, who'd been watching them outside, entered the lounge, a cup in her hand. She walked over to the coffee pot. Roth turned to leave.

Towers stood and whispered, "Do you have her current address, Mr. Roth?"

Roth was thinking about his next move, to the Manila Hotel where Lori MacMillan had stayed. But there was also an open item: MacMillan's passport had an arrival stamp into the Philippines, but no departure stamp, since he supposedly died here. If a stand-in body was used, how did the entry stamp get there? Easy. Marcellus obviously had an Immigration inspector in his employ. He looked again at the arrival stamp in the photocopy of MacMillan's passport. The tiny, circled red number of the Immigration officer was illegible. Purposely illegible, no doubt. Therefore, Warner could have entered on MacMillan's ticket and passport, then have Marcellus' stooge enter Warner as an arrival as well. One man came in, but with two passports, and obviously, the dead man's passport was missing. Roth would have to check if MacMillan's arrival ticket had been used. If so, that's what happened. Warner then gave MacMillan's passport and return ticket to Marcellus, and used his own passport from there on.

Warner had also taken out a travel policy in Brisbane under MacMillan's name. But how did he manage to do that without a visa for Australia in MacMillan's passport? Simple, the insurance agent in Brisbane—probably someone at a travel agency licensed to sell insurance—hadn't checked for a visa, probably only looked at the fly-page of a *photocopy* of MacMillan's passport when he wrote the policy. Tourists often traveled around with only a photocopy of their passport, particularly when they left it at an embassy for a visa stamp. Also, Warner checked himself in at the Gellert under MacMillan, but had flown to Europe on his own passport.

He likely registered with a credit card issued to MacMillan, but paid cash when he checked out. So the spa records would be under MacMillan, which would be necessary to file for the hospitalization claim. But why leave a trail on MacMillan? Why not? Warner never expected the trails to cross.

Towers moved in front of Roth. "I asked if you have Mrs. Mac-Millan's current address?"

"Sorry," Roth said, an evil grin on his face. "That's confidential. Non-government business. You'll need authorization for that." He reached the door, stopped and turned. Millie was puttering around, eavesdropping with her back to them. It wasn't much of a reach to see that her interest was personal.

Below the belt time. He looked wickedly at Towers. "Shame on you, sir," he said, his voice raised in indignation. "Sniffing around Mrs. MacMillan, that poor, sweet widow." He tossed a look at Millie as she turned around, eyebrow arched. Towers turned beet red. Roth went out the door, chuckling. *Fuck the stuffy little bureaucrat. Fuck him to tears.*

On the way back to his hotel, Roth made a detour to the address shown for Peter MacMillan's so-called associate, Mr. Morales. As he anticipated, it was a blind. The street existed, but the house number didn't, and the telephone number Morales had given to the embassy rang, and then emitted a busy signal. It was a telephone company test line. It was an old trick that investigators used. Well, investigators *and* con men.

———

Towers sat in his office that afternoon, pondering this business, feeling very much out of touch with everything and everyone, particularly the American community. It had never dawned on him how isolated government employees actually were.

Still, Roth was no gentleman to implicate him and Lori with such intimacy. Millie had bit her lip, left the staff room without a word, and avoided him all afternoon. Well, to hell with her, anyhow.

Who did Roth represent?

Towers plucked Roth's business card from his jacket hanging on the chair. There was a New York number. He looked at the wall clock. It would be 9:00 a.m., New York time. He dialed the number. . . .

In a small, windowless office at Premier Services on Long Island, the light on the red telephone lit up as it rang. Nina picked it up on the third ring, answered with only the last four digits.

"Hello," Towers spoke loudly in the receiver, even though the connection was perfect.

"Yes. May I help you?"

"I'd like to speak with Mr. Roth, please." Of course, he wouldn't be there, but he wanted to verify the business affiliation.

"I'm sorry," Nina said. "There's no Mr. Ross here."

"Roth," Towers repeated. "Roth. Not Ross."

"What can I do for you, Mr. Roth?"

"Is this . . . no, I'm not Mr. Roth." He squinted to read the card, moved closer to the lamp. "My name is Mr. Towers." He noticed that no company name was shown on the card, only Roth's name, his title—*investigator*—and a telephone number. "Is this an investigation company?"

"No," Nina replied. "This is an import-export concern. Who are you? Who are you calling?"

"Towers. Mr. Towers. For Mr. Roth."

"What number do you have, Mr. Roth?"

He rolled his eyes. "No. No. Mr. Towers." He read the number on the card, beginning with the 516 area code.

"Well, that's the right number, but there's no Mr. Towers here. And we're not investors."

"*Investigators*, I said."

"What are you investigating?"

"*No . . . no . . . no . . .* I'm not an investigator. I asked if *you* were."

"Me? Heavens no. I'm a receptionist."

Towers slammed the receiver down, cursed. Roth had bullshitted him.

At her end, Nina logged the call on a sheet next to the phone. The line had an unlisted number, registered to a Thomas Paine. The number was given out by their field reps when they were working a pretext, or a sting. Before giving out this number, the rep first alerted Nina that someone might call in connection with a case he was handling. Often an alias was given by the investigator. In any event, she spieled out an introduction commensurate with the particular sting the rep was working. She always answered with the suffix, and if she hadn't been instructed otherwise, always said that it was an import-export business, while—under all circumstances—denying knowledge of anyone's real name. That meant someone was suspicious, trying to uncover the investigator.

Nina checked Caller ID. The call came from 'Out of Area.' The caller was probably named Towers, probably Caucasian, and had asked to speak with Roth. Towers? Towers? Wasn't the US consular officer on the MacMillan claim named Towers? She shrugged, noted this in the log, and went out of the office. It was insignificant, or Roth would have forewarned her.

Towers poured himself a whiskey; something he never did alone, and never at the office. Before he'd met Lori, that is. Sure, she had betrayed him. But maybe she couldn't have helped it. Maybe she had to do what she did. He thought again of her sad, sweet face when she'd cried those times they were together. That couldn't have been acting. Then, as he had a thousand times, he thought of her fascinating body up against his, and his brain went limp.

He thought to call Morales' number again, but didn't bother. The man was never home.

———

In his hotel room, Roth replayed the meeting with Towers as he packed his bag. The embassy had heard nothing further from Kevin O'Toole. Perhaps Brian eventually surfaced, which was usually the case. But O'Toole was a Mick, and many Micks had red hair and freckles. Like the dead man.

He telephoned and registered into the Manila Hotel, unhappy about paying 200 bucks a night, which was a discount rate at that. He left a message with Otero where he'd be, then checked out of his hotel and took a taxi over to the Manila.

He normally stayed at hotels that figured in an investigation. It was bad form to poke around a hotel, asking about guests, and information was usually refused. But as a guest himself, management couldn't very well stop him.

At the Manila, he dropped his bag in his room, called down to room service for a bottle of rum, Cokes, and ice; then called reception and asked for the assistant manager to come to his room. Fifteen minutes later, an attractive woman—circa late twenties—arrived at his door at the same time as the room-service boy. She asked if there was a problem. Roth said there wasn't, introduced himself and the reason for his visit. He signed the tab and offered her a drink which she politely refused. He handed the young woman Lori MacMillan's name and the dates she stayed at the hotel, and advised her that he'd require information on telephone numbers she'd called and other charges made to her account, plus he wanted to interview some of the hotel staff. Miss Rosales-Sy, in turn, provided her card, explained that her last name was pronounced "See," then diplomatically refused this information on the grounds of confidentiality, explaining that, as a guest himself, Roth could appreciate their policy. "I'm sure you take my point," she finished politely.

Roth said that the Manila Hotel was hereby free to tell anyone absolutely anything they knew about him. So there! He added that, firstly, this was a government inquiry—just feel free to check with Mr. Towers at the American Embassy—and secondly, he didn't want to pester the girls in the telephone room, all three shifts; the clerks at the front desk, all three shifts; the waiters, bartenders, chambermaids, all three shifts; plus a hundred guests if he found it necessary to canvass door-to-door for repeat customers who might recall the widow MacMillan. No. In his opinion, handling these matters properly, through management, in the person of Miss Rosales-Sy—pronounced "See"—was the only way to guard against intrusive, insensitive inquiries conducted day and night, pestering everyone under the roof, starting unfounded rumors, even creating doubts as to hotel security. He smiled, drew a breath, and summarized, "I'm sure you take *my* point."

Miss Rosales-Sy gauged him at length, weighing his determination. She'd checked his registration before coming upstairs. His Platinum American Express credit card was on file. He'd booked in for three nights. Seventy-two hours was too long to keep this creep hanging around. His registration card read that he was going next to the US. Good. *Let's move his* cano *butt along. Give him what he wants as soon as humanly possible and get him the hell out of the hotel.*

She relented, saying that she would be only too happy to oblige the US government. However, she added, she could only provide handwritten details. No copies of anything. Roth remarked that that was just okee-dokee by him, then asked her to send up the maid who'd cleaned Mrs. MacMillan's room. That would be a woman named Rosalinda, Miss Rosales-Sy advised, asking if it was necessary that she stay for the interview. Roth said that it wasn't, only that Miss Rosales-Sy should explain to Rosalinda that she was expected to be completely candid.

He asked her how she knew off the top of her head which maid it was. Rosalinda remembered Mrs. MacMillan, Miss Rosales-Sy answered. She stayed for a total of three nights, on two separate occasions split by a few days when she visited Puerto Azul. It was common knowledge that Mrs. MacMillan had just lost her husband, and the staff had tried to be especially helpful. Roth read more into it than that; the Manila Hotel was a large operation and usually quite busy. So what if there was a recent widow amongst the guests? Just what made Lori MacMillan stand out?

"What else?" he asked. "There's more."

Miss Rosales-Sy seemed to search the floor for an answer. "Well, hmm, Mrs. MacMillan encouraged several rumors, it seems."

"Yes?"

"There's a rumor that Mrs. MacMillan had been a little forward with some of the staff." Miss Rosales-Sy looked embarrassed.

"I'm all ears, my dear."

"Well, sir, uh, it was suggested that Mrs. MacMillan propositioned some of the staff members."

"Tsk, tsk. Who would have believed it?"

She shrugged apologetically. "These are just rumors."

Which meant, of course, that there were no reports in writing. He could just picture the general manager reading the morning report: *"Housekeeper Rosalinda observed the lovely widow Mac-Millan galloping the room-service waiter on the serving cart."*

Roth chuckled to himself, and to Miss Rosales-Sy's relief, he didn't ask her to single out any of the staff.

He asked playfully, "Was that 'staff members' she propositioned?"

"Uhm, yes."

"Isn't that redundant. . . ?"

"I, uh, don't understand? Oh!"

Roth cracked up, enjoying her innocence. Her face blushed crimson. He thanked her for her assistance, showed her out, but asked if she was available for a drink later, during which time he'd advise her on the progress of his investigation, hoping of course to carry his investigation further into her knickers.

She apologized that she couldn't, her boyfriend was picking her up for dinner. Roth shrugged, said he understood, and wondered what the maid, Rosalinda, looked like.

Approaching her pension years, unfortunately. Rosalinda didn't provide much information at first, but Roth prodded her along with specific questions. She said that Mrs. MacMillan carried few things with her, only one small suitcase—carry-on size—but purchased several items from the hotel gift shop. During her two brief stays, her room had a very strong albeit pleasant scent of musk, presumably from an expensive fragrance she wore.

Embarrassed, Rosalinda said that she was certain on at least one occasion, two people had been in Mrs. MacMillan's bed. She grew quiet, preferring specific questions.

"Gimme, gimme, gimme, Rosalinda. What else?" Roth called out, changing into a pair of swimming trunks in the bathroom.

"Well, sir, it appears Mrs. Mock-me-laan traveled with a sizeable collection of—of. . . ." She had difficulty getting the words out. Never in her life had she spoken such words to a man. "*Especiale* condomes.*"

Roth emerged from the bathroom. "What was *especiale*? Bells and whistles?"

She couldn't meet his eyes, quietly replied that they were "Of the French variety." It was stressful for her to speak so frankly with a strange man about such intimate things. She wondered if she should include this in the confessional on Saturday. But what could she do? Miss Rosales-Sy had instructed her to be candid.

Roth laughed heartily, which didn't make this any easier for Rosalinda. Every kind of condom was on the market these days: colored, studded and ribbed, and the ones with alien-like tentacles. It wouldn't be long before someone engineered a condom that could whistle, maybe shrill an off-key *Rhapsody in Blue* during the ol' in and out. And chambermaids saw them all.

He thanked her, tipping her 500 pesos. Rosalinda pocketed the note reluctantly, thinking of it as sin money. She'd wash it off downstairs

———

"It's my ass if this gets around," Antonio whispered, looking over his shoulder, tucking the 500-peso note in his pocket. They were sitting by the pool, Roth enjoying a Sunset Surprise—the merry widow's favorite.

"I collect information, Antonio. I don't give it." Besides, everyone probably already knew. Despite Antonio's modesty, Roth was certain that he wore the widow MacMillan episode around his neck like a medal.

Antonio shrugged. "Sure, sir. I popped her. She asked me up to her room. Both times she stayed here. Hot bod. To die for, but—"

"But what?"

"She was like lightening, Mr. Roth. So the second time, after she returned from Puerto Azul, she had me doing handstands to ring her chimes, and afterwards I said, 'Hey, how about me'? You know? I didn't get mine. Know what she said?"

"I can guess."

Antonio's eyes went incredulous, looking into Roth's *mano-a-mano* like. "She told me to get out, or she'd scream rape."

Roth laughed. Whenever Western women vacationed alone, it was Club Meat. They gobbled up the young brown boys in Italy, Greece, Beirut, wherever.

"What could I do?" Antonio protested. "Please don't tell anyone, Mr. Roth. She could still make trouble for me."

"I don't think so, Antonio," Roth said distractedly, thinking he should visit the bungalows in Puerto Azul. "She was here for something too big to bother with a scandal."

"Yes? Like what?"

He looked around conspiratorially, leaned over to Antonio who moved closer. "She's a communist spy, Antonio."

"No kidding?" Antonio drew back, wide-eyed.

"Yeah. With ties to Middle Eastern terrorists and the NPA, IRA, and Mata Hari." Roth threw pesos on the bar to cover the drinks. "Your assistance has been very important."

Antonio smiled, impressed with himself. His tryst with Mrs. MacMillan had been ignominious to him, yes, but still, she was a great looking head, and to his co-workers she represented something of a trophy. A cocky smiled crossed his face as he shrugged nonchalantly.

Roth couldn't have that. "You were very fortunate, Antonio."

"Why's that?"

"She usually gets her victims alone. When she finishes using 'em, she ties 'em up, gags 'em, and castrates 'em. Balls and all."

"Oh, Jesus, Mary, and Joseph!" Antonio flinched, slammed his knees closed involuntarily, made the sign of the cross.

———

The next morning, Roth was having breakfast in bed when a bellboy knocked on his door. He handed Roth a plain envelope. Inside, there were several handwritten notes on unmarked paper. One was Lori MacMillan's total expenditure at the hotel, which included her purchases in the gift shop, her meals, even what she'd ordered in the coffee shop. Another note listed her overseas calls during both stays at the Manila. There were only two calls, both to the same Manhattan number and lasting less than a few minutes.

It was Friday morning, and he wanted to be in New York City Monday night. He reserved a seat to LA for Monday, connecting to New York. But first, Puerto Azul.

He made a reservation at the bungalows where Lori MacMillan had stayed, arranged for a car and driver from the hotel to take him down there.

As he was checking out, the receptionist gave him an envelope that Nestor Otero had left for him. On the way to Puerto Azul, he studied the photographs, a dozen blow-ups of the back of the man's hand. The pale ring around the man's wrist was prominent. Roth studied the knuckles: large, perhaps twice their normal size, rough looking, damaged. It was the karate hand Florentino had spoken about.

Roth put the envelope away and chatted with his driver. Gyp was a roly-poly type of guy with a pleasant smile. After a while, Gyp asked him if he was a friend of Mrs. MacMillan. Word had gotten around to the staff that he was making inquiries. Gyp recalled Mrs. MacMillan. At first, he'd been assigned by the transportation desk to drive her down to Puerto Azul, but when she saw him, she demanded another driver. Gyp didn't understand why until the young man chosen to drive her—a strapping 23-year-old named Claro—returned to Manila and let fly a secret. Mrs. MacMillan had demanded sex from him. Claro feared for his job as she'd threatened a complaint of sexual harassment if he didn't service her. Claro relented, doing the deed in the back seat behind a gas station on the road down to the resort.

Roth howled, and funnier yet was Gyp's replay of his conversation with Claro, who confirmed that the widow was a rabbit indeed. Their tryst in the back seat ended within seconds, then the merry widow reverted to a cool, indifferent passenger. She didn't

speak to Claro for the rest of the trip, and—adding insult to injury—
she hadn't even tipped him.

"Risky business," he added.

"Whaddya mean?" Roth asked.

"She liked risky business, sir. You know, doing it right there in
broad daylight in the back of the car." Gyp laughed, recalling Claro's
consternation. The beautiful *cana* barked orders, demanding that
he wear a condom, which she whipped out from her purse like a
smoking six gun. Poor Claro shook throughout, relieved when the
ordeal was over.

At the bungalows, an added ha-dee-ha-ha to his conversation
with Gyp came from Ernesto, the big security guy:

"So this *cano* came along, see. I think she'd been watching for
him. Trying to meet him, you know? They had dinner, and later they
were in the pool. She was dressed for murder, man. Then they went
to the beach where she got it on with him. We were watching,
man—the other guard and myself—through the fence. When she
finished with him, which was real fast," Ernesto snapped his fingers, "she left him bare-assed on the beach lookin' for his shorts.
She came in laughing, didn't see us, and went to her bungalow. So
I switched off the lights real quick so the guy wouldn't come back
in here. He was looking for his shorts all night, stark-assed naked
on the beach."

Roth cracked up. Towers hadn't disclosed that ignominious tid-
bit. Lori MacMillan was becoming more interesting with each
interview, and one thing was clear: she enjoyed exercising power
over people.

"You didn't get some?"

"Naw," Ernesto shook his head. "She flirted a lot, batted her
eyes, accidentally on purpose flashed some titty. But she was coming and going a lot, maybe following this guy around. It was more
like she was working than taking a vacation."

24 Los Angeles

A three-hour layover at LAX. Roth cleared Immigration, then went outside in the pre-dawn for a smoke. He waited until it was nine o'clock in Boston before calling the O'Toole Trucking Company. The receptionist said that Mr. Kevin O'Toole was on another line, and there was another call holding ahead of him.

"I'm calling about Brian."

The receptionist was quiet. Then, "Yes, sir. Please hold the line, sir."

His first question was answered—Brian was still missing. Roth remembered more about the family. The O'Toole's were interstate truckers. Ten years ago, there had been a bloodletting between some Massachusetts trucking firms and the mob down in Providence, Rhode Island. The O'Toole's were involved somehow, but he couldn't recall the details.

"K. O'Toole here." A gruff voice came on the line, sounding urgent. Kevin O'Toole, KO for short. A former middleweight contender who'd almost made it, but lost the title shot, then lost the rematch to the lightening-fast Puerto Rican champion. The rematch ended his aspirations. He quit the ring at 26, joined his father and brothers in the family business. The O'Toole's also figured in Boston politics and were prominent folks since they'd emigrated from Ireland in the 1880s.

"Why da fuck you wanna know about Brian?"

Oh, tough guy, huh? Yeah, this must be K. O'Toole, the guy who couldn't whip a skinny Spic without a dozen goons behind him. "The name's Roth. I'm a private investigator. About Brian. He never turned up?"

"How'd you know about that?" O'Toole asked. "Never mind. What's it to you?"

"Pop quiz, Mick. I got the PI license. The way this goes is like this, so pay attention. I ask the questions and you answer them. Now, if I wanna rent a fuckin' truck, guess who gets to ask the questions?"

"You wouldn't be making with the mouth if you were here in front of me."

"How would I recognize you after what that Spic did to your face?"

"Where are you, wise guy?" O'Toole was hot. Roth imagined he was standing at his desk, ready for the bell.

"Heading for New York. Out of Manila. But hey, killer, I'll be in New York tonight. You wanna come down for another pummeling, or you wanna tell me about your brother?" In fact, there was no way Roth would square off with this guy. O'Toole had been a meat grinder in the ring, but he lost the title shot because he went berserk whenever he got hurt. The champion had wisely paced O'Toole, jabbing and moving, cutting and dancing. He out-pointed him. Simple as that. "You find him yet?"

There was a long silence. Then, "No. No, we ain't." O'Toole asked again who he was.

"Roth. R-O-T-H. Take my New York number. I'll go real slow, so you can write it down with your crayon." He gave the number.

O'Toole repeated it slowly. "So why you calling me, Roth? I don't need to hire another private dick who can't find his own ass with both hands."

"Saaay, that's clever. 'Can't find his ass with both hands.' I gotta remember that. Look, you fuckin' leprechaun, I'm not a private dick. I'm divorced, so that part of me's gone public. I'm a private investigator. Get that straight. And I ain't lookin' for a job. I'm trying to help."

"Yeah? Why?"

"Maybe it'll help the case I'm workin' on. But you're asking me questions again, and I warned you about that, didn't I?"

He could hear KO breathing heavily on the other end, fuming. Long seconds passed before the Irishman calmed down. "So whaddya wanna know?"

"That's better. Did Brian wear a Cartier? A watch?"

Silence again. Roth had used the past tense, the question hung heavily on the line.

"Yeah," O'Toole answered finally, more quietly. "Dad gave it to him when he graduated from community college. Whaddya sayin' here?"

"Was Brian into karate?"

"Yeah! He was. Big time. Even before he went into the navy. Stayed with it and got an honorary brown belt over in Asia. Continued when he got home. Had a black belt by the time he was 22."

A lot of good karate did him. "Did Brian visit the Philippines when he was in the navy?"

"He was stationed there for a while. Subic Bay. About a year before Pinatubo closed the place down. He was a machinist's mate." O'Toole went quiet again.

"Keep talking, KO. Whaddya need, a fuckin' roadmap? Tell me about Brian."

"He, uh, liked Asia. Went back once or twice a year, whenever he could get time off. Liked the girls there, although I never understood why. I'd seen pictures of him with a lot of Filipino chicks. Never saw the attraction. They're uh, you know, dark."

"You don't like dark people?"

"Uh, no. No, I mean, uh—" O'Toole was vaguely aware of political correctness in America. "I mean, uh, they're all right."

"So why don't you own any?"

"Huh?"

"Never mind. Go on,"

"So, like I said, he went back every year or so. Took a month off each time. Those brown birds cost him his marriage. His wife divorced him. We're Catholic, see, and he got a divorce! Broke Mom's heart. And he's never been much on the job after that. We had him managing accounts, trouble-shooting, things like that. What could we do? He's our kid brother, you know, but, shit, how do you stop a guy from fucking up his life?"

You couldn't very well kick his ass. Not a guy with a black belt, even if his brains were in his pants. "He ever talk about anyone special in the 'Peens?" Roth asked.

"Once. After his trip last year. He was writing to her, sending her money. Was thinking about marrying her. That's who he went to see. She had a kid. From some other guy, you know."

"Brian like baseball? The Red Sox?"

"Yeah! How'd you know?"

Beer-drinking, blue-collar Mick from Boston. Not a giant stretch for that one. But Roth remembered Lolita's kid, little Pauley, wearing the baseball cap. "Do you remember the woman's name?"

"Naw. I never really paid attention when he went on about her and her kid. He's got a kid from his own marriage, you know. That was the kid he should have been talking about, thinking about. You know what I mean? But Tracey, his ex-wife, never let him near the kid. Not for the past couple of years; not after he brought home a dose of the clap."

"So what happened?"

"Brian phoned me when he got back over the last time. He found out the bird was seeing other guys all the while he'd been sending her money."

"Whores'll do that."

"Right. He was drunk as shit. Called me two, three times after that. Always drunk. Poor fuck even cried once. I felt sorry for him, told him to get his ass home. The broad, uh, Lolita was her name. I remember now. She told him to piss off because she had another guy who was gonna take care of her and her kid. She told him to forget about her, go home."

"But he didn't?" Roth asked, focusing on an attractive woman in her late thirties waiting near the phone bank in Arrivals. She wore stylish glasses and a conservative, well-tailored two-piece suit that didn't hide her curves. Her hair was chestnut, long, pulled off her neck, up into a bun. Maybe a lawyer. His type. Refined. Educated. With a quiet, gentle, unassuming nature; a lover of the classics, creative cuisine, wines, and film festivals—the good things in life. Warm, intimate conversations; thoughtful, sensitive, beautiful. And what a dynamite set of jugs!

A throng of nieces and nephews came wheeling luggage carts out from Customs in front of their parents. The kids spotted her, screamed "Auntie Lois," broke and ran to her. Roth pegged them as an expat family returning to the States after a year or two away.

"Naw," O'Toole said. "He didn't come home. Said he was gonna hang around, try to change her mind. Offer to marry her himself."

"Woulda gone down like the Dalai Lama sayin' Mass at St. Paddy's. Brian use drugs?"

"No way. He's dumb, but he ain't stupid. He likes to drink. Likes his brew."

"An Irishman drinking beer? Quit it. Your investigator found no trace of him?"

The children surrounded Auntie Lois, who embraced them in turn, the smallest first, working up to the oldest. Big hugs. Yeah, they'd been away a long time, and Auntie Lois was very popular with them. Roth studied her long, trim legs, well turned ankles. She could be popular with him, too.

"He found nothing," KO said. "No trace of him. Brian called from an exchange office in Manila. Cheaper than from his hotel, I guess, and he didn't say where he was staying. Cops had nothin', our embassy had nothin', Philippine Immigration had him going in, but no record of him coming out."

"All right, KO I'll be in touch," Roth said.

"Hey! You tell me what you got. You're on the job. Whatever you need."

"I don't work for Micks," he said, hanging up.

Roth had been talking about Brian in the past tense, but KO only heard what he wanted to hear. Roth picked up his bag and walked over to the welcoming group. As the oldest niece finished hugging Auntie Lois, he handed his bag to a nephew, threw out his arms. Lois shyly accepted a hug as the parents looked on, smiling, the niece-nefs exchanging sly glances, a silent taunt on their lips: Lois has a boyfriend! Lois has a boyfriend!

"God, Lois. You look fabulous," he growled, squeezing her tight. Yep, those headlights were proud suckers. He disengaged, held her at arms distance, looked her up and down. "And you feel great." He sighed, took his bag from the nephew and said, "Sorry, gotta catch a connection." He turned away, walked towards the terminal exit.

Lois looked after him, turned to her sister frowning. "Who on earth is *that*?"

Smiles faded and eyes widened as the parents and kids asked in unison, "*You* don't know him?"

25 Little Neck, N.Y.

Premier maintained a corporate apartment in Little Neck. It had once been Roth's place and he still kept a lot of his clothes there, plus artifacts he'd collected from his travels over the past 15 years. Souvenirs covered the walls, including primitive masks that stared at him as he went through the apartment turning on lights.

Representatives from around the globe crashed here when they came through New York. Premier recruited reps worldwide to keep up with their growing business, bringing them to New York for training, sometimes for court testimony. They had a good track record for getting convictions.

Clients never wanted to go to trial, satisfied just to get off the claim. But some cases were too big to ignore, and others went to trial when beneficiaries sued on weak cases, tried to scrounge a little parting cash. Piss-ass nuisance suits. Too often it worked; insurers abandoned principle in the face of high legal fees. Suicides, for instance. It was easier to settle than go to trial. Favorable judgments on suicides were iffy, unless the insured left a note and for good measure His Holiness the Pope witnessed it.

The three-bedroom apartment was buttoned-up tightly, unused for weeks. The windows were closed and locked, water turned off. Roth detected an aroma. Curry. Their man from India was the last to camp here. Before that, their guy in Cairo came through New York on his way to Nashville for a deposition.

Roth went back through the apartment, throwing windows open even though it was chilly outside. The smallest bedroom was converted to an office in the days when he bounced between Asia and New York.

Eleven o'clock. He was hyper after a long trip. He checked the office. A message on the answering machine. Nina called earlier to welcome him back, said she'd be up until midnight if he needed to call. He decided not to disturb her, tomorrow was soon enough. He splashed water on his face, took a whizzer, and walked up to Patrick's restaurant on Northern Boulevard. Maybe he could pick up a broad. But from what he saw on these occasional trips to the States, Americans weren't fucking anymore. They worked-out, ate flower salads washed down with mineral water, and hung on the phone and masturbated. Depressing. No, he wasn't home. He was only visiting his furniture.

He took a taxi to the office the next morning. Nina was in already, even though it wasn't yet 7:00. He hadn't seen her for six months although they communicated weekly, sometimes daily, from wherever he was in Asia. They greeted each other with hugs and he tried to squeeze her ass, a habit from working together for all these years. They exchanged gossip over coffee in the library, then got down to cases. Literally. Nina outlined some of the bigger, more problematic ones. They had over a hundred active jobs: a dozen in Africa, thirty or so around Europe, about the same number in Central and South America, the Middle East and Asia. She'd just sent a package of cases to his apartment in Bangkok for China, Taiwan, and more in the Philippines, plus a few scattered elsewhere. The package would have arrived in Bangkok while he was in the air. She was also working up cases in Papau New Guinea, Malaysia, and Vietnam. When the embargo against Vietnam was lifted, fraudulent cases came rolling in. Vietnamese-Americans could go back home now. And they took a lot of travel policies with them. It totaled eight new cases he needed to handle when he got back, so he couldn't stay around long with that kind of volume waiting for him.

"Where's all this comin' from?" he groused.

"Our website. Don't complain. One more thing," she said. "A guy named O'Toole called yesterday. From Boston. Wanted to speak to you as soon as you got in. Knew you were coming. Bossy, tough-guy type. What's the latest on MacMillan?"

Roth ignored her question and said, "Call him back. Tell him I'll be in touch when I'm ready, and tell him to send his investigator's report on Brian to me in Bangkok."

"Who's Brian?" Nina was jotting everything down.

"Just tell him. And if he gets pushy, just tell him you'll send up some little Puerto Rican to smack him around. A Puerto Rican. Got that?"

"Sure. I'll tell him," she said pensively, her question sitting somewhere out in left field. "When are you going to interview Mrs. Mac-Millan?"

"As soon as I get to it."

"Mrs. MacMillan has called Kincannon several times, demanding they take some action. But aside from the interview with the Chase-Hampshire rep, she's heard nothing more from them, either. I told her you'd call as soon as you got in. Before you ask, no, she has no idea you've been to Manila. I told her you were just out of town. She knows we represent Amalgamated Life, but probably not that we handle overseas. I didn't mention we also represented Chase-Hampshire now."

"I'll take it from here," Roth said. He took a vacant office for visiting reps, closed the door. Nina had his old office, where a once fully stocked bar was now piled high with case files and her desk looked like a hand grenade had exploded on it. Roth marveled at how she kept anything straight. But she did, keeping her pulse on all the reps and cases. A moment later, she knocked on the door, came in with the report from the Gellert in Budapest.

"Hot off the fax," she said.

"Is it the same MacMillan?"

"Can't be anyone else." She stood by the door. He knew what she was thinking. She was a good investigator, and her question about why the companies weren't to be notified about the hospitalization claim remained unanswered. Roth didn't look at her. She went out, closing the door behind her.

He then placed a call to Sid Sydow of American Travelers, and after a few minutes was put through to him. Sydow ran the claims operation for American Travelers in Chicago.

"Sydow."

"Sydow, this is Roth. With Premier. On the MacMillan case. We're working it for two companies, Amalgamated and Chase-Hampshire, but I understand you guys already paid it?"

"That's right. It's out of the contestability period. We checked it out." Sydow sounded his usual pompous self.

"Who'd you use in Manila?" Roth asked.

"I'd rather not say. But we're satisfied."

Roth already knew Sydow had used Loggert, who in turn, used Dubbs in LA to interview Mrs. MacMillan, then had Associated Insurance Adjusters in Manila verify the death. He'd seen their business card at Las Flores Funeraria. How they accepted the death certificate was curious. Had Boy Carrera entered it in the death register after all? Not likely; Boy probably just certified Associate's copy of the death certificate and their rep didn't have the brains to check with the NSO. They hadn't contacted the embassy, but it wouldn't have mattered anyway. Towers would have blown them off; he was above answering to Filipino investigators.

As for Associated in Manila, Premier tried them a few years back on a case. They were inept at best, or on the take at worst. They'd reported a clean case whereas Roth knew it was dirty just from looking at the death certificate. He rehandled that one—it *was* fraudulent. Confronting Associated with the results of his investigation, they gave him polite, shit-eating grins and shrugged it off, asking nevertheless when their bill would be paid.

Loggert never traveled further than the other side of his desk, and had never been to the Philippines. He was as pompous as Sydow, and held himself out as an expert on international claims.

Sydow wouldn't know about Associated, because Loggert probably took their report and retyped it on his own stationary to project an international image. Loggert was a master at fluff, and had once said that if you can't dazzle a client with brilliance, baffle them with bullshit.

"Look, Sydow. Loggert doesn't know the Philippines from the Philistines. He used some dummies in Manila. Pays them seven bucks an hour. What can you expect for that?" He wanted to know exactly what Sydow had. It could be important later.

"We've paid and closed the case." Sydow wouldn't believe he'd erred in his choice of investigators, because he knew less about the Philippines than Loggert. Even if he did think there'd been a screw up, he didn't want to hear about it now. For starters, he'd look bad. Secondly, he'd doubt the chances of recovering the money forked over to Mrs. MacMillan. It was best to let sleeping dogs lie.

"Listen," Roth said, "the case is complicated." *But it's fine with me if you won't listen.*

"Your partner, Miss, uh, Davis told me a few things already, and what you're saying is *your* opinion. Not fact. We have a death certificate *plus* the police report, which includes an autopsy from the Philippines FBI, *plus* a bill from the undertaker, *plus* a Report of the Death of an American Citizen Abroad."

Plus, plus, plus. Yeah, yeah. "Look," Roth persisted. "Death certificates in the Philippines are spurious, the cops are corrupt, the NBI's pathologist could have opened the wrong guy, and the funeral home has no idea who they fried." There. Sydow had every chance to reverse himself. If he didn't, all the better.

"You have nothing, Roth."

"Try this: maybe a certain Peter MacMillan was somewhere else a week after he was supposed to be dead."

The line went quiet. Then, "MacMillan's a common name." Sydow was reaching.

Roth groaned audibly. "The dead guy's ashes were left in the funeral home in Manila."

"Mrs. MacMillan's prerogative. We understand she and her husband hadn't been on the best of terms."

What did Sydow need? A diagram? Didn't matter. He wouldn't reinvestigate the claim and would never hire Premier. He didn't like

Roth's attitude. He was irreverent. That's the word Sydow once used. Loggert was his old army chum. They hung together at claims conferences, Loggert doing the back-slapping, drink-buying routine. Sydow was no international player, lacked field experience. Worse yet, he was an attorney, which entitled him to sit on the right hand of God. So, he'd be seen as mortal if he reversed himself. To have erred was out of the question. Asshole.

"You've made no mistakes?" Roth said. "Got it all, huh?"

"We got all that we need," Sydow replied, signaling the end of the conversation.

"Okay, Sydow. Oh, one last thing."

"Yes," he answered, very bored.

"Is Loggert still sucking your dick to get your business?"

The line went dead. Roth slapped his knee. By the way, what did that word mean, 'irreverent'?

If one company wouldn't believe fraud, maybe others wouldn't either. The conversation had been very telling. Not that Roth said everything he could have. He wasn't very convincing, hadn't laid out the solid details of the case. But he laid the foundation and it didn't take with Sydow. And Sydow wasn't really so different than most claims people these days.

But Kincannon was another story.

His next call was to Lori MacMillan, at the number she'd been leaving. An answering machine came on, a woman's voice said that this was Marcia—no last name—that she was out and would return the call as soon as possible. Her voice was one of those light, giggly ones, chronically happy, sounded like she was *so* happy she could just fart.

Roth left his name, the private number, and why he was calling.

An hour later, the phone rang in the private office. Roth went in, answered with only the last four digits of the number.

"Hello. Mr. Roth?"

Roth checked the number on Caller ID. It read, *"Unavailable."*

"Uh hum," he answered.

"This is Mrs. MacMillan. You telephoned me?" Her question was like a challenge, her voice matching what he'd come to expect: low, sultry, and direct. No happy farts in the wind with this one.

"Yeah. I need to see you."

"It's about time."

"Just flew in last night," he said. "From Manila."

The silence on the other end was deafening. Roth snapped his fingers, spun his chair around to see Nina leaning on the door jamb. She made a pistol with her hand. After a while he asked, "Are you there?"

"Yes. I'm here, Mr. Roth," Rachel said. She gave him an address on East 68th Street, said that she was staying with a friend temporarily—a Miss Marcia Post—and repeated that it was about time she heard from Amalgamated. They set an appointment for 10:00 the next morning at the Post apartment and Rachel hung up.

Nina hung over the desk, reading "*Unavailable*" on the Caller ID. "Must be a different number, a different instrument. Marcia Post is listed. Under M. Post."

Roth telephoned Marcia Post's number again. Got the answering machine. He didn't leave another message.

"Either she didn't call from there, or there's a second instrument in the apartment," Nina said. "Maybe she's screening calls. Maybe she has caller ID also."

"If so, she'll know I called right back." Roth pulled out his notes from the Manila Hotel. The number Mrs. MacMillan had called from Manila was the same number that Lolita had in her address book. He dialed the number. Mrs. MacMillan answered. No mistaking that voice. He hung up. So, she was getting calls at one number and making them from another. If she had Caller ID, his number would also appear as "*Unavailable.*"

Roth then telephoned a long-time source with the telephone company. They chatted whenever he visited New York, always about getting together for a few beers in the city. But both knew they'd never get around to it. Aside from business, they had nothing in common. Roth asked him to get Jordan Warner's unlisted number, wrote and circled "*100 dollars*" on a pad, handed it to Nina.

In ten minutes, his source called back, gave Warner's address on Fifth Avenue, and the telephone matched the number he'd just called for Mrs. MacMillan. Jordan Warner's Fifth Avenue address was just a few blocks from Marcia Post's apartment.

He'd gotten Lori MacMillan's PO box number from Towers, which also matched the PO box in Lolita Perez's address book. From

Ben's report from Budapest, the signature on Peter MacMillan's registration at the Gellert matched the signature on the insurance applications for the Amalgamated and Chase-Hampshire policies.

It was all one case. And a big one. But why was Lolita Perez whacked? To shut her up? Or was her death planned all along for the insurance? Did she have anything to do with murdering Brian O'Toole? Marcellus hadn't done the job, so that meant bringing someone else in, but why bring in a new witness to murder just to eliminate an old witness to murder? And why whack her so violently? Of course, for insurance. Double indemnity would apply if she'd been a hit-and-run victim.

He called outside for Nina. She came in, perched on the edge of the desk. He gave her the accident report on Lolita, instructed her to start calling around for any companies who might have insured her. Two things were likely if there was insurance on her: the policies would be under her real name, and they would surely be for double indemnity.

"Another thing. Remember Mrs. MacMillan's voice?" he asked.

"Sure, it's a smooth, come-fuck-me, voice," Nina mimicked.

"Call this number." He handed her a slip of paper with Jordan Warner's number on it. "When she answers, give her a 'Problem on the Line' routine. I wanna know what apartment she's in. Use this phone."

"Where'd you get the number?"

Roth just looked at her.

"Okay. Okay." She scooted off the desk, called one of the investigators. "Lou, get in here. Bring the radio."

Lou came into the windowless room, and plugged in the radio next to the desk, placed it up next to the phone. Roth stepped out of the office, sat on a desk near the door. Nina dialed Warner's number. Rachel answered, and Nina held the receiver up against the radio. Rachel asked several times who was calling, then Nina pressed the plunger on the cradle. She waited a few minutes, then signaled Lou. He moved over to another phone, lifted the receiver, punched 'Conference' as Nina dialed the Warner number again. Nina and Lou began jabbering, improvising a script.

In the Warner apartment, Rachel picked up the receiver. "Hello?"

Nina said, "So I told the bastard I was leaving him."

Lou asked, "You didn't tell him about us, did you?"

Rachel's voice interrupted: "Hello? Who is this?"

"Of course not. D'ya think I'm crazy. He'd go ballistic."

"Hello . . . HELLO!"

"Will he give you a divorce?"

"Will Sherri give *you* a divorce?"

"Who's on the line?"

"Honey, if it weren't for the kids—"

"Don't throw those brats in my face again, buster."

The Warner line went dead.

Nina and Lou hung up. They waited a few seconds, then Lou called the Warner number again.

Rachel picked up, her temper apparent. "Hello!"

"Uh, hello ma'am. Dis is the phone company. You're havin' problems with your line?"

"Yes. I certainly am."

"Uh, yeah, we're down in the basement. Dis whole PBX has gone haywire. Everybody in da building's gotta problem. What unit you in?"

"Unit?"

"Yeah, lady. What apartment you in?"

"I'm sorry," Rachel said, "but this number is unlisted."

"Not with the phone company, it ain't. Look lady, we're freezin' our noogies off down here, unscramblin' da lines. So if you wanna free your line, I gotta know da unit. Uddawise, we're outta here an' good luck to ya."

"Four A."

"Four A," Lou repeated. "Okay. Dat's a help. I see it." He turned his head from the phone. "Ova' here, Joe. Here's da fuckin' problem. Can you fuckin' believe this? Rats ate right through the fuckin' line." He let go with a king-sized provolone burp, hung up.

Roth smiled. Lou was good. Perfect blue-collar De's' and Doe's', interjecting Brooklyn's favorite adjective in every sentence. He called in to him. "Where ya from, Lou?"

"Brooklyn, Mr. Roth," he called back, disconnecting the radio.

"Who woulda guessed."

Roth phoned Jim Kincannon at Amalgamated Life. Miss Walsh answered. He had spoken with her before, but never met her. She sounded efficient, and Kincannon sang her praises. Roth flirted with her but it didn't take. She put him through.

"Kincannon," the voice came on the line.

"Jim. This is Roth. Hey, I gotta question before I get into business."

"Yeah?" Kincannon snickered. "I hire you to answer questions, Roth. Not ask them. Okay. Whaddya wanna know?"

"You punchin' Miss Walsh?"

"What!"

Roth could tell that he was in a bad mood. Kincannon was a no nonsense guy, which is exactly why he liked to screw with him. He'd asked him about most females they knew in common and some they didn't. Kincannon was always brusk.

"I'm a married man, Roth," he bawled. "I told you that before. And that kinda talk has no place in business and certainly no place on the phone."

"Oh. Damned sorry, Jim. I didn't know you felt like that. Okay, listen, just a second. I'm turnin' off my tape recorder. Now, tell me, are you two doin' it? Don't hold anything back."

"I'm gonna hang up, buster."

"Okay, okay. . . . On the MacMillan case. I'm seeing Mrs. Mac-Millan tomorrow."

"About goddamn time. She called here twice last week."

"The case is just about wrapped up."

They were both thinking the same thing: would they need to report it to a state insurance fraud bureau? The problem, however, was that fraud bureaus were small and couldn't handle all the work in their state. A case like this, however, would grab their attention, especially if it was wrapped up nice and neat—a case that they could prosecute successfully. There'd be good headlines, which led to bigger budgets, promotions, and accolades. That was okay by Roth; he just wanted the money, and few bureaucrats made what he earned. Accolades? He'd promoted himself to company president years ago.

"Should I set up a file?" Kincannon asked, in reference to the fraud bureaus.

"Not just yet. I got some loose ends and it's a tough one. It's gonna take some slick, fancy footwork." He hesitated. "Who knows, maybe I'll fuck up and can't bring it off."

Kincannon grunted, the line went quiet. Neither man said anything. Roth pinched his lip, wondering what Kincannon was thinking. Kincannon was sharp, analyzing what *wasn't* said as well as what he heard.

"Yeah, well. Keep me posted," Kincannon finally said, then asked Roth to transfer him to Nina. He wanted to talk to her about another case Premier was handling—the disappearance of a Mexican businessman. Roth had read the case notes. Nina was certain the guy was faking his disappearance with bogus ransom notes to his own family from a purported terrorist group. It was a 5-million-dollar life policy, and, last year, he'd been turned down for kidnap and ransom insurance. It was a refreshing change, if that's what the guy was doing. If the insured never turned up, the assumption would be that the terrorists whacked him even after a ransom was paid. So, the million-dollar ransom would also vanish. Smart. Roth appreciated the imagination. No one wanted the media getting hold of the story. A rash of copycat claims would follow, giving K&R insurers conniptions.

"Last thing," Roth said, whispering. "That cute little thing at reception, you bangin' her, Jim? Doing the ol' in and out? The ol' up 'n' down?"

"Have Nina call me back," Kincannon barked. "Go back to Asia where you belong, you disgusting degenerate."

"Ouch! Jim."

"And Roth, maybe you ain't as goddamn slick as you think you are." He slammed the phone down.

Maybe, Jim. Maybe. Roth smiled, hanging up. *But I ain't never been caught.*

After work, he went into the windowless office where a safe was kept, locked within a fireproof cabinet. He unlocked both and removed a .38-caliber revolver. He checked the pistol. It was clean and lightly oiled, the way he'd left it six months ago. He took some rounds from a box of cartridges and dropped them into his coat pocket along with the revolver. In a small card file, he found his New York City carry permit, and checked the expiration date. It was valid for another year.

He and Nina went for some drinks. They talked about company finances and personnel, then she dropped him off in front of the apartment building on Little Neck Road.

"Hey," she called. "So you're not married yet? Any prospects?"

"Naw. Frequent honeymoons, though. They count for a tax deduction?"

"You ever coming back to the States?"

"I'm here, ain't I?"

"To live?"

"This ain't living, girlie. In Bangkok, I work in a towel, maybe in swimming trunks if I wanna dress up. Call Lou. Tell him to pick me up in the morning. I wanna use him a few hours. Any problem?"

"I can spare him in the morning. But he's got to be back in the office to take a telephonic statement at one o'clock. What time you want him?"

"Have him here at seven. He'll be back by one o'clock."

Nina pulled from the curb, mobile in hand to call Lou.

26

Lou pulled up in front of the apartment building at exactly 7:00 a.m. Roth was ready, sipping his second cup of coffee. Through the curtains, he watched Lou behind the wheel. Would he just wait, or get out, go up and ring the bell. After a minute, Lou tapped out: 'Shave and a Haircut, Two Bits,' on the horn. Roth smiled in appreciation: Lou was assertive; seven o'clock was seven o'clock and president or not, he was being summoned New York style.

Roth drove—something he rarely did in Asia, where most car rentals came with a driver. He had to remember to drive on the right. Traffic moved on the left in Thailand, and some *farangs* got clipped daily, looking the wrong way when crossing the street. He thought of Max Pollock in his wheelchair.

They stopped off at a bakery, bought coffees and bagels—the New Yorker's breakfast—then took the Northern Parkway to the Triboro Bridge. In Manhattan, Roth skirted south along the East River Drive to East 96th Street, cut west to Lexington Avenue, turned south, arriving at eight o'clock in front of Marcia Post's apartment building on East 68th Street between Lexington and Third Avenue. The building was a four-story walk-up. Roth jumped out of the car, ran up the steps, and rang the bell next to the name, *"M. Post."*

As he expected, no answer. He got back into the car and drove around to Fifth Avenue where he parked on the east side of the street, opposite Central Park. He edged the car forward to let it idle at the curb thirty feet from the entrance of the MacMillan apartment building. He adjusted the rear-view mirror to where it fell on the glass doors under the awning. Fifth Avenue was one-way, downtown, strictly no parking at any hour. However, limousines stood on both sides of the street with engines running, drivers at the wheel, waiting to pick up executives from the luxury apartment buildings.

While they waited, Roth kept his eyes on the mirror and grilled Lou for his impressions of the business. Lou had a good attitude. His father and brothers were cops with the NYPD, but Lou didn't want to join the force. No pulling shifts or having his income limited by a pay schedule for this boy. He didn't care about security. He'd taken care of himself, opening a pension plan three years before. He wanted to travel and pick up a few languages.

Police cars passed occasionally, their routine punctuated by the appearance of meter-maids and tow trucks. As long as a car's engine was idling and a driver was at the wheel, they were ignored.

"I was wondering, Mr. Roth, why we don't make more arrests. I mean, we catch a lot of scammers, but we only arrest a few."

"There are three elements to a fraud, Lou: intent; setting about the mechanisms; and finally, the fraudster's gotta collect, gotta realize some gain. Without grabbing some bucks, it's only attempted fraud, and that isn't worth prosecuting, because the perp will only get a slap on the hand."

"I got it."

"So, despite not making a lot of collars, or stomping the holy shit out of a lot of people, do you like the business?"

"I do, sir. I'd like to open an office somewhere when I finish training."

"Call me Mike. How about Prague? We need someone in Central Europe."

"I was hoping for Asia, maybe South America."

"South America's covered and I handle Asia. Of course, we could use another guy in the Middle East. You like to fuck camels?"

"Prague sounds wonderful, sir."

They grew quiet and settled into their own thoughts until, at 9:30, Roth spotted an attractive blonde emerge from the apartment building and turn their way. She wore three-inch heels, was tall and lean, a rich mink coat blowing open to reveal jeans, dark-blue turtleneck sweater. Fifth Avenue casual elegance. Roth kept the woman's face in the mirror until he saw the mole on her right cheek, then turned towards Lou and tugged at his ear lobe, keeping his left hand across his face. The woman was stunning, her make-up perfect, professionally done, it seemed, not a hair out of place. Her fur coat was open, breasts poking out. Accidentally, of course.

Roth said, "A million bucks says that's our subject."

Lou caught her in the corner of his eye. "For her, I'd pay it. Wotta *bambino*!"

As soon as she passed, approaching the corner of 70th Street, Roth jumped out, told Lou to take the wheel. He shuffled up to the apartment building, approached the doorman, and asked for Mrs. Warner.

"You just missed her," Gus said, pointed outside.

"Mink coat?"

Gus nodded.

Roth withdrew a photocopy of Peter MacMillan's passport from his coat pocket and handed it to Gus. Hank walked over and looked as well.

"Is this Mr. Warner?"

Gus held it away from his face at arms length and adjusted his glasses. He looked over the rims at Roth, wondering if he should co-operate.

"Don't look at me, bub. Look at the picture." He stuffed a twenty in Gus' breast pocket. Money carried a distinct aroma for these guys.

"His hair's shorter and he wears glasses, but, yeah, that's Mr. Warner."

Roth looked at Hank, who also nodded.

"Is he upstairs?"

"Mr. Warner's away."

Roth snatched the copy back. "Don't tell them that anyone's been around asking questions." *Which is exactly what you guys will do.* Of course they'd tell Warner, and that's what he wanted. A big part of their earnings came from tips, and information that someone was checking on a tenant—possibly even watching him—was good for at least fifty bucks, especially with Christmas coming. Naturally, however, they'd say that they'd divulged no information. They'd also inform Lori MacMillan, or Mrs. Warner, or whoever she was, when she returned. He hurried back to the car.

They spotted the blonde a block down Fifth Avenue. He got in on the passenger's side and ordered Lou to follow slowly. At East 68th Street she turned the corner, walking towards Madison Avenue. The Post apartment was three blocks over, and apparently she was going to walk there. The car crept along 68th Street, and as they crossed Lexington Avenue, Roth jumped out.

"One more thing, Lou. Scoot downtown. Check building records for that place on Fifth Avenue. Get the floor plans and determine where the A line of apartments are. Got it?"

"Yes, sir. Anything else?"

"That'll cover it for now. Nina wants you back in the office."

Lou pulled away, cruising past the woman known as Lori Mac-Millan for a closer look at her, for a mental imprint of her face should he have further surveillance on her.

Roth followed her towards Third Avenue. Near the corner, she reached the Post apartment building, walked up the steps, and went inside. It was 9:45 a.m. Roth stopped outside the building. He lit a cigarette, then strolled to the corner of Third Avenue where he checked the shops. He noted the coffee shop on the northwest corner of East 68th Street and Third Avenue, named The El.

He entered, looked around. Old photographs of an elevated subway platform lined the walls, it being the inspiration for the name of the place. He asked how late breakfast was served. All day, the waitress behind the counter said. Her name tag read, *"Ethel."* He made his way back to the apartment building, and at exactly ten o'clock, walked up the steps and rang the bell for the Post apartment.

"Who is it," a soft voice came across the intercom.

"My name is Peter MacMillan." Roth smiled into the intercom.

"What?" the voice asked incredulously. Then angrily, "Who's there?"

"It's Mike Roth."

Silence again, the intercom still open. Waiting.

"We spoke yesterday," Roth said. "We have an appointment."

The security lock buzzed and he pushed the door open. The Post apartment was on the third floor. Roth walked up, looked left, then right. At the end of the hall, Rachel stood at a half-opened door, watching him as he approached.

"Mr. Roth?"

"The one and only, sweetheart."

Sweetheart. Rachel frowned and warily closed the door a few inches. What kind of claims adjuster called grieving widows 'sweetheart'? Roth was casually dressed in slacks, a black crew-neck under a black leather coat. Not exactly officious. No briefcase, standard equipment for adjusters. Roth stopped at the door, inches from her face, and leaned against the wall. "Well? You wanna talk in the hall?"

Rachel's fur coat was off and nowhere in sight. His eyes took her in, devouring her, pouring down her frame. She looked better without the fur coat. Large breasts—the natural kind hopefully—flawless complexion, shoulder-length blonde hair with a nice bounce, beautiful chiseled face, and deep green eyes. Roth could see why Towers tripped over his own dick for this one.

"Do you have identification? A badge?"

"We don't need any stinking badges," Roth quipped with a Mexican accent. "But funny you ask; ID is what I need from you."

"I—I don't understand."

"You understand. Now, you gonna let me in or do we forget about it?"

"I think I'd better call Amalgamated Life."

"Ask for Jim Kincannon. Whaddya going to tell him? That you don't wanna talk to me. That you don't like me?"

"I don't know who you are. You said yesterday on the telephone—"

"That I represented Amalgamated. And I do." He reached into his coat and pulled out a business card.

Rachel took the card and studied it. "It's just that you don't seem like an insurance representative."

"Save it, lady." Roth pushed the door open. "We've got a lot to talk about and I'm lonely out here."

Rachel stood aside, nervously looked into the hallway, marking out a path of escape if Roth became threatening. Adjusters didn't act like this or say such things. When she'd returned Miss Davis' calls, the line was always answered with four digits. No name was ever given. She'd reversed the number, but it was unpublished, so she'd had no business name to check. Maybe Roth was just a one-man shop.

Roth stood in the middle of the small living room and turned in a wide circle. "Anyone else here?" he asked, not looking at her. He walked into the kitchen, a tiny room barely wide enough to turn around in. He stopped in front of the refrigerator, turned back to Rachel.

"I'll bet you can't tell me if there's a beer in here."

"A beer?"

"A beer," he repeated, looking at her as though she was dim-witted. "You don't have a clue what's in this box. Beer? Bologna? Boston baked bullshit?" He shoved his hand into his jacket pocket, around his .38-caliber revolver, and walked through the apartment opening doors. He checked the bathroom, swept back the shower curtain, then went into the bedroom where he looked in the closet and under the bed. He returned to the living room, turned slowly, taking in the apartment's furnishings. The place was sterile, lacked character, the furniture inexpensive and boring. He'd been in cozier bus stations.

"It's a friend's apartment," Rachel offered.

Roth looked in the coat closet, nudging her out of the way.

"What are you looking for?"

"Dead husbands. Got any in here?"

"I'm sure I don't know what you're talking about."

"I'm sure you know *exactly* what I'm talking about."

"I think you'd better leave."

"We're both leaving. I want some breakfast." He swept past her, out into the hall. "Get your coat."

Rachel stood at the open door. "I'm not going anywhere," she braved. "I'm calling your employer." She reached for her purse and fumbled it open, searching for Jim Kincannon's letter. "Your conduct is inexcusable. Your insinuations are insulting."

Roth laughed, booming in the hallway. "Cut the shit." He pointed his finger at her. "That's the second time I've told you to cut the act. Now get it together. I said I was hungry. There's a diner on the corner that I like. You can watch me eat breakfast while I tell you how you fucked up this little scam. And what we're gonna do about it." He went down the stairs, leaving her undecided as to what she should do. Whatever Roth wanted, aside from breakfast on which he placed the highest priority, he wasn't threatening her with arrest. He wanted something, and she knew what it was. She grabbed her coat, looked around the apartment. She didn't want to leave traces that someone had been here. While Marcia knew she had a key, she told her that she was staying with a friend on Fifth Avenue while her apartment was being painted. In the hallway, she heard Roth walking down the stairs. She closed and locked the door.

Roth stood outside on the sidewalk, lighting a cigarette. Rachel walked down the steps and didn't look at him. Silently, they walked towards Third Avenue. She bundled the fur collar high around her throat, although the weather wasn't that cold. He touched the fur on her sleeve.

"Nice coat. Where'd you get it?"

"My husband bought it for me in Paris," she said coolly.

"You're a good looking woman," Roth declared, studying her face. "Even better looking than I thought you'd be."

Rachel said nothing, taking in the quiet street, watching if Roth had a partner lurking around. She mulled over his words. *Even better looking than he thought I'd be?*

They crossed the street where Roth stopped in front of The El coffee shop. He took her arm, squeezed tightly until it hurt. "That's a compliment, beauty. Say 'thank you.'"

"Thank you," Rachel murmured. Roth was strange; frightening actually. Unpredictable. And probably dangerous. "Who do you work for?"

"Amalgamated of Illinois. I told you."

"I mean what's the name of your organization? You're not an employee of Almagamated Life." She couched her question as though his answer would bring dreaded consequences for him.

"Alcoholics Anonymous."

"Mr. Roth. I'm asking you a serious question."

He studied the breakfast menu in the window of the coffee shop. "Okay, if the truth be known, I'm affiliated with Mistress Sadie's Discipline Club."

She turned around impatiently, as though to hail a taxi. In fact, she had no idea what to do. She'd never encountered anyone like this guy before.

He took her by the collar of her fur coat, opened the door, guided her inside.

"Morning, Ethel," he called to the waitress. Ethel looked round and saw Roth, who'd just popped his head in ten minutes ago. He was calling her Ethel already? If he returned for dinner, would he think they were engaged? She grunted a reply.

Rachel followed Roth to a booth by the window facing 68th Street, his familiarity with the place not lost on her. He knew where they were going, where he wanted to eat. Even knew the waitress by name. He put her in the furthest seat. She'd have to get past him to reach the door.

The morning rush was over. Only one customer sat at the counter drinking coffee, talking with Ethel. Rachel and Robert once sat in this very booth, the night they'd met Marcia, just after they'd checked Marcia's mailbox with the duplicate key Robert had made.

Roth called Ethel. Not that she was far away; she seemed the type to hang over her customers conversations. Nosy type. "Ethel, doll. How about some breakfast?"

Unlikely a coincidence, Rachel mused, that Roth just happened to live in Marcia's neighborhood. No, he'd been here before, probably watching Marcia's apartment. She looked across the street, confirmed her suspicion; the stoop of Marcia Post's building was clearly visible from the window. Ideal for camping out on a stakeout.

Ethel came over and Roth smiled at her, looked at Rachel. "Ethel, you don't suppose you could whip us up a few Sunset Surprises, could you?"

Rachel locked eyes with Roth.

"A what?" Ethel frowned.

"No. I suppose not," Roth said. "Too cold for those. Tell you what, rustle me a big breakfast. Four eggs over easy, bacon, don't be chintzy on the bacon, home fries, wheat toast, orange juice, coffee." He smiled wickedly at Rachel, asked Ethel obliquely if she had any Darjeeling.

"Darjeeling? Naw. I know we got Lipton's."

"Got some honey?"

"Sure."

"Drop a little in the tea. Liptons if that's all you got."

Rachel stared at Roth. *How in the world does he know my preferences?* She tried for indifference, but felt trapped. He offered her the menu, but Rachel shook her head. Her stomach growled. Nervousness. She saw part of a tattoo on his right forearm. Roth looked more like a stevedore than a representative for one of the country's largest insurance companies.

Ethel brought his coffee and her tea, and studied them. "Anything else for you?" she asked Rachel.

Rachel shook her head.

"We'll let you know," Roth said. Ethel walked away. Then he said to Rachel, "Yeah, you've lost your appetite. I have that effect on people sometimes."

"Aren't you supposed to ask me questions or something?" Rachel asked, resuming the beneficiary's role.

"Questions? I got most of what I need, but there are a couple of things. Who's Marcia Post?"

"A friend."

"Involved in this scam?"

"I don't know what you're talking about."

"I'll let that pass for the moment. Involved in this claim, then?"

"No. She's just a friend I'm staying with."

Roth looked at her, disappointment etched in his taunting smile. "Friend indeed? Okay, moment's up. You lie like a rug, beauty. She's either a dupe or she's involved in this scam up to her butt. My money's on dupe. Why else use her apartment? Okay, let's try this one. Where's Peter MacMillan? Your, uh, husband, you say?"

"He's dead. He died in Manila."

Roth shook his head slowly, lowered his voice. "I can understand why he'd wanna be dead, given the way you throw a fuck."

Rachel moved for her coat, started to stand.

Roth kicked her in the shin beneath the table. "Did I tell you to stand up? Sit down. Unless you wanna take a little ride over to the Seventeenth Precinct where you can lay your bullshit story on the buttons."

She threw her coat aside and placed her elbows on the table, staring at him, ignoring a throbbing pain in her shin. She wouldn't give him the satisfaction by rubbing it. "What do you want?"

"I'll ask you again. Where's Peter MacMillan?"

"I already told you that he's dead."

Roth grabbed her wrist, squeezed it hard. "You keep this shit up and we've got nothing more to talk about." His voice carried across the restaurant. Ethel and her customer looked over. Roth lowered his voice.

"One more lie and you're goin' to jail. Once more, so help me and I can't do anything for you. Am I comin' in clear?" He released her wrist, pushed her hand away.

Rachel's heart beat faster. She tried to control her nervousness, and pretended anger. But she was scared. She should have detected it yesterday when Roth said he'd just arrived from Manila. What did he learn there?

Roth reached into his jacket pocket and removed the hospitalization claim form on Peter MacMillan. He flipped it at her, hitting her on the tip of her nose with it.

"Read this, beauty. You people fucked this scam up so bad you oughta be jailed for stupidity, let alone fraud. You get the Dumb-Fuck Award of the Century." Roth looked over at Ethel who was holding his plate, standing away from their booth. He waved her over.

"We're not gonna have any trouble here, are we folks?" She asked.

"Ask her," he said, pointing to Rachel. "Are we gonna have any trouble here, beauty?"

Rachel said nothing, her head down, stomach in knots, trying to concentrate on the paper he had thrown at her.

"I don't think so, Ethel. She's on her way around to seeing things my way."

Ethel returned behind the counter, grimacing to her customer.

Shaking, Rachel read the hospitalization claim form, saw the date and Robert's handwriting. She had to read it several times to understand.

Roth watched her, an evil, humorless smile working on his face. "That was dumb, girlie. D-U-M-M. Did you know he did this?"

Rachel wanted to scream. Moreover, she wanted Robert right here so that she could rip his face open. The stupid, greedy, little shit! After all her precautions, all her cross-checking, data entering, and background research, he'd sneaked through a penny-ante hospitalization claim, then hid it from her. He'd blown a million and a half for a lousy 10,000-dollar claim. She should have known he'd pull something like this.

She thought fast. She had two options, neither good: either convince this guy that she was an innocent pawn—that Peter apparently faked his death without her knowledge—or run, contact Robert and warn him, tell him to get down to Mom's in Tampa. It was their emergency plan for this sort of eventuality.

But first, she'd have to get out of the restaurant. She appraised her chances of getting past Roth. He appeared to be alone, and since he wasn't arresting her, maybe she had a chance. She covered her eyes with her hand, took in the silverware on the table, her hot tea, his hot coffee, anything to throw at him. She might make it to the door, but then what? She looked out at the traffic on Third Avenue. It was flowing north, a lot of taxis cruising past. But unless she managed to hurt him, and hurt him bad, he'd grab her outside in a flash. Maybe if she jabbed her fork in his eye.

As if reading her mind, Roth scooped up her knife and fork. "You won't be needing these."

She still had her fingernails. A lightening-fast jab to his eyes to blind him momentarily, long enough for her to flee, get to the street. But someone just might be waiting outside. And if her attack wasn't successful, they'd surely arrest her right here.

No, the smart thing was to talk her way out of this.

"I—I can't believe this," she stammered. "This means—he's—he's not dead!" She looked up innocently, and found a tear. "What can I do? What should I do?"

"If it's advice you're asking for, I'd say, 'Save your money and take care of your teeth.' Is that the kind of advice you're looking for?"

"Please, Mr. Roth. Be serious." She stuck to her role, managed another tear and a sniffle.

Roth chuckled. He shoveled home fries in his mouth, chewed noisily. "Well, gosh, golly, and gee-whiz. All this time you thought Peter MacMillan was dead, and now you learn he's not. I believe it," he said, wide-eyed. "After all, you're the only beneficiary."

"You investigated this claim?"

His eyebrows went up in answer.

"I haven't collected anything yet." *Big mistake.*

Roth shook his head slowly and put down his fork. "There you go again, beauty," he said, sadly. "Just can't keep from lying. One of these days I'm gonna teach you a very hard lesson about lying to me." He picked up his fork and concentrated on his breakfast. A few moments later, he said, "You received two hundred grand from American Travelers. I represent Amalgamated Life and Chase-Hampshire." He paused. "Also, I represent my very own insurance company: Transylvania Life. It's my very own pension fund. I even have a motto." In a thick Eastern European accent, he said: "Et goes like zis: 'I vant to suck your blood.'"

His jocularity confused her. This was a serious matter, yet he bantered on like they were old friends chatting over breakfast. She'd dealt with a dozen adjusters. Some could have been turned, on the take, had the circumstances been right. But none acted like this lunatic. Still, he was on the take, all right.

"Okay, beauty, this is what happens now. I can help you, but you gotta tell me why I should." He rubbed his thumb against his first two fingers.

"How much?" she asked, a whisper.

Roth put his fork down, removed a pen from his coat, pulled a napkin from the dispenser, and wrote, "*500,000 dollars,*" turned it to where she could read it.

"You're crazy! I don't have that kind of money."

"But you will have that kind of money. You'll collect a million and a half. We're partners. Me, you, and Mr. MacMillan from Budapest." He chuckled, shoveled in more home fries.

Rachel started to speak, but he held up his hand as Ethel came over with a refill for his coffee. She tried again as Ethel left, but once more Roth held up his hand. He continued eating in silence, his eyes roaming over Rachel. She looked out the window, ignored his inspection, wishing that Robert was here in the hot seat, since he created this mess. But he wouldn't know any better how to handle him. She'd better learn what Roth knew, which seemed to be everything.

Roth finished his meal, called for another coffee, and when it came, he lit up a cigarette, inhaled luxuriously, stretched his arms over the back of the booth. He picked up his pen, put it inside his jacket.

"You're *really* a good-looking piece." His eyes poured over her again and he screwed up his face, reflecting. "You remind me of someone. No—not someone—something." He snapped his fingers, his eyes resting on her breasts. "I got it. The front bumper of a '57 Cadillac. Yes, ma'am. A good lookin' piece."

Rachel ignored him.

"Say 'thank you,'" he said, smile fading.

"Thank you. You're very kind," she said facetiously.

"I am, you know. In fact, you're gonna like me." Roth took another drag from his cigarette, dropped the butt into his coffee cup, stood up. "Let's go."

Nervously, she asked, "Where are we going?"

"I'll drop you at your place."

"I can walk."

"Let's go, I said."

Rachel scooted out of the booth and put on her fur. She started to walk in front of Roth. He pulled her back by her collar. "Let's get the order of things straight, right off, beauty." He handed her the check. She made a face, dug into her purse, pulled out some bills, and threw them on the table.

Roth winked at Ethel as they left, and outside he hailed a taxi, directed the driver to Fifth Avenue. He sat close to Rachel, put his hand on her thigh. "Tomorrow morning. There's a diner on Little Neck Parkway and Northern Boulevard, in Queens. Ten o'clock. Bring 66,000 cash. That's my third of what American Travelers has shelled out already. And bring Peter. I know he's away, but get him back here."

"I don't have that kind of money."

"Yeah, beauty. You do. Take it out of your account in LA. If I don't get mine, you won't see the rest of the money. Tomorrow, I'll tell you the next step." He handed her another business card, this one with his apartment phone number written on the back.

On Fifth Avenue he told the taxi driver to pull up in front of Rachel's apartment building. She tried to look indifferent, wondering how he knew where she really lived. Roth reached over her and opened the door.

"You're home, Mrs. Warner," he said, squeezing her thigh, nodding to the entrance of the building. He smiled. "Of course, it's not Mrs. Warner, but that doesn't matter right now. Let's keep it as Beauty. Will it be all right if I call you that? Beauty?"

It was unnerving that Roth was this close to them, knowing where they lived, knowing the Warner alias. She started to step out of the taxi, unable to imagine all he possibly knew.

"Oh, one more thing," Roth said. "Your first reaction will be to bolt, skip out on me. You were thinking about that in the restaurant. But don't even try, because you've got something that's mine." He smiled at her. "Plus, I'll think you don't like me. And that'll *really* crush me." He put on a hurt face, then leaned across to the door on her side, brushing his hand against her breasts. She saw the revolver in his pocket.

"Get out," he said. A cruel expression replacing his smile.

She got out, stood on the sidewalk, and watched as the taxi pulled away. Roth didn't look back.

27

"You stupid, greedy little shit," Rachel screamed into the phone.

On the other end, Robert winced, held the receiver from his ear.

"A lousy hospitalization claim! A few thousand measly bucks and you jeopardize a million and a half. What are we gonna do now, shit-for-brains? Huh? Huh?"

Robert's instinct was to run, clear out the apartment, have her slip out of New York, and they'd meet down at Mom's. Thanks to American Travelers, they were 200,000 dollars ahead on this scam. "Get out, Rachel. Just burn everything, trash everything, download your laptop, and mail the disks to Mom. Take the first plane out, doesn't matter where. No! On second thoughts, don't fly. Take a train. It'll be easier to get lost at Grand Central Station, and you won't be trapped in the sky."

"He called me Mrs. Warner, stupid. And he knows that's not my real name. I think he knows everything. I don't know how he found out, but he's been asking around about you, too. Showed your photograph to the doorman. He's probably watching me, waiting for me to run."

"Can we trust him?"

"How the hell do I know?" she screamed, almost hysterically.

A man walking his dog past the telephone booth stopped, looked at her. She made a face at him and he walked on. "Oh, Christ," she said, slapping her forehead.

"What?" Robert asked. "What is it?"

"Nothing. Nothing," she replied. For all she knew, the man walking the dog might be Roth's agent. She'd better think hard and fast from here on out. Roth was dangerous and too goddamn quick for her, and apparently wasn't even worried that she'd skip out.

"You must have a feel for it," Robert said. "How greedy is he?"

She'd been thinking about that. *Real greedy. And scary.* She remembered his eyes pouring over her, and his compliments. *And he's hungry for me.* Why hadn't she thought of that before? Probably because he scared the bejesus out of her this morning. He was a loose cannon, liable to do anything, and everything was a joke to him. Why not? He was in the driver's seat and feeling pretty smug with himself. But could she get control of him?

"Just get back here," she said, calming down.

"Maybe he wants to grab both of us."

"No," she said. "He's had a chance to do that already."

Robert was at a payphone outside his motel in Nashville. Rachel had telephoned his room, left the time to call and the number at a pay phone on the corner of East 70th Street and Madison Avenue.

"So he gets a third," he said. "That still leaves a million for us."

"Just get back here. Tonight," Rachel commanded. "Stay at the Hilton, near LaGuardia Airport. I'll pick you up in the morning." She left him with a parting sentiment—"You stupid shit"—and slammed the receiver down. She placed an *"Out Of Order"* sticker across the coin slot. This was going to be *her* telephone for the foreseeable future.

Robert crossed the road to his motel, Rachel's bitter words ringing in his head. *You need your mouth washed out with soap, bitch. That, and a good fucking.*

28

It was dark when the taxi dropped Roth in front of his apartment building. After the meeting at the coffee shop, he'd spent the afternoon at a storage facility in Long Island City, digging through personal effects he wanted shipped to Bangkok.

On the opposite side of the street, Roth spotted a dark sedan with two men sitting in it. Black-wall tires and an antenna on the trunk. Unmarked police car.

The light was flashing on his answering machine. There was a message from Nina, and a call from Lori MacMillan. The message from Lori MacMillan, aka Julia Warner, aka Whoever, was brief. She simply said, "Call me," but didn't leave her number. This was either to determine if he had the Fifth Avenue apartment phone number, or maybe she didn't want to say anything on the phone that might be incriminating. If he didn't have the number, that would tell her that the line wasn't tapped.

Roth went to the refrigerator, liberated a can of Budweiser, the only thing in there aside from condiments. He popped the top and gulped it, went to the front window, pushed back the curtain an inch. The unmarked police car was pulling away.

He went into the office and sat down, dialed the number for Lori MacMillan. She picked up on the first ring.

"Whaddya want?" he demanded.

"About tomorrow." Her voice was low, sultry.

"You're not gonna do something dumb like disappoint me, are you?"

"No. Well, yes and no."

"I like the 'no' part. What's the 'yes' part?"

"I can't raise it all that fast," she said. "I transferred some money into another account the other day. I would have told you if you'd given me a chance."

Roth guessed much of their booty was laundered, tied up in stocks, out-of-state banks, sheltered under other names and tax ID numbers, leaving only a small portion liquid.

"Well now, beauty. I wouldn't want you to get hit with an interest penalty," he said. "How much?"

"I pulled out 26,000 this afternoon. It's all I could free up."

"It's a start. Anything else?"

"Yes. Peter. He's away."

"I told you to get him back here."

"Yes. But I'm not sure if he can get here that fast."

"Bullshit. You've already spoken with him." The line was quiet. He wanted to give the impression he knew her every move.

"Yes," she said. "Yes, I did. But—"

"But nothing. I wanna see him."

"Can't *we* just handle this?"

"Do like I tell you."

She changed the subject. "What is the money buying? I need to know."

"Subtract a third of everything. That's what you're buying."

"Is that a guarantee?"

"Nothing in life is guaranteed, beauty. You know that. But if you don't get yours, I can't get mine. Now can I?"

"I suppose," she said.

"Anything else?"

"You're an interesting man. Are you going to tell me how you figured it out?"

"Maybe someday."

"I'd like to hear it." Her words were soft and Roth could hear her punctuated breathing. "You're very sure of yourself. Aren't you?" Before he could answer, she continued: "Determined. Very capable. Tough, too. How did you get to be like that?"

"Dancing with people like you."

"Like I said, you're interesting."

Roth smiled into the receiver. Beauty was cranking out the syrup. "I told you, you'll like me once you get to know me."

"Maybe," she said.

"Definitely," he replied. "Anything else?"

Silence. Clearly, she didn't want to hang up. And she hadn't steered away from incriminating herself on the phone. "No. I guess not," she said. "Not now."

Neither spoke for long moments, each wondering what the other was thinking.

"Ten o'clock, sharp," he said, and hung up. He wondered if she'd been recording the conversation. But, if so, why? She would only be incriminating herself as well as him.

He called Nina and they talked for an hour. When he hung up, he showered and went up to the diner where he'd meet Lori and Peter MacMillan in the morning. He ate a hamburger, then went across to Patrick's for a few drinks.

29

Roth entered the diner at 10:00 a.m., carrying a paper sack. He stopped at the cashier's counter, bought a copy of the *Daily News,* whose headline screamed at the reader in two-inch-high letters. The mayor was declaring war on street crime. Of course. City elections were next week.

Rachel was seated at the busy counter near the entrance. He motioned for her to follow him into the back section where there were booths. The area was nearly deserted, the breakfast crowd having gone off to work. He selected a booth next to a large plate-glass window, slid in, waved Rachel down opposite him.

A young man with a familiar face sat a few tables away, his profile buried in a copy of the *New York Times.* Roth said to Rachel, loud enough for him to hear, "Tell Mr. MacMillan, or whatever his name is today, to come over here and join us."

From the corner of his eye, he saw him flinch. Impatient, Roth raised his voice: "Hey! We gonna tango, or what?" He chuckled. "You read *The Times* in Queens, son, people are gonna think you're queer. It's worse in Brooklyn; they throw bricks at you."

Robert folded his newspaper, stood up and walked to the booth in front of Roth's and sat down, his back to them.

"Fucking shy, aren't you, fella?"

Robert didn't answer.

"So be shy, already. Just listen up and do like you're told."

The waitress came into the back section with a carafe of coffee. She saw Robert's abandoned cup on the table, carried it over to his booth, asked if he wanted a refill.

Roth ordered a full breakfast of bacon and eggs, same as the previous morning in The El. Rachel ordered a coffee.

When the waitress left, Roth held out his hand to Rachel. "Let's have it."

"Here?" Rachel whispered. "You want the money here?"

"No. Give it to me in the fucking office of Amalgamated Life Insurance Company. Where do you think? Yeah, here." He looked around, wide-eyed. "What's wrong with here?"

Rachel's eyes slid sideways and she nodded over her shoulder, indicating Robert. "He wants to know what we get for it."

Roth sighed. "We went over that yesterday. Cut the stalling."

Rachel dug into her purse, pulled out an envelope, a thick rubber band around it. She looked around, then slid it across the table.

Outside, a dark-blue van with tinted windows sat at the curb on the opposite side of the street. Inside, a man and a woman worked away with cameras. The man used a video camera and the woman took 35-mm stills, her camera's motor drive humming, clicking off shots. They'd be clear pictures. No reflection off the glass, no haze. Just good clean shots of Roth and the MacMillans inside the restaurant.

"Shoot the envelope," the man said, concentrating on his view in the video cam. "Zoom in on the envelope."

"I got it. I got it. Beautiful," she said, snapping away. She ran off twenty shots in quick succession. "Yeah, it was fast, but not fast enough, folks," she added, concentrating. "I got the transfer real good."

"She moved fast," the man said, zooming in on Rachel's face.

"Not fast enough," his colleague repeated triumphantly. "Not fast enough."

"Quick, he's holding it up. Shoot the envelope."

Roth felt the envelope, hefted it. "When will you have the rest?"

"In a week," Rachel answered. She looked around the diner, but no one was paying them the slightest attention.

Roth tucked the envelope in his jacket pocket and pulled a Polaroid camera from the paper bag. "I'm going into the men's room to count this, and while I'm gone, you beauty, will scoot over into Peter's booth and snap a couple of shots of him holding this up to his chest." Roth unfolded the copy of the *Daily News*, whose lead story was accompanied by a photograph of the police hauling a suspect into the Midtown North precinct station.

Robert spun around in the next booth. "Is this guy nuts, Rachel? I'm supposed to be dead."

She flinched. It had gone completely over Robert's head. He'd called her Rachel. Maybe Roth missed it. She shot him a glance. No. He hadn't missed it.

Roth slid out of the booth, reached across and smacked Robert hard on the side of the head with the newspaper. Robert jerked back, shocked, uncertain what to do. "Do like I tell you, or you *will* be dead."

"Why do you want his photograph?" Rachel asked.

"Let's just call it a matter of trust, shall we."

"You want me to take his photo here?"

"Yes, here. Right here, beauty. Look around. Do you think anybody gives a fuck what you're doing?" Roth headed for the toilet. In the men's room, he entered a stall, bolted the door, and counted the money. The bills were all hundreds; 260 in all—26,000 dollars. He snapped the rubber band around the envelope and dropped it back into his jacket pocket. It made a bulge over his left breast.

Returning to the table, Rachel had finished taking Robert's photo. Robert had turned away, his back to them, again faking interest in the *New York Times*. Roth's breakfast came, and when he sat down, Rachel pushed two developed Polaroids in front of him. A third negative was beginning to take form. He ate his breakfast silently, studying the pictures.

Rachel suddenly grew impatient. "What now?"

"Now I finish my breakfast." Roth poured ketchup over his home fries.

She reached for her coat.

"I'll tell you when to go," he said, stabbing the fries on his plate. "First, I wanna know a few things. Hey, butt-fuck," he said to Robert. "Turn around so I can see your face."

Robert moved against the glass and leaned back, turning sideways, but didn't look at Roth.

"All right," Roth said. "Next week, beauty, you bring me 40,000 more. My place in Bangkok." He wrote out his address on a paper napkin, pushed it across the table. "Got it?"

"We want to know *how* you're going to help us," Robert asked obliquely.

"First, I ask the questions, then I'll tell you what I'm gonna do to be sure you collect on the outstanding claims."

"How soon will the claims pay?" she asked.

Roth grabbed her wrist. "Are you fuckin' deaf? I've heard of dumb blondes, but not deaf ones. I said I ask the questions." He released her hand. "You, beauty, will bring me the cash next week in Bangkok." He pointed his fork at her. "That'll take care of my cut on the American Traveler's policy—"

"I have other plans for next week," she cut him off.

He looked at her in total disbelief, shaking his head. "You're incredible," he boomed. "This isn't a debating society. This isn't a fucking democracy," he continued, his voice rising. He slammed his fist on the table. "Last time, idiots. You do as I say, exactly as I say, exactly when I say it. If I say shit, you, beauty, will ask how much and what color, and then you, butt-fuck, will come sliding in on a shovel. Are you idiots clear on this?" He pointed with his fork toward the customers sitting at the counter who were looking back at them. "Even those fuckin' people over there understand that by now."

Rachel sat frozen. Roth had gone ballistic over a simple contradiction. But she was testing him. Maybe he knew it. Maybe that's what threw him into the tirade.

Roth threw out his hands and started working them like an orchestra conductor, his voice lower, softer, more soothing: "This is simple. Easy. Truly, a no-brainer. You do as I say. When I say it. End of story."

He settled back in his seat and held their eyes. Both looked away. He resumed eating, bit into a piece of wheat toast, washed it down with coffee. "Now, I wanna know if there are any more policies out there on Peter MacMillan?"

"N—no," Rachel stammered. "Just the three."

"If I find out there are more that you're not telling me about, I'm gonna be real pissed. Because, you see, if there are more policies, then there could be someone else out there investigating this thing. Somebody I don't know about. Somebody who can fuck me up. Get it?"

Rachel shook her head. "Only the three policies."

Roth nodded. "I ain't going to jail for no half million." He looked at Robert. "Are there any more hospitalization policies on Peter MacMillan?"

Robert shook his head.

Roth looked at Rachel and said, "Now we know that butt-fuck here doesn't tell us about all of his adventures, don't we?" He was sure that the hospitalization policy was unknown to Rachel before yesterday. Her face when she read the document that first time told him. She was the smart one here. She wouldn't have screwed things up with a piddling claim like that.

Her face confirmed this. She glanced back scowling at Robert. Roth chuckled to himself. There'd been some nasty words over that little screw-up, and Rachel's attitude squared with his. She was siding with him on that point.

"Now, of course, you two are thinking that if there were more policies on MacMillan's death, I'd want a third. And you'd be right. Because I'm risking my ass. If I report one thing and somebody else says differently, then people might start comparing notes. I could look stupid. Worse, people would know I'm on the take. More questions will follow, payment will get stalled, then denied, and the case gets reinvestigated. Got it?"

Neither Rachel nor Robert spoke. Rachel kept her eyes on Roth. He was starting to get angry, something that happened when people didn't agree with him. All of a sudden, he balled his fist and crashed it down on the table. His plate jumped and his silverware rattled, some bouncing off the table. Rachel jumped almost as high as the plate as people at the counter looked round into their section.

"If you people think you're gonna screw me, you're crazy," Roth yelled, his voice carrying across the restaurant. "I've been in this goddamn business twenty years and nobody's gotten away with screwing me yet." His face was beet red, his voice jerky. He stared straight at them. Rachel studied her lap, Robert buried his face in the *Times*.

The waitress was coming over and the manager at the cash register stood in front of the counter, arms akimbo, waiting to see if he was needed.

Roth lowered his voice. "I'll take your heads off if you try to screw me. I told you, I ain't going to jail for no nickel and dime scam. If I learn there's more hospitalization policies out there, you're dead meat."

"There are no more life policies," Rachel whispered desperately. "For God's sake, Robert," she urged, her head down. "Tell us, are there more hospitalization claims out there?"

"No. No others."

Rachel swore under her breath. *She'd* messed up this time, calling him Robert. Not Peter, not Jordan. It was clearly spontaneous with Roth rattling them so.

Roth swore. "You're brilliant, you know that, butt-fuck? A dead man submitting a hospitalization claim!"

In the van outside, the cameras were working overtime. The woman was on her third roll of film. She said matter-of-factly, "I think Roth's crazy."

"They must be arguing about something," her colleague observed. "Damn! I wish I could hear what they're saying."

In the restaurant, the waitress stopped a safe distance away. "Everything okay here, folks?"

"A little misunderstanding, sugar. Sorry about the disturbance. Caught my girl here naked with this guy. Thought they were screwing. But it turns out he just likes wearing her clothes. Panties, especially. Gimme a refill, will you?" He turned to Rachel. "Anything more for you?" Then, to Robert, "How about you, sweet lips?"

The waitress filled Roth's cup, studied the trio briefly, moved off. Had she not recognized Roth from the other times he came in for a late breakfast, she might have called the police. But a few patrolmen would start drifting in around this time anyhow.

The third Polaroid was clear now. All three photos showed Robert in the booth holding the *Daily News* up to his chest. He was clearly recognizable if the snaps were compared with MacMillan's passport.

"Okay, here's the agenda." He pointed to Rachel. "I see you in Bangkok next week with the additional 40,000. Then I wait. Three, four weeks, during which I delay my report. You, beauty, will make polite yet firm requests for payment from both companies. You don't get nasty. You don't get pushy. You don't make threats. Got it?"

She nodded.

"I will then provide you with the name of an attorney. You go straight to him and hire him. He'll write a strong demand letter. He won't know anything other than what you tell him. You got all that?"

Rachel nodded again.

Roth continued: "The companies will pressure me for a report, but I'll still drag my feet, say that I've got some good dope on the case which will contest the claims, and that I'll finalize it in a week at most. But I won't. It'll be a few more weeks. By that time, it'll be too late for them to reassign the case to another investigator. Just to be sure, I'll muddy the water so a new investigator couldn't find his own reflection.

"The attorney will then give very short notice that he's filing a lawsuit. He'll stipulate punitive damages. That always gets their attention. Then, I turn in my report at the eleventh hour, which says the case is clean. The companies won't like it, but they'll reach for their checkbooks fast, because the clock has run down and they can't do anything else."

"Won't the attorney want a cut?" Robert asked.

"Pay attention, dummy. I said that beauty will hire him. He won't be in on it. He just gets paid for his time. A grand or two should cover it. If there's no litigation, he gets no percentage."

"Why do you want these photos?" Robert asked. "You could quite easily screw us over after Rachel gets the money and you get your cut."

"On the contrary. These little mementos are to ensure that you darlings don't screw me. If you do, I drop the photos in the mail."

"You'll hang yourself."

"Why? Who says a little birdie didn't drop 'em in the mail? I'll just say I know nothing. I'll look dumb, but so what? These companies won't use me again anyhow after I finish screwing them around with all the delays, then come up with nothing. They'll even suspect me, but what can they do?"

"You could drop the photos in the mail after you get your split," Robert objected.

Roth smirked, looked at Rachel, pointed to Robert. "Is there inbreeding in his family? Think about it, butt-fuck. Why would I stir up shit once I get my cut?"

Robert and Rachel studied each other, then Robert looked away. They liked the deal. But Roth wasn't getting 500,000. No. It would only cost them a one-time 66,000 payout for his third of the American Travelers payment. Once Rachel got the other two checks, they'd skip out. Let Roth drop the photos in the mail. He'd end up looking stupid and no one knew their real identity. Sure, Roth would kill them—if he ever found them. That is, if they didn't kill him first.

"That's it, then?" Rachel asked.

"Not quite. First, Robert drops the claim for the hospitalization policy. Got it?"

Robert nodded.

"Just walk away from it. Even if you're contacted, don't respond. You're getting your mail at Marcia Post's apartment, right?"

He nodded again, avoiding Rachel's eyes.

"So, keep checking the mail. If anything comes from the companies, just toss it out. Second, I wanna know everything. I know most of it, but I gotta know all of it. I gotta cover my ass and account for anything that the companies might know that I don't know they know. Understand?"

The waitress brought Roth more coffee and cleared away his other dishes. She worked slowly.

"Why don't you just pull up a chair," Roth quipped. She made a face and moved away.

A police car pulled up at the curb outside. Two officers got out. Rachel stiffened, but Robert didn't see them since his back was to the window. The cops walked up the flagstone steps, came in, took stools at the counter.

"Okay," Roth continued. "Next item, a little show and tell, and you people better be convincing."

Robert saw the officers then. He watched the waitress who went up to the cops.

Roth looked over, saw the cops taking a seat. "Hey, dummy," he said to Robert. "Don't worry about the buttons. The new patrol cars have global donut positioning systems, that's all. You need to worry about me. Listen up."

He looked nervously back at Roth.

"Now, you guys *think* you're gonna try to bullshit your way through this, then once beauty collects the money, you *think* you're just gonna skip out because you *think* I can't find you. So let me straighten you out.

"I know a lot more than you can imagine, and the first lie gets you, beauty, a shot to the head." Roth balled his fist again. "Right here. Right now. Believe me, beauty, I'll hit you so fucking hard, those cops over there will ticket your pretty head for speeding across Northern Boulevard."

She knew he'd do it. Robert wouldn't do anything about it. He couldn't.

"You." He pointed to Robert. "Go to the toilet. Pull your pud while I ask beauty some questions. When you come back, your answers better match hers."

Robert hesitated. They hadn't planned on this, or they'd have rehearsed some bullshit story. This way, Roth would get their real names, their background, everything. If he didn't already have this information. So, if Rachel used an alias, there was no way he'd know which one because he'd be in the toilet waiting for his turn to be questioned. That was a problem with these scams: too many aliases, too many backdrops, too many claims. He couldn't begin to guess which story she'd use. And if their stories didn't jive, there'd be big trouble. Right here, right now, like Roth said, and the whole game would be over. They would kiss a lot of money goodbye just on what happened now. Roth would go berserk if he tripped them up, caught them trying to bullshit him after his warnings. Maybe he'd tear the diner apart, go for their throats. Maybe he'd call the cops over, press charges on the spot. He had enough evidence. Robert's photograph on the MacMillan passport and a copy of the Form 180 was all he needed to bring this whole thing crashing down right now.

"Get in there," Roth thumbed towards the bathrooms.

Robert scooted out of his booth, walked sullenly to the rear of the restaurant. He looked back at Rachel.

She shrugged. Roth had outsmarted them, and she wasn't surprised.

And somehow, she wasn't even disappointed.

Roth watched Robert go into the toilet, turned back to her, his smile evil. He chuckled. "There's no way in the world he can guess what you're gonna tell me. Rehearsal or not. Because you haven't the faintest idea what I'm gonna ask. Maybe I'm gonna ask you things I already know. Or, maybe I don't know the answers. You're not gonna know which. Now, beauty, we start with your *real* name." He balled up his right fist again, leaned forward, and took hold of her jacket lapel. He pulled her face within inches of his, worked his shoulders, loosening up, and whispered lightly, "You know what's gonna happen to your lovely face if you lie to me, don't you? It'll break my heart to smear that beautiful nose across your face, but I guarantee that it'll hurt you a lot more than me."

———

Twenty minutes later, Roth finished grilling Rachel and Robert. They left their booths, Roth stuffing the restaurant check in Robert's shirt pocket. Robert took it out and handed it to Rachel without bothering to check the amount. It was clear to Roth who handled the money; explained why Robert had resorted to the petty hospitalization scam.

As they walked down the steps at the side exit of the restaurant, the cameras in the van sprang to life.

No sooner had the trio left the diner, a man having coffee at the counter quickly jumped up and hustled towards the back section where they'd been sitting. He moved so fast that the cops looked up in surprise and turned to watch him. He snapped a rubber glove on his right hand, popped open a plastic bag, and reached the booths just ahead of the waitress. To her surprise, he lifted glasses, coffee cups, and silverware, slipping them into the bag and sealing it. He walked over to the cashier's counter, threw down a 100-dollar bill, and left the restaurant. The cops sitting at the counter looked at the manager behind the register for his reaction. He returned their look, a question on his face, but held up the note, shrugged. The cops looked at each other, went back to their breakfast.

Outside, the man watched Roth and the Tierneys walking into the parking lot behind the restaurant. He walked across the street to the van and got in.

The Tierneys got into their car, a late model Audi, and Roth walked north on Little Neck Parkway. He was filmed walking off, and when the Audi pulled out of the parking lot a moment later, it too, was filmed and the license plate recorded.

――――

Back in their apartment on Fifth Avenue, Robert seemed indifferent about the meeting. He didn't talk about it, didn't say a thing about Roth, didn't ask what Rachel had told him before it was her turn to visit the ladies room. They knew that he'd gotten the best of them, and Robert seemed resigned to splitting the booty.

Rachel watched from the bar and shook her head as he sat in front of the television, watching the ticker-tape, listening to his stereo with the headset on, leafing through magazines all at once, tuned out to the world.

"You're really quite a stupid fellow, aren't you, Robert?" she said matter-of-factly. "But why am I being so smug? That sonofabitch snagged me, too." She shook her head, clapped for Barbie who came running, and took her in for a bubble bath. Barbie liked baths. She also used a cat's litter box, being more feline than canine. Rachel hated walking her, and it was the one thing Robert absolutely refused to do.

――――

"Christ, chief, where ya been?" Nina inquired over the phone. It was Thursday night.

"Been busy."

"When are you heading out?"

"Tomorrow afternoon. On those new cases."

"How'd it go with Mrs. MacMillan?"

"You'll get my report. I got things to clean up in the office tomorrow, then I'm outta here. Flight's at 4:00 p.m."

30 Manila

"Yesssss," Towers hissed, smiling. "I'm outta here."
Two long years in purgatory in the bag, logged in the State Department's history books.

John Warbell returned the smile, handing him the transfer orders. "Washington. Effective January 3rd," he said. "You've got another week's leave still on the books; should put you home for Christmas."

Towers studied his transfer papers. He'd be stationed in D.C. for a year. Training interns. Not bad. Not bad at all. He wondered if Warbell just wanted him out of Manila. Maybe so; John and Millie had something going now. Maybe nothing serious yet, but he saw the signs, saw what was coming. Well, that was fine with him. Why not? She got on better with John than she ever did with him anyhow. Was there anything else behind the transfer? Rumors about the MacMillan matter were flying around the embassy. Was something up that he didn't know about? Was something behind his transfer? For the past two weeks, he hadn't been invited to play bridge at the ambassador's residence. Didn't matter. Just as long as nothing went into his record, and apparently it wouldn't or he'd have been notified.

"You're cut from the Manila roster effective December 12th. Your replacement arrives December One. Snap her in for us in Citizens Services, will you?"

"Sure, John. Who are you moving into Visas?"

"Millie."

"That's great. She deserves it."

"The ambassador thinks so. And I agree."

You would.

John swiveled his chair around to look out the window. He made a tent with his fingers, crossed his knees. "Bill. I've been thinking a lot about Millie these days."

"Do tell."

John did. "I mean, a *lot* of thinking."

So when's the wedding already? "She's a fine person," Towers said without feeling. "Well, I gotta get back to the section. If there's nothing else, John?"

"Just wanted you to know, Bill."

"Sure."

Towers left Warbell's office. He was finished with the Philippines. Finished with this wretched heat, the lonely nights, the eternal waiting for his life to take on meaning. Back to the land of the Big PX. No more working in air-conditioned glass-encased cubicles, or living in what amounted to dormitory apartments, riding around in buttoned-up autos against the pollution, the potential terrorists. No more bottled water, diarrhea, commissary supplies, or wretched bimbos invading the embassy, looking for a visa out of here. What was it that bastard Roth said about returning to the States? Back to the land of big tits and solid shits. Aptly put, considering the source. Yeah, back to a chance at pursuing a real life. Good ol' American women. God bless 'em. And Washington was loaded with women. Maybe somewhere, the future Mrs. Towers was waiting for him. But first, maybe Lori. He had to know.

31 Bangkok

Bangkok was sweltering at ninety degrees when Roth's flight landed from Hong Kong at 3:00 p.m. In the taxi heading into the city, he thought about Rachel, as he had all week. She had a way of invading his thoughts. Evil was like that, carried its unique brand of fascination, an irresistible allure. She'd arrive tonight with his money. He'd need to hold her here in Bangkok for at least the weekend, instead of her turning around for New York. He needed a few details filled in.

He dropped his bag at his apartment, then checked his mail. Gunnery Sergeant Austin from the US Embassy had mailed him two tickets for the Marine Corps Ball, scheduled for the 10th. He'd stop in at least, since the gunny went to the trouble, remembering him from last year. He checked to make sure his tux was ready. He found it in the back of his closet, hung in the dry-cleaning plastic cover, then tucked it into a suit carrier.

There was an e-mail from Nina concerning one of the cases he'd worked in China. There was also a fax from Rachel. She'd sent it from New York before leaving, asking him to book a hotel room for her in Bangkok. That was about 16 hours ago, so by this time she was in the air and would arrive around midnight. He checked her airline schedule, booked a room for her at the Hilton, then busied himself with reports.

He switched off his laptop at ten o'clock; showered; shaved; and dressed in lightweight slacks, loafers, and a Hawaiian print shirt. He took a taxi to Bourbon Street, a popular Cajun restaurant in Washington Square, off Soi 22. He ate a blackened redfish, washed it down with Mekhong and Cokes, had a dessert of Cointreau and coffee. At 11:30, he made his way to Don Muang Airport.

In the Arrivals hall, he rested his elbows on the railing that cordoned-off visitors from passengers. Several hundred people waited for arriving planes, a dozen drivers held up placards.

For some reason, the Yu case came to mind, all the little details that had given Yu away, the tiny clues he had followed to locate Yu alive and well at his brother's restaurant. A sobering thought. Were all *his* bases covered with this MacMillan business? Had *he* made any mistakes? What little details had *he* overlooked? None that he could think of. But didn't most scammers think that? Over-confidence was like the kiss of death in the confidence game.

He checked the arrivals board. Her flight from New York via Narita had landed twenty minutes early. Shortly after, he saw Rachel pushing a cart loaded with luggage. Apparently she had no plans for a quick turnaround. Either that or she was traveling beyond Bangkok. He went upstairs to the airline offices which were getting ready to close. He asked if the manifest from the Narita flight was in, and a clerk pointed to a stack of papers on a nearby desk. It was on top.

Roth ran his finger through it and found Rachel's name under "Warner, Julia," her latest bogus persona, and not her real name, Rachel Tierney. She had flown business class, occupying seat 7A. In 7B had been a Chinese gentleman. Probably no connection, but Roth noted the name anyhow. He scanned the entire manifest, noted no other names of interest. But if the Tierneys were sending some-one to hit him, he could be on any flight.

Rachel was apparently traveling alone. She'd checked in three pieces of luggage, and carried another on board, for a total weight of 66 kilograms.

This little piece of sleuthing would have taken weeks if not months in the States, using authorizations or subpoenas. Thais didn't bother with such crap.

He went downstairs and walked outside, watched Rachel for a while from a distance. She was definitely alone. No one approached her or seemed to be moving in concert with her. A lot of eyes were on her as usual. Men studied her legs as though committing them to memory, like maybe they'd be tested later.

Roth eyed a few limousines at the curb opposite the line of taxis. They were empty. She was patiently waiting for him. He lit a cigarette, sauntered up behind her. "Hey, lady. Wanna fuck?"

Startled, Rachel spun around. "Oh! Hello," she said, unfazed by anything he might say.

"Have a nice trip?"

"I'm beat."

To Roth, she looked fresh. And smelled marvelous. "Couldn't sleep on the plane?"

"Off and on, but not really."

"Push your cart over there. Into the taxi queue."

"You don't have a car?" Rachel asked, disappointed.

"Never use 'em in Bangkok. Traffic's terrible and taxis are plentiful and cheap."

"You could have a driver."

"Didn't want to bother."

"I'm a bother?"

"You're a fuckin' headache. That and a Jewish mother. Just get in line."

She received his insults gracefully, smiled at him, wheeled her cart into line. She'd have her moment. And probably soon.

Roth stood close to her, looking her up and down. She ignored his inspection, knew what he was thinking. What he'd been thinking about since New York.

Traffic was still heavy going into town. Roth's hand rested on Rachel's thigh, a move she hadn't objected to after the obligatory raised eyebrow.

"A lot of luggage. Planning to stay for a while? Like ten or twenty years?"

"I read about a spa down in a place called Hua Hin. Thought I'd spend a few days there. . . . If that's all right with you," she added facetiously.

"I'll let you know."

She dabbed her forehead with a handkerchief. It was warm in the taxi, even with the air-conditioner turned on high. "Where have you booked me?"

"The Hilton."

Rachel was surprised, expecting that he'd suggest she stay at his place. But he'd taken away her thunder; she couldn't deliver a 'thanks, but no thanks.' She looked out the window at the cars they were passing, disappointed that she could never gauge his next remark, his next action.

At the hotel, Roth told the driver to wait while a bellboy stacked her luggage on a cart. "You're on my tab," he said. He got back in the cab. "Don't forget my present."

"Want it now? It's right here." She glanced around surreptitiously and ran a finger across her purse hanging from her shoulder.

Roth studied her face. It was like she didn't seem to mind giving up the money, like she was handing it over gladly.

"In the morning is soon enough." He began rolling up the window. "Bring a swimsuit."

She smiled after him as the taxi headed for the exit. Yeah, she was getting to him, and he was making efforts to hide it.

———

As Roth stepped into his apartment, the phone rang and the fax signal came on. He made himself a drink as the first papers snailed out of the machine, until eventually there was a stack of documents lying in the paper tray. Financial reports on Robert and Rachel Tierney. Nina's sources in New York could pull up any credit profile, locate any bank account, track all credit-card activity, even alter credit-card records.

He'd read them in the morning before Rachel arrived.

He donned trunks, opened the terrace door leading to the pool. He briefly thought of calling in a girl. But somehow, a hooker would be a disappointment after seeing Rachel again. That bitch could seduce a dead pope.

32

Rachel stood in the shallow end her eyes closed, face tilted back for the morning sun to caress her. Roth might be right, she thought; if one spent her days in a swimming pool under a sun like this, life in the tropics was good. She supposed there were some benefits to having seasons, but right now, she couldn't imagine what they were.

She knew he was watching her. She cupped water in her hands, splashed her face, pushed her hair back, bunching her breasts in her bikini top.

She was wearing the Day-Glo lime job—the bikini that had turned Towers into an instant idiot—for now it was time for management analysis with Roth. She turned in the water to fix his position.

He sat on the diving board at the other end, watching her. She shaded her eyes against the sun with both hands—that ballooning effect again—and returned Roth's stare. She liked that kind of look from a man, regardless of how she felt about him. She despised the quick, furtive peeks most men stole at her.

Forty thousand dollars in a thick envelope was lying there on the table on his terrace. Roth had tossed it aside without comment. In fact, she'd been here for nearly an hour and not a word had been exchanged yet. The terrace door was open when she arrived, a breeze wafting through the living room, flagging the sheer curtains back into the apartment. She'd found him reading some papers, drinking a beer. She sat down, pulled the envelope from her handbag. He hadn't looked at it or at her, just tossed her a towel and nodded towards the pool, as if to say it was time to show the *other* currency. She changed into her bikini, threw on Roth's bathrobe, and he had her drink waiting on the terrace, a Sunset Surprise, à la Manila Hotel. One hour ago and not a word.

Was their business concluded? She had questions about the timetable, like when she should contact the attorney. But she said nothing. Roth would speak when he wanted to, and that suited her fine. Robert should be more like that. Roth would take care of things. He'd tell her what he wanted and when. Fine with her. Let someone else do the thinking for a change.

Roth dived in. He swam underwater, his strokes leading directly to her. He surfaced in front of her, standing so close without touching that it was awkward. She covered her eyes from the sun and peeked up into his eyes boring into her.

What *was* he thinking, if not the obvious? Clearly, he was attracted to her, but he wasn't slobbering over her. Aside from his crude words, he had revealed absolutely nothing of his feelings. Puzzling.

She'd always had an effect on men, ever since that summer when she turned 14 and grew a few inches. Grew everywhere. She learned that men didn't have all the power, after all. She began seeing the way they looked at her. She held the power now. But not with Roth.

At least not yet.

"What?" she asked at last, the first word between them.

He motioned to the terrace. They got out of the pool, dried off, and went on over. Rachel sat down, crossed her legs, threw her towel over her shoulders.

Roth sat down opposite her, fingered the envelope. "I want something else from you."

"What's that?" she asked, a smile coming to her lips.

Roth's eyes dropped to her thighs. "You're sitting on it."

"You want my chair?" she asked innocently.

Roth returned her smile. Nice smile, she thought. A different smile.

He was warming to her. But then his eyes went hard. "Get in the bedroom."

"No." She shook her head coyly.

He stood, his smile disappearing, replaced by that cruel look. "And don't even think about throwing a Manila Special."

"A *what*?" Rachel's voice cracked.

Roth took hold of her towel, pulled it up around her neck, balled the end in his fist. "A wham-bam thank you Sam, Manila Special." He pulled her out of her chair, grabbed her wrist.

"That's not part of this," she said, pulling back. But he was too strong, his grip tight on her wrist, hurting her. He held the towel firmly, twisting it tighter, like a harness, and pulled her inside. "Whenever I want, you'll lay down for me or I'll think we're not friends." He spun her around and yanked the towel away, grabbed her by her hair.

At the bedroom door, she tried to resist. Roth put his finger under her nose, forcing her backwards, head first, and she had to back up or fall. He spun her around again, slid his other hand beneath her legs and lofted her onto his bed effortlessly.

This wasn't on her terms and it angered her, yet she was curious about what came next. "I don't like rough stuff," she said through clenched teeth, drawing her legs up as he covered her with his body.

He grabbed her wrists, crossed them, held them with one hand, and slapped her butt so she'd drop her legs. She tried to bite his face. Dumb move. He butted heads with her, so hard that she saw stars and went limp. Above her head on the wall was the hysterical facade of an elaborate *barong* mask, a demon face that barred spirits from Roth's bedroom. She told herself she wasn't being raped, that this was really her idea, that she needed to get inside of his mind to know how to deal with him, that this was just part of what started in New York. She stared up at the mask as he ripped off her bikini and took her.

But what she didn't see was the tiny red light aglow within the mask.

———

They had sex all day, dozing off intermittently, then waking and screwing time and again. Her legs ached from the work, and her body was tender from his ruthlessness. She had always hated the affection some men pretended, in order to shield the frankness of lust. Roth hadn't bothered with that crap. No romance, sentimentality, or affection; gentleness or kindness. He'd used her like a cheap whore.

She stirred awake around midnight. Roth was on his back, asleep at her side, his arm under her head. She sat up and scanned the bedroom, looking for something heavy to crush the bastard's head in. Instead, confused as she'd never been before, she moved against him, hesitated, and then began kissing his chest, dropping her hand down to his stomach—and down.

She smiled in fresh wonderment at how her emotions had betrayed her, and how she felt about his attack. That she was going to sleep with him was a given fact after that meeting in the diner. But she was supposed to use *him*, as she'd used Towers and so many others, starting with Jack Scarlett.

Cops always say the guilty feel better when they've confessed. That's how she felt now; plus, trying to read Roth's mind was stimulating. He'd known the truth about MacMillan from the get-go, and had just crossed the t's, dotted the i's. Methodically and meticulously.

Daylight peeked through the curtains. They ate a meal he prepared—eggs scrambled with mushrooms, and some sort of pâté on crackers—and later, he lay next to her, massaging her with oil as she sobbed quietly, her nervous system racked from countless orgasms. The pillows were wet from her tears, the sheets soaked from their bodies, and now, each time he touched her in those places, her body shuddered, anticipating the excitement.

She dozed off and on, not knowing or caring if it was day or night.

Stirring eventually, she murmured, "Why are you doing this?"

Roth turned his head. "Because you're a delectable slut and I can't keep my hands off you."

She smiled, kissed his chest. 'Delectable slut' sounded marvelous; it was nice to be understood.

"Not this," she said. "I mean, why are you helping me?"

"*You're* helping *me.*"

"Yes. But why?"

"For the money, dummy. Why are you doing it?"

It was noon. She was half lying across Roth, his arm over her back, his hand massaging her buttocks. They'd been in bed for a full 24 hours. Plates were scattered across the bed, on the floor, and the sheets were soiled from food, booze, oil, and sex. The bedroom was a pig pen, but neither cared to move a muscle.

"Because it's all I've ever known," she answered. "But you're different. You're an investigator, and people in your profession are supposed to be solid types. So, tell me why?"

"Why I'm doing it? Because I got expenses. That's why. Booze, whores, comic books."

"I want to know. You can tell me. I've told you everything."

"Everything?"

"Everything." She propped her chin on her arm and made a hurt face. "At least everything important." Her eyes narrowed. Roth kept his thoughts to himself, had secrets so deep maybe he didn't even understand them, things he probably never talked about. Like why he went berserk whenever he suspected a lie, no matter how innocuous. She'd bet anything that a woman had once done a number on him.

Roth sat up and lit a cigarette. He took several long drags before reaching round for an ashtray. Not finding one, he flipped the ash on the floor. Didn't matter; the place was a disaster area and smelled like a whorehouse. Homey.

"Tell me," she coaxed

"It's all a big game. It's all about money," he said. "A huge sum of money that insurance companies don't even know they have. But it's more than that. My clients are inept idiots, narrow-minded little shits who cheap-charlie their investigators, fuck us at every turn. They screw over guys like me who do their dirty work."

He came up on his elbows. "I used to go out of my way to break a case, and all I ever got for my troubles was a lot of cheap chicken-shit. Most inside claim examiners are narrow-minded little snot-noses." Guys like Sydow came to mind.

He continued, venom in his voice: "One thing will always stick in my craw. I once investigated a claim in Yemen. Nearly got my ass greased breaking it. Risked my life and spent a week in a fuckin' toilet the Yemenis call a jail. I got scabies, and I fought off the jail-house proctologists. Then my property was confiscated and I was thrown out of the country.

"The claimant planned to waste me when I refused a bribe. When that didn't work, he ran to the authorities and accused me of spying, then he complained to the client that I was maligning his reputation.

"I convalesced for a week, and Nina, my partner, invoiced for my time in jail—a few thousand measly dollars. But you know what? The client said that it wasn't their problem. The fuckers re-fused to pay up, even though they knew all along their claimant was a crook."

Roth dropped his cigarette butt into an empty beer bottle. "In-surance people always take the easy way out for everything: it's easier to screw their investigator than face down their claimants. A couple of grand to do the right thing and the client won't do what a man should do. My clients are sniveling little humps with no not-ion of character or integrity, certainly incapable of handling their own cases, but shit on those who do. Disloyal, two-faced bastards."

Rachel sat up, silent at his tirade. She had her answer, an im-portant one given their alliance.

"*That's* why I'm doing it," he spat.

"Sorry I asked," she said emphatically, sliding out of bed.

"Where you goin'?"

"To pee?" she replied like a mouse, learning to be very cautious around him when he was angry. She went to the bathroom, closed the door.

Roth lit another cigarette and looked at the closed door. *Now you know. Don't you, beauty? Now you have your answer.*

33

They lazed the afternoon away. She didn't want to get out of bed, but he forced her up and called in the maid. Her legs were rubbery, her body sore, her equipment ravaged. They sat in his hot tub for a while, took a swim, then showered and dressed for dinner. They ate at L'Opera, an Italian restaurant nearby, then Roth took her to a traditional Thai massage parlor in Pratunam. He ordered two girls for each of them instead of a single masseuse. The girls worked on her for two hours, during which Roth ordered in a third girl to massage her feet. Reflexology, they called it. Nearly orgasmic.

By midnight they were back in Roth's hot tub sipping champagne. He'd brought two girls back with them, and the massages continued in the swirling water. The girls were naked, and while Rachel had no proclivities in this direction, the experience was erotic. She was certainly rethinking life in the tropics.

Back in bed, Rachel, although tender everywhere it mattered, was anxious for more, and an added stimulation were the girls who pranced about nude serving drinks and food, indifferent to the bedtime maneuvers. Initially shy, Rachel soon found their audience strangely delightful—another first. But then there'd been many firsts with Roth these past 48 hours.

She dozed off to an oil massage. Later—she didn't know how much time had passed—she stirred in response to Roth's voice in the dark. He was propped up in bed, smoking a cigarette, making designs with it in the black night air. The girls were gone.

She turned to him. "Hmmm? Did you say something?"

"I said, tell me about Lolita." Roth's voice was little more than a whisper.

"Lolita who?" she replied groggily. "I don't know any—"

"Maybe you never met her, but you know her."

Rachel came up on her elbows, blinking sleep away, thinking. How the hell did he know about the Lolita girl? She hadn't mentioned it, that's for sure. "Oh, yes. Robert's girlfriend, you mean? In Manila?" She looked at the luminous dial of the clock. It was exactly 4:00 a.m.

"Tell me about her," Roth said.

"How do you know about her?"

"What did I tell you about answering my questions with another question?" His tone was mild but she sensed an undercurrent of impatience, a stepping stone to anger, and from there, well, she didn't want to dwell on that.

"I—uh, only know what Robert told me. Which was, uh—"

"How much insurance you have on her?"

Rachel froze. The air was suddenly heavy with tension.

"I know about everything," he said quietly, anticipating her question. "You should know that by now."

Was this leading to Roth wanting a cut? "Robert's not going to like this." She put her hand on his chest.

Gently, he removed her hand, tossed her arm aside. His fuse was getting short.

"I couldn't care less what Robert's going to like. Has he filed the claims on her yet?"

His question was a challenge.

"Yes. I think so," she said.

"Oh, I see," he said. "We're partners, but you only think so? Wrong, beauty. You know so." Roth's breathing was deepening. He was about to explode.

"Okay," she hastened. "He has filed the claims." She sat up, spoke quietly, as delicately as she could muster for what she was about to say. "But those claims don't involve you."

"How much money?"

"I'm not sure."

Roth stubbed out his cigarette. "You wanna reconsider that last answer?"

"All right. There are four policies. Each for 100,000. All with double indemnity."

Eight hundred grand. Not bad for the life of a little island girl, Roth thought. He looked at her.

"But this doesn't concern you."

"No?"

"You're not involved, are you?"

"Another question to my question? Yes. I'm involved. Every insurance claim in the Philippines comes to me," he lied. "Who whacked her? Reno?"

"Whacked her? I don't know what you're talking about, and I don't know any Reno."

"Who do you know?"

"No one. That's Robert's end. I never met that man, Morales, or whatever his name is. He was just a mechanism for getting Peter MacMillan's death notification to the attention of the embassy."

"So you could get the F180?"

"Yes."

"Who whacked Lolita? Second time I've asked. There won't be a third."

"I don't know what you're talking about. Her death was faked."

In a flash, Roth gave Rachel a resounding slap on the side of her head, the blow coming out of nowhere in the dark. She cried out and slid out of bed, her ear ringing. "You sonofa—"

Roth flew at her. He grabbed her by the hair. She couldn't make him out in the dark, but he had no trouble seeing her. He swung his foot, sweeping her legs from beneath her, and she dropped hard to the parquet floor. She cried out.

Roth held a fist of her hair. "I told you what was gonna happen if you lied to me again, didn't I? And your mouth, beauty, how nasty. Were you gonna say 'sonofabitch?' Is that what you were gonna call me?" He slapped her hard across the face. "Sonofabitch?" he questioned, incredulously. "Sonofabitch?"

She covered her face and begged him to stop.

"Stop hitting you? Hell, woman, I'm gonna kill you if you lie to me again. Fraud is one thing, but you're mixing me up in murder, and the price tag on that is half of everything."

"I swear I never wanted to know, and I didn't know that you did. How could I?"

He raised his hand to hit her again, and, sensing it in the dark, she cowered, shielding her face with her elbow, holding Roth's arm to keep him from yanking her hair out of her scalp.

"I—I swear, Mike." Rachel's mind was in a whirl. "I don't know what happened to her."

"You knew she was dead, didn't you?"

"No. No—"

Roth slapped her face again, knocking her back against the wall. "Now, *you're* dead, girlie," he raged. From beneath the mattress, he withdrew a butcher's knife. Her eyes locked on the blade's glint in the light coming from under the bathroom door.

"No. Oh, my God. No!" She screamed. "I—I knew she was dead, but I don't know what they did to her."

"Robert told you she was dead?"

"Y—yes. He told me after it happened."

"That makes us both accessories."

"But I didn't do anything," she pleaded.

"How'd they whack her?"

"All I know is that she was run over. Robert wasn't even in the country when it happened. He knew a cop, or someone." Rachel spoke fast, the blade just inches from her eyes, the cold gray steel terrifying. "The cop took care of it."

"Why was she whacked?"

"She was always strung out on crack or something. Robert said she was unreliable. She threatened to run to the authorities, to expose

Robert to the insurance companies. Robert as Jordan, I mean."

"How'd you get the coverage on her?"

"We bought policies on Lolita and Robert, as Jordan Warner, each being the other's beneficiary as fiancées. Small policies, so there weren't medical exams. All except for one company who required a medical examination at the last minute."

"For which you had a stand-in?"

"Y—yes."

"Who?"

"A Cuban girl from South Florida."

"Name?"

"Why does it matter?"

"There it is again, a question for an answer," he hissed. "You're never gonna learn, beauty." He pushed her against the wall with his knee and held the knife to her throat. She felt the blade against her flesh.

She spoke fast. Any second now and Roth would cut her. "I don't remember her name. It was someone Mom, uh, our mother, sent up from Miami. Carmen. A Carmen something or other."

"Let's go back to Lolita," Roth directed.

"She believed Robert was going to marry her. At first, we, uh .
. . he was only going to fake her death, but she got out of hand, couldn't be controlled."

"And policies were taken on Robert also, so it wouldn't look lopsided when he claimed on her life?"

"Y—yes."

"Your idea, right?"

"Yes."

Roth let go of her hair, stood back. "Had to be your idea. Robert's not that smart." He turned and walked into the living room, switched on the light over the bar. He threw the knife in a cabinet, smiled towards the darkened bedroom.

"Oh, beauty," he called melodiously. "Would you like a drink?" He heard her sobbing in the bedroom. She tried to stand, but fell back against the wall.

"I guess you could use one," he muttered, chuckling. He made some Margaritas, the sound of the grinding ice in the blender angry in the blackness of night. He carried them in to the bedroom, put them on the night table, and turned on the bedside light. He pulled her up from the floor, sat her on the bed.

"Beauty, our first fight!" Roth said with mock concern. "Drink this," he ordered.

Rachel started to shake her head, but saw that 'no' wasn't an option. She took the glass in shaky hands, spilling globs on the floor. She slurped the drink, spilling more across her shaking fingers. The crushed ice hurt her teeth, and the drink was strong, tasting mostly of tequila. The bitter snap made her wince, and she tasted blood in her mouth.

Roth looked at the clock on the night stand: 4:16 a.m. Sixteen minutes had elapsed since he'd awakened her.

"There," he said, his voice soothing. "Doesn't the truth make you feel better? Of course it does. Now, I know that you're going to tell me the truth from now on, because you see, darling, like I told you before, I need the truth to keep us out of trouble. If I operate in the dark, well, things would get screwed up." He put his face next to hers. "It's not fun in the dark, is it? Bad things happen in the dark, don't they?

"Now, whacking people puts a whole new light on the picture. I want half on both cases and, of course, half when the Jordan Warner scam is pulled off."

Rachel thought. So this was why Roth wanted the money here in Bangkok. So he could get her alone. Lay her bare in every way. Work on her. She wasn't only defenseless, but literally naked.

And she'd planned to work on him. If her head didn't throb so much, she would have laughed. She should have known better from the way he handled things in New York. She'd let her ego get in the way, let past successes blind her. The world wasn't full of guys like Robert and Towers. Roth was a completely different animal altogether. Not so different than Jack Scarlett, and their type couldn't be played. Mom's favorite saying, 'Don't bullshit a bullshitter, honey. Never snow the snowman.'

Roth had been light years ahead of them. Still, fifty percent? In the MacMillan case and the Lolita case, the answer was obviously yes. Without him, there'd be nothing. He'd see to that.

"And there's a bright side to all of this." Roth hovered over her, gently stroking her hair. "We're going for bigger paydays and I got a few ideas that'll blow your skirt up, tickle your plum to giggles. Multi-million-dollar claims, instead of these nickel and dime scams. Start thinking in eight-digit figures, beauty." He walked into the bathroom, took a face towel, ran hot water over it, wrung it out. He returned, flapping the towel open to cool it. "With inside contacts, I can guarantee jumbo policies *and* fast, no-questions-asked claim handling. It'll cost us for the inside people, maybe a hundred grand a throw, but that's beans compared to millions. We won't even need stiffs all over the place. Just creative writing."

He administered the warm towel, wiping her face as though she was a child. She looked up at him, afraid to say anything he'd take the wrong way. Robert would have to agree to a fifty-fifty cut for Roth or have him killed. And if Robert killed him, what would become of their claims? But aside from that, killing Roth wouldn't be easy. Moreover, she realized that she didn't want him dead despite this beating. Maybe she deserved it for lying to him after all his warnings. Plus, he had the experience and the contacts. He'd get things done and he'd take care of them. Just as long as they operated on his terms, jumped when he said jump. Maybe that was as it should be. Yes, he was light years ahead of them.

That left her new relationship with Roth to square with Robert. He'd be livid to learn she'd slept with him. Especially if he knew she'd enjoyed it. She'd just have to bring him around. Or else. What was the 'or else'?

"Now," Roth said. "Let's have a nice little chat about Mr. Brian O'Toole."

———

When Rachel finished telling what she knew, it was 4:50 a.m. Roth had plied her with drinks in quick succession, and she'd become more talkative, but still wary of his fury. Murder was out in the open now, and surprisingly she felt relieved. Like a weight was taken off her and was now on Roth's shoulders. Robert never shared the pressures. Roth was willing to, and managed them easily.

He settled into bed with her, and soon pushed her head under the sheets. She performed on him as he spoke in a soothing, loving voice even, telling her to never again lie to him because if she did, he'd just have to kill her because he was beginning to feel things for her. She turned this over in her mind, relaxed in his warmth, and vowed to be truthful from now on. That wouldn't come easy for her, but she'd try. Was he really starting to have feelings for her? Did that square with his nature?

A moment later, he asked, "Would you like me to perhaps sing something while you're sucking my dick? Maybe hum a few bars from 'Some Enchanted Evening'?"

She exploded with laughter. It was impossible not to love him, and she stopped trying not to.

Well, sort of.

34

Rachel left for Chiva Som, the spa down in Hua Hin. She nagged Roth to go with her, but he called it a waste of his valuable time, insisted she go alone. He had things to do, he said, and promised her some adventures when she returned to Bangkok.

The more she thought about it, the less she minded. Had it been Robert, he'd have dragged himself along, suffocated her with the wrong kind of attention. A health spa was no place for Roth. He'd only lust after the women in the place, and the more she pondered that, a tinge of jealousy worked into her thoughts. Like everything with Roth, this too was a new experience, yet not one she was sure she cared for. On the other hand, maybe she did. At any rate, a reunion would be fun.

The evening she left, Roth attended the annual Marine Corps Ball at the Marriott on Sukhumvit Road. He met a few clients for whom he and an associate handled de-bugging work, then with a small group of party-goers, he hit a few clubs in Patpong. He bar-fined a dancer from the Tiara Club, took her home, but sent her away after a quickie, wondering why he'd bothered.

———

Rachel stayed in Hua Hin for five days, returning like a new-born babe. She'd been exercised and massaged, marvelously fed and pampered. Had she not missed Roth, she would have stayed for a month.

Back in Bangkok, Roth, true to his word, showed her the town. Her first night back found them in a gambling den off Soi Thonglor, in the home of a police colonel. She won at roulette. Not much, but she'd never won at the wheel before. Later that evening, they took in a sex show in Patpong, then went for supper at the Dusit Thani Hotel.

They slept the next day away, then in the evening attended a symphony, supped at the Royal Orchid Sheraton, and ended up rolling dice until the early hours in a go-go bar in Nana Plaza. Rachel dropped 80,000 baht—approximately 2,000 dollars—but Roth won 200,000.

The following afternoon, they flew up to Hong Kong for night racing at the Happy Valley racetrack, and stayed at the Peninsula Hotel in Kowloon. She shopped and saw the sights for a few days while Roth forayed into China on business, the nature of which he didn't confide to her. He returned and collected her, and they flew back to the Land of Smiles.

She'd originally planned five days in Thailand, but it was nearly two weeks before she returned Robert's calls.

He was frantic. "Is anything wrong, Rachel? Why the hell are you still there?"

"Mr. Roth has been showing me around."

"Around where? What's going on?"

"A few places. He's being a gracious host."

"You're not closing a deal, you know. We're not exactly signing a contract here. When are you coming back?"

"Day after tomorrow."

He called again four days later, and she lied that there was a problem booking a return flight. She blamed it on Chinese New Year, and said she'd been on standby all this time, but had a definite reservation in three more days. Robert burned on the other end of the line. Rachel scrunched tin foil next to the mouthpiece. It sounded like white noise on his end. Robert cursed, grew impatient and hung up, but called her back. She did it again when he asked why she wasn't staying at a hotel. Frustrated, he slammed the receiver down with a torrent of profanities, and then it dawned on him that Chinese New Year wasn't until February. He called back again, this time seething. But Roth's line was busy, or, more likely, was off the hook.

They went clubbing that night, their third in a row. Rachel had forgotten how she liked to dance. On the way home, they stopped off at the Long Gun bar on Soi Cowboy where they had drinks and watched the go-go girls, much to Rachel's fascination. Roth laughed; straight women were always intrigued by bargirls. Rachel studied the dancers until Roth was certain of one that had caught her eye the most. He selected a shapely twenty-year-old named Noi, who seemed equally interested in Rachel. Roth bar-fined her, and back at his place they all swam naked in the pool, then drank champagne in the Jacuzzi until the sun came up. They giggled and chattered throughout the night, with Noi answering Rachel's questions about her occupation. But anything further didn't take. Roth abstained, neither taking Noi, nor pushing her on Rachel, even though Noi unmistakably demonstrated her interest in the American woman. He packed Noi off in the afternoon with 5,000 baht in her purse.

Finally it was time to leave Bangkok. Roth said he had things to do, places to go, people to see, mentioning more work in China. Their last night was steamy as always, and in the morning he saw her off at the airport with a surprising farewell thought.

35 New York City

Rachel returned to New York glowing, though not entirely from the pampering at the spa. As Roth had instructed, she telephoned both insurers each week, inquiring about her claim, and each time, as Roth said to anticipate, she was only told that her claim was being processed. The people at Amalgamated and Chase-Hampshire were very polite, even apologetic. Sometimes, they repeated, foreign claims were difficult to resolve, and delays were expected. She gave sighs of exasperation, but otherwise kept her composure. Don't overdo it, Roth had instructed. Be persistent, but not nasty.

Nasty would come later.

Other men held not the slightest interest for her now, and she wanted Roth with growing urgency, irritated by their separation. But steadily, her failure at dealing with him to her full advantage gnawed within her, despite her satisfaction with him at the helm. She wanted something more; just desserts for being played-off like an amateur, not to mention getting slapped around. Revenge pushed increasingly into her thoughts. Maybe something harmless. Maybe something humiliating. But, it had to be *something*. She juggled between erotic daydreams of their moments together, and exacting a furious revenge. He confused her, which only added to her resentment.

She rarely spoke to Robert, who nagged her endlessly with questions about Roth, trying to pick out his weaknesses, anything that offered a way out of this new partnership.

Roth had promised that after the MacMillan claim was put to bed, she'd return to Bangkok for a long vacation. They'd visit Singapore, Bali, and Fiji next time. This is what she thought about, plus their play time and the endless partying. She read up on Bali and Fiji, inquired over the Internet about immigration and real estate values in these places, since Roth hinted that he was considering property investments in paradise.

She'd briefed him about the Warner claim, gave a status of the Lolita matter and the Bishop personas Robert was setting up, including the companies targeted. But she begged him to let her break the news to Robert first, and promised to bring him around to accepting the fifty-fifty split, as well as their special relationship. The fifty-fifty cut really didn't matter, did it? Not in the long run. But she needed to explain it to Robert, one item at a time.

Her departure from Bangkok had taken a completely unexpected turn. Roth threatened to drop kick her ass from one end of Manhattan to the other if she so much as looked at another guy. This was a surprising twist. So, she'd gotten under his skin after all. He didn't seem the type. That helped temper her desire for revenge, and, equally surprising, his jealously fueled her emotions for him. Never in her wildest imagination would she have fallen for Roth— of all people. On their first meeting in Marcia's apartment, he'd been crude and intimidating, ill mannered and hostile. She smiled when she thought of him, how he'd seen through her immediately, tossed all that feminine mystic crap right out the window. It felt good to be understood.

But still, the beating he'd given her. That took some thinking about.

She eventually explained the new fifty-fifty division to Robert, but withheld her feelings for Roth, knowing it would send him over the edge. There was no telling what he'd do. But she'd let Roth handle him when he got to New York. Robert's usefulness in this partnership was going to be reduced.

But Rachel hadn't told Roth the entire story concerning her relationship with Robert. That could wait, too. Eventually she'd tell him everything. It had no bearing on the business at hand.

Robert had conniptions over the fifty-fifty split, and spat venomous accusations at her sleeping with Roth. He seethed for days, damning her for all things filthy, disgusting, and perverted which, "I have no doubt, you performed with that bastard." Actually, she had, so while she admitted nothing, she also denied nothing, her silence aggravating Robert all the more.

"It's never fifty-fifty with you, bitch," he raged on. "You and I are fifty-fifty, huh? In a pig's ass, we are. You're 100 percent and I'm zero. Now that bastard is in for fifty, which means you end up with all of that, too. What does that leave me?" He stopped rambling, trying to work mathematical logic out of what he'd just said. It wasn't true really that he had nothing. Half of everything up to this point was his. He just never got his hands on it.

Rachel considered dividing up their spoils and sending Robert on his way. But there was MacMillan and Lolita to collect on, then the Warner claim had to be worked. A clean break wasn't possible just yet. She'd let Roth decide how to handle him.

As December rolled into the second week, Robert seemed to be cooling off, and Rachel wrestled a promise that he'd visit Mom and Doc in Tampa with her for Christmas.

On December 7th, Roth telephoned. Robert answered the wall phone in the kitchen and was curt until Roth threatened to stomp his head into pulp if he didn't clean up his manners. Robert thrust the phone at Rachel. She took the receiver, hiding her excitement as Robert loomed behind her. She turned her back to him and he eventually retreated to the couch in the living room.

It was wonderful to hear Roth's voice, but he got right into business. It was time to contact a certain attorney named Hewlett and retain him to pressure the insurance companies. He instructed her to inform Hewlett that she planned to change her residence by Christmas. She asked why.

"Coupla reasons. First, baby, I want you out here with me just as soon as MacMillan's finished. We're gonna operate from Asia. Also, when it comes time to tweak noses, relocating is a plausible reason why you want funds fast. Have you broken the news to Miss Roberta?"

"Robert? Uh, not everything."

"Better do it. And you better not be fucking, baby. That pussy's reserved. Stuff a cork in her."

"Yes. Yes, I will." She grinned. "What are you doing right now?" she asked quietly.

"Sitting here sniffing your panties and jerking off."

"You always say the sweetest things."

In the Jacuzzi, Roth changed the portable phone to his other hand, poured more champagne. He toasted the two girls in the tub with him then told them to shut up. "I'll call soon," he said, and hung up.

Rachel heard the line go dead. She cursed, wanting to talk longer. But Roth always ended phone conversations abruptly.

Robert called from the sofa. "What did he say about me?"

"He asked how you were."

"Bullshit!"

"Would I lie to you?" *You little shit.*

"I'm telling you, we don't need the sonofabitch."

Another tantrum, she thought. Didn't answer.

"You hear me?" he shouted. "We don't need him."

I need him, she wanted to scream. At least right now, I need a strong partner. That stupid move with the hospitalization claim in Budapest was the last straw. Robert was limited. Even Mom was more helpful with indexing, and Doc assisted her with research. The whole Jordan Warner death scenario for Brazil was Doc's creation. But the auto accidents Doc and Mom pulled were a far cry from death claims, and light years behind what Roth was planning for them. Roth appreciated how she indexed the insurance companies. She knew what she was doing even if Robert didn't. But Roth conceded that he made a good front man when policies were purchased. Robert presented himself well as a prospective insured, whereas Roth was too well-known within the industry. Also, he was older, making bonafides more difficult to create, and underwriting requirements stricter, not to mention higher premiums on policies applied for. No, Robert was ideal for posing as the insured, providing he kept his mouth shut and did exactly as he was told.

Still, she thought, any stand-in would work. Except that a new player brought into the loop would have to learn the routine, and would eventually demand a bigger piece of the action. She'd have to think on that. How to use another stand-in without giving up a large slice of the pie. Maybe not so difficult; they'd gotten rid of Lolita, hadn't they? She'd run it by Roth later, after the MacMillan claim paid off.

Robert returned to the kitchen, baited by her silence. He wanted this thing at a head. "All right," he conceded, as though he had a say in anything. "Roth gets half on MacMillan and Lolita. But that's it. After that, he doesn't get anything. Doesn't know anything."

"He knows about Warner," she said quietly.

"How does he know *that*?" Robert shouted, incredulous.

"Duh, wasn't hard to guess, Mr. Warner," she answered. Barbie, at Rachel's feet, sidled out of the kitchen. "You're upsetting her."

"Upsetting her? Upsetting her? She's a fucking dog, Rachel. A dog. How about *me*? I'm upset."

She might as well tell him the rest. "And he knows about the Bishops."

Robert spun in a 360, as though he'd been shot. "Holy shit, woman. You've told him everything. We'll never get free of the fucking guy. Don't you understand? A guy like Roth will never let go of you."

You got that part right, buster. He didn't let go once in three weeks.

Robert stormed to the closet, grabbed his coat. "He's getting out of our life, you hear me?" He left the apartment, slamming the door after him.

The storm over, Barbie waddled back into the kitchen, looked up at her owner. Rachel angrily scooted her away with her foot, immediately said, "I'm sorry, baby. You hungry? No?" Barbie yapped. "Yeah, you're right, precious. He's an idiot." She went into the living room to turn off the stereo, and when she returned to the kitchen, Barbie had burrowed into the cabinet beneath the sink. Rachel squatted down to scoop her out.

She paused as her eyes fell on a box of rat poison.

Down on the street, Robert hailed a taxi, went over to the West Side, found a bar. After his third drink, he decided it was time to make a telephone call. Time for action. Roth was becoming a sickness, like a terminal illness that got you if you didn't get it first.

———

Rachel phoned Hewlett the following morning. He was out, but called her back later, made an appointment to meet that afternoon.

His office was just a block south of Trump Tower, high up overlooking Fifth Avenue. Pricey. He was senior partner in a law firm carrying a litany of crusty names. They'd started as litigators, representing plaintiffs against insurance companies, but many of his clients now *were* the insurance companies. Still, he didn't forget his origins, and if a client needed representation against the insurance industry, he'd provide it, as long as the defendant wasn't one of his clients.

He looked over the claim forms, discreetly looked over Mrs. Peter MacMillan, and asked how he came recommended. Roth had prepped her on that. She answered that she'd looked him up in directories, asked around, and learned that his reputation was the best in the business. He was flattered, not to mention slightly infatuated with Rachel, yet he would nevertheless double his already ludicrous hourly rate. He tossed the policies aside, pronounced it was a simple matter. He required a 1,500-dollar retainer, which she paid by check, and said he'd get off strong demand letters in the morning to both companies. As it was already 4:00 p.m., he announced he was quitting for the day, and invited her for cocktails over at the Plaza. To his regret, she declined. A pity, he was currently between mistresses. Perhaps another time.

36

On December 17th, Roth telephoned Rachel again. It was midnight, New York time. She said that Hewlett advised her today that the companies had answered his demand letters, pleading for a few more days to 'clear up' some pending matters.

"Yeah, I know." Roth chuckled. "They've been screaming at Nina and she's been screamin' at me for my report."

"Have you sent it in?"

"No. I'll let them squirm for a few more days. Time to play hard-ball. Listen up: call Hewlett in the morning. Tell him to demand payment by the 24th, or file suit against both companies. No later than the 24th on both claims. Got it?"

"Gotcha."

"And tell him to be sure to stipulate punitive damages. It's been over three months since Peter's death."

"Won't he wonder how I know about such things?"

"Not necessarily. If he asks, just tell him you've been reading and talking with people who've been stonewalled by their insurance companies."

"Okay, but I wish you were here."

"I'll be in New York next week."

"You will? That's wonderful."

"Why, sure, beauty. I wanna be certain that I'm not forgotten once you've collected."

"Mike! How can you say such a thing? Do you really think that?"

"Is your pussy behaving?"

"Uh huh." She smiled into the receiver. "She's waiting for you. But I'll bet you're sitting by the pool right now with some little plaything."

"You got the pool right. But no birds. Woodrow's anxious to see *you,* baby."

Rachel started to answer, but the line went dead. She looked at the receiver like it was broken. She thought of calling him back. Maybe he'd been disconnected and would call back. She made herself a drink and waited, but he didn't. She called his Bangkok apartment and got his answering machine. She shrugged, dialed Mom in Tampa to chat. She decided to take Roth to meet her and Doc for Christmas, and had forgotten to squeeze it into the conversation. Roth was all business on the phone, never liked to just gab about things. She'd tell him next time he called. He wouldn't mind, she was sure. He'd like Mom and Doc.

Roth stepped out of the telephone booth and scratched his bristled chin. He was tired after thirty hours traveling. Miami International was busy, flights were still arriving at midnight. He had a beer at a snack bar, decided to crash for the night and drive over to Tampa in the morning. He found the transportation counters and rented the biggest, most ostentatious car available, then drove to a nearby motel.

37 Tampa

"Hi." The stranger smiled like the Cheshire cat.

A confidence man if ever she saw one. "Hi, yourself." Mom smiled back. "Can I help you?"

Mom was twenty pounds overweight, he gauged. Wrong side of fifty. Resembled someone's sweet little auntie.

With a slight southern twang: "I *am* truly, truly sorry to disturb you, ma'am."

Mom's eyes narrowed. His drawn out 'ma'am' placed him for Tennessee, maybe Arkansas. A grifter from Arkansas? Why not? A bigger Arky con artist previously occupied the Oval Office. Her eyes slid past the stranger, taking in the street as far as she could see. The only car parked out there was his. She'd seen him knocking on doors across the street. Probably casing the area.

"That's all right," she said. *Just make one wrong move, buster, and Wolf will rip your fucking throat out*. Her German shepherd sat obediently behind the door, watching his owner's every move. "Can

I help you?" she repeated. She smiled her nicest smile. "Providing that you're not selling anything, that is."

They laughed, sizing each other up. "Well, if I were," he said, "I'd see right off that I knocked on the wrong door."

"That'd make your eyesight twenty-twenty," Mom agreed.

They laughed again.

Okay, bub. Game time. Let's have it.

"But I'm not," he said. "I'm looking around the neighborhood to buy. Looking at that corner property." He nodded up the quiet street and Mom followed his direction. A *"For Sale"* sign hung on the vacant townhouse. She hadn't noticed that before and wondered when it was put on the market.

"Yes?"

"Well," he continued. "I think it's always a good idea to check around, talk with locals first—about property prices, taxes, municipal services, the neighbors, things like that—before I even consider buying."

Mom held her smile. *Pretty smooth garbage you're handing out, bub. Neighborly. A square would probably buy it.* "So how can I help you?"

"Just that. Are the city fathers planning on tearing a viaduct through these backyards? Is the golf course behind us going to widen the green? They've got a good 100 yards yet on their side of the fence to widen that fairway. That'd put the drives on the ninth green in flirting distance to a lot of windows. Things like that."

"Why not ask the owners?"

"Of course. But frankly, if you were selling your home and it was about to be swallowed up in a stadium-sized cesspool, would *you* tell a prospective buyer?"

"I take your point." *All right, bub. I'm hooked. Good spiel. Rehearsed. You've even got me thinking about property values. You're slick. Sharp dresser. Grifter on big scams. Safe. Not a confidence man who uses violence if there's an easier way.*

Mom took in the yellow Cadillac convertible. This year's model. "Is that your car there?"

"Yes, why?"

"The neighbors are always curious about strange cars in the neighborhood. I'm the block captain."

"Yes. I saw the sticker in your window. Knew you'd be the person to talk to."

Mom smiled. *Then you also know that it's the best way to watch for anyone who might be watching me, without attracting suspicion.*

"Speaking of which," he continued. "Is it a safe neighborhood? Pricey neighborhoods can fool you, you know. What's the crime rate? Do the police coop in their cars swigging down beers out on the golf course at night? Things like that."

Mom held his eyes. *You're good, honey. Haven't heard 'coop' in a bunch of years. You've been working New York, maybe—the cop-cooping capital of the world.*

"Just a second." Mom called over her shoulder, "Doc." She smiled at the man at the door. "Let me put the dog in the bedroom." She closed the door, clapped her hands at Wolf, and pointed to the bedroom. A bark echoed through the home. A few seconds later, she returned to the door. Coming up behind her was a silver-haired man. He was around sixty, well groomed, dressed like a weekend golfer, and, like Mom, his smile was ear-to-ear.

"This gentleman here may become a neighbor," she relayed to Doc.

"Really?" Doc exclaimed, his voice pleasant. Mom looked back at Doc, and with her small finger, flicked an imaginary speck of dust from her eye. Doc answered, his pinky finger digging into the corner of *his* eye.

"Please come in," Doc said. "We're having tea on the lawn out back. Care to join us?"

"Why, thank you!"

"You wouldn't be adverse to a spike of vodka in your tea, now would you?" Mom threw in.

"Why, ma'am, you've just answered my question about one of my new neighbors. Pleased to meet you folks. Doc, is it?" He stepped across the threshold, extended his hand. "Davis. Jefferson Lee Davis."

Out in the garden Doc poured drinks, and after a few minutes Mom disappeared—no doubt to check their visitor's license plate. That was okay, the plate would match the family name he'd given. He'd looked up Davis in the phone book, cruised past a few Davis homes, settled on one, and stole the guy's license plate. Of course a check would come back with a different first name and make of the car, but folks down here changed plates rather than pay to register more than one car. And he alluded to having kin hereabouts.

———

He spent the next few days cultivating Mom and Doc, making inquiries about them in between lunches, cocktails, and dinners. He checked births, deaths, real estate, chattels and property, police records, and litigation records.

He played golf with Doc, whacking a few balls around on the course behind their home. Ever the con, Doc inveigled their way onto the course without paying. No point in forking out those high country club prices, he said. In the evenings, they went out for dinner, Davis usually picking up the tab. Damn, but Mom could put away the sauce! And Doc was no slouch, either.

Davis had broken the ice that first afternoon, alluding first to some stock irregularities he'd been accidentally caught up in over in Louisiana, and thereafter he, Doc, and Mom swapped war stories about insurance scams and confidence games, neither party incriminating themselves, per se, just talked hypothetically. Just the way kindred souls would—people who knew their own.

The evening before he departed Tampa, Roth considered taking down the "*For Sale*" sign he'd placed on the vacant corner property. But he decided not to bother; Jefferson Lee Davis had changed his mind about buying the place.

38 New York City

Marcia Post's tinny voice crackled over the intercom. "Hello?"

"Oh, hello," Towers said excitedly, surprised that finally there was an answer. He'd tried four times already today, and a voice caught him off guard. He practically kissed the metal intercom plate, so close he stood to it. Was it Lori?

"Lori?" he asked nervously, his heart pounding. So close. He was so close, now. He'd moved into his temporary apartment down in Arlington last week, but instead of flying home to Denver for Christmas, he hopped a shuttle up to New York.

He deserved some answers. His career had barely avoided disaster, and his emotions had been toyed with. Bullshit, they'd been trampled on. If nothing else, she'd certainly be surprised that he'd tracked her down. Impressed, maybe. Who knows, maybe Lori was in trouble. She was obviously in with the wrong kind of people judging from that creep Roth.

"You have the wrong apartment," the voice came back.

"Uh, no. Is this the apartment of—" He clutched the notepaper in his fist, read it. "Of Marcia Post?"

A reluctant "Yeah" hung on the line.

"I'm Bill Towers," he said, as if that explained everything. "I spoke with you some time ago. On the phone."

"Who do you want?"

"Lori. Mrs. MacMillan."

"There's no one here by that name. You have the wrong apartment."

"That's impossible," he said. "I was told that Mrs. MacMillan was staying with you as of two months ago." He tried to remember when he'd spoken with Maureen in Los Angeles. The first week of October, for sure. "As of October," he added.

"Who told you that?"

"The people who rent her apartment in Los Angeles. Lori gave them your name and address."

"Well, I don't know anyone named MacMillan. So, please go away."

"Please. Please, Miss Post," Towers croaked pathetically. Then it hit him. Maybe Lori was using another name. Her maiden name, perhaps.

"This—this is extremely important. I must speak with you."

Marcia bit her lip. Doormat time. She wished her apartment faced the street so that she could get a good look at him before she buzzed him in. He sounded so sad, but still, that didn't mean he wasn't a crazed killer or somebody like that. Some funny things had been happening lately. Someone was definitely getting into her mailbox. She was certain of that. So she'd done little tricks with the box. Things like placing a length of hair across the opening. She'd seen that in a spy movie. Sure enough, someone was opening it, but as far as she could tell, she wasn't missing anything. Could this guy be behind that?

"There's a coffee shop on the corner of Third Avenue," she said. "The El. I'll meet you there in 15 minutes."

———

"Her name isn't Lori MacMillan." Marcia Post studied the photocopy of Lori MacMillan's passport. "This is Julia Warner. Jordan's sister." She shook her head in wonderment, put her coffee down, screwed up her face.

Towers took the paper back. "Julia Warner?"

"Yeah," Marcia said suspiciously. "Where'd you get her photograph?"

"From her passport. When she came to Manila to identify the body of her dead husband." Towers dug into his coat pocket, searching for the Form 180 and a passport photograph of Peter MacMillan.

"Husband? She's not married," Marcia said.

"Who's Jordan?"

"Who are you?"

Towers explained. Again. This time Marcia listened. She wondered what happened to Julia and Jordan. She hadn't heard from him for over a month, and realized for the first time that she had no idea where Julia lived. Just somewhere on Fifth Avenue. She guessed Jordan hadn't returned from his last trip.

Towers handed her the photograph of Peter MacMillan and explained again how he'd learned her name and address. Ethel came over to refill their coffee.

"That's Jordan Warner," Marcia exclaimed, reading Peter MacMillan's name next to the photograph.

"No, it's Peter MacMillan," Towers argued.

"No, it's Julia's brother," Marcia said, tapping Robert's photograph. "I should know. I date him." That wasn't exactly true, was it. They'd had a few dinners, and he'd jumped her. Once.

Ethel, at the next table, twisted around, took the photograph from Towers. "Uh, yeah, he's a regular here."

Towers and Marcia looked up at Ethel. *"He's a regular here?"* they asked in unison.

"Yeah. Almost every day now. He was in this morning."

"He was in this morning!" Again Towers and Marcia chimed out together, and then looked at each other.

"Yeah, name's Bobby, I think." Ethel worked hard on a mouthful of gum.

"Bobby?" Again incredulously, in unison.

"Maybe you guys should put it to music," Ethel said, cracking her gum. "Maybe take it on the road? Yeah, like I said, he comes in, reads his mail over breakfast."

"That's what's happening with my mailbox," Marcia mumbled, even more confused. "He's been in town all this time?"

"Who?" Towers asked.

Ethel put her coffee pot down, listened. Neither paid her any attention.

"Jordan," Marcia answered. "Julia's brother. I used to hold his mail for him. But now he's picking it up himself, I guess. But I never gave him a key to the mailbox."

"This man?" Towers tapped MacMillan's photograph.

"Yeah. I guess he doesn't want me to know he's around." It hurt to admit that, but there wasn't any other explanation.

"Where does she live. This Julia Warner?"

"I've seen *her*, too. A couple of times," Ethel chimed in, picking up Lori MacMillan's photograph.

Towers and Marcia yo-yo'd back and forth, looking up at Ethel, at each other.

"Yeah," Marcia said. "She used my place a few times. For business. They were painting her apartment and she needed a place to crash. But she never stayed over, just came a few times in the afternoon while I was out. That's Julia Warner."

Ethel shrugged. "She was once in here with some other guy who didn't treat her none too good. I thought maybe he was going to realign her teeth or something, you know?"

A customer came in, sat at the counter. "Got to go," Ethel said. She picked up her coffee pot, left.

Towers began to worry. He'd been right, after all: Lori *was* in trouble.

———

Marcia was a doll. She let him drop his bag at her place while he canvassed apartment buildings on Fifth Avenue. Maybe she'd even let him crash on her couch tonight. He hadn't thought to make a hotel reservation and didn't look forward to paying two or three hundred a night in a midtown hotel, even if he could find a vacancy, what with this being the holiday season.

The operator confirmed that there was a Jordan Warner with an unpublished number on Fifth Avenue. Marcia thought it was in the East sixties, maybe the seventies, remembering that Jordan said he walked to Julia's from her place. That's when she'd first met Julia at The El. So, Julia must live nearby.

It was Saturday afternoon and it would be dark soon. Towers tried apartment buildings starting from East 61st Street, just north of the Pierre Hotel. Thankfully, there was only the east side of the street to work, Central Park being on the opposite side running all the way up to 110th Street.

———

By dusk, he'd only gotten as far north as East 70th Street. It seemed hopeless. Maybe because he was trying to match the wrong name to Lori's face. He'd continue in the morning.

As he'd hoped, Marcia offered him the couch. He countered with an offer to take her out for dinner, assuming that her trash was taken out more often than she was. They huddled in the restaurant, swapping their perspectives on Julia Warner. No doubt about it, Lori was Julia Warner, all right. Right down to the mole on her cheek.

Back in her apartment, Marcia was hospitable to a fault. Annoyingly so. She offered him pillows and sheets and blankets, even offered to take the couch herself if he was too uncomfortable. Such a big man shouldn't have to squeeze up all night on a tiny couch, she said, then asked if he wanted a third cup of hot chocolate, maybe a late-night snack. She offered to run to the deli around the corner for anything that he wanted. Towers was only glad that she didn't offer up herself.

39

In the Warner apartment just five blocks from where Towers and Marcia were turning in for the night, Robert paced the floor, swearing. "You wanton whore." He replayed the conversation between Rachel and Roth for the third time. Each time, pangs of hatred wrenched his guts. That she had screwed Roth was one thing—business was business, after all—but that she actually loved the sonofabitch stung Robert to the core.

He changed tapes in the micro cassette recorder daily, ever since he'd installed it under her bed when Rachel was off running around with Roth in Bangkok. She didn't really believe he'd bought her bullshit about getting stuck over there, did she?

He'd eject the tape from the recorder and insert a new one, then listen on another recorder when he was out of the apartment. It was a simple ten-dollar phone recording switch attached to the tape recorder that activated when the receiver was lifted. Most of the calls were Rachel's conversations with Mom, initiated from Florida,

268

and Rachel hadn't spoken with Roth since the 17th. But he was coming.

Did she think he was stupid? Giving half the money to Roth was insane. Sure, he promised big things, high-flying million-dollar scams, using insiders. But for all Robert knew, it was just talk. They'd done all right before he barged into their lives. And he intended to see that they continued that way. No, sir. Rachel wasn't going to cash him in for a new partner. Not in this life.

———

Rivera was late.

Robert felt edgy waiting in the restaurant. The bar was packed, but he'd managed to grab a deuce behind the brass railing that separated the tables from the standing-room-only bar action. The cheerful patrons agitated him. Three shopping days until Christmas, folks, so get the fuck out there and shop, already. This business was bad enough without having to wait for Rivera in a public place. Why had he allowed Rivera to choose where they met? After all, he was the fucking client, wasn't he?

The restaurant, Mexican cuisine, was essentially a singles place. Guys and gals crowded two, three deep at the bar, hoping to meet that special someone to exchange blood tests with. He scanned the bar, his eyes settling on a tall, attractive redhead chatting with an awkward guy who looked surprised that she'd even given him a second glance. But the nerd didn't notice her making subtle eye movements, giving the place the once-over, checking out the guys. She looked at Robert and they played eye tag until she turned to the bar, maybe to give him another perspective. Great ass. But he wasn't interested at the moment, he just enjoyed distracting women from other men.

He saw the Cuban enter the restaurant, look around the throng. After a few moments, he spotted Robert's red bow tie. They locked eyes momentarily, the connection made. Rivera came over, sat down.

"It's a cold motherfucker out there." Rivera rubbed his hands together, blew into them. From the corner of his eye, Robert caught the redhead turning, quickly eyeing the Cuban. Rivera looked up at her, smiled, but she lost interest in their table, since she obviously wasn't going to get any attention from men talking business.

Rivera was a large man, cramped in the chair at the table. Early thirties, maybe. Light skinned. His head was big, his complexion, once ruddy, had either cleared up or he'd undergone dermabrasion. He was well dressed, smelled of musk. He had a friendly face despite his cold eyes.

"Jones," Robert said by way of introduction.

"Jones?" He shrugged. "Sure, man. Whatever you say." He looked around for a waitress, then looked at Robert's drink for a suggestion, but ordered an Irish coffee instead. He worked himself out of his overcoat in the confined space and dropped it back on his chair. "You a friend of Vinnie's?"

Robert shook his head. "Never met him. Just spoke to him on the telephone. Got his name from a guy in Florida."

"By name of?"

"Does it matter?"

"It matters."

"Campobello."

Rivera searched his memory. "Oh, yeah. Soupy! Tampa, St. Pete?"

Robert nodded.

Rivera's drink arrived. "Soupy's okay." He sipped gingerly, let out a long sigh. "So, now we know everybody. Whaddya need?"

Robert took a photograph of Roth out of his jacket pocket. It was a snap taken in Bangkok, a picture of Roth and Rachel real chummy like, together in a pool. Roth smiling that confident, knowing smirk of his. Robert had found it in Rachel's cosmetic kit, hidden in the lining. He'd had it rephotographed and blown up.

"He'll be in New York. Soon. Maybe tomorrow. Don't know where yet, but I'll let you know."

"Slow down," Rivera said, studying the photograph. "What's his business?"

"Insurance."

He looked at Robert, his hand signaling 'gimme.'

"An adjuster."

"Don't look like no adjuster, man." Rivera flipped the photo back across the table. He sipped his coffee and took a look around the restaurant, anywhere but at Robert. He was finished talking if Robert had nothing more to add.

"An investigator." Robert shrugged.

"No shit?" Rivera said. "Now that ain't the same fuckin' thing, is it?"

"What's the difference?"

"You know the difference, man. Or else you wouldn't lay that adjuster crap on me." He picked up the photo again. "Who's the cunny?"

"She's my wife."

"Will he be alone?"

"Yeah. He doesn't want people around for what he's doing."

"Twenty should do it."

"Twenty? For what? Ten minutes work?"

Rivera shrugged. "Do it yourself, then, if it's so easy."

"I can't. He knows me."

"That'd make it all the easier. Right? Don't jack me around, my man. Either you ain't got the balls, or you wanna be someplace else with a lot of witnesses when he goes down. So cut the crap. Twenty. Half now, the balance when it's done, or I'm outta here."

Ten thousand represented every loose dollar Robert was carrying on him, compliments of that hospitalization claim. He'd told Rachel he'd dropped it, but he hadn't. Roth had been wrong. The check from the Australian insurer arrived, no questions asked, in Marcia's mailbox last week. Still, 20,000 to have Roth hit was a lot of money. Too late to shop around; he was out of time. Roth would be here any day. Also, right after Roth was hit, he'd have to get the balance from Rachel. Rivera didn't work on the installment plan. Rachel would be furious about the hit, but she'd have no choice, not once she knew the kind of guy Rivera was. He glanced over at the redhead. She was talking to another guy at the bar, the nerd trying to remain in her orbit of conversation. Fickle cunts, he thought. Yeah, it was a lot of money, but the redhead's flightiness helped make up his mind. Rachel and Roth; that tore it.

He looked back at Rivera, nodded. Surreptitiously, he removed a wad of money from his breast pocket, pretended to count out 10,000 dollars under the table. Actually, it was every dollar he had. He put the stack of 100-dollar notes into a menu, slid it to Rivera.

Rivera chuckled at Robert's attempt at stealth, opened the menu, and counted the money openly. Just as Roth had taken his down payment at the diner on Northern Boulevard.

These were reckless men, Robert thought.

"Only thing remaining is when and where?" Rivera asked.

"Don't know where yet. Probably a hotel. He should be here tomorrow, like I said."

Rivera finished his drink, stood up. "You got my number. I'm all yours for the next few days." He pulled his coat from the chair, threw it over his shoulders, winked at Robert and left.

Robert watched the big Cuban outside bundling up against the cold. He paid the check and worked his way up to the bar. The redhead had gone. He didn't see where. He scouted the room, pleased that a few women gave him a discreet double-take. He edged into a small opening at the bar, brushing against a guy next to him. That was okay, the girl he was with—about the caliber of Marcia—gave Robert a wide smile, pulled the guy closer to her. Not that she liked him; she just wanted Robert to have a place at the bar next to them. She then drew him into their conversation—some Christmas gibberish—asking what was a good present for a man.

How about a fuckin' stick to keep you in line, bitch. He smiled. "A cane is always good. Fashionable these days."

She liked that; a novel idea, she said. She asked the guy she was with. He shrugged, hoping that he wasn't getting a walking stick for Christmas.

Robert looked around. The redhead was definitely gone, but he spotted a brunette at the end of the bar talking with two other girls. Their eyes met, he winked. She held his gaze, looked back at her girlfriends, one of whom was wearing bright, freshly laundered workout clothes, as though she'd just come from a gym. Robert bet that the girl never worked out, just wore the outfit for a conversation starter. *Phony twat. You should get the stick for Christmas.*

He ordered another drink, knew it wouldn't be his last. Not the way he was feeling. He replayed Rachel's words to Roth. How could she ever want to screw the guy? He was forty-something, with a face that looked fond of accidents. He smoked, drank like a fish, and was probably diseased from whoring around. And the crude bastard didn't know how to talk to people. His thoughts went graphic, seeing Rachel's beautiful body against that bastard's, seeing her doing things to him. He slammed his glass on the bar, headed for the door.

But he didn't go back to the apartment. He hit another bar, this one less crowded. That was all right; he didn't want a woman. He wanted to think. Needed to think. About how to handle Rachel once Roth got his head blown off. How to get control of their money. That was the problem. She controlled the checkbook. And when a broad does that, well, things can't be good between a man and a woman. He'd let it happen, though. Little by little, she'd gotten stronger, bossier. That would change. What else? He ordered a drink, told the bartender to make it a double. What else? Oh, yeah, he'd let her refuse him. That would fucking cease, also. She belonged to him, goddammit. What else? Oh, yeah, the sassing would stop. Her smart-mouthing would come to a screaming, screeching halt. She'd know that he wasn't to be fucked with after Roth got his.

Rachel was in bed when he staggered in at midnight. A small shopping bag from Elizabeth Arden sat on the kitchen counter. She was now spending her afternoons, not to mention small fortunes, at beauty salons, yet he was supposed to feel good when she doled out beer money.

He staggered to the bedroom door, pushed it open, and plopped on the bed beside her.

She stirred. "You're drunk. You reek."

Robert stood clumsily, started stripping off his clothes. Rachel sat up, shaking her head. "No, Robert." She took a pillow, started to get out of bed.

Robert splayed his hand across the top of her head, pushed her back. But she rolled to the other side of the bed, stood up. She was wearing a pair of his pajamas, something she'd been doing since returning from Asia. So she wouldn't excite him. Strangely, it aroused him more. She came around to the door carrying the pillow.

"I'll take the couch," she said, but he grabbed her and pushed her onto the bed, falling down on top of her.

"You're sleeping here," he slurred. "With me. Like always."

'Always' ended four years ago. That kind of always, anyhow. She pushed him off of her, got up again. Robert grabbed at her, caught her wrist.

"I said I want you, bitch."

She broke free, scratching his wrist with her other hand. "Get out of here, Robert." She stood back, breathing heavily. Robert rolled off the bed, hearing nothing she said, and advanced on her. She slapped him. He stood dumbfounded, holding his cheek. Then he went into a rage, swung at her, connecting with her jaw. Rachel went down, hitting her ass hard on the floor, like a puppet whose strings had been cut. But she bounced up and flew at him with her nails. He tried to protect himself from her fury, but was too drunk. She scratched his face and neck with a flurry of slashes. He fell backwards, hit the floor, cried out, and rolled away from her. She pursued, kicking him with her bare feet as he crawled towards the door.

"You sonofabitch," she screamed. "I'll kill you." She grabbed a lamp, hurled it at him, striking him on the back of the head as he managed to get on all fours. He crawled and squeezed out of the door, which she banged repeatedly against his legs. Outside, he rolled along the floor, balled up, holding his shins, howling in pain.

Shortly, the phone rang in the living room. Building management, no doubt. Robert stood, hobbling, and she gave him a final kick and pushed the door closed and locked it. "Answer the phone, you fucking animal," she screamed through the door. "It's probably the police. They wanna talk to you."

But the phone carried on ringing. He didn't answer it. Finally it stopped and Rachel heard her voice on the answering machine. Whoever called, probably the guys on duty downstairs, didn't leave a message. She went into the bathroom, rinsed her face, and pressed a cold towel against her jaw. She'd have a welt in the morning. Robert was quiet outside. She studied her reflection in the mirror.

This shit was at an end.

40

This was the place, Towers thought. Had to be. The way the doorman and elevator man exchanged glances when he showed them Lori's passport photo. He hadn't missed it. They knew her, all right. Just not under the name of Lori MacMillan.

"I think her name is Julia Warner," Towers offered feebly.

"It don't say that," Gus said, his thumbnail on the name, Mac-Millan. He showed it again to Hank. "Whaddya think? You know her?"

Hank shrugged, studied Towers. "My memory's not too good these days." *You certainly ain't a New Yorker, chum. President Jackson would improve my memory marvelously. Funny, though, you're the second guy in the past few months showing photos of Mr. or Mrs. Warner.*

"Yeah, mine neither," Gus said, winking at Hank.

Towers put on a serious face. He whipped out his Department of State ID card. "Does this help your memory?"

"Well, la-de-fuckin'-da," Gus quipped. "A Fed." *We should prostrate ourselves now?* It was dumb trying to muscle a New York doorman.

"Doesn't help a bit, J. Edgar." Gus turned his back, adding, "Say goodbye. We're busy."

Towers put his ID card back into his coat pocket, shot them a stern look, then left.

Hank chuckled. "Didn't anybody tell him it's Christmas?" The conference over, they went back to what they were doing.

Fuming, Towers took up a position on the sidewalk across Fifth Avenue. He'd wait. If Lori lived here—and he was certain she did—she'd have to come out sometime. It started raining lightly, and he cursed at the thought of these insignificant building employees blowing him off like he was nothing—a nobody. How he wished he could walk back across the street and slap a subpoena on them, threaten them with arrest, maybe handcuff the bastards. They'd beg to talk to him then. The rats. Sometimes government people refused information to civilians, but it shouldn't be the other way around. Who did these damn people think they were, anyhow?

Upstairs in the Warner apartment, Rachel stood at the kitchen sink, listening for the shower. Robert had said nothing this morning. Not a word. Avoiding her eyes, he went into the bathroom as soon as she'd come out of the bedroom. His left eye was bruised, but the scratches weren't deep. A moment later, she heard the shower running.

Rachel shook rat poison in the milk container, the orange-juice carton, and into the tuna she'd mixed with onions, celery, and garlic—lots of garlic. She wrapped a tuna salad sandwich in cellophane, put it on a plate, and opened the refrigerator. A tub of cottage cheese, another of Robert's favorites. She took it out, popped the lid, shook poison in that, too, whipped it with a spoon, then smoothed down the surface and resealed the cellophane across the lip of the container. She looked up at the fluorescent lights in the kitchen. Better leave them on; wet rat poison tended to glow in darkened areas. She'd learned that when Jack Scarlett's time had come. Robert never lifted a finger in the apartment, so the lights would stay on forever if she didn't turn them off. He never thought about costs. She stopped what she was doing and thought about the Warner claim. There'd be no Robert for her to trek through the bush with down in Brazil, no expedition photos, and no witnesses who would see them together. So what? Either she'd change the death scenario or get someone else to travel down there with her. Whatever. She'd leave that to Roth. He'd know what to do.

The telephone rang and she jumped. Probably Mom again. She thought not to answer it, but that might bring Robert out of the bathroom before she finished. She lifted the receiver, cupped it in her shoulder, snapped, "Yes."

"Hi, baby!"

"Mike! Finally. You're here?"

"Nowhere but."

"Oh, God! That's wonderful!" Wonderful and not so wonderful. She needed time. Time to clear out anything that could identify her and Robert. She heard Robert turn the shower off, and she hurried to finish what she was doing. He came out of the bathroom as she cupped the cottage cheese, put it back into the fridge. She washed off the spoon, put it in the dishwasher.

Robert sauntered into the living room, drying his hair. He eyed the stock ticker working across the television screen, fingered the remote, turning down the volume, and watched pensively, studying Rachel's body language on the phone. She looked around the corner at him, moved out of view. Robert turned his attention back to the television.

"Downstairs, baby," Roth said into his cellphone. "Holding a cab. Get down here. And bring your pussy with you."

"I never leave home without her." She'd have to return later, after Robert was, what? Unconscious? Dead?

As always, Roth hung up without another word. Rachel flew into the bedroom to collect her coat, emerging a few moments later after a quick facial touch-up. She opened the linen closet, removed Roth's Christmas present from between the folded towels, dropped it in her purse. She went into the living room.

"I'll call later," she said.

"Where is he?"

"Downstairs."

Robert said nothing, but his eyes were misting.

She softened. "Things end, Robert. New things begin." She went over to him, sat at the end of the couch. He'd put cream over the scratch marks on his face. She nearly touched his face with concern, didn't, but ran her fingers through his hair. She was going to miss him, in a way. She wondered briefly what she'd tell Mom. Oh, well, she had time to think about that before she got down to Tampa. A pity it had to be this way, otherwise she'd be able to make a claim on his death as Jordan Warner. As it was, she'd have to come back without Roth and erase their identity here at the apartment as best she could since this address wouldn't work for the Warner claim later. Jordan Warner couldn't very well die in the jungles of Brazil *and* in a New York apartment. So Fifth Avenue could never come into play. A lot of time and money wasted. That thought made her angry with Robert again. Even with his elimination, he somehow managed to screw things up.

Robert didn't look at her. He blinked rapidly, turned up the volume on the TV, whispered, "Go on. It's all right."

Rachel kissed him on the cheek and studied his beautiful face. She almost felt like crying herself. But it was too late for tears.

She walked to the door, opened it and stood there, her back to him. "I've left a sandwich for you. In the fridge."

He didn't say anything.

"I'll call later. When I know where I'll be." She closed the door softly after her and walked down the hall to the elevator. When it came, Hank didn't look at her. He'd probably heard about the commotion in the apartment last night. At the door, Gus didn't look at her either, confirming her suspicion. Fuck 'em. They'd only see her one last time anyhow.

In the apartment, Robert stood and crossed to the door, listened for the elevator. He threw the deadbolt in case she returned, having forgotten something, then hurried into the bedroom and crawled under the bed. He reversed the tape without bothering to crawl back out. He listened to the conversation, then scooted out from under the bed, and headed for the phone in the living room, mimicking Rachel, his inflection feminine. "'I never leave home without her.'" *Cute, you fucking bitch.*

He dialed Rivera's mobile. The Cuban answered on the third ring, with a customary clearing of his throat.

"He's here," Robert whispered. "But I don't know where. Hotel, probably. I'm checking the places in the area."

Rivera stood on the sidewalk across the street. He'd seen Roth in the back of the taxi. "I have him," he said. He closed his mobile and looked towards the guy who'd been watching the apartment building for the past hour, ever since he'd arrived.

Robert called Rivera back: "You have him? You have him? Okay, be careful. My wife will be with him." He hung up. He didn't want Rachel to get hurt, but if she saw Roth wearing his brains on his shoulders, that would be lovely. "It'll do the bitch good," he said to himself. Rivera was good, right there on the job, just like he said he'd be.

The rain obscured the windows of the taxi from where Towers stood. He couldn't see who was sitting in the back seat. It was a man, though.

"Excuse me."

He turned absently to the large Cuban under an umbrella who was asking him for a light. Towers shook his head, mumbled that he didn't smoke, and looked back across the street. His heart suddenly lurched as he saw Lori running out from under the canopy in front of the apartment building. The taxi's rear door opened and she got in, closed it, and embraced the man inside. The taxi pulled away from the curb.

"Lori," Towers called, running into the street. Cars braked and honked their annoyance.

Rivera watched Towers, lit his own cigarette, saw Roth's taxi ease into traffic moving south on Fifth Avenue. Towers tried hailing an unoccupied taxi, but they cruised down the avenue with their off-duty lights on. Not enough taxis, traffic up the wazoo, and a million shoppers with lots of cash—a hack's dream, a sellers market. Traffic was backing up at the light at East 65th Street. Rivera held up a twenty, and two taxies pulled over, dueled with blaring horns for President Jackson. Rivera got in the first one.

"That taxi there." He pointed ahead. "With the poster for *Les Miserables* on the trunk. Follow him, but not too close. Got it?"

The driver nodded, turned on the meter. Rivera dropped his hat in his lap, looked at the driver in the rear-view mirror. He removed his automatic from his overcoat, reached into his jacket, removed the silencer, screwed it onto the muzzle, all the while keeping his eyes on the driver who didn't look back.

Rivera watched Towers running down the sidewalk across the street, trying to catch up with Roth's taxi. Who this dipshit running after the broad was, he didn't know—but he'd better find out. He cursed Robert under his breath. "You better not be holding out on me, fucker."

The traffic on Fifth Avenue snailed south once the light at East 65th Street changed. Rivera kept his eye on Roth's taxi, occasionally looking back to see Towers hurrying along the pavement. There was no doubt about it, he and schmucko were interested in the same taxi. Rivera chuckled.

More empty taxis with off-duty lights on rolled past schmucko, who glanced skywards just as the weather turned nasty. Now and then a taxi pulled over for a savvy New Yorker, but the drivers ignored Towers who looked dangerously like a quarter tipper, a less desirable fare than a gang of kids Harlem-bound with ghetto blasters.

Towers ran 12 blocks, once nearly catching-up with Roth's taxi. He dodged Christmas shoppers who hurried past him, their faces down against the gusts of cold rain, falling heavily now.

At Central Park South, Roth's taxi turned west, then U-turned and pulled up in front of the Park-Strawberry Hotel. Rivera instructed his driver to pull over. He looked back at Towers, cutting the corner across 59th Street and Fifth Avenue, sopping wet, panting, and holding his side.

Rivera got his first good look at Roth as he stepped out of the taxi, holding his hand out for the woman. A doorman hurried down the steps with an umbrella.

Checking the area, Roth made note of a dozen things, a dozen faces. He saw a big Latino getting out of a taxi across the street, then scanned along his side of Central Park South, just as a dark-blue van pulled up near the hotel entrance. He saw Towers humping towards the hotel, looking like a half-drowned rat about to have heart failure. He took Rachel's arm and they went up the steps and into the hotel.

Towers stopped running and bent over, hands on his knees, gasping for breath.

Rivera crossed the street. It had been an expensive ride, but at least he knew where his mark was staying—no thanks to his client—which meant that Roth didn't want his client to know where he was staying. Roth was being cautious? Did he smell a hit?

Rivera bounced up the steps, looked back at Towers who was fifty yards from the hotel, hardly moving. Inside, he followed Roth and the woman through the crowded lobby to the elevators. Apparently, Roth was already checked in, had a room key in his hand. Rivera crammed himself into the same elevator car, listened as passengers called out their floors. From behind him, Roth called "tenth floor." Rivera called the eleventh. By the time the car reached the tenth, there were only five occupants in the elevator. Roth and Rachel stepped out and the operator started to close the gate, but Rivera blocked the door with his foot. He watched Roth and the woman push through heavy glass doors leading to the corridors.

"I'm on this floor." He apologized to the operator, stepping out. His eyes scanned the area, spotted the security camera high up on the wall, monitoring the elevator bank.

Roth and Rachel turned into the corridor alone. Roth held his .38 in his coat pocket.

Rivera pushed through the glass doors. No cameras covered the corridors. He reached under his coat, fingered the automatic's safety off, and followed them down the corridor. But his luck wasn't holding; a large party was coming out of a room on the same wing. Too many witnesses. Either he took the whole bunch down right now, or just identify Roth's room. Later would be better. Whacking a flock of Christmas shoppers from out of town would be sloppy. Besides, the client didn't want the woman with Roth to get hit.

Room 1019. Roth and the woman entered, closed the door. Rivera heard a deadbolt thrown. He walked back to the elevators, dropped his head as he passed under the closed-circuit camera, and went back downstairs with the crowd.

Roth occupied a bedroom suite complete with bar. He reminded Rachel of Jack Scarlett in so many ways. As she was taking off her coat, he whisked her into the bedroom, threw her coat and purse on a chair. He kissed her, running his hands across her body, then caught himself, pulled away. "Later for this. Call Hewlett first."

"Now?"

"Right now. The ultimatum's up, baby. As of today. Hit 'em quick and hard. Don't let 'em think. Hewlett will know what to do. Tell him you want the checks tomorrow."

"Just like that?"

"Just like that. Acid-test time."

She started to pick up the phone in the bedroom.

"Use the one out there," Roth said, thumbing towards the sitting room.

Rachel shrugged, went into the next room, found the phone on the bar. She called Hewlett's office. He was in, and said he was just about to call her to suggest the same thing. He'd make the calls and get back to her. She gave the hotel number and Roth's room.

In the bedroom, Roth went through Rachel's purse and coat, since she wasn't carrying anything on her body. No weapons in her coat, none in her purse. There was a gift-wrapped present. He started to read the card tied to it as Rachel hung up the phone. He dropped the purse back on the chair.

———

From his eyrie on the forty-fifth floor, Hewlett looked down on Fifth Avenue mobbed with shoppers. Ants from up here, scurrying along the sidewalks, crossing at intersections in an orderly fashion. He'd heard nothing from Amalgamated Life or Chase-Hampshire since their pathetic requests for just a little more time, the language in their letters being almost identical. He went to his desk, called Amalgamated Life's New York office, and was put on hold. He scribbled a reminder for a few Christmas gifts he still needed to pick up. At least he was spared having to buy another mink this year. He thought of the lovely Mrs. MacMillan again.

"Kincannon." His voice came on the line.

"Robert Howell Hewlett here, Mr. Kincannon. On the MacMillan matter. My watch reads eleven o'clock. Five hours until the county clerk's office closes. Shall I dispatch my clerk, Mr. Kincannon?"

"No. No, Mr. Hewlett. That won't be necessary," Kincannon said into the receiver. There was defeat in his voice. "No need to file a suit."

Hewlett smiled. He liked striking fear into the hearts of grown men. Especially at Christmas time.

"We can have the check ready for you on Monday, the 27th." Kincannon said.

"You can have the check ready tomorrow, Mr. Kincannon," Hewlett countered, rubbing his chin. He looked into the mirror on his credenza, took a comb from his breast pocket, stroked it through his beard. "My client is leaving on an extended trip, and won't be returning until after the 1st. She'd like to pick up the check, and I agree that it'll be safer in her bank than remaining with Amalgamated Life."

"That puts quite a rush on me," Kincannon objected.

"Rush? My dear Mr. Kincannon, you've had precisely 110 days since my client filed her claim. Nations have risen and fallen within that time, ancient galleys have sailed new oceans in lesser time. That doesn't strike me as a rush, so, regrettably, it's tomorrow or my clerk takes that subway ride this afternoon."

"All right. All right. Tomorrow. But before three o'clock. We're closing early."

"Merry Christmas, Mr. Kincannon."

"And two words right back at ya," Kincannon growled, slamming down the receiver. He looked up to find his assistant, Rowena Walsh, standing at the door. They stared at each other for a moment, and both shrugged.

———

In the hotel lobby, Rivera found Towers standing by the elevators, anxiously looking around. A duck out of water. The hotel was packed, being two days before Christmas, but it wouldn't be long before the dicks noticed both of them. Christmas brought pickpocket opportunities galore. He hummed a Christmas tune lightly, adding his own lyrics: "Tis the season to be jolly, fleece the marks, but quick, by golly." Whistling that tune, Rivera approached the reception desk. A young man, dapperly dressed, leaned on the counter, gave him a ten-cent smile. His name-tag read, "Craig."

"Have you anything available, Craig? A last minute thing, I'm afraid."

"I'm terribly sorry, sir. We haven't anything available until the New Year. Not until January 15th, actually." He was somewhat pleased with the hotel's exclusivity.

Rivera pushed folded bills across to the clerk. Craig's eyes fell on three 100-dollar bills. Rivera smiled. "Are you sure?"

"Let me just go and check to be certain" he said, a smile on his lips approximating Ben Franklin's. He disappeared, and returned shortly with a key. "What luck, sir. We've just had a cancelation. A single, and I'm afraid it's only for one night."

"My business will only keep me here one night," Rivera said.

Craig deftly palmed the bills, quoted the room rate, slid a registration form across to Rivera, asked if he would be paying by cash or credit card.

"Cash."

"That'll be 350, sir." Craig smiled.

Rivera forked over another four 100-dollar bills, completed the registration with not one true fact, and waved Craig off when he returned with fifty dollars change.

"Oh, thank you very much, sir," Craig said crisply, pocketing the extra bonus. In all, Rivera was out 700 dollars. He'd add that to his client's bill. He pocketed his room key, tossed a salute to Craig, and walked past Towers, who looked lost and was checking faces, his head ping-ponging across the lobby as though he was watching a tennis match. Rivera stood directly in front of him. Towers looked past him, didn't recognize him from just 15 minutes ago on Fifth Avenue. One thing was certain, he's no copper, Rivera thought, as he headed for the elevators.

His room was small, at the end of the eighth floor, facing West 58th Street. He checked around, examined the lock—which should be the same type for all the rooms in the hotel—then hung the "*Do Not Disturb*" sign on the doorknob and returned to the elevators. He pressed the service button, studying the security cameras by the elevator bank. At the gift shop in the lobby, he bought a can of shaving cream. He found Towers again, wandering around the lobby. He strolled over, stood next to Towers, and without looking at him said, "Have you checked the bar?"

Towers looked at him. It still didn't register that Rivera had asked him for a light on Fifth Avenue. "What?" Towers asked, uncertain whether the stranger was talking to him.

"Follow me," Rivera said. "The bar." He walked off, and a confused Towers followed, wondering who the hell this guy was. The Cuban took a seat at a cocktail table near the window facing Central Park. The bar was starting to get busy for lunch. Christmas music spilled across the spacious room as tourists began pouring in, fresh from shopping adventures. Towers stood next to Rivera's table, wanting to know what he wanted. Whoever he was, he obviously knew what was going on. Rivera gestured to a seat opposite and Towers sat down.

"Cards on the table, huh, fella?" Rivera said. "You tell me who you are and what you want with Roth, I'll tell you who I am."

Towers looked like he'd been hit in the face with a sack of shit. That was Roth in the taxi? Lori was with Roth? "Who are you?"

"I guess it's no deal, huh?" Rivera started to get up. He knew how to play this jerk.

"Yeah, yeah. Okay," Towers agreed, fearful he'd lose any hope of learning what the hell was going on. He identified himself, even showed his ID, and told his story, right up until this morning when he'd left Marcia's apartment. He showed Rivera the photographs of Peter and Lori MacMillan.

Stupid fuck. Rivera's interest turned to the insurance angle. Roth must be muscling in on his client's scam, and, apparently, on his wife as well. This wasn't just a jealous husband thing. But Towers had no idea how much insurance money was involved. Rivera glossed over his interest, hinting that he was with the DEA, maybe CIA, anything with initials. He was completely astounded at Towers' gullibility, especially since he was a State Department guy. Rivera studied him, thinking over his story. *This fucker's got his head into the woman so far he can't think straight.* He wondered if maybe he'd even get to poke her when this business was finished. Why not? So far, it seemed like she was laying down for everyone else in the game.

"Let's go see this Miss Post," Rivera said.

"But what about Lori and Roth?"

"We've got them covered," Rivera assured him, suggesting that he wasn't working alone. "They're not going anywhere."

"Why do you want to meet Miss Post?"

"You'll see," Rivera replied.

"I'd better call her." Towers stood, looking for a phone. "Make sure she's home."

Rivera handed Towers his mobile, had to instruct him how to use it.

Towers called while Rivera scanned the area for hotel detectives. An uneasy feeling swept over him. No one was watching them as far as he could determine, but the situation just didn't have a good feel to it. He casually checked the diners, the waiters, the traffic in and out, and then the drinkers at the bar. Nothing he could put his finger on.

"Okay," Towers said, closing the phone. "She's at the apartment."

Towers followed Rivera outside. They caught a taxi discharging passengers. The driver immediately switched on his off-duty light, waved them off without apology, but Rivera jumped in and slid across the back seat, beckoned Towers in. He handed the driver a twenty-dollar bill, said, "Seventy-second Street and Third Avenue."

To Towers' amazement, the cabbie didn't argue. All it took was money. He should've done that on Fifth Avenue instead of getting a hernia chasing Lori's taxi in the rain.

"She lives on 68th Street," Towers objected.

Rivera whispered, "We'll walk a few blocks."

Okay with Towers. This guy apparently knew what he was doing.

———

Marcia Post proved to be Towers' intellectual equal. As Towers hung his wet overcoat up, she got him a towel and went through his overnight case, looking for a dry shirt, said that he should change out of his wet clothes. Towers smiled at her when she called him Willie. She related to Rivera everything she'd already told Towers, not thinking to even ask who Rivera was. Another government guy, she guessed, rather impressed with herself being at the center of all this intrigue. She rattled on as she absently appraised his leather gloves which he hadn't removed, wondered briefly if they were a Christmas gift from someone. She pondered if she shouldn't pick up a little something for Willie. It wasn't really appropriate, since she'd only known him for 24 hours, but maybe he'd appreciate it, being how he was away from home.

Rivera sat patiently as Towers added more, addressing Miss Post as Marcia, probably for the first time. They made a cute couple: Confederated Idiots Unlimited. Rivera listened, then nodded, stood and asked to use the bathroom. He went in, leaving Towers and Marcia shrugging and making stupid faces at one another over the mystery. Rivera closed the bathroom door. He withdrew his automatic, thumbed off the safety, and placed the weapon on the toilet lid. He examined himself in the mirror, checking his teeth. He ran a comb through his long black hair, straightened his tie. He glanced at his reflection sideways, stood close to the mirror and made a face to see if he needed to trim his nose hairs. Then he picked up his automatic, returned to the living room, and pumped two rounds each into cute Willie and Marcia.

This was really going to cost his client.

He removed all of the ID from Towers' body and overnight case. No way he could conceal Marcia's ID, it was her apartment, after all. But, she lived alone. He dragged their bodies into the kitchen, emptied out the refrigerator, turned it around, and laid it down. He stuffed Marcia's body in first, crammed Towers in on top of her. But one arm hung out, so Rivera stepped into the refrigerator and stomped both bodies into the box. For good measure, he turned off the heat in the apartment and opened the window, flooding the place with an immediate chill. It would be days before their bodies started to stink. He sat on the refrigerator door, heard a bone break, and reloaded the automatic's magazine.

———

Early evening. In the Warner apartment, Robert went to the fridge. He took out the tuna sandwich, peeled the cellophane from around the plate, poured a glass of orange juice. He was just about to bite into the sandwich when the phone rang.

It was Mom. Yes, he said, they were coming down for Christmas. Tomorrow evening. No, they wouldn't be late. Their flights were on schedule and the weather was co-operating. Love and kisses, Mom. Say 'hi' to Doc. He picked up his sandwich again and thought of Rachel, where she was right now, and what she was doing with that bastard. Losing his appetite, he dropped the sandwich back on the plate, put it on the floor.

"Barbie. C'mere, girl. Mommy slut has made something for you." He carried his orange juice into the living room as he heard Barbie padding into the kitchen across the tile floor.

———

Rachel's passion soared, her lust surpassing even their time in Bangkok. The separation from Roth had been unbearable, an eternity. Not once had she even looked at another man and, as always, she'd had opportunities galore.

Roth was an animal, devouring her like there'd never be another time. She felt an inexplicable sadness in him, a longing to hold her, to possess her forever. Well, they had forever, hadn't they? At least until she got bored of him, until she no longer needed him.

Their play was interrupted by the bedside phone at 8:00 p.m. Roth answered it, listened briefly, then hung up. He turned the ringtone volume down, and resumed that delightful thing he'd been doing to her. She resisted the pleasure, asking who called. He told her there was a queue of women forming in the hallway, demanding their turn. She giggled, guessing that it was the hotel operator.

Around midnight, she dozed off, only to awaken shortly after from the glow on the TV set. No sound. Roth was standing by the set, adjusting a VCR.

"What are you doing?"

Roth stepped back, viewed the screen. A black and white picture of the hallway appeared, as seen from the bottom of the door in the living room. Rachel noticed the camcorder for the first time, and her eyes followed a line that snaked down from behind the bureau, ran out into the living room, and across the floor to a point where it disappeared under the door to the corridor. The TV set in the living room was also hooked up. It was a pin-point camera set-up, similar to the one in her apartment.

"Why are you doing that?"

"You tell me."

"I've no idea."

"Then don't worry about it."

"You think we're being watched?" She pulled the sheet up to cover her breasts.

Roth reeled in the snake camera from under the door, smiled at her. *"We're* not, but—" He pointed it at her. The images on the TV went berserk for a moment, then finally she appeared on the screen. She let go of the sheet and snuck a quick look.

Although shy at first, she pushed the sheet aside and admired herself on screen. Roth scooted next to her, his crotch coming into view, next to her face. His position suggested what Rachel proceeded to do, watching her progress as she worked on him. She'd never done a video before, but decided to buy the best technology available. As soon as possible. Tomorrow. A Christmas present for herself. Damn, but this was fun! Roth always did the craziest things.

He lit a cigarette. "Heard from Towers lately?"

She stopped what she was doing. "Towers?"

"Yes. William Towers. Manila?"

"No," she said, hesitated. "Well, he wrote me several times, and left messages on the machine in LA, but I never answered. Why would I want to see him? Why are you asking?"

"You know me, babe. I'm crazy jealous about you," he said without conviction.

―――――

Robert's stomach hurt. He felt hungry, yet he didn't feel like eating more cottage cheese. He went into the kitchen, poured a large glass of milk. That's what people with ulcers did. Milk must be soothing. He drained the glass, and after a short while, his stomach did start to feel better. He returned to the living room, crashed back on the couch, wondering when Rivera would call to tell him that Roth qualified for morgue benefits. He put the earphones back on, placed the phone close by.

In the bedroom, Barbie twisted in agony beneath Rachel's bed, whining occasionally, yelping when a sharp pain ripped through her tiny abdomen.

―――――

In Roth's suite, Rachel dozed off again and didn't hear the phone ring in the living room. It was 2:00 a.m. Roth grabbed his trousers and moved quietly to get it, picked up the extension on the bar. He cupped the receiver to his shoulder, listened as he pulled his trousers on, then hung up. He went back in the bedroom, pulled the camera eye from under the bedding, snaked it into the living room and over to the door. He stooped and pushed it under the crack, twisted the neck, working it into position to view the hallway. He looked back at the TV monitor.

A familiar face jolted him. Rivera stood on the other side, head turned sideways against his door, listening. He was facing down the corridor towards the elevators, and hadn't seen the camera eye peek out by his feet.

Roth backed away from the door, his heart pounding, eyes glued to the TV. Rivera reached into his pocket, produced a set of lock picks. It would take him only seconds to open the door if he was any good. Roth moved to the closet and fumbled through his clothes, found his revolver in his inside coat pocket. He glanced over his shoulder into the bedroom. He could only see the foot of the bed. Rachel didn't stir. He freed his pistol and backed away from the closet, stood in front of the TV, watching Rivera, who was concentrating on the lock. Roth aimed his pistol at the door, to fire as soon as it opened. One lock clicked and Rivera held the tension bar, holding the latch unlocked as he pulled an automatic pistol from his coat. A silencer—looking as menacing as the pistol itself—made the piece look like a cannon. Roth cocked his .38-caliber snub-nose, controlled his nervous breathing, braced to fire. The last thing Rivera would ever see was Roth's .38 exploding in his face. Roth's pistol hand shook, his forehead a shower of sweat. He hadn't killed anyone in a long time.

But Rivera couldn't defeat the deadbolt. Roth watched the TV as the Cuban mouthed a curse having to do with his mother, then leaned into the door to ensure the bottom latch stayed free. He stuffed the automatic back into his overcoat, brought out his pick again, and started working on the deadbolt.

Then he froze. Seconds passed and he didn't move; the door didn't move. Was he going to try to kick the door open, spray the room? Did he sense a trap inside? Smell it? Roth's eyes kept jumping between the door and the TV, unsure which to trust, the door's movement or the screen. He looked back into the bedroom, at Rachel, to be certain she wasn't sneaking up from behind to plunge a knife into his back. He listened for the door to creak, but heard only the raw fear of his heart beating in his ears. He moved closer to the door, out of viewing range of the TV, his pistol arm extended.

The door still didn't move.

Was the assassin checking his piece, wondering if he'd chambered a round. Maybe he'd just knock and when Roth answered, empty the automatic through the door. Roth edged out of the way, in case the assassin knew he was just on the other side, in case he decided to fire blindly through the door. Roth reached over, silently turned back the deadbolt. Now the assassin could just turn the knob and open the door.

But Rivera worked the pick furiously, which only relocked the deadbolt.

Roth heard someone else in the hall. Talking. Laughing. He backed up, jerked his eyes to the TV screen. A couple was coming down the hall. The assassin's automatic was still in his coat.

On his side of the door, Rivera paused once he'd heard the elevator doors open on the floor. He dug into his pocket, as though searching for his room key as the couple sauntered down the corridor towards him.

He turned and walked slowly towards the elevators, fiddling with his own room key, and passed the couple who seemed to take forever to reach their room. It was risky hanging around on the floor too long. Security dicks checked at regular intervals and there was the camera, its view obscured by shaving cream. It was unlikely that the cameras were monitored constantly. That would require too many eyes. There were hundreds of them in a place this big. Still, someone would look eventually, and see only a blurry image on the screen that monitored the elevator bank.

The couple was laughing, the man hanging all over the woman. *Having a goddamn great ol' time.* Rivera swore silently, trying to appear casual. The woman reached into her handbag. It was her room they were going to. Bitch probably picked up some guy and was dragging his drunken ass back for a quick romp for legal tender, a pro working the Park-Strawberry for Santa Claus money. High-class doll, at that. A good-looking bitch—redhead. They passed behind him, the man glancing back, maybe suspiciously, Rivera thought.

He continued down the hall towards the elevators, not wanting to alarm the couple as they reached her room, unlocked the door, and entered.

Roth stooped down and manipulated the pin-point camera, twisted it over to see the couple enter the room three doors beyond his. He twisted the neck back towards the assassin in time to catch him rounding the corner, going out of view.

Roth opened the door, slipped out, flipping the security bar across the path of the closing door so that he wouldn't lock himself out, then raced barefoot along the plush carpet towards the elevator, revolver first.

Rivera doubled back through the glass doors, thinking about the redhead. He'd seen her somewhere. Where was it? He shrugged, neared the corner of the corridor. He stopped. The redhead. Where *had* he seen her? Wait. It was that place where he'd met his client.

Roth rounded the corner, ran into Rivera who was just standing there, his automatic still in his coat, his mind on the redhead. The Cuban's eyes widened. He reached into his coat for the automatic.

"Go ahead," Roth urged, the barrel of his .38 in Rivera's face.

Rivera dropped his hands, backed away, and Roth advanced to the point where they both glanced up quickly at the security camera whose lens was covered with shaving cream. Rivera backed out of the glass doors to the elevator bank. The silencer's length. Damn, it would be easier to pull a howitzer from his pocket. He backed up further and Roth waved the nose of his revolver, directing Rivera to the fire door next to the elevator bank.

"If you want my money," Rivera tried, "please take it, but don't hurt me, mister."

"Yeah, that's it. Your wallet. It's that bulge right there in your coat pocket. Why don't you take it out for me? Huh, fella?"

Rivera backed through the heavy stairwell door. "Sure, mister. Just don't shoot."

Roth inched closer, the barrel of his snub-nose two feet from Rivera's head. He threw his shoulder against the stairwell door to keep it from closing in his face, and let it ease shut behind him. Rivera backed against the railing behind him—as far as he could go, unless he started down the stairs. He looked down. The stairwell was dark except for a single light bulb on each floor, circling the shaft from which a draft of cool air rushed up, carrying a dull breathing sound, as though the concrete walls were alive.

Roth suddenly rushed forward. Rivera threw up his arms instinctively to cover his face, and tumbled backwards over the balustrade. His hands shot out with a cat's speed, and he grabbed hold of the railing. He swung back and forth wildly, then dangled there. Roth stood above him, looking down at him, his eyes cold, unfeeling. He put the barrel of his .38 on Rivera's nose, looked down into the dim void of the circular stairwell, a five-foot-wide funneling abyss straight down to hell.

Another gush of chilly air blew up the shaft, yet Rivera was sweating. "Give me a chance, huh?"

"Like you were gonna give me?" Roth said, his voice shaking.

"I don't know what you're talking about."

"'Course you don't, fella." Roth cocked his revolver.

Rivera went for his automatic, hanging by one hand, jabbing his right hand down into his coat pocket. He struggled to free the gun, wondering why Roth didn't fire. He yanked back and forth. The silencer was caught on the pocket lining, and his overcoat flapped as he worked to free the weapon. His gloves didn't help, he was losing his grip. He was dead and knew it. He managed to free the automatic, swung his body, bringing the weapon up to fire, to take this sonofabitch with him.

Roth smashed his revolver down across the bridge of Rivera's nose, and the assassin's hand slid off the railing. He dropped his .45, threw his other hand up, but too late. He fell, clawing at air, his eyes the size of saucers, terror closing his throat. He made not a sound, but sickening thuds echoed up the circular tunnel as his body struck the railing on several floors, ricocheting from one to the other. He was dead before he hit the bottom, blood and brain matter decorated the stairwell on half the floors.

Roth stared down into the void for long moments. He inched open the fire door, checked the elevator area. It was empty. He darted past the elevators and through the glass doors to the corridor and hurried back to his room.

Inside, he went to the bar and poured a drink, shaking so badly he had to use both hands. He slurped at the whiskey and carried his glass to the bedroom door. Rachel stirred and turned over. Dead asleep. He drained the glass, poured another, drained that.

He watched the hallway on the TV screen. Within minutes, there was activity in the corridor. Hotel security men followed by police officers appeared for a few seconds, working frantically on their radios, then vanished. They were trying to determine from which floor the assassin fell. Not an easy job; Rivera's head struck the railing on the eighth floor first. That would mean he fell from the ninth or higher. And there was no indication of another person's involvement. Not unless the landing was dusty and Roth had left his footprints. Roth checked his feet. They were a little dirty. But by now there were a dozen house dicks and cops running up and down the stairwell. If he'd left footprints, a hundred shoes might obliterate them. But the assassin's automatic with silencer would rule out a suicide or likely accident. Shit. He carried his drink into the corridor and walked down to the elevator bank. Two uniformed cops and a hotel security guy stood guard. The steel door to the stairwell landing was held open by a wooden wedge.

"Hey, what's happening?" Roth inquired.

One of the cops answered. "Nothing, sir. Just go back to your room, all right?"

"Is there a fire?" Roth asked, concern in his voice. He walked out onto the landing, up behind a plain-clothes hotel security officer.

"There's nothing to worry about, sir. Just go back to your room."

Roth looked over the railing. Flashlights were visible on all the lower floors and a few above them. "That's what the captain of the *Titanic* said: 'Nothing to worry about, folks.'"

"Sir," a stern voice called from the landing above. "You can't come out here. Go back inside. We ain't telling you again."

Roth looked up at a plain-clothes detective. "Okay, okay. Just don't let the hotel sink." He raised his glass in a salute, went back to his room.

His ass was covered. Four people had seen him out on the landing.

Soon, police and security staff converged on the floor en masse. Initial investigations had determined that the dead man's gun had been fired recently, and upon finding the shaving cream on the security camera, they concluded that the tenth floor was the likely place from where the man had fallen. They checked the doors along the corridor to see if any were left ajar. While they wouldn't wake up a hundred guests, they did start checking registrations, and would spend the night quietly investigating if Rivera had harmed anyone before he sailed down the stairwell.

The unfortunate guest in 1012 had priors for petty gambling charges: running numbers in Brooklyn and taking bets on the ponies. He was rousted from his sleep and interviewed downstairs in the manager's office until morning, but none of the other guests were interviewed, since the police believed they had the connection to the dead man.

From the moment Roth picked Rachel up the previous afternoon, he'd been on guard. That was the earliest the Tierney's could've organized a move against him, since they couldn't realistically place him anywhere up until then. But why? If they whacked him now, that would have placed their claims in jeopardy.

Still, this must have been Robert's doing. A solo act. Had Rachel known about an attempted hit, she wouldn't have wanted to be around, and she certainly wouldn't have been asleep.

Roth closed the door to the bedroom. He poured another drink and moved a chair up near the door to the corridor. Even with police prowling around the hotel, a second, more determined assassin might make another move. Two men, he'd been told earlier. Was there a second gunman? Roth wouldn't be able to sleep, but the shakes finally stopped with his third double whiskey.

41

Cesar Surces, aka Anthony Rivera, aka Tony Rivers was in the morgue on First Avenue. Multiple cranial fractures. His head looked like a coconut that an elephant had tap-danced on. The silencer was homemade, and his automatic, of course, wasn't licensed. Given his extensive rap sheet for everything from aggravated assault to manslaughter, the police weren't concerned that he was an innocent victim. This wouldn't be a high profile case.

Dawn. Roth shaved and showered with the bathroom door open, then called room service as Rachel started to stir. But she just rolled over, mumbled he should come back to bed, then dozed back off.

The *New York Times* slid under the door, but Roth called down for the *Post* and *Daily News*. There was nothing in the early editions about last night; the item probably hadn't reached the City Desk this early, and the hotel was probably trying to quash the story. Gunmen rampaging through a five-star hotel wasn't good for business.

Rachel opened her eyes finally, thoughts of Robert waking her fully. He should be dead by now. She slipped into the bathroom, brushed her teeth, and turned on the shower.

Hewlett called at nine o'clock and Roth answered. "Yeah?"

"Uhm, who is this?" Hewlett asked.

"Well, who the fuck are you?" Roth snapped back.

"Mr. Hewlett."

"Hold the phone, *Mr.* Hewlett. Next time identify yourself before asking who's answering. Or didn't you learn any manners at Harvard?" He handed the phone to Rachel. She spoke briefly with Hewlett, amused by Roth's way of putting a fine point on things. The lawyer's romantic notions were squashed.

Hewlett coolly told her that the checks would be cut today. Roth, listening on the line in the other room, cupped the receiver, called to Rachel. She told Hewlett to hold on, cupped hers.

"Tell him you want to pick up the checks yourself."

"Pick them up personally?"

"Why not? You told him you're moving, didn't you?"

"Yeah, but—"

"But nothing. Pick up both checks today, then we're outta here."

Rachel gave Hewlett his instructions and hung up. On his end, Hewlett wondered how the man had known he was Harvard Law. Whatever, Mrs. MacMillan seemed to keep rough company, indeed.

"He'll call back when it's arranged," she said. "I assume your report went in to the companies?"

"Yeah." Roth laughed. "My clients were very dissatisfied. Nina was, too. Said that she expected a lot more than what I gave them."

"I'd like to read them sometime."

"Sure. If you like fiction."

Roth poured himself another coffee and lit a cigarette. He stood at the window overlooking Central Park while Rachel fussed with her hair. Central Park South was heavy with traffic, but the weather was better. Not so cold, and no rain.

Rachel needed time alone. To take care of the mess in the apartment. She called to Roth. "You're not going to your office?"

"No. Nina thinks I'm in Bangkok. I'm yours for a week, kiddo."

She went up to Roth and hugged him from behind, thinking about the money, about next week in Florida. "I didn't have a chance to tell you, you always cut me off on the phone so fast," she scolded. "We're going down to Tampa. I want you to meet Mom for Christmas. Just for a few days. I've reserved the tickets and we can pick them up at the airline office across the street. Then we'll jump across to Bimini or somewhere—"

"We?"

"You and I. Robert was going, but he's not, after all."

"Why not?"

"Uhm, he's got something to do here."

"What?"

"I—I don't know."

He grabbed her bathrobe at the collar, pulled her to him. "Try that again."

"I think there's a girl he wants to spend Christmas with here in the city," she invented.

They studied each other, both wondering what the other was thinking. He was wondering about Robert; she was wondering if he suspected that Robert was being eliminated.

"Who?"

"He didn't say."

Roth smiled. She was lying. Again. But why? He relaxed his grip on the bathrobe, patted her ass.

She smiled. No need for him to learn about Robert until next week. Then she'd tell him that she'd had to do it. For them. She remembered her Christmas present for him and went to her purse, took out the package. "Here, you never wear one," she said.

He read the card and she bit her lip, watching his reaction to her gift. *"To a Great Private Dick."* Roth chuckled, unwrapped the box. It was a gold Cartier wristwatch. He met Rachel's twinkling eyes, saw her pleasure, her delightful willingness to please him, like when she'd handed over the money in Bangkok.

"It's beautiful, baby," he said.

"I knew you'd like it. You never wear a watch. Merry Christmas." She threw her arms around his waist, hugged him, admiring the piece which had set her back 7,000 dollars. She buckled the leather band around his wrist, taking in the gleaming gold, the tiny diamonds in the face.

"What made you select this?"

"Robert mentioned it, actually. He saw one somewhere and was hinting." She shrugged apologetically. "I got him one, too. Had to, you know?" *No problem, I can return his.*

"Sure," Roth said. "I've got a surprise for you, too."

"Oh! What?"

"Uh uh, beauty. You get my present later."

Hewlett called back and said that she could personally pick up both checks, anytime before 3:00 p.m. He asked if she wanted him along. Her eyes deferred to Roth, listening in on the extension, and he shook his head.

"It won't be necessary, Mr. Hewlett."

Good, Hewlett thought. After his 'chat' with her crude friend, he was only going to send an associate along with her anyhow. He looked at his watch. He'd make the 1:10 to White Plains, be home in front of the fireplace by 3:00.

"Do I owe you anything on account?" Rachel asked. *Not that you'll ever see it.*

He said that she owed another 1,000 dollars—*thanks again to your crude friend, Mrs. MacMillan*—but he told her just to send a check at her convenience. When she hung up, Roth plopped on the bed, pulling her next to him. He picked up the receiver, called the Warner apartment.

Robert answered a dull "Hello."

"Hey, dickhead. How you doin'?"

Rachel froze. So, Robert was still alive!

Robert froze. So, Roth was still alive! He was expecting to hear from Rivera, or maybe from Rachel, frantically screaming that Roth was lying dead in a pool of blood.

Silence. Then, "I'm doin' okay." He wasn't. His stomach ached something terrible. "Packing for Florida."

Roth glanced at Rachel, who could only hear one side of the conversation. "You sound surprised to hear from me. Listen, Rachel's picking up the checks today, and you're going along. Then, she's got something to handle." He threw open his robe, put her hand on his manhood, winked at her. She curled up at the head of the bed, listening, her mind racing.

"It's not necessary for me to go with you," Robert objected.

"Sure it is, buddy. You and I'll wait outside for Rachel while she makes the withdrawals, so to speak. That way I know my partners won't forget me, maybe run off without me."

Rachel pulled away and sat up, looking hurt. Roth stroked her cheek, then took her hand and put it back on his member.

"It's not necessary I go along," Robert repeated, feeling again like he needed to bolt to the toilet.

"I said it *is* necessary," Roth snapped. "Call you later. Stay close to the phone." He hung up.

Robert fingered the buttons on the phone. Should he call Rivera? No. Better not. Let the man do his job. He'd report in when he had something to report. He was a professional.

Rachel rolled over in bed. Her plan wasn't working. No immediate concern, however. Roth was here now. He'd keep Robert in line until she had another chance to take him out of the picture. Maybe after they picked up the checks, she'd find a way of getting Robert back to their apartment alone. Roth would insist on holding the checks, of course, but he wouldn't want to go back to the apartment for something as mundane as packing. She'd pull Robert aside, hint that she had a plan, anything to get him back to the apartment alone, where she'd dispatch him once and for all. She'd get him naked, no task that, maybe for a bubble bath. He was just stupid enough to fall for that. She'd do the business on him with a bludgeon or a butcher's knife. Her mind turned to reviewing what weapons she could improvise from what was in the apartment. After she killed Robert, she'd take Barbie and her bag, remove all traces from the place. That would take a few hours. Robert had no priors, had never been in the military, and she couldn't think of any reason why his fingerprints would be on file. Good; she wouldn't have to chop his fingers off. But why risk it? Off they'd come. A butcher's knife could accomplish that. Dental records? They were in Florida. No chance that they'd ever cross with Robert's corpse if he couldn't be identified. What else? What else? She'd need three hours in the apartment.

Hewlett called back with more details. Chase-Hampshire had just called him and said that 2:00 p.m. was the deadline to pick up their check. She could pick it up at the cashier's office on the fourteenth floor of the building bearing its name. For the Amalgamated check, their office was at Rockefeller Center. He gave the details and she wrote them down, Roth reading over her shoulder.

"Convenient," Roth whispered, his lips to her ear as he studied what she'd written. "They're only a few blocks apart."

Rachel hung up, peeled the note from the pad.

"Things happen when you got the right attorney," Roth said, rolling on his back.

"How do you know Hewlett? Have you two played this game before?"

"Never met him, actually. He's a ball-breaker. Makes the insurance boys squirm when he enters the picture. A kick-ass litigator who knows insurance law better than the people who write the policies."

"Well, he got action quick enough."

"No, sweetie." Roth reached over, tweaked her chin. "Just to keep the record straight, *I* got the action. The companies didn't know what hit 'em. What were they gonna do? Start investigating all over again? Not a chance with Hewlett on their ass."

She watched Roth's face. His eyes were fixed hard, his words venomous whenever he talked about insurance companies. That's why she trusted him from the first. He loathed the companies with dedication. "You *really* hate insurance companies. Don't you?"

Roth rolled over and put out his cigarette, then laid on his chest between Rachel's thighs and took hold of her wrists, his arms on the outside.

"Damned right, I hate the sonsabitches. My mother was a day late in paying insurance premiums, after carrying her insurance with the same company for twenty years. One day late and there was a fire. The bastards refused to cover the damage." Roth kissed her belly, buried his mouth in her navel and raspberried her. She howled and tried to squirm away, but Roth held her wrists and blew harder. She screamed and Roth looked up, rolled his eyes, licked his lips. "Didn't you know that I trained at the navel academy?" Rachel burst out laughing, and Roth looked up again. "If you laugh too hard, you'll fart."

That made her laugh all the harder, and she was turning red-faced. He stopped, released her so she could regain her composure.

"I thought you hated insurance companies because they refused to pay you for that time you spent rotting in jail, wherever that place was."

Roth frowned, then nodded. "Yeah. That, too."

They had sex again, then showered together at Roth's insistence. He had no intention of taking his eyes off her, not for a minute. But she was clean—the closest thing she had to a weapon was a nail file. Just the same, she might find his revolver if he didn't watch her. Moreover, he didn't want her to discover the crate in the closet.

She got out of the shower first and stood by the mirror, started working on her face. He finished, stepped from the stall, and jumped back startled—her face was covered with green slime.

"Fucking hell! You look like the Incredible Hulk in drag."

She flashed him a breast, went on with her facial. When she finished, she went into the bedroom while Roth shaved. He watched her in the mirror as she moved around the room, then sat at the foot of the bed. Shortly after, Rachel exclaimed, "God! Isn't she ugly?" She was lying on her back in bed, head propped up on a pillow, her legs spread wide, guiding the snake camera here and there, watching the monitor.

Roth dried his face, caught her position on the TV. He came out of the bathroom and laughed at her contorted posture, a *Kama Sutra* position for God only knew what.

"No, baby. It's beautiful. The thing my dreams are made of."

"Ugh." She grimaced, dropping her legs. "What was God thinking when he made this."

"Be thankful you've got it. It's the only reason I bother talking to you."

"Mike!" She pouted, acting hurt.

He stood before the mirror in the bedroom, slapped cologne on his face. "I'll get you one of those exploratory probes from a medical supply shop. Built-in flashlight. Then you'll see where they made that disaster movie about people trapped in a tunnel."

She stuck her tongue out at him and rolled off the bed. As they dressed, Roth called the Warner apartment again.

Robert picked up the receiver after the first ring. "About fucking time you called." Wait. Maybe it wasn't Rivera. "Uh, hello?"

"Ohhhhhhh, Roberta," Roth sang out.

Damn! Roth should no longer be in the equation. Where the fuck was Rivera?

"What?" Robert answered, thinking fast. Had something happened?

"One o'clock. In front of Tiffany's."

"I'm busy packing. I told you, you don't need me." He held his stomach as an intermittent pain ripped through him again. As much as he felt like it, he just couldn't take a crap.

"I want you with me," Roth snapped. "Then we'll go and celebrate. Exchange presents. You did buy me something for Christmas, didn't you?"

"Well, uh, no. No, I didn't."

"I'm crushed. But then you probably didn't expect me to be around this long, did you?"

Robert stared wide-eyed at the phone. *What did he mean by that?*

"In front of Tiffany's. One o'clock. Be there, you little shit, or I'll come up there and get you." Roth hung up.

Robert slammed the cover on his suitcase. He found Rivera's mobile number, dialed it. After two rings, the line was connected. No voice, Rivera's way of answering.

"What's going on?" Robert demanded. "Where the fuck are you?"

Silence. Then, "At the Park-Strawberry."

Rivera sounded different. "So that's where he is? What the fuck's the delay?" Robert demanded. He frowned. Rivera definitely sounded different.

Detective Weber, sitting behind his desk at the Midtown North Precinct, tried for as much brevity as possible. "Gotta problem."

Robert winced at another sharp pain in his gut, then screamed into the phone. "Thanks for telling me. Why haven't you called?"

"Been busy," Weber replied.

"Not busy enough," Robert shouted into the receiver. "The bastard just called me."

"Who?"

"Who? Who the hell you think?" Robert exploded, as much from the pain in his gut as from rage. Then he froze. *Who? Who? he asked. This isn't Rivera! Rivera wouldn't ask 'who?'* Robert slammed the phone down. He sat down at the breakfast table. What was going on? Someone else was using Rivera's cellular.

Detective Weber hit the disconnect button on Rivera's phone. Whoever called wasn't in the phone's memory. In fact, there were only a few numbers in there: one for Rivera's mother, his sister, and, Weber presumed, a couple of steady bimbos.

———

Rachel called Mom in Florida to say that Robert wasn't going down that night, and that she'd be there in a day or two. She'd invent something when she arrived with Roth, then break it to Mom gently. No. On second thoughts, maybe she wouldn't tell Mom anything at all. Mom and Doc hadn't seen Robert for over two years. She'd make up stories as time went by, just let Robert fade out of the picture, eventually say that he went off on his own, that she lost contact with him. Sounded plausible. Robert never called Tampa, never wrote, and rarely bothered to even take the phone when Mom called. Guys were like that.

Mom rambled on with her holiday plans. She was throwing a small party for some friends from the old days. Rachel asked if any of them would be on crutches or in wheelchairs. Mom laughed, said that the gang was working Atlanta at the moment. She was inviting some neighbors.

Roth, on the extension, winked at Rachel. Mom said that there was someone she wanted Rachel to meet. Roth threw a jealous look at Rachel, but she shrugged, then told Mom that she wasn't interested in meeting anyone new. In fact, she said, there was someone she wanted Mom to meet.

"Oh!" Mom exclaimed, not disappointedly, at which point Roth motioned to Rachel and drew a finger across his throat. When she didn't hang up, he walked into the bedroom and depressed the plunger on the phone.

"Call her back later," he said.

Rachel shrugged, said okay. Why not introduce Roth to Mom and Doc? She had enough on him to ensure that he kept his place until she got tired of him. Guys like Roth and Cracker Jack Scarlett came and went, and lately, for some inexplicable reason, she'd begun dwelling more on that time in Bangkok when he'd knocked her around.

But before that day came when she moved against him, she needed to learn all the things he knew, needed his contacts, learn about his 'inside' plans to scam the insurance companies. She could keep him placated. He was becoming increasingly enamored with her, just as Cracker Jack had. Besides, until then, there was more fun in the offing. Roth would be a barrel of laughs right up until the end.

When they left the suite, a uniformed cop posted by the elevator gave them the once over. Downstairs, Roth left Rachel with a cup of tea in the lobby coffee shop, said he was going to the airline ticket offices on East 59th Street, across Fifth Avenue. Instead, he made a phone call in the lobby, then bought a late edition of the *New York Daily News*, scanned through it until he found what he was looking for. He ripped out a news item, stuffed it into his coat pocket, and returned to the coffee shop. "Pull it together, beauty. We gotta split."

"Let me see the tickets!" she begged, childlike.

"Later," he said.

She stood and he put her coat on. "First class?"

"For me, yeah. *You're* sitting in baggage."

She laughed obligingly.

———

At 12:45, Robert lifted himself off the toilet where he'd been for the past 15 minutes without doing the business. He didn't understand why; his guts were wrenching and he was light-headed and sweating. He dressed wearily, and before leaving the apartment, knocked back another glass of milk. *Can you fucking believe that— ulcers at 26? No doubt from the aggravation that bitch gives me.* He'd have Doc look him over in Tampa, get this thing checked out. He left the apartment with no thought of feeding Barbie. Out of sight, out of mind.

Barbie didn't have much of an appetite anyhow. She lay dead beneath Rachel's bed.

In the elevator, another painful spasm gripped his stomach so tightly he nearly doubled over. Nausea swept over him, followed by dizziness. As fast as it came, the pain left again, as it had throughout the night. He hailed a taxi in front of the building. His face was slick with perspiration, and he wiped it away with a gloved hand, looked at it. How in the world could he be sweating in New York in late December?

———

Roth and Rachel left the Park-Strawberry at 1:00. Roth checked the area, looking for another possible threat. Several security dicks milled about the lobby and avoided eye contact. Rachel usually stopped traffic, but these guys were inspecting the ceiling, the carpets, anything but her. At the curb, two detectives were talking with a patrolman. One of the dicks eyed Roth. By this time, they'd have background information on all of the guests from the tenth floor up, and his name would have popped out, grabbed their interest. Roth was a licensed PI with a carry permit.

They walked two blocks to Tiffany's on Fifth and 57th Street. Roth chuckled when they spotted Robert waiting on the corner. He looked lost and uncertain, glancing around furtively, trying to look incognito behind sunglasses and a cap pulled down over his face in a rakish manner. He certainly didn't appear anything like the late Peter MacMillan.

In fact, Robert didn't look at all well. His complexion was pasty and he was perspiring profusely.

42

Robert watched nervously as they approached. But Roth gave no indication that anything was wrong. Robert scanned the intersection of Fifth Avenue and 57th Street, looking for Rivera. A fusion of people, hundreds, maybe a thousand, right here at this famous cross-street. Was he around somewhere, waiting for an opportunity? Would he take Roth out right here, amidst a sea of holiday shoppers? Cuba style. But who was the guy who answered his mobile?

Roth suddenly grabbed Robert by the lapels, pushed him off balance up against the building, and planted a kiss hard on his mouth. Pedestrians gathered around the busy intersection craned and gawked, some laughed. New York was a crazy town. Robert stared wide-eyed at Roth, tried pushing him away.

"I wanted to meet you here at Tiffany's, Roberta. To buy you a ring. Say that we'll be together forever." Roth released him, and

Robert had to scramble to keep himself from falling, but managed to regain his balance.

"Cut the shit, Roth," Robert barked. He looked around, confused and embarrassed, wiped his mouth with the back of his gloved hand.

Rachel read nothing in Robert's eyes that *he* suspected betrayal. He looked like hell, but otherwise seemed all right. Damn! She'd just have to do him later.

Roth linked arms with them, and ushered them south along Fifth Avenue, like the Tin Man, the Scarecrow, and Dorothy off to see the Wizard.

"Okay, kids. It's Santa Claus time," Roth announced. He guided them across Fifth Avenue to West 54th Street where they stopped in front of the Chase-Hampshire Life Insurance Building.

"Well," Rachel said. "It's show time." She looked at Robert with concern. "You look awful, Bobby. Have you eaten?"

"Yeah." He shrugged, as a fresh pain gripped his abdomen. "Some cereal. My stomach's off, that's all."

She took a handkerchief from her purse, wiped beads of sweat from his forehead. "Some sun will do you good," she said with concern in her voice. She smiled at him. *Yeah, you're going down, Bobby.*

"You look like you've been shot at and it missed, partner," Roth said. Adding, "But shit at and hit." He hadn't missed what Rachel said, some sun *will* do you good. Like Robert *was* going to Florida. In the room she'd said he wasn't, that he was staying in town. On the telephone, Robert had said he was packing. They weren't on the same page with this story.

"Don't worry about me, Roth," Robert answered. *Yours is coming. Yours is coming.*

They waited outside while Rachel went up to Chase-Hampshire's offices. Robert said, "I don't think it's smart for me to be waiting here in broad daylight while she's picking up a check for my death."

Roth lit a cigarette. "Relax, Bobby," he said dismissively. "I can call you that? Bobby?"

Robert didn't reply, bored with Roth's antics. Where *was* Rivera? Maybe the greaser was gonna take a powder, rip off his ten grand, not come through. But Rivera came highly recommended, so that couldn't be it.

Roth mumbled, "These insurance idiots could walk right past you without giving you a second look."

"Yeah, but they know you, don't they? What if one came out and saw you standing here talking to me. Don't they have a copy of MacMillan's passport. With my picture on it?"

Roth flipped his cigarette away. "You're in disguise." He smirked. "Besides, I'd introduce you as my fiancée." He moved next to Robert, mock passion on his face, in his voice. "I meant it about the engagement ring, big guy. Don't you believe me, or are you just fishin' about for another kiss to prove it."

Robert moved away, tired of his antics. "Fuck you, Roth. I'm sick of your crap. Fifty percent. We don't need you."

"Sure you do, pard. You wouldn't be getting dick without me."

"You're cuttin' in on everything."

"Learn to love it," Roth said. Then, "Rachel does."

"I shouldn't be here," Robert repeated. "Anyone could be watching us right now."

The crowd swelled as people leaving work poured out of the building. A redhead came out, walked past them. Roth checked her legs, watched her cross the street, but Robert didn't notice her as another spasm ripped across his gut. This one much sharper. He grimaced. *Come on, Rivera, wherever you are. Hit this bastard.* As if expecting it, he stepped a few feet further away from Roth.

Minutes later, Rachel came out through the revolving door. Without a word, the trio moved off, crossing West 54th Street, and continued south along Fifth Avenue.

"No problem?" Roth asked.

Rachel patted her purse. "Easy as pie. I had to show some ID, sign a few things, and that was all."

"Let's see it," he demanded.

She took the envelope from her purse, handed it to him. As they walked, Roth opened it and pulled out the check just far enough to read it. Robert leaned over and read it also.

"Three hundred big ones, kiddies," Roth said. He closed the envelope and slid it into his coat pocket.

"I believe my name is on the check?" Rachel smiled.

Roth tapped his coat. "Safe keeping, beauty. Safe keeping."

Rachel didn't care. The check was in her name and, besides, with the 65,000 they'd already given him, this 300,000 still represented less than half of Roth's remaining cut, using the fifty-fifty formula. But once she picked up the next check from Amalgamated, the one for a million, they were heading straight for her bank.

They entered Rockefeller Center, walked down the line of shops leading to the plaza. Roth and Robert moved to the railing overlooking the ice-skating rink as Rachel walked further to 30 Rockefeller Center.

The skating rink was packed. The gigantic Christmas tree behind the rink loomed sixty feet into the air, and thousands of holiday shoppers wandered about, taking pictures of the giant tree, pointing out the sights to toddlers bundled against the cold. Street performers danced, played instruments, and mimed—anything to separate the generous Christmas shoppers from a few bucks.

Roth watched Rachel enter the building. He looked down at the skaters, lit another cigarette. Robert stood apart from him, still wondering about Rivera. Maybe he was here, melting into the crowd, watching and waiting for his opportunity. The area was packed with people, shoulder to shoulder in some places.

He inched further away from Roth. Maybe when Rachel returned with the second check, Roth would be lying in a pool of blood. Right here. Greetings, Christmas shoppers. The crowd was perfect cover. Murder in plain sight. He edged further away, expecting him to go down any second. If he did, Robert would just turn away and move off, disappear into the crowd, like he hadn't known him, hadn't seen the bastard's head explode or his back buckle like he'd been kicked by a horse. Shoppers would stop, look, gasp, then scream and scatter. He wondered what Rivera was using. Silencer, no doubt, but he had no idea how loud the gun's report might be.

A sharp pain shot through his guts and he winced, becoming woozy.

Roth, watching the skaters, glanced at him. "You really look like hell, boy."

Robert struggled against the pain, leaning against the railing.

"You didn't read the papers this morning, did you, Roberta?"

"What?" he asked, sick to death of Roth's abstract jokes, his asinine insults. *Hit him now, Rivera. Hit this low-life, usurping sonofabitch now.*

Roth handed him a newspaper clipping. Robert swabbed beads of perspiration from his forehead, took the clipping and unfolded it. *C'mon, Rivera. Shoot the bastard.* He started to read the clipping, his fantasy of Roth's death consuming him, the pain in his gut excruciating. He was oblivious to three big men in heavy overcoats edging through the crowd towards them.

The newspaper headline was blurry, but he managed to read it: *"LONE GUNMAN FOUND DEAD AT THE PARK-STRAWBERRY HOTEL."*

He looked up at Roth and began to faint, sinking to his knees.

43

Rachel got out of the elevator on the twentieth floor. Only a few employees were on the premises of Amalgamated Life of Illinois. She gave her name at the reception desk, asked for the man Hewlett told her to see—James Kincannon. She recalled the name from correspondence, and had spoken with his secretary in Chicago a few times.

The receptionist asked her to take a seat and called someone on the phone, then leafed through some papers, looked over every so often at Rachel, smiled. She was in her late twenties, maybe early thirties. Pretty face, but Rachel thought she wore her hair too short. If she gave a shit, she'd tell the woman that short hair wasn't fashionable these days, maybe give her a few tips on how to look better. Fuck it. Maybe she was a dyke.

Ten minutes passed. From somewhere off in the distance, an ambulance siren wailed, the sound getting closer. Rachel asked the receptionist if it would be much longer. She said that she had banking to do before 3:00 p.m. The receptionist made another call, and a few moments later directed Rachel through frosted-glass double doors leading into a general bullpen area. Here, another young woman beckoned her into a back office. She introduced herself as Rowena Walsh, said that Mr. Kincannon would be with her shortly. Rowena went out and closed the door.

Aside from some richly appointed furniture and a plush carpet, the office was stark, minimally furnished, like a space used by visiting executives. There were no personal items on the desk or credenza. There was a door leading off to the side. A private bathroom, she assumed. She sat down in front of a large executive desk, checked her watch: 2:00 p.m. She looked around for an ashtray but there wasn't one, then she noticed the "*No Smoking*" sign. A small mirror hung on a side door. She stood and checked her make-up, thinking that she looked better as a blonde than a brunette. She sat down again, bored with waiting. Even this high up, she heard Christmas music from the street, and somewhere off in the distance the wail of the ambulance came closer still.

A short time later, Jim Kincannon came in, apologized for the delay. He said that Miss Walsh was bringing in the check directly. He moved behind the desk and Rachel noticed his limp.

She gave him an ingratiating smile that said 'eat shit and die.' Roth was right: these insurance types were buffoons. Kincannon sat down, cupped his hands on the desk, and made small talk about the weather. It wasn't going to be a white Christmas, he was afraid. Rachel said that it really didn't matter as she'd be in Florida shortly.

Rowena came in with a folio and sat it on the desk before Kincannon. He turned it around to Rachel, and asked her for ID. She produced a passport, a driver's license, and several credit cards in the name of Lori MacMillan. He asked her to sign some papers acknowledging receipt of check number such and such. She signed, and Kincannon placed a check from Amalgamated Life Insurance Company on the desk, pushed it towards her.

She picked it up, counted the digits. Seven of those beauties. One million dollars, plus a chunk of interest amounting to 12,500 dollars for the period of time between the reported date of death and today.

"Now, that's some Christmas present, isn't it?"

Rachel spun around at Roth's voice. He leaned against the door jamb, hands shoved down in the pockets of his overcoat.

What are you doing up here? She glanced at Kincannon, back to Roth. "Uh, Mr. Roth, isn't it?"

Roth stepped into the office and rapped his knuckles twice on the side door. The door opened and two men pushed into the room. They were cameramen, each holding a camcorder, the film lights blinding. Behind them, three other men in suits pushed into the room followed by the woman Rachel had met in reception. Only now she wore a New York City police officer's badge on a chain around her neck. Two uniformed officers were behind her, and suddenly the room was packed with bodies. Rowena peeked in behind them.

"Got it all, Mr. Roth," one of the cameramen said. He pulled the mirror off the side door, revealing a gaping hole. He reached in, retrieved his battery pack.

"Keep them running," Roth ordered.

Kincannon stood, and, almost formally, introduced the men in suits as a special agent for the New York State Insurance Fraud Bureau, Assistant District Attorney Hoffman of the New York County DA's Office, and his young assistant.

The policewoman lifted Rachel from her chair, spun her around, pressed her against the wall, and started frisking her. Down on the street, the ambulance siren stopped.

Her head swam as Kincannon came around the desk quickly and took the check from her hand. The policewoman drew Rachel's left arm behind her, started to handcuff her. But Roth stepped forward and took the cuffs, nudged her aside.

Rachel started to turn, to look into Roth's eyes, to ask what was happening. But he leaned into her, mashing her face roughly against the wall with his forearm. "My Christmas present to you, beauty. Something for *your* wrist."

"Let the officer cuff her, Roth," Kincannon said.

"The collar's mine," Roth grunted. "Anyone can cuff her. Even that jive-ass breakdancing to "Jingle Bells" down on the corner can cuff her." He slapped the cuffs on her, pressing the clasps hard into her wrists. She winced. He took her shoulder, spun her around, pushed her back into her chair. The policewoman began reading

Rachel her rights from a card, and ADA Hoffman advised her that she was being placed under arrest for insurance and mail fraud.

Rachel began shaking, reality hitting home. She stared at Roth in disbelief, but he was looking at the ADA.

"It's a good collar." Hoffman nodded.

"It should be," Roth said. He sat on the edge of Kincannon's desk, lit a cigarette, ignoring the "*No Smoking*" sign. "I busted my ass on this one. Worked this case night and day, wading up to my ass in Filipino thugs and Manila whores, sacrificed my purity and innocence to droves of wanton women, just to make this case." He winked at Kincannon. "I want you to remember that, Jim, when you get my bill." He looked coldly at Rachel. "Add murder to all this."

"Murder is Filipino jurisdiction, Roth," the Bureau agent named Marsh interjected, shaking his head.

"Not for those." Roth held Rachel's eyes. "Not for Brian O'Toole and Lolita Perez. Seems there was a stepfather down in Florida nailing you, wasn't there, beauty?"

Marsh and Kincannon exchanged looks. This was news to them, but not to Hoffman. He'd been contacted by the Hillsborough County, Florida, District Attorney's Office. Roth had filed a complaint there the week before, alleging the probable homicide of one Jack 'Cracker' Scarlett eight years ago. The DA in Florida acted on his complaint after contacting Hoffman about the MacMillan matter.

Rachel started shedding tears and her face contorted with rage. "You *bastard*," she spat.

"You might have something there," Roth returned. "Mother was always vague when I asked why I didn't look like Dad."

She sprang at him, kicking and going for his face with her teeth. The policewoman blocked her, got kicked in the shins for her trouble, but managed to throw Rachel back into the chair. The uniformed cops scrambled over and held her from behind. Rachel screamed at Roth, running a string of curses, nearly insane with rage. How could he betray her after all they'd done, after what they'd been through? She sobbed, pleading, "Help me, Mike. Please."

Roth's smile was pure venom. He turned to one of the cameramen, Premier's employee, the same operative from the van. "Keep that thing running," he said again.

Rachel began denying her involvement in Scarlett's murder. She'd only been 15 at the time. She denied any involvement in this scam, pleading that she believed all the while her husband was dead. "Mike, you know the truth. Help me. I know nothing about all this. I guess my husband, Peter, set this up with someone in Manila."

Roth laughed. "Give it up, beauty. I've got tapes from every conversation we had, even those intimate little pillow talks. Plus videos from the breakfast parlay at the diner." He stubbed out his cigarette on a piece of paper. "What these boys don't know about is Jack Scarlett's death. Only learned about that last week. Mom and Doc were most courteous, us being such good chums." He looked into Rachel's eyes. "I'm the guy Mom wanted you to meet." He checked his Cartier. "They should be under arrest right about now."

"Where's Robert?" Rachel asked, trembling.

"Midtown North," one of the cops said. "Where you're going."

"Uh uh," Roth cut in. "He's on his way to Roosevelt Hospital. He collapsed on the sidewalk." He watched tears running down her cheeks. "Now some people wanna take your picture, fingerprints, autograph. Things like that." He turned to Kincannon and Hoffman. "Here's the bribe money. From the diner and from Bangkok." He pulled a thick envelope from his coat, held it up to the video camera, and tossed it on the desk. "It's all tagged, and what I want from you, Hoffman, is a count and a receipt." He smiled at Hoffman. "Wouldn't want this cash to get lost down at the DA's office, would we?" He turned to Premier's cameraman again. "Keep it rolling."

The DA's cameraman had turned off his video camera. He looked at Hoffman, turned it back on.

"Hello, chief."

They turned to see Nina Davis edging into the room. Laura, the redhead, followed.

Hoffman and his deputy were counting the money, and Nina studied Rachel, the woman whose name she'd lived with for the past three months.

When the count was finished, Hoffman wrote out a receipt, handed it to Roth.

Rachel was weeping uncontrollably, head down, murmuring how she'd been so stupid to trust Roth. "A boy scout in the end," she muttered. She started swearing again, her face ugly with anger. She cursed Roth and everyone in the room, even cursed herself, the men silently staring at her.

Roth read the receipt aloud for the cameras, and handed it to Nina. He removed the Cartier from his wrist, read off the serial number, held it up to the cameras. "Part of the bribe. It'll be in my report," he announced. He looked at Hoffman. "I don't wanna see any of you boys downtown wearing this thing." He dropped the watch on the desk next to the money. "Film everyone present," he ordered Premier's cameraman.

"Yes, sir," the operator said, panning slowly across the room. The Fraud Bureau investigator and Hoffman looked darkly at Roth, but stood still for the camera.

"Damn right, boys," Roth said. "I want it documented who was present when I handed over the booty." He turned to one of the uniformed officers. "You'd better radio Roosevelt Hospital, suggest they check Tierney for poison. He had all the signs of it." He looked at Rachel. "Yeah, life woulda been a pip with you, beauty. You, me, and my food taster strolling off into the sunset."

Roth turned to Kincannon. "You'll also be getting transcriptions of my taped conversations with the suspects."

The young DA's assistant whispered into Hoffman's ear that Roth's tapes hadn't been ordered by the court, and therefore, might be inadmissible.

"Back to law school for you, junior," Roth snapped, poking his finger into the young man's chest. "I was part of those conversations. So I could record—federal and New York State statutes."

"Weren't some of those tapes made overseas—?"

"Where there are no statutes," Roth cut him off. "The only thing that remains to be seen is how long you can remain with the DA's office."

"Easy, Mr. Roth," Hoffman said.

"Sure, Hoffman. Junior's your problem. But I don't like idiots telling me my business."

Rachel was moaning now, rocking back and forth in her chair, babbling, cursing hysterically. She looked like she was going over the edge. Roth looked at her with hate in his eyes. "Some class act, ain't she?" He shook his head. In the end, Rachel had no grace, no dignity whatsoever. "Guess we're about wrapped up here. But keep the cameras on her until she's out the door."

He motioned Jim Kincannon aside. Kincannon, proud of Amalgamated Life's contribution in this matter, huddled contentedly, almost smugly, with Roth off to the side. He knew the laws of evidence, every insurance investigator did, and Kincannon knew that Premier recorded most interviews. Amalgamated was delivering a very solid case to the DA's Office. Now came the usual jurisdiction squabble and, hence, who got the credit that translated into political glory.

"Just one more thing, Jim," Roth whispered.

"Sure, Roth. What's that?"

Roth eyed him sternly, whispered, "And I want the truth, Kincannon."

Kincannon's smile faded. "Of course."

"Tell me straight. Are you fornicating with little Miss Walsh?"

Kincannon's face fell. He spun away, indignant, given the solemnity of the proceedings. He asked Nina for a final report and bill as soon as possible, and mentioned a new case in Costa Rica, asked her to meet with their attorney next week.

Then they watched as the uniforms hefted Rachel from her seat, led her from the office, followed by the policewoman. Rachel was still sobbing, seemed unable to stand on her own. But she halted at the door, turned back to Roth, struggling with her hands behind her. "Can I wipe my face, goddammit," she snapped.

The female officer took a handkerchief and wiped the tears from Rachel's eyes and cheeks, wiped her nose. She pulled her face away, glared at Roth. "Why did you insist on half of everything? When you'd be getting nothing in the end?" She looked around the room. "Do you people know that he wanted half of everything?"

"My greed appealed to you, convinced you that I was going bad."

Rachel thought about that. For sure, had Roth only wanted a small percentage, she wouldn't have trusted him. It was his greed and hostility towards the insurance industry that earned her confidence. She'd never once suspected a sting. Not from the moment they met at Marcia's apartment.

"You'll have plenty of time to think about it," Roth said. "But when I grabbed for half, you and Robert squabbled, went for each other's throat. It worked with you, but Robert remained loyal, didn't he? He knew who the enemy was."

"Why us?" Rachel asked.

"You and me? To split you and Robert apart."

"I trusted you."

"You were supposed to."

"You rotten sonofabitch." Her eyes burned at Roth. The police-woman yanked her from the room and Rachel began fighting again. She screamed more obscenities at Roth, vowing to kill him some-day. She kicked the officers and tried to bite them. They managed to pull her down the corridor, where, at the elevator, they threw her on the floor. One sat on her and they cuffed her ankles.

"I'll kill you, you bastard," she screamed back again, snapping at the officers with her teeth. "It doesn't matter where I end up, you're dead, you motherfucking piece of garbage."

The officers gagged her so that she couldn't bite. One of the cops, huffing loudly, radioed for a straightjacket and a wheelchair down-stairs, and it took three men to cram Rachel into the elevator. Her muffled screams echoed up the shaft until her voice faded, then was no more.

Roth looked around at the faces staring at him. Even in the pres-ence of a murderer, he'd turned out to look like a bastard because of his treachery. He wanted to say that it was the only way. But to hell with them.

He wasn't in business to teach school.

44

The next afternoon, Christmas Day, Roth sat at one of the computers at the office and typed out transcripts of his last conversations with Rachel. He was nearly finished after working for six hours. It was tedious work, playing the micro cassette tapes on a transcriber, controlled with a foot peddle, headphones boring into his ears as he hammered out the dialogue.

He'd declined Nina's invitation for Christmas dinner with her family, and had made calls to friends and family throughout the States wishing them a Merry Christmas. In vain, they always asked him when he would visit. Maybe next year, he always said. He was alone and it didn't bother him. Away from paradise, it was just one more dismal day. Last year, he'd spent Christmas Day in a hot tub with three lovelies and champagne. He wished he were there now, surrounded by young cuties wearing Santa Claus caps and very little else.

He finished the transcripts, typed his final report on the case, for a total of thirty pages. He itemized the final bill and placed everything on Nina's desk except for the tapes, which he put in the safe.

He hated paperwork, but unless the Tierneys copped a plea, he'd still have to testify at some future date, and the transcripts would prove vital. He looked at the framed picture of a little boy sitting on the crapper, clutching a roll of toilet paper, with the caption, *"The job ain't done 'til the paperwork's finished."* He'd hung that sign in his first office nearly twenty years ago, and its message still rang true.

He turned next to the report on the Lolita Perez case. Nina would eventually round up the companies and mail them a case synopsis. Essentially, it was the same case as Peter MacMillan, and many of the same transcripts would be used. As incredible as it seemed, Jordan Warner, aka Robert Tierney, the beneficiary, could still pursue the claims against the insurance companies for Lolita's death. Knowing that stupid bastard, he'd probably try. If he survived the poisoning. So the Lolita case required closure as well. Then he dictated letters to the companies who had insured the Bishops. A dozen claims, present or potential, were being resolved at the same time. The non-client companies on the Lolita claim would have to buy Premier's reports, and Nina would take care of all that.

Rachel and Robert Tierney would be denied bail—even in a liberal New York courtroom—given their multiple passports, myriad IDs, and pattern for defrauding insurance companies, immigration services, the Internal Revenue Service, the US State Department, and just about everyone else. It would be a prosecutor's field day, the kind of case they loved to build their reputations on. In a few days, news headlines would scream out capsules like, *"Brother-sister confidence team snagged by the DA's Office."*

Premier's name would never appear in the dailies; the politicos would grab the thunder.

He wanted to call Kevin O'Toole, but felt it would make a sour Christmas present. He finished the paperwork—at least this part of it. He called a taxi, locked up the office, and went down to the waiting cab. He took it into Manhattan, to the Park-Strawberry where he decided to keep the room for the next few days. Let the clients pick up the bill.

Near the reception desk, two hotel dicks were watching him, whispering. Roth picked up his key and strolled into the bar. It was deserted, the proper setting for the buttons who would be coming along soon. Better to chat with them here than in his room. For all he knew, they might have an arrest warrant. He climbed on a bar-stool, thinking that maybe he'd call an escort service, wondering if Mrs. Claus worked Christmas night. A take-out would come at a premium. No Christmas spirit with hookers. If they were going to get stuffed on Christmas, so were their stockings.

A part-time student named Jack was filling in for one of the regular bartenders. Jack appreciated the company, buying Roth's first drink with a "Merry Christmas, sir."

After his second rum and Coke, two detectives entered the bar, walked over, and stood on either side of him. The older one looked more like a professor than a cop.

"Mr. Roth?" the senior man asked. "Would you step outside with us, please."

Roth shook his head. "I'm happy here. What can I do for you?"

The detective looked at him sternly. Interrogations went better when they had a subject alone. But they couldn't demand that, unless they were arresting Roth. "The other night, a man fell to his death on the stairwell."

"Yeah. I read about that. Chambermaids really getting tough on bad tippers, huh?"

The detectives glanced at each other. Roth thought that the young dick looked anxious to make trouble. But the professor was in charge here. Probably a lieutenant.

"Maybe he was *thrown*," the lieutenant suggested, moving closer. Jack moved to the end of the bar and began wiping glasses, didn't look over.

Roth said, "It's true then, what they say about New York—it's really a dangerous place?"

"Cut the crap, Roth," the young cop said. "Whaddya doin' here?"

"Having a drink. You guys want one?" He waved Jack over, pointed to a position behind the bar, directly in front of him. "Stand here, will ya, Jack."

Jack looked at the cops. He didn't want to be brought into this. The lieutenant thumbed him away. He started to move off.

Roth rapped his knuckles on the bar. "I said stand here, Jack. *I'm* your customer, not these guys. They can't tell you to do dick unless there's an emergency. You got that, son?"

Jack looked at the two detectives, who didn't contradict Roth, didn't say anything, didn't even look at him. He returned, leaned against the shelves, folded his arms, and wished he was somewhere else.

"Don't get wise with us, Roth." This was the junior detective. "You live in Bangkok, don't you? Whaddya doin' in New York?"

"Tryin' to pick up women?" Roth answered with a shrug. He looked around the empty room.

"Once more, buster," the cop said, "and you're coming with us." He pulled a wallet from his overcoat pocket, flipped it open to reveal a detective's shield.

Roth thought he hadn't been in grade for very long, proud to flash the gold shield. His ID card read, "*Jon Bell.*" Roth took it in. "Damn!" he exclaimed. "Did you get a whistle with that?"

"That's all, buster," Bell said, taking Roth by the arm. He felt the revolver beneath the coat. "He's carrying!"

"Hold on," the lieutenant ordered. He knew Roth had a carry permit, had checked for that earlier. Bell should have, also.

Roth put his hands on the bar. "I'm doing some Christmas shopping," he said soberly. "I return to the States occasionally. Business."

"How does Surces come into this," Bell asked.

"Don't know what you mean. Don't know what a surces is?"

"The man who fell."

Roth shook his head, shrugged.

Bell looked to the older cop, persisted with the old tactic: "Let's pull him in, Lieutenant."

"What for?" Roth demanded. "You'll be wasting your time, get nothing outta me but my attorney's name."

The lieutenant leaned closer. Roth could smell the spearmint on his breath. "Maybe, Roth, but you'll spend an interesting night in the lock-up."

"On what charge? The city gets sued, you end up with paper-work up your crack, maybe draw an official reprimand. Plus, not to be overlooked, you lose me as a friend. And all for what? Because this guy with you can't talk nice to people."

The lieutenant held out his hand and said, "Let's have it."

Roth held his eyes on Jack. He pulled open his lapel, with right thumb and forefinger withdrew his .38 slowly from his shoulder holster. "Want it cleared?"

"Never mind that." The lieutenant snatched the revolver from Roth, put it up to his nose, sniffed it. He shook his head at Bell. There'd been no shooting the other night, nothing to try for a ballistics match.

Jack finished building Roth a fresh drink, placed it in front of him. He leaned back against the shelves, folded his arms, waiting. He was beginning to enjoy this: hard-ass cops getting jerked around by his customer.

"You workin' on anything?" Bell asked.

"I'm always working on something," Roth said.

"Working on anything here at the hotel?"

Roth shook his head. "Just my drink, maybe a hooker later."

The lieutenant held Roth's revolver, hefted it, like he was weighing something in his mind. He handed it back to Roth, who holstered it.

It was unlikely that the DA's Office would even connect Roth to Surces' death, or even think to ask him where he'd spent the last few nights in New York. The only connection to Roth could be if some bright dick came into contact with both cases—Surces and the Tierneys. Not likely. Surces was a homicide case and the Tierney's were white-collar crime. So far. The DA's Office had the Tierney case, while Homicide was handling Surces' death, and the DA in Florida had the Scarlett case. The cops had nothing on Surces' death and Roth knew it. They'd found no footprints, had no solid idea which floor Surces flew from. It would be next to impossible to pin down something like that. Besides, Surces was a thug and the police hadn't come up with his victim. Did they really care what happened to a piece of shit like him?

"We have the videos," the lieutenant said. "The one with you out on the tenth-floor landing."

Roth shrugged. "I thought there was a fire. Came out to investigate."

The first thing the cops had done was check the cameras on the tenth floor. If they'd looked harder, they'd find an earlier tape where Roth and Rachel had gotten off the elevator, followed by Surces. So far, they'd just been looking for the time on the tape when Surces fell.

"You're registered under the name of Nina Davis," the lieutenant said.

"My partner."

"Room 1025 was also registered to Miss Davis. A few of your people were in and out of the room all day yesterday and the day before."

"Shopping," Roth said simply. "I held meetings in the city, so we could all get in some shopping. She made the reservations weeks ago, when I made plans to travel to the States. Ever try to register just before Christmas?"

"The guy who fell did," Bell put in.

Roth couldn't resist it: "He dropped in then, hmmm?"

"You flew into New York from Miami day before yesterday," the lieutenant said. "What were you doing in Florida?"

These guys had done some homework. "Pleasure," he said.

"You rented a car in Miami. Where'd you go?"

"I cruised around."

"Cruised around for 500 miles?"

"Yeah," Roth said. "Drove down to the Keys for a few days."

"That ain't a 500-mile round trip."

"Cruised up and down the Keys. Bad idea; I won't do that again. Not a hooker in sight."

"Anybody see you?"

"Just the hooker I took down from Miami."

"What's her name?"

"One of those African-American names. Uhm, something like Nomoni—Nomoni something." He sipped his drink.

"She was black?"

"Yeah. Probably still is. I remember her name now. "No-money, no-honey. Well, that's what she kept saying, anyhow."

"Funny," Bell said. "Where'd you pick her up? And why were you cruising for a pro if you already had one?"

"Near the place I was stayin' in Miami."

The lieutenant and Bell exchanged glances. They could work this story forever if it was an alibi. The lieutenant dug out his calling card, crammed it into Roth's coat pocket. "Don't leave town without checking with me." He started to leave, but turned back. He hadn't forgotten Bell's second question. That's why he was a lieutenant.

"Why were you looking for the second girl?"

Roth smiled. "To make a sandwich. Cute little chocolate gals. Picture this: an Oreo cookie streakin' up and down the Keys in a yellow Cadillac, corn rolls flapping in the breeze, big black melons bouncing all over the dashboard, slappin' me in the face, the three of us waving to all those rednecks."

The detectives looked at Roth like he had a contagious disease. The lieutenant shook his head and they left the bar.

"Merry Christmas, officers," Roth called after them. No question about it, they were just fishing.

He finished a few more rum and Cokes, tipped Jack twenty dollars, and went up to his room. He called Nina, told her to expect a visit from the cops about the other night.

"Some idiot called earlier," she said. Roth heard her boyfriend ask who was calling.

Roth chuckled. "Was his name Bell?"

"Hmm, not sure. I think it was something like Dopey."

"That's him. What'd you tell him?"

"It wasn't 'Merry Christmas.' Whaddya think I told him? Told him to call our attorney."

The next morning, Roth had breakfast in bed, then called downstairs, requested a typewriter be delivered to his room. There'd be a problem, the business office said, since they didn't use typewriters. He told them to do their best, and an hour later, a clerk appeared at his door with a heavy, old IBM Selectric, whose cover had just been dusted off. Roth spent the day composing letters which he'd mail from Tokyo, on his way back to Bangkok.

The first was an anonymous note to Major Rodrigo Santos including blown-up photographs of Reno's tryst with the waitress. To be sure that Rodrigo acted, Roth sent similar packages to three other

Manila police stations, including photos clearly showing Reno giving the waitress a tonsillectomy, violating the holy sacrament of his marriage to Major Rodrigo's beloved baby sister. The good major would have to recover his face, although he probably needed no such impetus.

His next letter, also anonymous, was to Lolita's brothers in Masbate. Roth typed out the story of Lolita's relationship with Marcellus, and his plan with Robert Tierney to murder her. In this envelope he included gory blow-ups taken of Lolita on the morgue slab, guaranteed to incite even a pope to a murderous rage. He enclosed photos, addresses, and known haunts of Officer Reno Marcellus.

The next one was to Kevin O'Toole in Boston. While it was anonymous, O'Toole would know the author. Roth didn't care. He just didn't want any of the letters traced back to him legally. He outlined the entire story and fingered Robert, Rachel, and Marcellus, whose photos he included in the envelope.

The Tierneys would remain locked up awaiting justice, and they'd surely get time. Marcellus would get his, too. Soon. And even God couldn't guess who'd get him first.

His last letter was to the directors of American Travelers, complete with a detailed case synopsis, and overwhelming proof: transcripts of selected tapes and the names of those in charge of the criminal case against the Tierneys. Roth detailed the date when he outlined the case to Sid Sydow, who refused to reinvestigate.

Roth offered to have Premier recover the 200,000 dollars that Sydow had forked over to Rachel. Premier's fee would be 40,000 dollars for a *guaranteed* recovery. All Nina had to do was direct American Travelers to the Tierney's assets. She was eons ahead of the authorities on that score, so American Travelers could get their legal paperwork in first, freeze the Tierney accounts.

Rachel had moved their assets immediately after that meeting in the diner, once Roth had their real names. But Nina had quickly tracked most of the transfers. Over three million dollars sat in banks, and some was invested in annuities with the very insurance companies the Tierneys had ripped off.

Roth offered a claims payment review on anything that Sydow had touched since joining the company two years ago. He outlined a few other cases he knew of where payments had been made on mutual fraudulent cases, and alluded to Sydow's penchant for directing investigative assignments to his buddies. He was careful to couch his letter, with only a hint towards collusion, to avoid a libel lawsuit from Sydow. But he would be too busy covering his ass and dragging out old claim files until they gave him the door.

American Travelers was a mutual company, and, after all, bad claim payments involved their policyholders' money. God forbid, Roth hinted, that the media got hold of this.

Yeah, they'd do business with Premier. And fast.

When he finished with the typewriter, he ejected the ribbon, unsnapped the type ball, and removed that as well. He covered the Selectric and called downstairs for it to be removed. Ten minutes later, the clerk reappeared at his door. He gave the man a fifty, told him that he didn't want to see a charge for the typewriter rental on his bill.

Finally, he called Nina to have her advise Immigration that the passport for Brian O'Toole had been stolen. No doubt someone was using it, probably a Filipino with a passable likeness. Marcellus wouldn't have overlooked that money-making opportunity. Immigration would eventually pick up whoever had it.

He spent ten more minutes apologizing to Nina for not having taken her entirely into his confidence with the sting from the beginning. Instead, he'd pulled her in only the week before he returned to New York, just in time to get the Tierneys under surveillance. The more people who knew about it—especially insurers—the more dangerous it could have become, possibly even for Nina. His partner listened quietly, and Roth knew she wasn't completely satisfied. But she said to forget it.

Time to haul ass back to Bangkok. He thought about Mac, and grimaced. If the maid hadn't been feeding him, the poor little finger-eating fucker would be hanging upside-down in his cage.

He ordered up dinner and thought again about calling in a pro, wondered if they ran After-Christmas sales.

45

Roth flew out the next day. As he was about to board the plane, he called the Midtown North Precinct in Manhattan, said that he could be contacted through his New York office.

At Narita Airport outside Tokyo, he mailed the letters to Kevin O'Toole, the Perez Brothers, Major Rodrigo and the other police stations. Then he changed planes for Bangkok.

During the flight down to Bangkok, he went over the entire matter, as he would many times before the minutia slipped from his memory, fading into time like a hundred cases before.

Rachel's father had died when she was eight years old. Mom remarried a slick redneck from Georgia. 'Cracker' Jack Scarlett taught the family insurance fraud: slips and falls, auto accidents, any personal injuries that could be faked. They prospered under his tutelage and the chips rolled in, what with Mom, Robert, and Rachel falling down all over South Florida. But Cracker drank too much, squandered their booty on women, booze, and gambling. He'd taken his protégés for granted and was even abusive. Until Doctor Will Rossiter came along. Doc had been kicked out of medical associations from Texas to Alabama by the time he arrived in Florida. He tied up with Cracker and Mom, and began filling out bogus medical certificates for alleged accident victims. Mom built up her crew of lay-down artists, and she and Doc hit it off big time while Cracker Jack was paying too much attention to budding, 13-year-old Rachel. He raped her over a two-year period on the quiet, until Mom learned about it. Along with Doc, they dispatched Cracker, Doc conveniently signing the death certificate.

Cracker Jack's body had been exhumed and autopsied. His system was lousy with arsenic. For the time being, Mom and Doc were long-term guests in the Hillsborough County jail, awaiting trial.

Cracker's death had brought Rachel and her brother closer, since Robert had secretly watched Cracker taking sister Rachel. He fell in love with his sister, who carnally loved him right back until she grew out of it. Indeed, a family that lays together, slays together.

The MacMillan case was one of Roth's most prolonged stings. However, with Rachel, it hadn't been entirely unpleasant, and he really hadn't gone out of his way. The Hong Kong trip had been on his itinerary, anyhow.

He'd miss Rachel, all right, but she was a murderer without remorse, a dangerous mess whose therapy bills would bankrupt a millionaire. Maybe the prison shrinks could straighten her out. After all, everyone was a victim in America these days.

Roth jotted down a reminder to call the travel insurance company down in Brisbane, and thank them personally for their assistance. He'd asked them to pay the hospitalization claim on Peter MacMillan if Robert pursued it, as expected. He posted a bond for the 10,000 dollars. The company wanted to know what it was about, but they were told nothing, except that although the claim was bogus, it was important it be paid as part of another ongoing investigation. With the bond in hand, and several waivers that their legal people insisted on, they co-operated.

Nina meanwhile was claiming Brisbane's money from the Tierney assets. As best she could figure it, there was a 300,000-dollar surplus which couldn't be laid off to any particular scam. The Tierneys could use whatever was left for their defense.

———

A week later, when Roth returned from a case down in Jakarta, he received a telephone call from Kevin O'Toole.

"Thanks for the note," O'Toole said. "And for Brian's urn. The family appreciates it."

"*De nada*," Roth responded.

"This cop, Marcellus. You sure he's the one?"

"You'll find Brian's Cartier on the bastard's wrist."

The line went quiet, then, "You wanna do him for us? Just name your price."

"Not my thing," Roth said. He wouldn't tell O'Toole that a line was forming to take out Marcellus.

"Look me up, you ever get to Boston," O'Toole offered.

"Likewise, if you ever get to Bangkok. You'll be safe, no Spics out here."

O'Toole laughed and hung up just as a DHL man knocked at Roth's door. It was a package from Nina. Inside were more assignments and a copy of the *New York Post* that carried the story about the murders of William Towers and Marcia Post in Manhattan.

Nina called also, feeling miserable that their surveillance team had only been downstairs at the curb when the murders took place. If only they'd known.

Roth put it together how Surces ran across Towers and Marcia Post. Once Laura, cruising the singles action at the Mexican place, tied Surces to Robert, the big Cuban was under constant surveillance, right up to when Roth picked Rachel up and zipped her down to the Park-Strawberry. The meeting between Surces and Towers in the hotel bar was covered by the surveillance team who followed them to Marcia Post's apartment. Surces was tailed alone back to the Park-Strawberry, but the team had no make on Towers and was initially concerned that there were two assassins.

The *New York Post* had a layout on pages four and five, replete with a diagram of the death apartment and photographs of the victims: Marcia in her cap and gown from her college commencement, Towers' official State Department photograph.

It was a shame, actually. Towers was a goner from the moment he first laid eyes on Rachel. Exsanguination. Like a shark ripping into its victim, then waiting until it bleeds to death before gobbling it up. That's what Rachel had done to Towers. She was no less responsible for his death than Surces. She'd probably read about it in her jail cell.

As for Marcia; well, at least her killer paid with his life. The police tagged their murders on Surces with ballistics, but the trail stopped there. Apparently, no one tied Towers' visit to New York City with the Peter MacMillan business. Or, if they did, they didn't come forward. Maybe Towers' old girlfriend in Manila, Millie O'Hearn, would piece it together. The newspapers called it a mystery as to why Towers was in New York, and assumed Marcia was a girlfriend. The cops hadn't established Surces' motive for the killings.

Roth could clear it up, but he'd implicate himself in Surces' death. He could have come forward when Surces took the plunge, would have had to if there'd been a shooting in his room. No reason to come forward now, particularly with all the media bottom-feeders. A private investigator would be high profile. Lots of headlines, and the DA would hammer him for not coming forward immediately. But that would have jeopardized the set-up against the Tierneys.

There was no way he'd emerge from this without a bloody nose if he came forward now. Premier would lose clients and Roth would be wading up to his ass in detectives like Bell.

Towers' name would eventually surface in connection with Roth's investigation. In all, there were 14 insurance companies who would be getting reports, since those on Warner and the Bishops would also need this information. Towers' name was mentioned as the consular officer on the MacMillan case and in reports covering Premier's handling in Los Angeles. Maybe they'd want Towers to testify, at which time they'd piece together his murder. Plus the DA's Office and Fraud Bureau people would be subpoenaing these reports. Also, Rachel knew Towers, but not Surces. Robert sure as hell wasn't going to blab it around. For Roth, actual contact with Surces, much less homicide, couldn't be proven, and the episode with the killer certainly didn't appear in his reports. If it came back to haunt him, he'd worry about it then.

————

A few weeks later, a check for 10,000 dollars from O'Toole Transportation arrived by express mail. The check's memo read, *"For consulting services."* Ten thousand, a nice chunk in one pile, but not so much when divided into smaller piles amongst partners. Roth decided on his next visit to Manila to open a trust account for little Pauley.

Lolita would never see America, but maybe Pauley would someday.

That evening, Roth visited Soi Cowboy. The clubs along the street were priming for Chinese New Year, and a lot of bargirls were in town, down from the provinces. He hit a few places, then wandered into the Tilac Bar for Happy Hour. He took a stool at the bar, ordered a drink, watched a tall dancer grinding her body up on the catwalk to a Rolling Stones number.

When she turned his way, Roth saw her number button pinned onto her panties. Number 14. She scanned the bar, caught her reflection in the mirrors that lined the walls of the club, admired her own youthful body. She was watching the most beautiful body Roth had seen since Rachel. Her, again. She'd be like poison for a while, but maybe Number 14 up there was the right antidote. He caught her attention and mimed a drink. She nodded, winked at a girlfriend dancing next to her. She looked back down at Roth, his face the image of a 1,000-baht note. She liked faces like his.

The action from a dice game going on next to him caught his attention, and when he looked up again at Number 14, he shuddered at a vision of Rachel's face superimposed on the dancer's. He blinked, but Rachel's face remained. He shook his head, turned his attention to a commotion at the door, just in time to see Max Pollock rolling himself inside, assisted as usual by several bargirls who lifted his wheelchair over the door jamb. He was in the same electric vehicle. Max spotted Roth and wheeled over, pinching bottoms with impunity as the crowd parted, giving him and his hands a wide berth. He parked at the bar next to Roth, ordered a beer.

"Hey, Roth. Remember me telling you about my wheelchair."

"Sure I do, Max. You're never far from my thoughts."

"Those cheap fuckers at my insurance company. They refused to pay my claim. You know what they told me?"

"They probably told you to crate it up and ship it to them, that they'd repair it or send you a new one."

"Yeah! How'd you know?"

"Just a guess, Max." He watched Number 14 coming down from the catwalk. Rachel's image vanished as she edged her way through the crowd towards him.

"Just a guess," he repeated absently, bringing his drink up to his lips.

About the Author

Byron Bales was born in St. Louis, in 1942. At 15 he began working as an investigator until serving in the US Marine Corps, where he first visited Asia during the pre-Vietnam era.

Returning to civilian life in 1963, he continued working as an investigator in multiple specialities. He is a licensed investigator in New York State, the State of California, and is registered as an investigator and security consultant in the Kingdom of Thailand.

In 1979, he established an investigation firm which now has a worldwide network of agents. During his career, the author has handled assignments in over 170 countries and territories.

He divides his time between Southern California and Southeast Asia, and can be reached at: firstpi.com.